KEEPER OF THE KEYSTONE

A novel by

CL Barber

Text copyright @ September 2016
CL Barber
All Rights Reserved by
CL Barber & SatinPaperbacks

Published by SatinPaperbacks

© 2016, CL Barber & SatinPaperbacks except as provided by the Copyright Act January 2015 no part of this publication may be reproduced, stored in a retrieval system or transmitted in any form or by any means without the prior written permission of the Author and Publisher.

This novel is a work of fiction. Names and characters are the product of the author's imagination and any resemblance to actual persons, living or dead is entirely coincidental.

Author Biography

Cindy Barber is a Head of Faculty and teacher of History. She has won short story competitions and runs a local writers group. Cindy is a married mother of two boys, living in Essex.

Keeper of the Keystone is the first in the Chronicles of Kilion series. The second is currently underway.

There is a competition running until December 31st 2016 with two categories aimed at the under 16's and the over 16's; in under 500 words, create a character and explain who they would be friends or enemies with from the first book. Each winner will receive £50 Amazon voucher and a £50 book voucher for their school. Their characters will also appear in the book with their names being credited.

DEDICATION

This book is dedicated to Ashley Barber who has supported me despite my constant working when I could have spent the time with him.

Publisher Links:

SatinPaperbacks:

http://www.satinpaperbacks.com

http://www.satinpublishing.co.uk

https://twitter.com/SatinPaperbacks

https://www.facebook.com/Satinpaperbackscom

Email: nicky.fitzmaurice@satinpaperbacks.com

AUTHOR LINKS:

For more information please visit:

Facebook: https://www.facebook.com/C-L-Barber-153595361723011/

To contact the author:

Email: clbarber1977@outlook.com

Contents

Author Biography	3
Publisher Links:	3
AUTHOR LINKS:	4
Chapter One: The Assailant	1
Chapter Two: The Ring	9
Chapter Three: Missing	11
Chapter Four: The Birthday Present	17
Chapter Five: The Watch	22
Chapter Six: The Visit	26
Chapter Seven: Retribution	35
Chapter Eight: The Hopkin's Empire	43
Chapter Nine: Freak Weather	50
Chapter Ten: The Farmhouse	62
Chapter Eleven: The Prisoner	77
Chapter Twelve: Grimbald	88
Chapter Thirteen: The Castle	93
Chapter Fourteen: The Feast	109
Chapter Fifteen: The King's Men	121

Chapter Sixteen: Drugged	127
Chapter Seventeen: Reported Missing	132
Chapter Eighteen: Memory Loss	142
Chapter Nineteen: The Dungeon	157
Chapter Twenty: Richard's Return to the Castle	162
Chapter Twenty-one: The Second Ring	172
Chapter Twenty-two: Sisterly Love	182
Chapter Twenty-three: Breakfast	190
Chapter Twenty-four: Valkyrites	194
Chapter Twenty-five: The Forest	199
Chapter Twenty-six: Tour of the Castle	206
Chapter Twenty-seven: Relocation	222
Chapter Twenty-eight: The Forest	228
Chapter Twenty-nine: Dinner	230
Chapter Thirty: The Witch	238
Chapter Thirty-one: Regrets	251
Chapter Thirty-two: The Carriage Ride	255
Chapter Thirty-three: The Library	271

Chapter Thirty-four: The Cave	279
Chapter Thirty-five: Knowledge of the Rings	286
Chapter Thirty-six: Freedom	292
Chapter Thirty-seven: Deception	301
Chapter Thirty-eight: Potions	314
Chapter Thirty-nine: The Secret Passageway	324
Chapter Forty: A Change of Plan	342
Chapter Forty-one: Following his Lead	356
Chapter Forty-two: Finding Michael	367
Chapter Forty-three: Mistaken Identity	376
Chapter Forty-four: Gate to Dragon Falls	382
Chapter Forty-five: Re-united	395

Chapter One: The Assailant

Mathis battled through the stormy weather; his shoulders hunched forward, his head bowed; striving forward whilst still clutching a parcel to his chest.

The alley was gloomy, the pavement was slippery and puddles lined the uneven ground. He quickened his step, battling against the torrential rain, clinging on to the package he'd brought for his son's first birthday. He knew Michael wouldn't understand what was going on, but for Mathis, it was another milestone in his new life and a step further away from the one he'd left behind.

Hearing footsteps, he glanced over his shoulder and saw a dark figure gaining ground. As the hairs on the back of his neck prickled, he surged forwards at a greater pace, his heart pounding.

The end of the alley was in sight; he frantically wiped the rain from his eyes and tried staring in front of him, but it was so dark, he couldn't see if there was anyone nearby. Was it his imagination or had the footsteps behind him quickened? He ran towards the end of the alley which opened out onto a familiar street near the local farmhouse, and tried scanning the fields for possible assistance.

Lurching forwards, his ankle landed awkwardly and he clutched the wall for support, but by then it was too late, a strong hand had gripped his right arm. Stubby fingers pinched his flesh under the denim material, spinning him round with such vigour that the parcel slipped from his grasp and landed sodden in a muddy puddle. Mathis faced his assailant, determined to show no fear.

Although his attacker was wider than Mathis, he was a

couple of inches shorter. As expected, he wore black from head to toe, from his muddy boots to his woollen balaclava. The only feature Mathis could distinguish were the misty green eyes.

Straightening up to press his only advantage; Mathis gasped as he noticed a knife handle protruding from a belt behind the attackers back.

"Come wiv me and no-one will get hurt," he snarled.

"What do you want?" Mathis demanded, trying to stop his voice from quivering.

"Don't ask questions. You either come of your own accord or I'll force you to."

Aware of the knife but, unwilling to give in so easily, he tried wrenching himself free. His move anticipated; the attacker punched Mathis just above the chin, forcing his head back and cutting his lip. Blood trickled down his skin.

"So that's the way you wanna play it? Any wife? Kid p'raps?"

"What's it to you?" Mathis slurred, his mouth stinging.

"Have you or haven't you?"

Shaking his head, Mathis prayed his eyes didn't betray his lies. There was no way he was going to allow his family to suffer with him.

"Just as well, a family would only complicate fings."

"What... do... you... want?"

His attacker's eyes smiled gleefully and Mathis tried once more to pull away. This time the assailant aimed at his stomach. The force of the blow winded him, crunching into his ribs, causing such excruciating pain that he could barely breathe. As he was forced onto the floor, more blows pummeled down into his shoulders and back, bruising him physically as well as emotionally.

Pulling back Mathis black hair, the assailant pulled him upright and forced him to look directly into his eyes. "Next in line eh? Rather powerful position don't you think?"

How could he know? How had his past caught up with him? "But... what about my brother?"

"Dead. Killed in battle, and once you've helped us find his ring, you'll be joining him."

Nausea swept over him and he began to retch. His brother was dead and he'd known nothing? He was never going to see him again. Rage consumed him; he would make sure that no-one got their hands on the ring. Moving his arms behind his back, he mumbled a word he had used only once previously, then slipped the ring off his wedding finger until it dangled from his fingertips. Grappling to break free, he yelled as he struggled, disguising the sound of the metal as it landed, unnoticed in a murky puddle close to the discarded present.

Steel pierced his flesh and a sharp pain shot from his shoulder, reaching every part of his body. He watched his blood seep through his clothes and trickle down his chest as another nauseous sensation threatened to overwhelm him.

Struggling, Mathis managed to dislodge the knife from his attackers grip. Sighing, he forced his green-eyed opponent backwards and managed to connect an uppercut to the fiends jaw. Sensing an opportunity, he tried to grab the knife, but wasn't quick enough, and an elbow crashed down onto his shoulder. Exhaustion overwhelmed him.

Unable to take any more, a final shove saw Mathis fall to the floor, where he lay sprawled in a puddle.

His brain instructed his legs to stand, but they refused to obey. His energy evaporated; he was just too weak to fight back, too weak even to yell. Defeated, he lay still, his eyes so battered he could barely see, awaiting death.

Instead of finishing him off, the masked figure produced a frayed piece of rope from a small rucksack he had been carrying over his shoulder. He ran his hands over it playfully, as Mathis turned his head to one side and prayed silently. All hope lost, he offered no resistance as his arms and legs were bound together. As his attacker stoop up to observe his work, Mathis breathed a sigh of relief that at least the disguised figure remained oblivious to the fact that the ring he desperately wanted lay just inches away.

Although the wind had subsided, the cold night air filled Mathis' lungs and stung his half-closed eyes. He tried staying conscious but with each second that passed, he felt fainter, his vision blurring until his eyes closed completely, leaving only the darkness and the sound of his heartbeat to drown out the pounding of the rain and the heavy breathing of his captor.

Struggling to open his heavy eyes, Mathis noticed he was no longer outside lying on a hard, wet floor. Instead he lay on a leather settee near an open fire. He couldn't have been there long, for although he felt warm, his clothes were still damp.

Attempting to achieve a more comfortable position, he winced in pain; his shoulder throbbing from the untended stab wound. Blood, dark and solid, had clotted around its opening, while his jacket clung to him like a second layer of skin. Exhausted, he rested his head on an arm of the chair as he stared at the fire gathering his thoughts. He watched as the embers soared into the air as birds will in flight, only to die; their vivid redness fading to black as they drifted, like the mythical phoenix, into the flames below.

He had no recollection of how he had made it to the house, but knew that if he had been found by a stranger, they would have taken him to hospital. Knowing the attacker must be nearby; his eyes scoured the room for a means of escape. At the far end he noticed some bay windows, while halfway along the wall, to his right, a door was slightly ajar.

He tried swinging his legs on to the edge of the settee, but was prevented by the binding which held his ankles together. His arms, though in front of him, were also tied. Unable to pick either knot, he wiggled his body towards the side of the sofa but was soon out of breath and aching from the bruises he had sustained during the attack.

Then he heard noises. Murmurs at first; but it wasn't long before the sounds became words.

"You said you'd support me on on this!"

"You told me he wouldn't get hurt! You said he'd go along with it!" A high pitched voice trembled.

"He won't tell me where it is. I need to do this to get the answer from him."

"He's half dead in there. Surely that's enough?"

"Yer know I can't leave it like this," the man's voice growled.

For a moment there was quiet. Then the woman

responded calmly, "You don't have to go through with this. Let's take him back to the alley and make an anonymous call for an ambulance; no one need know what you've done." Her words caressed Mathis' ears as he listened, aware that his fate lay in the hands of the winner's voice beyond the wall.

"There's no goin' back. I ain't changing my mind." Pausing his voice, calmer than before, he pleaded, "I'm asking yer to support me in this. Think of the rewards we'll get when we 'and him and the ring over."

"I can't do it. It's not right," she sobbed.

"So you'll split up our family for a Prince who deserted 'is own country?"

"How could you resort to this violence, and kidnapping? What's happened to you?" her voice was hysterical.

Failing to get him to see reason, he could hear her words becoming more frantic, quickening, and tumbling incoherently from her mouth. With no response forthcoming, her arguments quietened; her sadness at his betrayal audible. Holding his breath, Mathis prayed she would make him see sense, though he like her, had given up hope.

"Think carefully about what you're doing. Soon someone will miss him and report his disappearance. He could have a wife at home waiting, calling the police even as we speak.

"He ain't got a wife, I've checked. And even if he does; what would it change?"

"But..."

"Stop it. Even if he 'ad told someone about his past,

which I doubt, he couldn't 'ave told them about us. He don't even know who I am."

"Go back to bed!" she shouted towards the sound of approaching feet. Her orders disobeyed, the feet made their way downstairs.

"Please don't hurt anyone dad. You're not going to kill anyone are you?" a girl's voice squealed.

"Dad, please put the gun down? I'm scared," a boy's trembling voice pleaded.

"'How dare yer tell me what to do! I'm in charge and you'll do as I say, do you 'ear?" The man's voice boomed filled with fury.

The pleas became louder as their mum joined in, building into a crescendo.

"I'm phoning the police," cried the woman.

"Put the phone down!"

"Richard, take your hands off the gun!" she screamed.

"Richard, stop it. Look..."

A sharp gasp and then a gunshot filled the air;

Then another. Then another. Then, the screaming stopped.

***

Conscious of the sound of heavy breathing, he was so confused he didn't even realise that it was him that was making the noise. All he knew was that his heart was beating so fast, he couldn't tell what was throbbing more; his head, his chest or his shoulder.

It wasn't until he heard the clumping of boots from the

hallway that he registered the implications of what had just taken place. Too frightened to contemplate the present, he was fully aware that any chance of freedom had just disappeared with the dying breaths of the hysterical woman and her two innocent children.

Chapter Two: The Ring

A ring, recently worn by an excited father and devoted husband, now lay as motionless as its owner's body, its gleaming band barely visible in the puddle it had landed in.

The air was still and calm, a gentle breeze replacing the wind and rain which, until an hour ago, had drowned the night. Since the attack not one drop had fallen. The moon had woken from its slumber and chased the rainstorms into the darkness. Its faint rays cloaked by the remnants of the clouds which allowed only the faintest glints of light to illuminate the streets below.

In the darkness of the alley something hid behind the safety of the bins; a mouse scuttled from its resting place, frightened by the intruder who, since the attack, had been crouching nervously in the shadows. Fearful eyes peered from the hiding place, darting from one end of the alley to the other.

For over an hour he had been sitting, in the wet, too scared to move. He kept thinking about the look of disbelief which had flashed across Mathis' face as he had heard of his brother's death. He recollected the pain he had felt as the metal had pierced the younger man's flesh and watched in horror as the weeping blood had laced the nearby puddles; he had wept, praying for it to stop.

If he'd been younger, he would have tried to help, but he knew he would be no match for the attacker. Despite feeling useless, he comforted himself with the thought that he could at least prevent the attacker from finding the ring and getting too much power.

He had tried arriving sooner, to warn Mathis of the planned assault, but he had been too late. Instead, he watched as his great-nephew was stabbed and even now, wasn't sure whether Mathis had survived. Trying to remember where he had seen Mathis discard the ring, he had waited until he was certain no one would venture down the alley, and then he'd scoured the puddles. All he could do now was to find the ring and guard it from those who craved its power.

Arm outstretched, his wrinkly hand felt along the wall as a growing ache spread through his body where the feeling in his limbs began to return. Within seconds, pins and needles had set in, signalling the return of blood to the lower part of his body.

For some time he inspected every crevice, scuffling around on his hands and knees. Almost ready to give up, he leaned back on his heels, and rubbed his hands together for warmth and picked up the discarded present. As he did so, he noticed a glint. Making sure no one was nearby, his hand darted to the shining object in the murky water and stowed the find in his pocket. Clutching the sodden present under his arm, he rose to his feet, his legs still shaky, and let out a sigh of relief as he turned round and disappeared.

Chapter Three: Missing

Swallowing a mouthful of stone cold tea, Catherine scrunched her face with distaste. She had made a fresh pot ready for Mathis' return from work, but his cup remained on the breakfast bar, with the two spoonfuls of sugar still unstirred in the bottom.

Tense with frustration, she considered her options, should she keep his tea hot? Or give up hope and throw it away? Picking up her book, she tried reading to stop herself from worrying but was interrupted by the chime of the clock; 11pm, he'd been missing two hours.

Awakened by the sound of chimes; Michael stirred in the second bedroom, but Catherine was too worried to notice. Rising to her feet, she headed to the window of their small, two bedroomed flat and peered down at the dusky street below in anticipation of her husband's arrival. The street was deserted and, for the first time since they had met, she was worried about him.

Anxious, she phoned his work place, hoping that they had asked him to stay on late. When a polite voice informed her he had left his usual time, the answer hit her like a blow to the stomach. Shaking uncontrollably, she hung up. Her heart pounded wildly, she knew something was wrong; he'd never been late without telling her before.

Hearing Michael for the first time, she stared into his room, sadly aware that in less than an hour, her baby boy would be a year old. His presents sat by the coffee table, lovingly wrapped by her and Mathis before he had set off for work.

She had clicked with Mathis from the moment they had met. Of course they rowed sometimes, usually about money, but they were happy. He wouldn't just leave them; something was wrong and she was forced to consider the possibility that he might not be there tomorrow, or the day after. She didn't know how she would cope looking after Michael on her own, she'd never considered having to be a single mother.

Her mind filled with morbid thoughts. What if he'd been robbed, mugged, murdered even? Her overactive imagination explored every possibility until her head ached and her eyes began to feel heavy. Returning to the comforting arms of the sofa, tiredness swept over her like a blanket; as her thoughts once more drifted over the day's events and into the future, what would happen to them now?

Catherine woke to the sound of Michael crying, wanting his morning feed. Exhausted, she dragged herself from the settee, straightened the creases on her skirt and staggered into his room, gazing lovingly at the blonde haired baby in the cot. Allowing his hand to grab hold of her finger, she halted abruptly as she remembered; Mathis, her husband, he hadn't come home! Adrenaline surged through her as she rushed to their bedroom. Flinging wide the door, she looked at their bed, but it remained empty.

Racing to the bathroom, she peered round the door, and then hurried into their tiny kitchen, hoping to find him preparing breakfast. Disappointment clawed at her as the rooms remained empty; he hadn't come home. Returning sadly to her son, she scooped him up and hugged him tightly to her chest.

As she carried Michael through to the front room the phone rang. Quickly she picked up the receiver, hoping to hear Mathis' voice on the other end.

"Catherine?" It was just Jane; her heart fell.

"Yes," was all she could manage, her throat dry.

"I need to talk to someone..."

"Well, erm..." Catherine wasn't ready to play agony aunt to someone but Jane didn't wait for an answer.

"Oh Catherine... it was awful, I still can't believe what's happened," she paused to gather her thoughts. "Last night, as John and I took Alfie round the farmer's field for our usual evening walk, we heard arguing coming from the farmhouse. At first we thought it was a normal argument so didn't want to interfere, especially as we don't really know the family. I mean, they've only been there a couple of months, we barely even say hello to them..."

"And?" Catherine encouraged, eager for her best friend to get to the point. She really wanted to focus on finding her husband, but didn't have the heart to refuse her closest friend, especially as she sounded so distraught.

"I wish I'd done something instead of ignoring it. It was horrific. The next thing we heard was gunshots, three of them, and they sounded so loud; we were literally only metres from the house. The noise was deafening; John lost his grip on Alfie's lead and the poor dog scarpered across the field. It took John ages to catch him; I was so scared the poor thing would get lost. Well, I couldn't help John catch him, what with my bad knee, and I was too scared to go inside, so I called the police."

Catherine could hear her breaking down on the other end of the phone. And no wonder, she thought, what a horrific thing to happen.

After a few deep breaths, Jane continued, her voice unsteady as she chocked back the tears, "When John came back with Alfie we hid behind a gate as we waited for the police. Neither of us saw anyone leave... so we presumed that whoever had fired the gun must still be in there. I can't remember ever being so scared"

"Oh Jane, how awful..." Catherine mumbled, trying to get her head around what she was being told. And at the farmhouse! Poor people, they hadn't been there long. She'd only chatted to the woman once, little more than a week ago, she even seemed quite kind as far as she could remember. She couldn't believe it had happened so near to her flat!

"Fortunately, the police were there within minutes, cordoning off the area. We waited nearby in case we were needed as witnesses, and so saw them bring out the bodies, covered in white sheets, just like in the movies. Catherine, the poor woman and her two children; they were dead, killed outright. It was so horrific, I couldn't stop crying. What if we had knocked on the door? Maybe we could have stopped the row? Prevented it from happening? They might still be alive."

Captivated by this tragedy, Catherine couldn't help but think how strange it was that this had happened the same evening that Mathis had disappeared. "What about her husband? Did he do it?" Catherine asked.

"That's the weird thing! I could have sworn I heard him, well, a man at least. But when they searched the house he wasn't there. No men were found, dead or alive. Yet both John and I were absolutely certain that we'd heard a man's voice." Catherine heard Jane sigh down the phone and wished she could give her friend the support she needed.

"So, any idea who was responsible?" Was it too much of a coincidence that her husband had gone missing the same night these murders had occurred so locally. Perhaps Mathis had seen or heard something suspicious. What if?

"I don't think anyone's been arrested yet. John and I were being questioned at the police station all last night. They kept asking if we'd heard what the row was about and if we were certain we had heard a man's voice. I don't think they can explain it at the moment. We've not long been home, poor Alfie was on his own all night, and after such a shock. He was so pleased to see me this morning, bless him."

So they didn't find anyone else? Then who shot them? What if Mathis had been involved? "Jane?"

"Yes?"

"What time did it happen?" Catherine asked tentatively.

"We went out for our walk about ten, so not long after then."

Sliding from her hands, the receiver landed on the floor. Staring into nothingness, tears rolled down her pale cheeks. Unable to explain why, she instinctively knew that somehow, her husband's disappearance was connected to the awful events at the farmhouse.

Taking hold of the receiver once more, she apologised to Jane, promised to meet up soon; then called the emergency services.

***

That evening she sat in front of a blank screen on the television. Michael, her one reminder of Mathis, shoved his toys in his mouth, enjoying the sensation of eating them more than playing with them. Torn wrapping paper littered the floor while the cake she had laboured over lovingly remained untouched on the plate.

She had reported Mathis missing. 'Nothing much they could do', they had told her, just as she had anticipated. Instinctively she had known, ever since her conversation with Jane, that he wasn't coming home. She didn't know what had happened, or why, or whether she'd ever know the truth; but she did know that from now on, she was on her own. The thought of being a single mother scared her, and not for the first time that evening, she sobbed uncontrollably for everything she had lost and everything she would never have.

Chapter Four: The Birthday Present

Michael was impatient for Science to end. He peered at his battered watch, with its plastic strap that held it together with a safety pin. Just five minutes left!

Mrs. Draygon, the fiery Science teacher hovered over his shoulder, her steely eyes penetrating his test paper, scrutinising it for errors, while her tobacco breath left Michael wanting to gag.

Holding his breath until she was at a safe distance, Michael watched gleefully as she stood directly behind Alvin and proceeded to exhale over the biggest lump of lard in the year. Her thin-lipped mouth smiled as she glanced at his paper, knowing he had, once again, managed to fail.

His test finished, Mike returned to his second favourite pastime; daydreaming. As usual, he imagined slugging Alvin across the chin, an occurrence which would never happen in real life. Just as his hand was connecting, he was brought back to reality by the sound of the bell signalling the end of lesson. Shoving his torn pencil case into his hand-me-down satchel, he placed his test paper in her wrinkly hands and then escaped the classroom before snotty nosed Alvin Aldwinkle tripped him up again.

At the end of the Science corridor stood his two best friends. In fact, thought Michael, they were his only friends. Hazel pushed her long, dark hair away from her flushed face; her blue eyes sparkling brighter than normal. Dan meanwhile, had his hands tucked in his pockets as usual, and was staring at the floor.

Dodging the onslaught of students cascading down the Science corridor, Hazel handed Michael a carrier bag. Today was July 5th, Michael's fifteenth birthday. He hadn't expected anything so was surprised and excited by their gesture. As they headed for their lockers, he pulled out his birthday card, tore open the envelope and gazed longingly at the red convertible on the front; he would have been happy with a Ford or Vauxhall.

"Thanks!" Michael exclaimed while wishing his mum had a car. But with only a cleaners wage to support them, they had very few luxuries, least of all a car!

For as long as he could remember he'd wished his dad hadn't left when he was a baby. At night, in bed, he prayed for his dad to return, to walk through the door with his arms open wide, but he knew it could never be any more than a dream because even if his dad was still alive, he was sure they wouldn't recognise each other.

"Come on Michael!" Hazel tapped her foot impatiently.

"Sorry." Shoving his hand in the bag, he pulled out a small, neatly wrapped present. Ripping the paper apart excitedly, he discovered a box, which when opened, contained the most exquisite ruby ring he'd ever seen. Although he couldn't help but think it looked a little bit feminine, Michael stared in disbelief. He'd never owned any jewellery before, except for his decrepit watch. His mum had promised to buy him a new one with a metal strap for his birthday, but Michael was certain she wouldn't be able to afford it.

"I... er..., it's... it's wicked! Where did you get it? It must have cost a fortune," Michael stammered.

Unexpectedly he felt a tear welling up, which he quickly wiped away, just in case Alvin saw him and really did make him cry; he'd never had such a lovely present. His mum was amazing but she had to work really hard just to provide essentials such as food and clothes; luxuries were out of the question.

"Like it?" enquired Hazel, who looked as excited as Michael felt.

"I love it! How on earth could you afford it?" he asked, hoping he wasn't going to have the police knocking on his door charging him with possession of stolen goods; which wouldn't go down well with his mum at all.

"You'll never believe it," said Hazel. "Go on Dan, you tell him."

Dan, who hadn't spoken since Michael had opened his present, began to explain. "Last week, as we were discussing what to get you for your birthday, we noticed a strange little shop on the corner of the High Street. Neither of us recognised it so we decided to take a look inside, it was empty except for an old man behind the counter; a very strange, very old man!"

As Dan got carried away with the shop owner, Michael took the opportunity to try the ring on for size. Sliding it over his knuckle, he stared at it in disbelief; it fit him perfectly which confused him somewhat, for when he'd first taken it out of the box, he'd felt certain it would be too big.

Obviously excited, Hazel picked up on the story, her arms flailing in the air like an octopus on caffeine. "We glanced around to see if we could find something appropriate and before we knew it, the old man had approached and asked if we needed any help. We told him we were looking for a birthday present but hadn't a clue what to buy."

"The next thing we know," continued Dan, "he shuffled towards us, gave us a strange look, closed his eyes and then asked us your name. I can't say I'd ever experienced that type of sales technique before! But with nothing to lose, we told him your name and age. Honestly Michael, it was unbelievable, as soon as he heard your name, his face turned deathly pale and he looked like he was having trouble breathing..."

Hazel carried on, "We thought he was having a heart attack so we grabbed his arms to stop him from collapsing. Then, as if nothing had happened, his face lit up and he muttered something under his breath. I could have sworn it was something about finally finding you," glancing at Michael, Hazel watched for his reaction but Mike, as dumbfounded as his friends, was at a complete loss as to who this man was. However, she had him fully captivated and he listened much more intently.

"Slightly concerned by his interest in you, we were just about to leave when he called out saying that he had the perfect gift. With that, he produced this magnificent ring from his trouser pocket. We couldn't believe our eyes!"

"Completely gobsmacked," agreed Dan.

"We tried saying it was out of our price range but he insisted we take it, that it was free, and that it was meant for you." Again Hazel gave Michael a quizzical look, but when he remained silent, she continued, "Then, as if things couldn't get any more curious, just as we were leaving he asked us to tell you it was from an old relative and that he'll visit you soon. I tried asking him what he meant but before I'd finished my sentence, he'd vanished… just disappeared into thin air! Sounds like something from one of your books, doesn't it?" joked Hazel.

Michael was stumped. He didn't know any strange, old men and as far as he knew, he had no living relatives.

"Come on Michael, stop day-dreaming," urged Hazel as she straightened the collar of her expensive new jacket. Feeling scruffy next to them, Michael pulled his arm out his jacket sleeve and shoved his sorry excuse for a coat in his satchel.

Chapter Five: The Watch

"A million love songs are made of... and here I am...."

"Oh no, not again!" Michael winced as he opened the front door. Entering his second floor, two-bedroomed flat after school had become something of a ritual for Michael who had grown up cringing at his mother's love of a pop group called Take That. He would approach with caution, check that no-one he knew was standing nearby, then dive in and slam the door quietly behind him.

Hazel and Dan teased him about his slightly eccentric entrance and his unreasonable fear, but he had become paranoid about anyone hearing his mum sing; especially since Alvin and Animal had overheard her warbling down the street and had proceeded to serenade him with the song 'Babe,' every day at school for a fortnight.

Why Take That? It was getting so bad that on a couple of occasions he'd caught himself humming their songs in class, which probably wouldn't have been so bad if he'd been female, (just as well his school reputation was non-existent anyway). He had hoped her infatuation would fade, and it had started to; but then, just as other artists had established themselves, what do they go and do? Launch a comeback! Her singing he could just about cope with, but it was her habit of gyrating her hips which banged into everything in sight that he would never come to terms with.

"Hello pumpkin, good day at school?" Outwardly he smiled, but inwardly he winced at the pet name she insisted on calling him, even in front of his friends and teachers.

"Not bad. Science test last thing but I think I've done okay," he slouched onto the ripped settee, but instead of switching on the television like most other children his age, he picked up his latest book. He was half way through Dickens' Hard Times, and couldn't help but think that it had been aptly named, because it was certainly giving him difficulties. However, he persevered as his English teacher insisted that he read these classics to improve his writing skills. Why she encouraged this he had no idea, he was already top of his English class, as he was in most subjects, giving him a reputation as a boffin. This, and the fact that his mother was a cleaner who could barely afford food to eat had resulted in a miserable existence at school, where bullies such as Alvin took great delight in calling him 'boff', 'Professor Pumpkin' and 'cleaners boy', in lessons.

Glancing at his hand, Michael wondered whether he should show his mum the ring and ask if she knew anything about the strange old man and his apparent family connection. Instinctively he rejected the idea, thinking that seeing it would make her feel guilty about not being able to afford anything expensive for his birthday. Too excited to read and unable to think of anything to say to his mum, he sat patiently, daydreaming of a time when he would be rich and popular.

"I've made your favourite, cottage pie, as a special treat." Wearing her best dress, his mum waltzed into the room and placed a tray on his lap."

Bloated from devouring his overlarge portion, he carried his plate to the kitchen before rushing to his room to change out of his uniform. Just as he was about to collapse onto his bed for a quick rest, he noticed a small, neatly wrapped present on his pillow. Hoping it contained the watch his mum had promised, he was thrilled when he gazed down at the metal face and strap, just like the one he'd imagined.

As the proud owner of a new ring and a watch, he couldn't believe how lucky he was. Fastening the new strap around his skinny wrist, this time without the aid of a safety pin, he rushed to the kitchen and flung his arms around his mum's neck.

She was thrilled. For the past year she had saved a small amount each month just to be able to afford it, and from the joy on his face, she knew it had been worth every penny. She only regretted she couldn't afford more and that he still didn't have any of the gadgets and computers that other children his age enjoyed.

"Better than that tatty thing you wear at the moment," she joked, her face glowing with pleasure at her son's approval. Though only fifteen, Michael seemed much older and she often worried that he'd missed out on the carefree stage other children had enjoyed.

Clinging to him, she savoured his joy, unwilling to let him go. For although she always wore a brave face, they were both aware it was also the anniversary of the day the police had classed his dad a missing person. Not knowing if he was alive or dead still haunted her, especially on days like this when it was brought to the forefront of her mind.

"You really look like him," releasing him, she looked into his slim, innocent face, "same blue eyes and bone structure, just different colour hair," she said, running her hand through his blonde locks.

Not wanting to wallow, he freed himself and rushed back into his room to change into something more comfortable. He needed some space to think about his dad, his ring and of the mysterious man at the shop.

Suddenly his ring finger started tingling; the gold band felt warm against his skin and the ruby in the centre started glowing. Michael gawped, blinking in disbelief.

Then, almost as soon as it had started, the tingling subsided and the band and ruby returned to their normal state. Shocked, he was left wondering whether it had been his imagination playing tricks on him. His natural instinct was to rush to the kitchen and confide in his mum. Yet he couldn't do it for fear of sounding ridiculous. How could he, a fifteen year old, tell his mum about a magical, glowing ring and a disappearing shopkeeper? She'd tell him he'd been reading too many fantasy stories or declare him clinically insane. No, this was something he'd have to work out for himself, obviously with the help of Dan and Hazel.

Chapter Six: The Visit

Brightly coloured birds chirp noisily in the tree under which he stands. Michael has never seen so many unusual species and stares at them wondrously.

Turning his gaze towards the landscape before him, none of it is familiar. In fact, he hasn't a clue where he is. Whilst scrutinising a round, hairy creature carrying its dinner up the misshapen tree, he feels a gentle tap on his shoulder. Unnerved, he swirls round quickly to discover what touched him.

Nothing… Nobody.

Shielding his eyes from the sun's glare, he cranes his neck left then right but finds nothing.

To his right a hazy mist is settling at the top of a mountain range and at the bottom, hundreds of tall trees stand like loyal subjects thronging round their King. Michael notices that the tree under which he is standing is inhabited by many creatures and birds, and yet he can't imagine anything making their home in the skeletal trees in the distance. Their emptiness fills him with foreboding, causing the hairs on the back of his neck to prickle. The only sign of life is the shimmering stream flanking the skeletal trees that flows round the perimeter of the forest.

Down the hill to his left, he spies a small village, with smaller clusters of houses scattered further in the distance. The closest houses are crooked and unsymmetrical, with smoking chimneys protruding from the brick walls instead of the roof. Most of the cottages are only one storey high, and their gardens like the houses, are tiny.

Further in the distance there is another hill. On it, a stone wall encases a huge expanse of land. In the centre stands a majestic castle which towers over its surroundings. It is exquisite, completely unlike his small flat back in Grays.

Another tap on his shoulder startles him. He pivots round, turning so fast he catches his foot in a small pothole and stumbles backwards. Regaining his balance, he faces a man who looks the best part of a hundred years old. Michael stares disbelievingly at the wrinkled old figure that had just appeared, disappeared and reappeared without so much as being seen or heard.

"Wondering who I am and how I got here, aren't you?" his voice is soft and reassuring, with no sign of his age given away in his speech.

Scrutinising the strange man; his bright red shirt, the black and white striped waistcoat, mustard tie and finally his matching brown cardigan and trousers, they all caught his attention. Despite being filled with anxiety, Michael can't help but feel an irrepressible desire to laugh at this bizarre and colourful ensemble of clothing.

"Is something wrong?"

"No, nothing... I was just wondering..." Michael stammers as he twists the ring on his finger nervously. Glancing round, his eyes search for anything which might explain his companion's sudden appearance, but he finds nothing, "how you got here? Why I didn't see you a moment ago? Who are you?" Realising the old man is struggling to keep up; he halts his barrage of questions.

"It's so good to finally meet you. I'm Abednego, though most people call me Abe, and I live in the castle over there…" Sensing Michael's unease, Abednego places his arm comfortably around his shoulder. "Don't look so scared, everything's fine. You might feel confused now, but it will all become much clearer soon."

Dumbfounded at the old man's knowledge of his name, Michael is lost for words. Instead he stands up, opening and closing his mouth like a demented goldfish.

"Please don't be alarmed. I'll explain later. Relax, no-one else here has a clue about your existence, so you've no need to worry."

Still speechless Michael continues to stare as Abe continues, "Just in case you're wondering, the ring was from me. Now, listen carefully. You must promise me that you will protect it with your life, for it will guide and help you. Hide it and tell no-one here of its existence for its value is more than you'll be able to understand, for the moment at least." Before Michael could respond, Abednego continued, "and beware; here in Kilion, people aren't always what they seem, just make sure you think carefully before talking to anybody. Many would sell their own mothers to get their hands on that ring. Make sure you let no-one influence you. Go with your instincts, and only then will you be able to fulfil your destiny." Abednego's face slowly turns red as the excitement of finally finding Mathis' son overwhelms him.

"I'm not sure I understand what you mean by my destiny? Who shouldn't I trust? Why am I here?"

"I'm your Great Uncle," he chirps, ignoring Michael's questions, "Oh, I'm so pleased I've found you, though it's taken some time. Never been to a place with so many houses! Never mind, now that I've found you, I know everything will be just fine."

Michael stares at Abednego, realizing he is still no closer to discovering why he is there. However, before he is able to repeat his questions, a clap of thunder makes him jump. Suddenly, in the space of seconds, the bright sky becomes dull and overcast as a blanket of greyness descends. Rain cascades in torrents and the birds stop their happy chirping; some freeze like statues, their bright colours fading to a stone grey; others take flight, heading away in the direction of the forest.

Within seconds his clothes are drenched and clinging to his skinny frame. Pushing his hair from his face, he is astonished to discover the old man has disappeared, leaving Michael desperate to find out more about him and this strange place.

"MICHAEL, WAKE UP!" Stirring, Michael awoke to his mother's concerned face.

"Get up or you'll be late for school."

"But I was in the middle of an important dream. Oh well, at least it was until it started to rain."

"Unless it's the winning lottery numbers, I suggest you turn your attention to getting up and dressed; I've been trying to wake you for ages."

"Sorry."

"You were talking in your sleep again, it's that overactive imagination of yours." Opening the curtains, inviting in the rays of sunlight, she headed towards the door, "do hurry; Hazel will be here soon. Oh and your breakfast is on the table."

Far too early in the morning to be that bright and awake, Michael thought to himself. Scrunching his eyes tight, he tried recalling his dream, but as always, although he could remember what he saw and what the old man had looked like, he had no memory of what was discussed other than his claim that he was a member of the family.

Suddenly a thought occurred to him; what if the man in his dream and the man in the shop were the same person?

Uncertain about the significance of his dream, he pushed it aside for he had no intention of Hazel finding him in his pyjamas.

Within minutes he was munching his breakfast, waiting impatiently for Hazel to show up so he could tell her about his dream. Regular as clockwork, she knocked just as Michael shoved the remnants of his peanut butter sandwiches in his mouth.

"See ya later!" he shouted, grabbing his old satchel.

"Have a nice day at school pumpkin."

Cringing, Michael slammed the door shut before she embarrassed him further by demanding as kiss.

Before they had finished descending the stairs of his flat, he was recounting his dream, telling her everything he could remember.

Hazel remained quiet for some time after he'd finished. Initially Michael was tempted to disturb her, but decided to wait a while because she wasn't known for pondering over things too long; usually Dan was the thinker of the group.

However, after a couple of minutes his impatience got the better of him. "So, what do think? Was he trying to tell me something important, or was it my imagination running away with me again?"

"I can't believe it," Hazel whispered disbelievingly. "You described him exactly how he was in the shop and I don't remember either of us mentioning what he was wearing. It can't just be a dream, there's got to be more to it!"

Michael knew she was right. Strolling, deep in thought, they made their way along the main road towards the school gates. Still in silence, glancing at Michael's hand, Hazel noticed he was still wearing the ring. "I'd take that off for school if I were you, unless you want it confiscated."

Unwilling to risk the only thing he owned which was actually worth anything being confiscated, Michael tried removing it only to realize it was stuck fast. Taking a deep breath, not that this would actually help in anyway, he tried again, this time pulling even harder; it was no use, the ring wouldn't budge.

After struggling for what seemed like several minutes but was probably no more than seconds, the only thing Michael had achieved was the reddening and swelling of his finger. Next he tried wetting it, hoping the moisture would remove the stubborn ring, but it was not use, the ring was stuck like a limpet to a rock, and it wasn't letting go.

At this point, Hazel, who had until now, been watching with amusement, offered her services. Although the thought crossed her mind that even if he was caught wearing it, they probably wouldn't be able to get the ring off him either. Nevertheless, she clasped both hands round his already sore finger and yanked in one direction while he pulled his throbbing finger in the other.

Several failed attempts later, Michael winced with pain as he gazed at his red finger. People passing by stopped and stared as they resumed the tug of war, each pulling as hard as possible.

Eventually, after much heaving and sighing, Hazel's foot slipped. With bothof them pulling in opposite directions, something had to give and unfortunately it wasn't the ring. Hazel stumbled backwards, tripping and falling, with Michael following closely behind. Onlookers howled with laughter as both landed heavily, sprawled on the dusty pavement.

The exhausted pair gathered their belongings together, aware of the laughter peeling through the street. Michael's vision became a blurry mixture of pointed fingers and callous faces as malicious shouts deafened him.

"OI MIKE, SEE YER IN THE DIRT WHERE YA BELONG. NEVER MIND PUMPKIN, I'M SURE YER MUM WILL CLEAN YA UP, AFTER ALL, DOIN' THAT FOR A LIVIN' SHE SHOULD BE USED TER IT!" Alvin Aldwinkle; the tallest, fattest and most uncouth boy in their year, who just happened to be in most of Michael's classes, hurled abuse across the street. Of all the people who could have seen him fall, it was just typical that one was Alvin. Now he would never live it down!

Shoving his equipment back into his ripped satchel, he could feel his breathing quicken and the blood rush to his cheeks. Falling was embarrassing enough, without the insults which were now being called out. Students who had continued their journey now stopped and returned their attention to him, fuelled with this new ammunition. A barrage of insults ensued; name calling, laughing, jeering and staring, simply because of Alvin's revelation that his mother was a cleaner. His face turned an even deeper shade of red and his head was now throbbing so violently he thought it would explode. Praying for the ground to open up and swallow him, he bowed his head in a bid to block out the faces permeating his vision.

Placing her arm round him comfortingly, Hazel smiled awkwardly, knowing how he must be feeling. Yet Michael was oblivious to her attempts. Instead, dwelling on his anger which was stirring inside of him like molten lava in an erupting volcano, he knew it was only a matter of time before he exploded. He hated the way they attacked his mum, insinuating that she wasn't as good as them just because she was a cleaner.

Michael hoped that someday, when he was watching, Alvin would fall over, and perhaps then he would know what it was like. He sighed; everyone knew things like that never happened to bullies like Alvin. Almost as soon as he thought it, his finger started tingling. He was horrified to discover that once more the ruby in the centre of the ring was glowing, only this time he noticed a black spot appear in the centre of the ruby which he hadn't seen before. It looked like an eye, and more worryingly, it seemed as though it was staring straight at him, which of course, was ridiculous. Desperate to hide it, he clenched his fist and shoved his hand in his pocket, praying no-one would notice. He was lucky; no-one did, for at that moment Alvin detracted all the attention away from him. Hearing the renewed guffaws of laughter, Michael looked up and took in the sight of Alvin lying on the ground; clutching his right ankle.

Astonished, Hazel watched gleefully. There collapsed on the ground, a stony faced Alvin glowered at those who dared to laugh at his misfortune. Michael stared in disbelief as Alvin struggled to his feet, clutching at his cronies who helped hoist his lumbering body off the pavement.

"Get me up!" he rasped, scowling at his three cronies.

Michael could imagine him making a mental list of all the offenders. "May take his mind off of bullying us for a bit," he whispered, as they surged towards school, determined to keep out of Alvin's way.

"Strange wasn't it?" remarked Hazel.

Michael didn't know what to say. Should he tell her what he had thought moments before Alvin's fall? Should he tell her that his ring had glowed? That it had made his whole hand tingle? Unable to contain his excitement, he knew he couldn't keep it to himself so the rest of the journey was spent discussing the last couple of days and wondering what was going to happen next.

Chapter Seven: Retribution

The first chance they had to talk to Dan was in the canteen at break time. Grabbing a seat next to him, Hazel couldn't contain her excitement. "You'll never guess what happened to Michael last night!"

"Or what happened on the way to school this morning," added Michael, who if possible, was even more excited than Hazel.

"I heard about Alvin's tumble," Dan grinned, "though only by catching the gist of whispering in the corridor. No one's brave enough to mention it too loudly in case he or his friends overhear."

"Not that, though it's part of it."

"What then?"

Dan sat in silence, his eyes unblinking. When Michael had finished, a smile spread across his face while his mind worked overtime to explain the events.

As the quietest of the trio, Dan contemplated everything thoroughly before commenting. Now however, he simply pictured the scene he'd missed earlier and his dark brown eyes sparkled with pleasure.

Stretching his arms above his head, he tensed his muscles; picked on by boys in his year, it didn't stop some of the girls secretly admiring the toned physique from his enforced tennis lessons. Despite his good looks and athletic abilities he wasn't one of the popular kids. In fact, like Michael, he was an outcast. Alvin and his lapdogs picked on him because of his good manners and posh voice. For years, Alvin, as posh as a portion of fish and chips, had made it his goal to ensure everyone regarded Dan as a social outcast. This suited Daniel who preferred having a couple of close friends to a group of people he barely knew. It had never bothered him that he wasn't one of the popular kids, for he had never been good at mixing with others, partly because he was an only child and partly because his parents were always parading him to their work colleagues like a token trophy. That was of course, when they weren't travelling on work related business and leaving him in the care of the live-in nanny.

Thinking carefully about the situation, Dan finally responded, "I think we need to keep a diary of everything that's happened so far so we don't forget anything. It may even help us work out why these strange things are happening."

"What a great idea," shouted Hazel.

"Shhh, keep your voice down," whispered Michael, "we don't want anyone else finding out what's going on."

Apologizing, Hazel rested her head on her hands thoughtfully. One reason Hazel was so likeable was her enthusiasm for everything; she had an aura about her which brought out the best in them. No matter how depressed or confused he was, Michael could always rely on Hazel to make him smile. Dan complimented this set-up by putting problems into perspective and offering sound and sensible advice.

Being a year older than the others in her year had alienated her from most students, while only starting half-way through the pervious academic year had increased her isolation. Fortunately, both Dan and Michael, knowing how it felt being an outsider, had offered her their friendship and ever since then, the bond between the three of them had become unbreakable. Hazel had immediately felt at ease with them, because unlike most in their year they weren't judgmental; they liked her for who she was, and hadn't asked any questions about her past or why she was re-sitting Year 10. Rumours had been rife among the other students, stories of a teenage pregnancy, and time in a detention centre taking the top spots in the fiction category that explained why she was a year behind. Hazel hadn't bothered to put anyone right, she really didn't care what people thought about her, except for her friends.

Michael was the third 'misfit.' Unlike Hazel and Dan who came from financially stable, even wealthy backgrounds, Michael and his mum were very poor. Dan was picked on because he was too rich, and Michael because he wasn't wealthy enough, these factors didn't bother them though; they were best friends and stuck together through thick and thin.

The bell rung loudly signalling the end of break, and Dan and Michael sighed. It was Maths next and no matter how hard they tried, Michael and Dan simply couldn't grasp the main concepts of algebra, relying on the mathematical genius of Hazel to get them through. This particularly frustrated Michael as it was the only subject he was unable to grasp and he hated the idea of failure.

Despite being one of their more pleasant teachers, Mrs. Moss, their Maths teacher, was completely incapable of controlling a class of 15 year olds. Now, he wasn't a person who normally looked to blame others for his failings, but

Michael did think this significantly contributed to his lack of ability. After all, how could he concentrate properly on the numbers in front of him while others in the class shouted and yelled like they were at and England football match?

Before they had even finished filing into the room, Alvin was already constructing paper airplanes to throw at innocent bystanders. These usually hit Mrs Moss square on the head, causing howls of laughter for the remainder of the lesson. How she had failed to work out the culprit, Michael had no idea.

"Can anyone tell me what x is?" Mrs Moss asked expectantly, while most of the class were still unpacking their equipment.

"Oi Mike, see yer mum's clean'd ya up. S'pose she's got all the rite cleanin stuff, ya know, wat wiv her job an' that." Shouted the slobbering Alvin across the length of the classroom.

Michael couldn't believe Alvin's audacity, especially after his fall. Typical that no-one seemed to remember that part of the morning! 'Probably too scared to mention it,' thought Michael.

"You're right, she does have lots of cleaning equipment. Perhaps she could lend it to you sometime, as it looks like you don't possess any," Hazel retaliated to a gobsmacked Alvin.

"Please Hazel, don't aggravate him too much, last time we ended up in the school pond, and I don't fancy having to explain another incident like that to my parents, they're already threatening me with boarding school," Dan pleaded. Respectfully, Hazel bit her lip.

"Don't yer eva talk t'me like that agen. Ya 'ear?" His threatening tone caused a hushed silence to sweep across the room. Daniel felt the hairs on the back of his neck prickle. Hazel sighed, annoyed that no-one else would stand up to him. Okay, so he was big, over six foot, and perhaps fourteen to fifteen stone which was gigantic compared to most of the students in the year, but that shouldn't mean he could act as he pleased at the expense of others. Mrs Moss, pretending not to hear, continued discussing algebra with a clearly disinterested class. The only consolation Hazel could find was the thought that his physical enormity was probably his consolation prize for his complete lack of looks, personality and intelligence.

Michael nudged Hazel and winked, "wish I'd said that. We'll just have to walk home as fast as possible tonight."

Hazel returned his smile, all the while praying the day would end better than it had started. The last thing she wanted was to have to pick herself off the floor twice in one day.

As the bell rang signalling the end of school, and more importantly, the end of the week; Dan, Hazel and Michael scurried like scared mice out of their English classroom. Walking twice their normal speed, they hoped to avoid bulky bully-boy Alvin. Michael struggled to keep up with Hazel and Dan as the sole of his shoe kept tripping him up.

"Hurry up!" Hazel yelled over her shoulder at a straggling Michael.

Trying not to trip over the sole of his left shoe, Michael broke into a jog as he clutched his satchel into his chest, making sure none of his belongings fell out where his zip had broken.

Michael and Hazel had decided to change their route home and go through the alley. Dan, who thought an isolated alley was the perfect place to lay in wait to beat someone up, had been outvoted. Hazel's persuasion and Michael's pleading had won the day and Daniel was starting to think they had been right as there had been no sign of Alvin yet.

"I can't believe we're going to such lengths just to avoid that big oaf," Hazel muttered.

"Let's hope he's forgotten his threat and decided to pick on someone else tonight," said Dan wistfully.

"Sumfin' tells me yer luck aint in," a malicious voice bellowed behind them; all three froze. How had he managed to get there? Surely they would have noticed him on their way home?

"Didn't expect to see me 'ere did ya?" A smile spread across Alvin's fat, spotty face, detracting only briefly from his goofy front teeth.

'Nothing like stating the obvious is there?' Michael thought to himself dismally. However he refrained from voicing his thoughts, not wanting to aggravate an already dangerous situation.

"Oi Weasel, come 'ere and 'ave a lookie at what I've found," Alvin roared between small bursts of laughter, relishing their scared expressions. Out of the dark shadows Alvin's three cronies emerged. Weasel first, the smallest of the group and aptly named after his sly nature. Everyone knew he was the grass, making enquiries, eavesdropping on unsuspecting conversations and then feeding his discoveries onto Alvin, the pack leader, who was much too dim to work out anything for himself. Despite being disliked by virtually everyone else, no-one dared attack him, for everyone knew he had Alvin's protection. By his look of glee, it was obvious it had been Weasel who had overheard their conversation and informed the others.

"Come on Alv, let's get stuck in," Beef urged. Despite being only a couple of inches smaller than Alvin, and almost as obese, Beef seemed awestruck by Alvin and did anything Alvin requested of him. He liked nothing better than attacking and humiliating students against whom Alvin had a personal vendetta; and as Alvin always had a vendetta against someone; Beef was kept constantly busy and happy.

Animal was the last of the fearsome foursome; his IQ was even lower than Alvin's, and he had an annoying habit of grunting approval every time Alvin made a suggestion. In all the time Michael had known him, too long as far as he was concerned, not once had he heard Animal mutter a proper word. He even seemed incapable of saying 'yes' or 'no' like most ordinary human beings; instead producing a noise rather akin to a snort through his overlarge, slightly reddish nostrils.

"What yer waitin' for?" Alvin's booming voice echoed through the alley.

The four faces edged closer, their eyes twinkling like a child opening his birthday present. Like a pack of wolves they slobbered as they contemplated their prey. Fearfully, Michael, Dan and Hazel shrank back, turned and raced towards the exit. Their hearts pulsed rapidly as they stumbled forwards, Michael clasping his bag to stop his work falling out, and Daniel swiping his hair out from his eyes. Stumbling over his loose sole, Michael crashed to the ground like a sack of potatoes. Dan and Hazel, having got slightly ahead, heard Michael's yelp; hesitated, then turned to help him… sealing their fate. Gripping an arm each they hauled him to his feet, all too aware of the lumbering bodies approaching. Quickly wiping himself down, Michael glanced behind him, only to see not two feet away towered Alvin, Animal, Beef and Weasel, all grinning wildly. Beef rubbed his hands excitedly as Michael, Dan and Hazel closed their eyes and started to pray.

Chapter Eight: The Hopkin's Empire

Daniel's kindness certainly hadn't been inherited from his greedy, self-obsessed parents who were more worried about attending a client's dinner party than their son's parents evening.

Mr Hopkins glared at his son who shrunk back into his chair, inwardly cursing Hazel for insulting Alvin in front of everyone.

"Been fighting have we? Think it's clever, fighting like common riff-raff do you? Once again you've shown complete disregard for our family name! I certainly don't expect this appalling behaviour from an heir to the Hopkins Empire; an Empire, may I remind you, that your mother and I have worked extremely hard to build up." His father's near black eyes were just inches away from Dan, who was conscious of the cold beads of sweat forming on his bruised skin.

Dan was too afraid to meet his dad's eyes. He hated that his father always believed the worst of him, never asking for his side of the story. Dan had given up trying to vindicate himself, now he simply sat; eyes downcast, praying for the lecture to end and for the self- discipline not to shout back. Dan was mad, not at Alvin, not even at his black eye and swollen lip, but at the lack of any sympathy and love from his parents.

"Have you seen yourself in the mirror? You look like a commoner, certainly not like a son of mine. It still amazes me how respectable people like your mother and I managed to end up with a hooligan for a son. No wonder your mother is always worrying about you, look at you! If anything like this happens again, we'll send you to boarding school like the other children of our Class." Daniel had been holding his breath; anticipating this threat. "And if I catch you hanging around with that poor, pathetic boy in future, there'll be trouble. I know he's the cause of all your problems... and your present poor attitude..." As Mr Hopkins continued insulting his friends, Dan's mind drifted to a place where his father's voice couldn't penetrate.

His dad's sudden bout of wheezing brought Dan crashing back to reality as his gaze rested on his dad's bright red face and swollen cheeks. This wasn't a new look, nor an attractive one; he always bore a slight resemblance to a pig. Dan had yet to figure out how his dad spent so much time at the local sports centre yet still stayed overweight. He was only a couple of stones overweight, but he was prone to high blood pressure which made him appear unhealthier than he really was.

His mother was the complete opposite, being exceptionally skinny and constantly preening herself in the mirror. She had no idea that she bore a closer resemblance to a giraffe than a model; for any beauty was overshadowed by her vanity and unusually long neck which meant she towered over her husband by at least four inches.

Rushing over, cursing Dan under her breath, his mother loosened her husband's tie, escorted him to the sofa and handed him a glass of water. "How are you feeling now dear? Better?"

She knew it wasn't Dan's fault, but glared at him anyway. "Look what you've done! Really, you'll be the death of us.

Now apologise immediately, and then go to your room to consider your actions."

"Sorry," he mumbled grudgingly before escaping upstairs.

After a quick rest they got ready to attend yet another dinner party. By then, Dan was so engrossed writing his diary he didn't even realise they had gone.

Mary, the live-in nanny, opened his bedroom door quietly before craning her head round. "Never mind dear, they're off again tomorrow for at least three weeks this time, something to do with a new deal they're working on. Then it'll be just us and no more lectures!" Her calming voice and soothing smile were a refreshing change from his parent's blank stares and grimaces. These mystery trips filled him with excitement, and with his parents away Mary took charge. She was more of a parent to him than his real ones had ever been.

"Thanks Mary," his swollen lips smiled.

"That's better; now let me see to those injuries of yours."

***

"Oh dear, what's happened? Sit down, I'll make you a cuppa and you can tell me all about it." Soothed Hazel's Nan, Rose, as she headed for the kettle and first aid box in the kitchen. Fortunately her Nan wasn't at all judgemental and never flew off the handle at anyone; except maybe for her step-mother.

"Drink it up before it goes cold." Perching next to Hazel on the cream leather sofa Rose sighed despairingly. It baffled her how Hazel, an attractive, intelligent and easy going girl, managed to encounter so much trouble at school. Luckily Hazel wasn't one to wallow in self-pity, which was just as well after all she had been through.

She regaled the story of Michael and her falling over, Alvin's immediate stumble and their conversation in Maths. Of course, she omitted any mention of the ring; that was their secret.

"It's all very well being witty, but some things are better left unsaid, especially if it's going to result in a black eye! I can't believe he actually hit a girl." Mortified at Alvin's effrontery, Rose began ranting about boys nowadays; it took a great deal of persuasion for Rose to agree not to report the incident; Hazel dreaded to think how bad things would be if Alvin found out.

"Anyway Nan, hadn't we better go shopping? If we don't go soon I'll be at a greater risk of starvation than bullying!"

"I'll just grab my purse." Rose scoured downstairs, her movements extremely fluid for someone of seventy. Even Hazel's friends were amazed at her fitness and well-being, she was so full of life, walked miles each day and Hazel couldn't remember the last time she had been ill. Rose declared it was the result of years of healthy living and constant exercise, though Hazel put it down to being blessed with healthy genes, which unfortunately, her mother had not inherited.

"With all the commotion, I nearly forgot, your dad called earlier, said he'd call back about eight, but I didn't get much else 'cause that thing he calls a wife was shouting in the background! How your dad fell for such a horrid woman, especially so soon after your beautiful mother, I'll never know, it's like she's put a spell on him." Rose's face started turning red and she only relaxed when Hazel placed her arm around her shoulder. "Sorry dear, I know I shouldn't get so worked up, I just wish things were like they used to be."

"So do I, but we shouldn't dwell on the past. Come on, let's get going." Putting on a brave face, Hazel manoeuvred her Nan out the house, trying to suppress the aching sensation which had engulfed her since the loss of her mum only eighteen months ago. She loved her dad, but found it hard reconciling herself to the way he had so easily replaced her mother, remarrying after only a year; and with someone so nasty!

***

Michael stared miserably at Charles Dickens' Hard Times, trying to distinguish the words through his swollen eye. His mum had tried comforting him when he told her what had happened, although he had omitted the comments about her job, knowing how much it would devastate her. She always felt that she let Michael down because she had so little money. This was ridiculous as Michael adored her, but she was always comparing herself to others and worrying she wasn't able to give him what other students had.

"What a great age fifteen is turning out to be! It's only been two days and already I've been beaten up and publicly humiliated," he sighed.

Then glancing at his hand, he scolded himself for his self-pity. After all, he was doing well at school; had a loving mother; two great friends and the mysteries of the magical ring and the man in funny clothing. His face brightened at the thought of writing everything down. Using an old notebook he'd found in the rickety drawer under his bed, he carefully wrote 'Michael's Diary – Keep out,' before writing everything down.

***

Grabbing his schoolbag the following morning, Daniel remembered just in time that he'd left his history homework in his bedroom. Rushing upstairs, he was brought to a standstill outside his parents study by the sound of their voices. Curious, he tiptoed closer to the door and strained to hear their conversation.

"Everything's going so smoothly, I reckon it'll be weeks rather than months before we lay our hands on it, and as soon as we do, the deal will be in the bag."

Daniel sighed. Their business was all they ever talked about, they were obsessed. Fortunately for Dan's sanity, their business often took them away for days and sometimes weeks at a time, which provided some much needed respite from their constant moaning and lectures.

"Just think of how rich it will make us!" Yvonne screeched excitedly.

"Millions I reckon, just think, we'll never have to work again!" his dad exclaimed with delight.

Daniel's heart plummeted. The thought of his parents retiring early was too much to bear. How would he cope with them constantly at home?

"Have you packed everything? Our waterproofs?" his father asked.

"I've been packed for days."

Curious as to why they would need waterproofs on a business trip, he continued to listen, and besides what would make them so very rich so quickly? Maybe they were oil tycoons!

As voices softened, Dan stooped in closer. Not once had they ever told Dan where they were going, they never even left a contact number in case of an emergency. Just as well nothing serious had ever happened while they had been away.

"… once it's completed we can finally send him to boarding school!"

Catching his breath, his mind raced frantically. Why would they want to send him to boarding school? And why did they have to wait until after the deal?

As silence descended behind the door, Daniel backed away, anxious not to be caught. His thoughts were troubled by the conversation; he was in autopilot as he rushed to his room, collected his homework and made his way to school.

Chapter Nine: Freak Weather

"Boarding school!" Exclaimed Hazel, "they can't do that! Tell them you won't go."

"I'm pretty sure that tactic won't work, my parents don't tend to care about what I think or want! They haven't done for as long as I can remember. Anyway, it's not so bad; at least I won't have to live with them."

"But why once the deal's completed? What's it got to do with you?"

"Nothing. I've never met their clients, couldn't even tell you their names. And as for the deal, it could be about anything. They don't even discuss what's on television with me, let alone business transactions."

"So you know nothing?" Michael studied Dan's face, trying to gauge whether he was withholding anything, but from his confused expression, it was obvious he knew as little as they did.

Bell rang, and while Hazel and Dan headed to Mr Stein's class, Michael shuffled to Mrs Dragon's science room, wondering whether their tests had been marked yet.

Fumes from the gas taps invaded his nostrils as he entered the room and sat at the front, as far away as possible from Alvin and Animal who were huddled at the back.

Animal stared at him like a crazed bull, making Michael feel nervous. However, he decided that as long as it was only Animal's stare boring into him and not a sharp object, he would benefit more from listening to the test answers than worrying about him.

"Michael dear, be an angel and hand these out please, that's a good boy." Shoving a bundle of answer papers into his chest, she bared her rotten teeth in what looked more like a growl than a grin. The rest of the class, following Alvin's lead, sniggered as the word 'angel' left her lips, leaving Michael, once more, in a state of embarrassment.

Glancing at the first paper, he flinched at the sight of Alvin's name scrawled at the top. Alvin leered at him as he cautiously walked over. Staring at the papers, Michael was unable to suppress a grin at the sight of 8% and a U scrawled at the top of his answer booklet. He didn't usually delight in the failures of others, but he couldn't help but relish the thought that the furthest Alvin would probably go in life would be the end of a dole queue.

Holding the paper out at arm's length, Michael prayed Alvin hadn't noticed him smirk at his paper. Alvin, sensing an opportunity to humiliate, slipped his foot directly in Michael's path.

Unable to react in time, he tripped and, seemingly in slow motion, fell flat on the floor, his arms flapping like a bird. As his cheekbone hit Animals shoe he opened his mouth, allowing a pathetic yelp to escape.

Everyone laughed as he lay helpless in full view of everyone; making the most of the situation Animal snidely kicked him in the ribs while the rest of the class, watched like spectators at a bear-baiting fight, continuing to delight in his discomfort.

Without Dan or Hazel, he felt lonely and embarrassed. Scouring the class for a friendly face, he noticed that only

Chloe in the corner of the room, looked sympathetic. Rather than laughing, she walked over to him,

"You alright?" helping Michael to his feet, she smiled at him.

"Yes thanks," he muttered, wishing he were invisible.

"Smile," she whispered, "pretend you're not bothered," bending down to gather up the papers with him she continued, "People don't hate you; they laugh because they're afraid if they don't, they'll be next. He'll soon move on to someone else."

"I hope you're right," muttered Michael.

After handing out the rest of the papers to giggling students, he slumped at his desk, cradled his head in his hands and stared at the old graffiti, forever ingrained on the wooden benches.

Rather than subsiding, his anger had steadily grown at the thought of Alvin's treatment of him. Before the ring had even started glowing, a strange feeling in the pit of his stomach warned him that something was about to happen. He was right, for within seconds the jewel in his ring glowed, with the dark spot in the middle once more appearing. Worried that someone might notice, he hid his hands under the table. His thoughts began to wonder, what would the ring do this time?

It wasn't until he heard tree branches banging against the classroom windows that he noticed the sudden change in the weather outside. The soft rain, so typical of English weather, now pounded against the glass, becoming hailstones. Storm clouds gathered so dark that the sky was almost black, and the wind grew so strong that the trees became pliable puppets to natures wroth.

As the weather reached a crescendo, without warning, the windows at the back of the classroom swung open, hitting Animal and Alvin so hard on their heads that both were hurtled from their stools to the floor below; with no movement from either body, all talking and laugher halted. No-one moved.

Michael's heart pounded furiously. Despite being pleased, he still felt slightly guilty; for although Alvin had made his life a misery, he certainly didn't want to be the cause of a serious injury.

At the back of the classroom the window slammed shut; the wind gradually dropped and the hailstones subsided, returning once more to gentle droplets.

Mrs Dragon stared at them, he face white with shock. "Quick, get help."

As the rest of the classroom buzzed with activity, Michael stared out of the window. Although he had no idea how the ring had changed the weather, he was fast becoming aware of the power it held. Stools scratched the floor as students rushed to assist the lumbering heaps. Only Chloe and Michael remained where they were.

It took minutes for the two boys to haul themselves to their feet and swagger out of the classroom door like drunkards, dizzy with concussion. Both glowered at Michael as they passed him, but neither said a word.

Class resumed but nobody could concentrate and Michael, like everybody else, was having difficulty focusing on the test answers. He spent the rest of the lesson making sure he kept his hand hidden, still unsure as to whether the ring was visible or not. Although he, Dan and Hazel could see it, his mum hadn't mentioned it and even though school regulations stated no rings should be worn, not one teacher had mentioned it. Common sense told him there was no such thing as a selectively visible ring, but was the thought of a completely invisible ring any more believable?

Walking home was their time to discuss new events and theories, and today was no exception. Eager to hear Michael's account of the freak weather, they listened as he explained what had happened, careful to leave nothing out. They empathised when he told them about falling flat on his face, and laughed so hard they could hardly breathe when he mentioned the fate of Alvin and Animal. All three thought it about time Alvin experienced some of the pain and humiliation he so eagerly inflicted on others.

"Still coming round tonight?" Dan asked once their laughter had subsided. With his parents away, he was determined to make the most of being allowed to invite his friends round.

"Of course."

"We could head into town after dinner? Maybe visit the small shop and see if the old man knows anything?" Hazel suggested.

"Cool idea! Why didn't we think of it earlier? Maybe he can shed some light on what's going on," agreed Michael who wanted to confirm that the man from the shop was the same man he had dreamed about.

"Maybe if you drew a sketch of the place, we could look it up on the internet? Google Earth perhaps?" Dan suggested, clutching at straws.

Cringing, Michael reluctantly agreed, although painfully aware he was to drawing what Hitler was to world peace.

"What time should we come over?" Michael cut in quickly before Dan got too carried away.

"Any time before half five is fine."

"Cool, see you later then," replied Michael before he and Hazel parted company from Dan who lived in the opposite direction.

**

The sun was setting behind a maelstrom of violet and grey clouds as Hazel and Michael arrived on Dan's doorstep, brimming with excitement. Dan beckoned them inside his grandly decorated hallway.

"Let me take your coats." Without waiting for a response, Mary removed them from the guests, and smiled warmly at them, aware of how important they were to Daniel. "Why don't you make your way into the living room while I grab some drinks?"

Sat around the marble coffee table, Hazel voiced what they were all thinking. "It's so exciting isn't it? I haven't had this much fun in ages."

"Did you bring your diary?" asked Dan, getting straight down to business as usual. "Let's add today's events in so we don't lose track of what's happening."

Pulling out his notepad, Michael held it protectively, embarrassed by its tattered state.

"Tell you what," chirped Dan, "I've an unused diary upstairs. We can use that for best and your notepad for recording notes and ideas. Having two copies might be useful." With no objections from Hazel or Michael, Dan dashed to his room.

His bedroom had become his physical refuge from his parents company, while the diary had become his emotional one. Having put so much effort into it, he was eager to share what he'd written.

Hazel and Michael laughed, amazed at his efficiency. "Come on," nudged Hazel while they waited.

"Come on what?"

"I don't know about you but I've never seen further than his hallway and front room." The mischievous glint in her eyes set alarm bells ringing in Michael's head.

"We can't just go wandering around uninvited," he countered, despite feeling curious himself. Surely all the house couldn't be as extravagant as the hallway and lounge.

Eager to explore, Hazel was already standing by the arm of Michael's chair waiting for him to follow. "Chill out, we're only looking. I promise I won't touch a thing."

Knowing she wouldn't take no for an answer, he followed dutifully as she guided him back to the staircase in the centre of the hall. Michael thought it looked like something out of 'Gone with the Wind,' a film Hazel and Dan had forced him to endure. Yet somehow, even with his vivid imagination, he couldn't picture Dan's mum and dad as Scarlet O'Hara or Rhett Butler.

"How amazing is that staircase?" wincing at her romantic tone, he hoped she wouldn't get all soppy and girlie.

Mounting the stairs, they turned right and noticed a door slightly open halfway down the hall. "Let's look in there," she suggested.

"We can't do that!"

"We can! We could say we heard a noise and thought it was Dan."

Before Michael had time to respond Hazel had dragged him to the room and yanked him inside. The sun's rays rested on the four poster bed that occupied the centre of the room.

Michael gasped in awe. Never had he seen anything as ornate; intricate carvings covered the wooden posts while a cream duvet matched the frilly pillowcases.

"Oooops," giggled Hazel, "think we'd better leave this room alone."

"I never had Dan's parents down as the romantic type." Shuddering at the vision of a pink pig cuddling a stony-faced giraffe, Michael and Hazel slipped out of the room.

Further along the hallway they heard a rustling noise and stopped dead. "That must be Dan."

Peering through the crack between the door and the wall, sure enough, they saw him standing in his room, a puzzled expression plastered across his face.

"Something wrong?" Michael queried.

Dan jumped, surprised by their appearance. "Oh, nothing," he muttered absent-mindedly. Unconvinced,

Michael could see Dan's bemused expression, but thought better of pressing it further.

"Can't find it anywhere," he mumbled. "I could have sworn I put it back in my top drawer." He cast his eye quickly over his bedroom one last time before shrugging dismissively.

"Doesn't matter," said Hazel, "we've still got Michael's notepad which we can use for the moment."

Making their way along the hall, they heard a noise from the room next to Dan's parent's bedroom.

"What's in there?" whispered Hazel.

"Just their study," replied Dan apprehensively.

"What was the noise? I thought your parents were away!"

"They are, and I've no idea what the noise was." He sighed, knowing Hazel well enough to anticipate her next statement.

"We should find out what it is!"

Dan grimaced. He'd never been in his parents study before for fear of being caught, and even though they were away, he was sure they would still find out somehow.

"Come on, they're away on business. They'll never know."

"Okay," Dan agreed reluctantly, curious to find out what they hid in their 'forbidden room.' Maybe he'd discover where they were and what their mysterious deal was about. Anyway, it wasn't as if he was going to steal anything, simply investigate what they were up to.

"We'll leave everything exactly as we found it no-one need ever find out."

Resigned to the idea, Dan took the lead. As Hazel opened the curtains, light filtered into the room to reveal a study as neat and tidy as Dan's bedroom.

"Don't go in there!" Dan exclaimed; but he was too late, the top drawer under the oak desk was already open.

"Where did your parent's say they'd gone?" asked Hazel as her hand dived in and pulled out two burgundy passports.

Colour drained from Dan's face. He'd assumed they were abroad on business, or at least, that's what they'd led him to believe.

Michael's attention was drawn away from the passports as the now familiar tingling sensation spread through his hand, and this time Dan and Hazel noticed. It was the first time they'd witnessed the ring in action and somehow, for them, it seemed to make everything more real.

"Why's it doing that?"

"You're not annoyed are you?" A slightly perturbed Dan queried.

"I don't think so," Michael stammered.

Without warning, the cupboard doors to their left flew open, exposing many strange artefacts, one of which stood out in particular, for it lay separated from the other articles on the bottom shelf. Picking it up, Dan looked at the tinged yellow paper. As he unrolled it, all three scrutinised the map it revealed, but none recognised any of the place names or symbols scrawled across the page.

"It looks ancient!" Exclaimed Hazel who peered closer at the almost tea coloured paper, "what country is it?"

Leaning closer to get a better look, Michael gasped, stepping backwards involuntarily. Closing his eyes, he pictured the scene from his dream. Once again, he imagined the castle on the hill and the skeletal trees standing next to the fast flowing stream. Shocked by the resemblance, his hands clasped the desk so tightly his fingers turned white.

Noticing the colour drain from Michael's face, Hazel rushed towards him. "Sit down and take some deep breaths."

"It's …, it looks like the place I dreamed of," stammered Michael disbelievingly.

"Are you sure?" asked Dan, who by nature was more reluctant to believe in strange happenings than either Michael or Hazel.

"Of course I'm sure, there's the castle with the wall surrounding it, and there are the scattered clusters of cottages nearby, the ones with the strange chimneys." Michael continued scanning the map, his eyes resting for a moment on the forest. "There," he moved his hand to the trees, "those are the trees next to the stream, beside the mountains."

Grabbing the map off Michael, Dan walked to the photocopier by the window and quickly made a copy, and then rolling the original back up, he replaced it on the bottom shelf, hoping his parents didn't notice it had been moved.

"Something really strange is happening!"

"I think the ring's trying to tell us something. It clearly wants us to have the map, perhaps it's going to take you there, or maybe you'll dream about it again." Hazel whispered.

"But how? Why?" Michael was confused, and Dan was so nervous he had to clench his fists to stop them shaking.

Taking the scrunched map from Dan's clasp, Hazel folded it and placed it in her pocket. "We'd better get back before Mary notices we've gone."

A stern faced Mary greeted them, "And where have you been?"

"Sorry. I needed the toilet and Dan was upstairs so I, well we," glancing at Michael, Hazel continued, "decided to find it. We got lost, this house is so big, but fortunately Dan found us." So innocent was Hazel's face, Mary couldn't fail to believe her.

Michael was shocked. He'd never known Hazel to lie, and was surprised at how convincing she was.

Mollified, Mary returned to the kitchen while a guilty feeling Hazel passed the photocopied map to Michael to stow in his bag

"Why do you think Dan's parents have a map of the place Michael dreamed of?"

All three sat in silence. No-one knew what to say. They had completely forgotten about finding the shop.

Chapter Ten: The Farmhouse

Flicking though his notepad, ideas filled Michael's mind, many of which verged on the fantastical. It was the last day of the summer term and this was the first chance they'd had to meet alone since discovering the map.

Early as usual, Hazel and Dan arrived just as excited as Michael. "Hi," he smiled, allowing them to enter his small but tidy flat. Wasting no time, not even offering to take their coats, he led them to the coffee table which his mother had laden with food and drink. It wasn't much, mainly cheap fizzy drink, crisps, sandwiches and some biscuits but they tucked in gratefully.

"See ya later pumpkin." Michael cringed as she ruffled his hair before placing a slobbery wet kiss on his cheek.

Catherine had planned to return home later than usual from work that evening to allow them some privacy. His bedroom was tiny and she didn't want to make them feel uneasy by being in the same room as them. Beaming with pleasure, she left them eating and drinking. It was the first time he'd invited friends round and she was delighted he wasn't ashamed of her or the flat.

After devouring the food, Michael stacked up the plates while Dan read out his notes so far, as though they needed reminding. It had been days since the ring had glowed, but as soon as the old man was mentioned Michael felt the familiar tingling sensation in his finger, spreading through his hand and up his arm. Gasping at the ferocity of the glow, Daniel ceased reading, his mouth agape; all three were momentarily speechless.

Pins and needles attacked Michael's hand with such intensity that his grip weakened and the plates shattered on the floor. Unable to control his actions, Michael made for the flat door.

"Where are you going?" exclaimed Hazel.

"I...I don't know. The ring's pulling me! I can't control it." Michael stammered.

Without hesitation Dan and Hazel followed, unsure of their destination, but determined not to lose Michael.

Down the concrete steps, through the street, turning one way, then another, their destination remained a mystery. Trying to hold Michael back had proved futile, his pace didn't even waver. So they followed, uneasy yet excited.

Gradually fields replaced houses as they were pulled in the direction of the old farmhouse. They shuddered at its derelict, weathered appearance. Uninhabited since the tragedy fourteen years before, it had remained the subject of local speculation, with myths and legends growing out of the murders for which no one had ever been prosecuted. Despite no solid evidence, it was commonly accepted that it had been the farmer, Mr. Arkwright, who had slaughtered his wife and their children. Yet the mystery surrounding his disappearance remained, for neither he nor the murder weapon had been found and so the police file remained open.

Since then the farmhouse had been on the property market. Yet its history preceded it and so it had remained empty; dilapidated and surrounded by a forest of overgrown weeds.

The door to the main building remained open, goading any one brave enough to venture in. Those who had dared enter said the walls held the secrets of that night in their foundations, and that if you listened carefully enough, you could hear the desperate screams of the wife and children. Others said they'd heard the faint whispering of truths, but all who entered the building had left before becoming overwhelmed by its sadness and mystery.

As Michael approached, the hairs on the back of his neck prickled, his pupils dilated and his pulse raced as though he was being confronted with death rather than an empty building. Dan and Hazel scurried behind, sensing his anxiety.

Approaching the unwelcoming door, they noticed the top hinge was broken, the paint was peeling and tiny shards of broken glass lay scattered on the floor.

No-one spoke as they ascended the wooden steps. Looking up, Michael's eyes absorbed every detail of the once beautiful house. The remnants of the windows were covered in dust and grime; the walls were enveloped in moss, while plants climbed up towards the bedroom windows like peeping toms, desperate to discover what was happening inside, but not willing to risk entering.

The force that guided Michael, though not allowing retreat; weakened, enabling slower and steadier movements. With trepidation they entered, treading on a threadbare carpet; the stains of blood still slightly visible.

Dan gazed in wonderment; his eyes scanning the hallway. The stairway seemed to lead into an eternity of darkness, one he wasn't prepared to explore. Broken wood jutted dangerously from the rotten banister while the stairs looked precarious from rot that had set in.

"We can't just stand here," whispered Hazel. "For some reason, we, or at least Michael, is supposed to be here, so we may as well look around. It wouldn't have brought us here for anything bad to happen, would it?"

"I'm not sure?"

"Until now it's always protected us, hasn't it? So I'm pretty sure it must be on our, or at least Michael's side." Her voice held a conviction she didn't feel inside. Yet she remained determined to wear a brave face, if only to reassure the others.

Tentatively edging down the hall, Michael halted outside the first door. Preparing for the worst, his slim, sweaty palm twisted the doorknob clockwise, revealing a dust-filled room. There were intricately woven cobwebs covering every corner; a dusty fireplace and a single gilt framed family picture hanging from the wall. The woman was smiling; her arms wrapped round two children protectively while a man stood behind, slightly distanced from the others. Unlike his wife and children, his face was so faded, it was unrecognisable.

"Must be the family who lived here," whispered Dan, unable to take his eyes off the scene. Their faces were full of laughter and he wondered what could have caused such a tragic ending.

"Let's go. Whatever we're supposed to find, it's obviously not in here." Hazel grabbed their arms and manoeuvred them out of the room towards the door at the end of the hallway.

Clenching and unclenching his fists nervously, Michael inhaled deeply then reluctantly pushed the door. It was stuck. He tried again, this time more vigorously. Again the door barred their entry.

"Perhaps we should try another room," suggested Dan, hoping to leave this awful place as soon as possible. He wasn't a coward, in fact he was usually considered quite courageous. However, exploring a house where three people had been brutally killed and many people had heard voices from was a little beyond the call of duty for any fifteen year old.

"Look!" exclaimed Hazel. "I think it wants us to go in, Michael's ring's glowing again! Perhaps it's going to help us solve the mystery! Wouldn't that be amazing?"

Shining so brightly, the ring illuminated the length of the hallway, and then slowly, with no assistance from Michael, the door swung backwards, allowing them access to the secrets beyond.

Half afraid, half excited, Hazel held her breath and stepped inside with the others following close behind.

A thick blanket of darkness encased them. Gripping each other's arms tightly, they huddled together, their steps small as they felt the walls for a light switch to guide them. Finding nothing, it soon became obvious that the room contained nothing that was going to assist their journey.

"Shhhhhh."

They stopped abruptly, too frightened even to breathe. In the distance they heard a noise, like footsteps, barely audible but there nevertheless. Hazel shivered, her sense of adventure battling against her sense of self-preservation.

She thought perhaps on this occasion, the urge to remain alive would win. Beside her, Michael, equally excited and scared, tightened his already firm grip on the others.

"What if it's dangerous? What if the murderer's still lurking in the house?" Dan's imagination was already in overdrive.

"We only got past the door because of the ring, so whoever the footsteps belong to, they can't be here to harm us."

"I'm not sure how you reached that conclusion but we have to decide quickly. We either carry on, or turn back now. We can't just stand here doing nothing." Bravely, Hazel started shuffling forwards, trying not to trip over anything.

"We should at least see what's in here. If we go back, we'll always wonder what if?" Hyped up, Michael's argument was confident and self-assured.

Hazel was quick to agree, her eyes already adjusting to the darkness, allowing her to see the shadows looming from large objects around the room. Tiptoeing forwards, surrounded by shadows, Dan was perturbed,

"Where's the end of the room?" he asked as he strained to see into the darkness.

"I don't know, but I'm certain the farmhouse wasn't this big from the outside. Perhaps it's sloped down and we've gone underground," suggested Michael who knew how daft the idea sounded.

"We haven't gone down any stairs and I'm pretty certain we haven't gone down a slope. Something weird is happening," Dan croaked.

"Well it wouldn't be the first time!" exclaimed Hazel.

It was a few minutes before they were confronted with a huge wooden door which, unlike the rest of the house, appeared relatively new.

Trembling, Michael expected the door to be locked so he leaned into it, using as much force as he could muster. With unexpected ease the door opened and Michael stumbled, losing his footing and landing head first onto a carpet of grass.

The musty room invited in the dim rays of the sun as enthusiastically as it would an old friend. As fresh air entered their lungs, Dan and Hazel left the confines of the farmhouse and helped Michael to his feet.

"All that worrying for nothing! Though you have to admit, the house looks much smaller from the outside. It was huge!"

"That's not what I was expecting. I had visions of confronting a crazed murderer and instead I'm faced with a lovely grass garden." Hazel confided.

Oblivious to the lovely setting, Michael felt overwhelmed by the ring's power. He alone was responsible for it; and the thought terrified him. The journey had made him acutely aware that he had no control over it. Perhaps it wasn't as good as Hazel imagined. "What if the ring turns out to be bad?"

"Nothing bad's happened yet, has it? We've simply walked through a farmhouse!" reasoned Hazel.

"What if we were supposed to find something important?" Pondered Dan, who couldn't believe the ring had taken them to the farmhouse so forcefully, simply for them to walk straight out of it.

"Well I for one, am not going back in there to find out." Michael responded.

Relishing the breeze on his face, Dan wandered forwards and inspected their surroundings. Soaking up the scenery, just moments elapsed before his eyes opened wide in astonishment. Instead of overgrown weeds and rotten crops, he beheld luscious fields extending for miles in all directions with the misty mountain peaks in the distance. It instantly it occurred to him that they were no longer in Grays, and it wasn't long before Hazel and Michael had reached the same conclusion.

"What's happened?" Dan gulped incredulously. "We're not at the farmhouse are we?"

"It doesn't look like it, though how can we be anywhere else?"

Staring in the direction of the mountains and streams, Michael pinched himself to make sure it wasn't another one of his day dreams. "I think we should retrace our steps."

Turning his back to the mountains, Dan stopped dead and stared incredulously in the direction of the farmhouse. It wasn't there! All he could see was a solitary oak tree with a trunk as wide as any of them had ever seen, supporting umbrella branches.

"Look at the sky, it's changing colour!" Hazel enthused, who had yet to take in the seriousness of their situation.

They gazed in wonderment, turning round in circles as they greedily digested the wonder of the view; the mountain range, the fast flowing stream and the silhouette of a castle in the distance, behind which the almost lilac sky and amber setting sun blazed in glory.

"It can't be!! Michael gazed for ages before continuing, "This is it, the place from my dream. I must have stood in this exact spot, the view looks so similar."

"I don't know what to say."

"What about, where is the farmhouse? In case you hadn't noticed, it's miraculously disappeared, which makes getting home rather difficult!"

"What an adventure!" shouted Hazel.

"What about your Nan and Michael's mum? They're going to be pulling their hair out if we aren't home soon." Dan, ever sensible, sometimes despaired of Hazel's cavalier attitude. "I could be gone days, even weeks before my parents noticed, and even then, I'm not sure they'd care."

"We could try to find an opening in the oak tree," Suggested Michael, slightly embarrassed that this was the best idea he could muster.

Knowing how ridiculous it sounded but, but unable to think of a better suggestion, they tugged at branches, prodded knots and fumbled to find any crevices in the bark that could lead to a secret entrance. Nothing happened.

"Common sense states that if you can go somewhere, you must be able to get back, so I'm sure we'll find a way home," Hazel reasoned.

"I hope you're right."

Glancing at his watch, Michael was horrified to discover it was already five to eight. "Mum's gonna be home in an hour, I must be back by then."

"Nearly eight! I told Nan I'd be home by half past to help with preparations for tomorrow's church jumble sale. What are we going to do?"

"Come on ring, take us home!" Michael commanded, praying it would work its magic. It didn't; not even a twitch... nothing.

Standing motionless, Dan closed his eyes tightly, his eyebrows furrowed, deep in concentration. "Got it!" he yelled, startling Michael who stumbled backwards, tripped on the sole of his shoe again and landed once more on the grass.

"What?" grumbled an irritated and even dirtier Michael.

"If this is the place from your dream, then it must be the place on the map. So why don't we use that? It's bound to show us how to get out of here," grinned Dan, delighted at his idea.

Pulling out the crinkled map, all three huddled together, peering at the faint text, which was even more illegible than that on the original. Seconds became minutes and still they were no further forward in deciphering the wording or working out which way would led them back to Grays, Essex, England.

"Who was that?" Michael looked at the others.

"Who was what?" Dan asked, still concentrating on the map, determined that his idea would work.

"Someone tapped me."

"Don't look at me," replied Hazel.

"Dan?"

"Not me."

"Well I didn't just imagine it, it must have been someone."

Looking up, Hazel's eyes widened as she clamped her hand firmly over her mouth. "L…l…l..look," stammering, she stared and pointed past Michael's shoulder.

Swinging round, Michael saw the man from his dream, still as uncoordinated and colourful as before. Extending his hand towards Michael, the old man's smile beamed from ear to ear, showing a full set of gleaming white teeth.

"You're from my dream, aren't you?" Feeling ill at ease, Michael's heart pounded as he finally faced the man who had haunted his thoughts for weeks.

"Nice to meet you in the flesh, so to speak. I felt you enter the old farmhouse and thought it only right that I should welcome you to Kilion. Not that it's a surprise to see you here. In fact, I've been expecting you for quite some time."

"You have?"

"Honestly, I expected you a couple of weeks ago, but it's not important, so long as you're here now."

"Why? How?"

"The ring. I expect you've already realised it's got a mind of its own, does things when you least expect it!" Clearing his throat he glanced at Michael's hand before continuing. "Before you go any further, I need to warn you about a few things, help keep you from harm's way, so to speak."

"Harm's way?"

Noticing Michael's confused expression he queried, "I don't suppose you remember our conversation?"

"I remember the birds turning to stone, and the mountains, and you, but very little of what was said."

"Typical teenager; more worried about what's going on around you than paying attention to what you're being told. Just as well I'm here… but listen carefully this time… all three of you." His smile was genuine and his eyes were kind. Instinctively Michael knew he could trust him.

"Most importantly, please, never, and I mean never, take anyone or anything at face value, things aren't always as they appear; always question people's motives if you want to remain safe."

"Safe!" Dan's expression transformed from one of curious intensity to horror. "What do you mean stay safe?"

"Don't get me wrong, Kilion is a nice enough place to live; but you're not Kilionians and you're not here to live. The ring has brought you here for a reason, one you'll find out soon enough."

"Honestly, I'm not sure I want Michael to find out, I'd much prefer to discover how to get home," an adamant Dan declared.

"The castle there in the distance should be your first port of call. But make sure that when you're there, you don't talk to anyone unless it's necessary and definitely don't tell them anything about yourselves, especially where you come from as they've never heard of it."

"All your warnings are worrying me. Are you implying something bad could happen to us?" A shocked Hazel asked as she ran her fingers through her dark, tangled hair.

Disliking the way the conversation was going, Dan interrupted. "We really haven't got time to visit the castle;

we just want to get home. So if you could point us in the right direction?"

Envisaging his poor mum worrying, Michael added, "we could always visit another time, once we've let people know where we are. So, could you point us in the right direction, please?"

As he wiped his forehead with his sleeve, Abe looked genuinely upset. "I hate being the bearer of bad news, but now you've entered Kilion, it's impossible to return home."

"You must be mistaken. Surely we can get back through the house? If you could just tell us where we can find it?" Hazel asked.

Seeing the looks of horror, he tried consoling them. "I'm afraid the farmhouse was created as a one way route, but there might be another way I'm not familiar with. I'm sure the King will be able to help but first, you must visit the castle."

"You're saying you don't know if we can get home?"

"We can't stay here!" squealed Michael.

"Can the King definitely help?" Dan asked hopefully.

"I can't promise anything, but if anyone can, it would be him. Anyway, a trip to the castle won't hurt. It's where the ring wants to take you, and at the very least you'll be given food and shelter while you figure out what to do."

They stared at the magnificent building crowning the hilltops. "The King and Queen know of your arrival already, and a feast is currently being prepared in your honour. Now, if you'll excuse me, I must return to help organise the festivities. Unfortunately, I can't take you with me; no-one can know of our connection until I've figured out a story to explain your arrival. But with youth on your side, walking shouldn't take you too long."

"But..."

"Oh, and don't let anyone, and I mean absolutely no-one, know about the ring, not even the King..."

"But we need to…" Hazel stopped abruptly in mid-sentence for the old man was no longer there.

"Where's he gone? He can't just have vanished into thin air!" Dan stared into the empty space where Abednego had stood just moments before.

"Afraid he does that kind of thing. In my dream, one minute we were chatting happily, the next it was raining and he vanished into thin air."

"The castle it is then!" Already striding forwards, Michael and Hazel hurried to catch Dan up, neither one relishing the idea of such a long walk in what was becoming an increasingly cold place.

"Are you sure we're doing the right thing," Shouted Michael as he shoved the map into a pocket.

Pausing, Dan replied, "Well, as far as I can see, we've entered a strange country through a disappearing farmhouse, our map is as useful as a Japanese guide book in China and the only person, and a disappearing one at that, has implied we may as well buy a house here because we won't be needing our old ones anytime soon." Dan was clearly fretting. In the past he had relied on common sense in difficult situations. Yet here in Kilion, nothing seemed to make any sense, and none of his ideas had worked. "So, if he's being truthful, and he seemed genuine, then the only option we have is to hope the King can assist us. Unless you've got any better ideas?"

Michael and Hazel wanted to comfort him, tell him everything was going to be okay, but deep down they felt as helpless as Daniel.

"What idiots, why didn't we think of this before? Why don't we call home?" Reaching into her pocket, Hazel pulled out his mobile phone, only to discover there was no reception.

Routing through his trouser pocket, Dan fumbled for his phone; perhaps his would have better reception. "I can't find it! It must have fallen out of my pocket on the way here." He searched his pockets again, hoping it would miraculously appear. After all, if the farmhouse and Abednigo could come and go as they pleased, why not his phone? His disappointment was palpable. Neither of them asked Michael.

With no other option, Dan said, "If we hurry, there's a slight chance we might make it home tonight. if we're lucky, that is."

More determined than ever, they scuttled towards the castle as the sun set over the mountains.

Chapter Eleven: The Prisoner

Jasper limped into the damp cellar, clutching a sealed envelope in his hands. His eyes gleamed with anticipation. "Sir, there's a letter for you, delivered by his special hunting hawk."

"Give it 'ere then, and don't dribble when you talk, it aint becoming." Snatching the letter from his faithful servant, he stroked the smooth envelope.

Richard watched as Jasper limped towards the door, his head hanging awkwardly on his chest. Since Richard's return to Kilion fourteen years ago, Jasper had served him faithfully, even acquiring his limp by protecting Richard from the creatures of the forest. Yet despite all they had been through, the only emotion Richard could feel towards him was pity. The stooping figure, looking older than his fifty-six years, could only be described as ugly, or at best, plain. Stopping to push his tangled, greasy hair behind overlarge ears, his sad eyes peered out from under thick, bushy eyebrows as Jasper spoke, "I'll be in the kitchen preparing dinner if you require anything."

Guilt, pity and loneliness were the reasons Richard tolerated Jasper's company. Both had no family left and neither were likely to find someone special now, especially situated in a dangerous forest with mountains on one side and a lake on the other; not exactly the ideal place to find a soul mate.

Isolated from society, their only way of communicating with the outside world was an occasional letter by hawk. That was of course, if you excluded 'him' downstairs; but he didn't count, because apart from delivering his food and drink, neither Richard nor Jasper had anything to do with him.

Most people hated isolation, yet Richard had come to believe that he could no longer live any other way, appreciating only the solitude of his thoughts. Frustratingly, Jasper would ramble on at the slightest opportunity, discussing trivial matters simply to get his attention. At first Richard thought it would drive him insane, yet over time he'd perfected the art of ignoring Jasper without him noticing.

Returning to the present, Richard inspected the newly delivered cream envelope with his name scrawled on the front in disjointed italics. Anticipation gripped him. Surely this was the order to finally kill him downstairs, an act he'd been desperate to commit ever since He had cost him his wife and children.

Remorse filled his heart every time he relived the events of that fateful night. If he'd known what the consequences would be, he would have handled the situation very differently. Every time he closed his eyes, a sense of loss consumed him. He relived the moment the shots had been fired every night in his dreams. Instinctively he'd known as soon as they had been shot that never again would he experience true happiness, never again would he feel truly alive.

Pulling his thoughts back to the present, he resolved to make a conscious effort not to dwell on the past. Every time he did, he always ended with the image of three cold bodies lying on the floor; their shocked eyes staring straight at him accusingly, unable to believe what he'd done.

Worse still, their lives had been sacrificed for nothing. Well, almost. Gold! He'd received a mountain of money, but what use was it? He had no-one to spend it on or share it with. Yet now, perhaps things would change, for he was certain the official order had finally been delivered and maybe he could finally start a new life, somewhere else.

Scouring the letter, a smile formed on his thin lips. His attendance was required at a meeting inside the depths of the castle at the break of dawn the following day. His heart pounded with anxiety and pleasure at the thought of finally meeting his Master face to face.

Settling himself down with a glass of water, he responded immediately. Signing his name, he checked it for errors, attached it to the hunting hawk, then reclined in his chair and fell asleep.

***

Haunted eyes stared listlessly at the crumbling walls of the cell. Initially he had counted his days in captivity. Yet as days had turned to weeks, then months, then years, he'd given up and resigned himself to a life of solitary confinement.

A tiny window to his right provided his only comfort in the cold, damp cell. It was his only source of light and was the key to the outside world, the trees and sky teasing him, reminding him of the life that had been snatched from him. His comforts were limited to a bucket, a cracked sink in the corner and blocks of wood covered by a mattress from which coils jutted in all directions, causing nights of discomfort and pain.

Bones protruded at awkward angles from his skinny frame which, in his youth had been slim and toned. Translucent skin barely protected him from winter nights; and his once thick, dark hair was now dank and lifeless, greying at the temples and reaching past his waist. His once sparkling blue eyes now contented themselves with staring into nothingness, hollows encasing his eyeballs through lack of sleep and nourishment; while a long, brittle and greying beard and moustache covered the majority of his face. Nothing mattered anymore; he simply lived to die, to be free of this hell hole.

For a while thoughts of escape and of returning to his family had kept his spirits high. Yet after years of being held hostage, cramped and isolated, he just wanted peace, and to free himself from the bars which imprisoned his body and soul night and day.

An unexpected noise from the window caused him to turn his head slowly, too weak to move with speed. Resting on the window sill stood a small, twittering creature. Wide, round eyes, protected by long, dark eyelashes blinked as it absorbed the sight of the cell, its furry body kept upright by thin, bandy legs, lightly covered in fur. The creature could have been no more than five inches tall.

"Hello," a faint voice chirruped.

Bewildered at the creature's ability to speak, Mathis rubbed his eyes, frightened that his years of isolation and malnourishment were causing him to hallucinate.

"I'm Siddons, a Snufflepug. Nice to make your acquaintance." The funny blue creature bowed low, his knees jutting out either side, making an amusing sight.

"Mathis," he croaked, coughing from the effort. Realising just how weak he had become, he decided that even if escape was impossible, he should at least practice talking and walking, just in case an opportunity ever presented itself.

"I know who you are. You don't think I've stumbled across you in a cell in the middle of nowhere by accident do you? I've been searching for ages," the funny creature petulantly remarked, "you do realise everyone thinks you're dead?"

A least it would explain why, to his knowledge, nobody had tried finding him. For years he had been annoyed by all that he'd been subjected to, resolving that if he ever escaped, he would seek revenge for the stolen years. Yet the appearance of this furry creature encouraged an even greater feeling, one of hope. Tears of relief and happiness sprang to his eyes, but pride stopped them falling. He didn't want anyone, not even a 5 inch bandy kneed creature, to see how close he was to breaking down.

"I, like everyone else, thought you'd been killed. Then one day, a couple of years ago, I overheard a conversation in the forest as I was gathering food. The snippets I caught gave me the impression they were speaking of you as though you were alive. But with no hard evidence I knew that if I mentioned it to anyone, they'd laugh at me, like they always do. But I was determined to find you. So with nothing to do except forage for food, I've spent most of my spare time searching."

Mathis tears evaporated, drying on his skin as a smile crept across his face. To have company, something real, meant everything to him. But to have that person determined to help free him, to give him his life back was more than he could ever have hoped for.

"Oh, I'm so glad you're alive."

"Only just…" Mathis croaked before spluttering again.

"No offence, but you look worse than I'd imagined. Not to worry, at least you're alive; we can work on the rest." The Snufflepug clasped his hands together gleefully.

"C… can you help me g… get out of here?" He knew that being discovered was not the same thing as being rescued.

"Of course. I wouldn't have spent so long searching just to say hello." His enthusiasm comforted Mathis, who was now confused and overwhelmed.

Siddons inspected Mathis who was in a dismal state, little more than an ensemble of hair, skin and bones. He shuddered. He hadn't anticipated how difficult the task would be, and yet despite his reservations, he had to keep Mathis optimistic, for only the thought of escape would help Mathis get better.

"What can I do to help?" Mathis asked.

"Let's start with trying to increase your fitness and stamina levels." Pleased with his first decision, a smile spread across the tiny face. Back at his village he was too young to be an adult, yet too old to be a child. So often he'd felt excluded, and now not only was he being taken seriously, he was making the decisions and it made him feel good.

Mathis wiggled his fingers, clenched and unclenched his fists, then bent and straightened his arm, determined to build up his strength as quickly as possible.

"Now I know where you are, I'll bring you as much food as I can. Eat everything, even if you don't like it; you need to put some flesh onto your bones, and exercise as much as possible; loosen your muscles, do some sit-ups, walk around your cell. And practice speaking, start off small to loosen your throat muscles and then, maybe have conversations with yourself, ease your throat a little before we get you out of here."

At the thought of fresh air stroking his skin, Mathis eyes brightened. Just being discovered had made his mind more alert. Subconsciously he was already making plans for the future. Again he smiled, too weak to offer verbal appreciation but his eyes said it all.

"Don't start getting emotional; you'd be better off using that energy to make yourself stronger! Now I've no food today but I'll collect extra rations tomorrow, though I can't promise I'll make it here every day, it depends on the situation in the village."

Mathis nodded appreciatively. Siddons, anxious for Mathis to regain his strength, continued, "Eat all food straight away, you can't get caught eating anything they haven't brought you. And don't let them catch you exercising, they'll get suspicious. Secrecy's the key; getting caught could prove fatal. They must see and suspect nothing." Winking, he turned his furry back on Mathis;

opened a large pair of wings Mathis had previously failed to notice and jumped, his wings flapping rapidly, carrying him into the forest, out of view.

Resting against the cell wall, Mathis rose to his feet, his muscles shaking from the effort. After a few repetitions he was exhausted but determined to do all he could to reclaim his own destiny. Staring past the door, his mind was focused on what needed to be done; all the while making sure the limping fool was out of sight.

***

"Everything's going as planned. Abednigo's informing the boy about the feast so he should be here soon." The messenger's eyes shone brightly in the darkness of the deepest room of the castle, where the flickering candles reflecting in the mirror, were the only source of light.

Content, the cloaked figure smirked, "But how to proceed once he is here?"

"Someone needs to talk to him, coax the information from him, man to boy, so to speak."

"Perhaps… though we'll have to be careful. We can't push him. We need him to co-operate willingly."

"Is there anything I can do sir?"

"No, let's gain his trust first, then we'll start planning. We've waited years. A few more days won't matter."

"I'll do what I can to encourage him to confide in me."

"Watch him and his friends closely, find out what they're like."

"Like a hawk."

"Make a note of everything he says and return in three days. We can figure out what to do from there." He rubbed his hands gleefully, a habit he'd acquired in childhood.

His servant bowed low then closed the door behind him. Scuttling through the cobweb filled passage; he twice turned the statuette of a trolls face anti-clockwise. Muttering under his breath, he pushed the stone wall, revealing the secret passage and squeezed through the tight space before pulling the handle and closing the wall behind him.

Feeling along the rough bricks, using his hands to guide him in the darkness, he manoeuvred his way along the narrow passage back to the hubbub of the castle. Peering through the crack in the stone, he was relieved to discover there was no-one on the other side. Straightening and dusting his robes, he wiped the cobwebs from his hair and then, after taking a deep breath, made his way into the corridor back towards the Great Hall which would be brimming with noise.

***

Scuffling along the passage, Abednigo braced himself for the feast that evening. Having taken a liking to Michael and his friends, he was excited about seeing them again.

"Have you heard? Three teenagers are heading for the castle."

"I wonder who they are!"

"No idea."

"Abe, do you know anything?" Zawi Chemi's wrinkled hand tapped his shoulder. As one of the fifteen wise ladies at Court, she had lived through five of Kilion's Kings and was renowned for her ability to find out everything that was going on within the castle walls.

"Zawi, how nice to see you! Michael's my great nephew from Zancaster and he's bought a couple of his friends to pay me a visit. I can't wait! The King's even been kind enough to honour them at his feast tonight!"

Baring her yellowing teeth, she hustled over to a group of younger Courtiers, perhaps to gather more information, or perhaps to disseminate what she had just discovered. Chuckling, he reached his private rooms, closely situated to the King and Queens suite, then slumped onto his bed. Closing his eyes, he reflected on the situation and wondered what the future would bring.

Fourteen years he had been waiting, anticipating Michael's arrival. Yet now he was here, Abednego was filled with confusion. He'd expected Michael to know something about his father, but it seemed Mathis had kept his promise too well, for it appeared Michael knew nothing, not even about his inheritance. His emotions were in turmoil as he considered his options, knowing that what was right wasn't necessarily what was best. If he offered Michael what was rightfully his, it would affect the whole Kingdom,and and not necessarily in a good way. He didn't doubt that Michael would have good intentions, but he was so young, how could he possibly cope with the responsibility of Kingship and all that it would entail? Equally as important, he'd recently detected an undercurrent within the Court which he didn't understand and it was unsettling him.

Recently he had kept his ears to the ground and knew there was whispering and secrecy amongst certain members of the King's circle. In fact, he was almost certain there was a conspiracy of some sort. Until he knew exactly what was going on, he thought it would be better for Michael if his identity remained a secret. This way, he wouldn't become embroiled in Court Politics. However, by withholding Michael's identity, he would be depriving him of the knowledge of his past, and who he really was. Confused, he opened his eyes, looked at his weary old face in the mirror and decided to leave any decisions until after he'd eaten. His mind was always clearer on a full stomach.

Chapter Twelve: Grimbald

Panting, they hurried towards the castle while still appreciating the sight of the cobbled streets lined with small, dainty houses, and their jagged stone walls held together by mud; a stark contrast to the bricks and cement they were used to seeing in England.

Weaving through the lanes, they encountered a middle-aged man who appeared to be returning home from a hard day at work. Instead of smiling or waving, he stopped dead as they passed, he neither spoke nor smiled, but simply watched them until they disappeared from sight.

"Why did he look at us so strangely? Like we're different?" asked Hazel.

"No idea. He didn't look very wealthy though, his clothes and his face filthy." Michael replied peering closer at the houses, amused at the way their chimneys protruded from the wall rather than the roof.

"He was wearing a cloak; we're heading towards a castle and the houses don't seem to have electricity. Do you think we might have travelled back in time?" A curious Dan asked.

***

"Grimbald, what's wrong? You seem on edge, has something happened?" Stoking the fire with an iron rod, his wife settled herself on the uncomfortable wooden bench.

Wiping a bead of sweat from his forehead, her husband stretched his arms out behind him and straightened his back. "Something's not right; I felt it as soon as I saw them."

"What's not right?" Intrigued, she picked up her darning, not wanting to appear too anxious. "And who's them?"

"On my way home from work I saw three youngsters wandering the streets. They definitely weren't from round here." Rubbing his hands together for warmth, he continued, "and one of them, a small lad with blond hair, well, I couldn't help but notice that he looked a bit like Prince Mathis."

"Lots of people resemble others, there's nothing strange in that."

"I'm not talking about a vague resemblance, I mean really similar, like a relative or something."

"Now you're being ridiculous. He can't possibly be a relative. Mathis has been gone for over fifteen years. How old did the boy look?"

"I don't know, thirteen, fourteen perhaps."

"Then it's out of the question. He died fourteen years ago, unmarried and childless."

"But how do we know whether or not he had a wife or child? They couldn't even produce a body as evidence of his murder in the end."

"I'll admit the circumstances surrounding his death seemed somewhat suspicious, but it was so long ago. I can't even remember why they couldn't bring his body back! You'd have thought as a Prince, he would have been buried properly."

"That's all in the past now, but it's not Mathis we're talking about, it's the boy and his two friends remember." Rising to his feet, he paced the length of the room, "and I didn't say he was a relation, I just said he really reminded me of him."

"For goodness sake, sit down and stop thinking about it. Tea'll be ready in five minutes."

"I can't stop thinking about it. Seeing him, well, it sent a shiver down my spine." Halting, he slipped off his heavy boots, placed them by the bench and wiggled his toes in front of the fire.

"I'm not sure what you expect me to say, there's no way you're going to find out about him now." Breaking from her darning, Ragetta looked at her husband as a thought struck her. "What if they didn't bring a body back because he isn't really dead? That it was all a cover-up so he didn't inherit the throne? And if he's not dead, what's to say he didn't have a son?"

"Ragetta dear, don't get too carried away, I only saw a boy who looked like him. It's been so long since Mathis died, it's possible I imagined the similarity. Maybe it was just my imagination playing tricks on me."

"You're right. As much as we'd love it to be different, he must be dead; otherwise he would have claimed his Kingship."

"Maybe, though his reason for leaving here in the first place was so that he would never have to be King, which means there's no motive for murder. Anyway, there's no way King Mazarin would have anyone killed, he's as soft as sand."

Grimbald comforted Ragetta; he'd been worried about telling her. Deep down he knew she'd never really accepted Mathis' death and this would only reignite her curiosity.

Glancing at her husband, his eyebrows were furrowed in concentration so she asked, "Well, what's bothering you then? If Mathis is dead and you don't think the boy's related to him, why can I still see that faraway look in your eyes?" After twenty five years of marriage, she could read him well enough to know when something was bothering him.

"We still don't know what they're doing here."

"Perhaps they're lost, or maybe they're visiting a relative."

She felt him tense. Knowing she hadn't stemmed his curiosity in the slightest, she waited for the inevitable.

"I'm going out," he grunted as he reached for the dirty boots he'd discarded just minutes before.

"Where?"

"To find out what they're doing here," Fastening his laces he added, "look at the weather, there are storm clouds gathering on the horizon and it looks like it's gonna' pour down. What if they need somewhere to stay for the night?" Adjusting the collar of his large green cloak, he stooped to kiss his wife goodbye, and then left.

"Don't be long!" She yelled as the door slammed shut.

Breathing in the damp air, he looked at the castle in the distance and noticed the three small figures standing in front of its walls.

Raising his eyebrow quizzically, he shoved his hands in his pockets and headed in their direction. He couldn't help it, and of course, he would never let on to his wife, but he too shared her secret hopes that the boy was somehow related to Mathis. As he had watched the lad earlier, he had seemed so familiar, Grimbald couldn't help wondering if Mathis had fathered a son without anyone knowing, a son to carry on the family name, to follow in his footsteps, to take the crown of Kilion.

Treading on the dusty path, he tried suppressing his thoughts, not wanting to raise his hopes too much in case they came to nothing. Continuing uphill, he prayed fervently that he wouldn't have to enter that awful place.

Chapter Thirteen: The Castle

They stared at the intimidating, wrought iron gate enclosing the gothic castle. Statues perched proudly atop the many turrets and towers, their watchful gazes falling on the huddled group of friends below.

"Those statues are spooky, it's like they're watching us," whispered Dan.

Michael once more glanced at his new watch, hoping the King would be able to help them return home.

Slowly the gates creaked open, unassisted, and beyond which the huge wooden doors followed suit, revealing Abednego who was wearing splendid robes. Standing beside him was an elegantly attired man, wearing purple and gold, clearly the King. Diamonds, amethysts and rubies sparkled on his crown, while matching jewels adorned the thick rings he wore on both hands.

"Welcome. It's a pleasure having you to stay. I thought you'd be hungry after your journey, so I've taken the liberty of having a feast prepared in your honour. But first I'll show you where you can freshen up." The King's smile failed to reach his hazel eyes and they wondered whether perhaps his attention was elsewhere.

Following obediently, they gazed in wonderment at the huge chandeliers and candles along the hallways. Tapestries and paintings, rich in colour and texture covered the otherwise plain walls. New tapestries glittered in the light, whilst older ones were faded and less easy on the eye. Those more ancient in origin mostly depicted battles in extensive detail, swords clashing furiously and animals rearing from the onslaught. Newer tapestries were mostly portraits of members of the royal family, past and present; their expressions devoid and haughty. Some looked so realistic it was as though their spirits were peering out from the confines of their canvas.

"Their eyes look like they're following us," Hazel whispered to Dan and Michael.

Dan, whose thoughts had mirrored those of Hazel, caught up with the King then coughed before quite rudely cutting in on his conversation with Abednego. "We're really grateful for your kind and unnecessary hospitality, but we really must return to our families in England. Our parents will be worrying about us."

Neither one acknowledged him, both as oblivious to his request as they were to the stares and whispers coming from the castles inhabitants. They were engrossed in conversation as Abednego explained to Mazarin the reason for their visit to the King.

***

'Please pay attention to what I'm saying, it's important!" Martha Malovski reprimanded as Viola, her eldest daughter, twirled her fingers in her hair sulkily. Her angular features, as always, sneering with contempt at the instructions they had been receiving from their money-grabbing mother for the past twenty minutes. Unaware of her daughters disdain, Martha smiled adoringly at Viola, mistaking contempt for concentration.

Sophia smiled sweetly at her mother, but received no acknowledgement by Martha who remained focused on her eldest and her favourite; the one who reminded her so much of herself when she was younger. "These three youths, whoever they are, must be important if the King's holding a feast for them. Wear your most alluring dress tonight and do all in your power to ensnare the blond lad. He's the important one."

The mention of the word 'ball,' caused Viola's frown to metamorphasize into the most engaging of smiles, "You mean they might be rich?" Her face beamed at the thought of money. Her sole ambition had always been to marry someone wealthy who would look after her and keep her. Love as a concept did not appeal to her, she considered it an emotion for the weak. For her, happiness was being rich and powerful, bathing in the adoration of others, living like her mother.

"They've just arrived so we must prepare immediately. We have half an hour until the feast, enough time for you to make yourself more beautiful than you already are."

"I guarantee they'll be eating out of my hand by the time tonight is over."

Pleased by this unexpected chance to further secure her family's future, Martha's tall frame rose from the bed and glared at her younger daughter, "and what are you staring at? Close your mouth and stop gawping. Honestly, how I gave birth to such a graceless daughter is beyond me. At least try making yourself look half decent, I'm sure Viola will allow you to borrow one of her old dresses… if you can squeeze into it." Her remarks cutting deeply, and yet unabashed by the look of sorrow in Sophie's eyes Martha continued. "Just smile politely and say as little as possible, that way there's less chance of you causing any embarrassment. Do you hear?"

Straightening her back, head held high, Martha shot one last approving glance at Viola before allowing them some privacy.

Although resigned to her mother's hurtful comments, she still wondered at the cause of her deep-rooted hatred. Sophie had always yearned for a close mother-daughter relationship, or at least, a strong bond with her sister. Unfortunately, she had been granted neither. Her mother was haughty and obsessed with looks and money; surprising considering she looked like someone that'd had all her flesh sucked away from her face, leaving little more than skin and bones. Despite her arrogance and self-importance, or perhaps because of these, people laughed at her behind her back, thinking her proud and foolish; knowing her luxurious lifestyle was merely the result of tricking a Duke into marrying her. Despite being so similar to their mother, it amused Sophie that while Martha doted on Viola, her sister openly showed condescension towards their mother.

Picking out a ruby red gown, Viola grinned smugly as she admired the image that greeted her in the mirror. Noticing Sophie's reflection, embarrassment flooded through Viola who was mortified that Sophie had witnessed such an open display of vanity.

"What are you grinning at?" Viola glowered.

"Sorry, I was j… j… just watching and wondering what I could wear tonight, that's all." She berated herself for smirking, hoping Viola didn't respond by choosing an awful dress for her to wear.

Scouring dresses of various shapes, styles and colours, Viola asked, "What do you think, this red dress or my new turquoise one?" She paused, expecting an answer, but Sophie remained silent, simply nodding in agreement, waiting patiently. "And what about you?" Skimming her finger across the medley of materials, she stopped near the middle of the wardrobe. "You can wear this blue one; it's a bit bigger than my other dresses so you'll probably have a better chance of fitting into it; can't say I cared for it much, lacking in elegance if you ask me, but it might just suit you!"

Annoyed at the slur, Sophie prevented herself from saying that she looked fit and healthy, whereas Viola simply looked like she'd been starved for weeks. Not a look Sophie found attractive or wanted to copy.

Sidling over to her side of the bedroom, she dressed in the castoff which fit her surprisingly well. Applying a touch of makeup to give her cheeks a hint of colour, she then concentrated on styling her honey blonde hair. She couldn't wait for the Feast.

***

Halting before a huge oak door, Abednego unlocked a room to reveal splendour beyond even Dan's wildest dreams. Handing the key to Michael, he indicated for them to enter the bedroom suite.

"Please feel free to freshen up. There are some clothes in the wardrobe which might make you feel more at home," after indicating to a wardrobe, he turned his attention towards Hazel and added, 'there's a separate bedroom through there with some more feminine clothes." Aware of the multitude of tasks he needed to fulfil before the feast, Abednego made to leave, "I'll be back up in half an hour to take you down."

They looked at each other worried. It was clear that both the King and Abednego expected them to remain at least one night, meaning the earliest they could return home was the following morning. With no way of contacting their families, they knew they would be worried sick.

"This would be so amazing if it weren't for the fact that my mum has no idea where I am." The image of his mum staring from their window, waiting for his return, was almost too much for him. Fiddling with his watch, he desperately tried to think of a solution.

"We could always leave and figure a way home ourselves," Hazel proposed.

"There's no way we can leave here without being noticed. And even if we did, the huge gates and wall would be impossible to scale, and where would we go? We don't know anything about this place," a dejected Dan reasoned.

"Suppose so."

"And Abednego said the only way we can get back is with the King's help. We just have to hope he helps us sooner rather than later."

"Okay, we'll stay tonight then discuss what to do tomorrow morning," agreed Hazel.

"We'd best start getting ready; making an effort to blend in might help win him over," reasoned Dan as he entered their en-suite. Hazel disappeared into the adjoining bedroom to get ready, more worried than she could ever remember feeling.

***

By the time Grimbald had reached the hilltop, the sun had virtually set and the air had turned cold. He gazed at the castle walls and the huge building, so intimidating in size that even he, a giant of a man, felt threatened by its expanse. Noting that the wrought iron gates at the front were barred and protected by four armour clad guards, he pondered the problem of how to get inside the castle.

Clutching his cloak under his chin, he started to follow the perimeter or the wall round towards the back of the castle. His enthusiasm was waning, it was getting late and he knew Ragetta would be worried. He was half-tempted to turn back, but a niggling feeling at the back of his mind made him push thoughts of his wife aside.

Unable to find another entrance, he realised his only option was to scour the wall. Estimating it at about eight feet high, he considered he was tall and strong enough to at least try. Rolling back his sleeves he clawed at the edge of the bricks, scraping his skin on their roughness. Jumping, his hands gripped the top of the wall, his veins protruding from the effort. Clambering up the sides, he paused for a final breath before hauling himself to a seated position on the top. Peering over, he assessed the drop, noting how slight the margin for error was. There was only a couple of feet of grass between the wall and the huge moat surrounding the parameter of the castle.

Positioning himself flat on his stomach, he manoeuvred his body so his legs dangled over the edge. Securing his grip, he slid down, landing safely on the soft grass by the murky water. Realising he was going to have to swim; he braced himself against the wind which howled like a wounded wolf. With little sunlight remaining and a sky devoid of stars, his only continued source of light would be the two moons in the distance.

Inhaling deeply, he resigned himself to the inevitable and dipped his foot in the water. It was freezing. Lowering himself into the moat, he cringed as the mud and slime clung to his clothes, seeping through to his skin. Once submerged, he began dragging himself through the filthy moat, shivering violently as he clawed his way across to the other side.

Though only a short distance, his arms ached and his hands stung where the infected water invaded the scraped skin he'd sustained from climbing. Exhaling, he watched his breath evaporate, as his shivering limbs became less co-ordinated with each stroke.

Finally he hoisted himself onto the bank and sat, holding his knees into his chest, his entire body shaking. His water-logged boots were like weights on his feet, his clothes clung to his skin and water from his hair dripped annoyingly down his face and neck. He was beginning to wish he'd never noticed the boy; or at least that he'd had the common sense to abandon his mission as soon as he'd been confronted with the wall and moat. The thought of a cooked dinner and crackling fire waiting for him at home did nothing to brighten his mood.

He wrung the muddy water from his clothes and cloak as best he could and tipped the excess water from his boots. Tying the laces together he threw his boots over his shoulder and trudged towards the castle, amazed at how little security there was. It almost seemed too easy, though somewhat uncomfortable, to be able to trespass on royal property.

Shaking uncontrollably, he reached the once familiar brick archways, there were five in total, and they led into a cobbled courtyard. Replacing his boots, he passed through the arches just as the light from the castle shone on the small statuettes lining the courtyard, while in the distance the comforting sound of water cascading down the beautiful figurines into marble pools made him stop for a second. Composed, he entered the building and his shivering instantly subsided as the heat warmed him, and the light allowed him to see properly.

Knowing exactly where everything was, and where everyone was likely to be at this time of the evening, he crept along the passages, his eyes darting cautiously from left to right to make sure no-one was unexpectedly around; he couldn't afford to be caught.

"What are you doing here?"

Startled at being caught so quickly, Grimbald turned. He raised his arms to chest height, ready to defend himself, until it registered that it was his old friend, Robespierre who stood in his path. "I, well, I." He muttered before falling silent, his arms dropping to his sides. With no idea how to explain his presence, he almost laughed at his complete lack of planning for the possibility that he would be caught.

"Not stealing are you?" A smile crossed Robespierre's lips, who appeared almost as startled as Grimbald at the situation.

"Of course I'm not!" His initial reaction was to lie about why he was there, but he figured Robespierre would never believe him, and anyway, he wasn't good at lying. The only feasible course of action was simply to tell the truth. "I know it will sound a bit far-fetched, but today, on my way home from work I noticed three youths, one of the boys in particular caught my attention. When I realised they were heading for the castle I rather impulsively followed them here."

"Why?"

"Well, now I'm here, I'm not really sure."

"So that's your story is it?"

"You don't have to tell me how ridiculous it sounds; I've just heard myself say it. I'll totally understand if you choose not to take my word for it, but I promise you faithfully, it's the truth." Grimbald stopped and silence followed. Reluctantly, he resorted to pleading, "please don't tell anyone. Just let me go and I swear I'll not enter the castle again." His heart pounded furiously as he held his breath in anticipation.

Robespierre considered his old friend whom he hadn't seen in fifteen years. Grimbald hadn't changed much except for a sprinkling of grey round his temples and a few extra pounds round his waist. Watching the intruder click his fingers nervously, Robespierre felt a surge of pity for the man he'd once counted amongst his closest friends. That was of course, until Mathis had left to start a new life and Grimbald, his personal attendant, had decided to retire from Court life rather than accepting another responsibility.

Grimbald felt regret and a tinge of resentment at how their lives had taken them in such different directions.

"You look frozen! I presume the swim was not to your liking?" Joking to lighten the situation, Robespierre attempted to put Grimbald at ease.

Fatigued and unwilling to play games, Grimbald remained silent, convinced Robsepierre would have him arrested.

"Look Grimbald, I know we parted on bad terms. I have often wished things could have been different. Don't you ever think back and wonder if we could have avoided it? We were so close once and I know you think it was easy for me… that I took the easy option… but I promise you there have been many times, even now, when I wish I'd been brave and left like you did."

Relaxing, Grimbald said, "I know it wasn't your fault, perhaps I shouldn't have been so stubborn, and for that, I'm sorry. It's all water under the bridge as far as I'm concerned. But right now, I need to know whether you plan to hand me over to the King." Determined to retain his dignity he looked Robespierre in the eye, his back straight, his posture defiant.

"No, I don't." The thought had crossed his mind, but he couldn't betray his old friend. He felt like he'd let him down once already and couldn't bring himself to do it again.

"I appreciate it." Relieved, he smiled before turning his back on Robespierre and continuing along the passage, water still dripping from him, staining the floor as he went.

"Wait!" Robespierre called.

"What?" The tired figure stopped impatiently, eager to get on with his task.

"You look a mess."

"Thanks."

"Don't take it personally but you're soaking wet and smell of mud. It's hardly an appearance that will go unnoticed in a castle where even the servants are dressed in velvet."

"I haven't much choice. I'll just have to hope I don't bump into anyone.

"Take my cloak; that at least will disguise your wet clothing."

Surprised, Grimbald wrapped it round him, the warmth encased him and almost immediately his shivering began to subside. "Thank you."

Without a thought for the consequences, Robespierre added, "Quickly, come to my rooms, you can borrow a towel and some clothes so you'll blend in better. We're about the same build so they should fit."

Following Robespierre, Grimbald thought for the first time that perhaps it might not be impossible after all.

"Thanks," Grimbald said minutes later, feeling warmer and looking much more presentable.

"I'm sorry I can't do more. The King's holding a special feast tonight and I can't be late, or it's the black list for me!"

Shaking hands in a gentlemanly manner, Robespierre headed towards the Great Hall where the music had already started playing.

Resembling other Courtiers, Grimbald strolled along the hallway, head bowed low, making sure his face was hidden from view. Passing a green liveried servant, his heart fluttered with fear but with his eyes cast downwards, they passed him by, unaware of his identity. With each Courtier or servant he passed, the more relaxed he felt, until finally he halted outside the guest rooms, staring at the door in bewilderment. Were they in there? Should he knock? What would he say? What if someone else was in there? How would he explain his presence? What if they were in there but didn't believe him? What would he do then?

"Good evening. May I be of assistance?"

His leg started trembling at the fear of being caught. Not quite knowing who he was talking to he managed to murmur, "no thank you, I'm fine."

"It's just that you look lost." The voice which was meant to sound kind had a slight edge to it, making Grimbald nervous.

"Really, I'm fine," he urged, wishing the stranger would leave him alone.

Determined not to let the matter drop, the interrogator strutted towards him and extended his arm towards

Grimbald's face. Placing his hand under Grimbald's chin he forced Grimbalds head up as both of them gasped.

Grimbald stared directly at Raglin, the Minister chiefly responsible for his decision to leave the castle. Meanwhile Raglin was amused to find himself confronting the trouble maker he thought he'd seen the back of.

"Grimbald, what a pleasant surprise. The King must have forgotten to tell me of your visit."

"Must have done."

"Now, now, Grimbald, we both know the King would not invite the likes of you into his Court. So, can you please explain why you're trespassing on Royal property?" Revelling in his superior position and Grimbald's obvious discomfort, Raglin's voice had changed from one of almost pleasant concern into a snarl.

If his assumption was even close to the truth, any word of the children could endanger all their lives. With no option but to lie, Grimbald stammered, "since an accident two years ago, I've had money problems. I thought, or my wife did, that if I managed to get to speak to the King, he might find it within his heart to give me a job, what with my previous experience of royal service."

"I'm afraid there are currently no positions available at Court for middle-aged trouble makers, though I'll let you know if the situation changes."

Clenching his fists, Grimbald fought back the temptation to defend his actions. "That was years ago. You must know how time mellows people?" The thought of crawling to this detestable man was almost as sickening as being caught in the first place.

"Unfortunately for you, age has not mellowed me. I've simply become older and wiser, and from where I'm standing, you've not only been caught breaking and entering into Royal property, you've also stolen clothing to disguise yourself."

"But…"

"Extremely serious charges!"

He couldn't possibly repay Robespierre's kindness by saying he'd been lent the clothes, so he remained silent and waited for the worst.

"Is there anything you'd like to say in your defence?"

Praying fervently for a miracle, he raised his head high but remained silent, staring at Raglin defiantly.

"I admire your spirit, if nothing else." Pulling a metal gadget from under his robe, he pressed a small green button and within seconds two armour clad guards marched towards him. Accepting defeat gracefully, Grimbald held out his hands. All his hopes evaporated, he sighed as they escorted him down corridors, wondering how long he'd be incarcerated for and whether they would at least allow him to inform his wife of his predicament. Walking along passages and descending stairwells through dark unused rooms, he was led from the castle's magnificence into wet, dull passageways where water dripped from the ceiling like sweat, creating a musky aroma within the dimly lit caverns of the castle.

Eventually, after passing along an underground canal which led out into the moat, he was shoved through a hole which appeared in the wall. Hauled along the far side of a rat infested chamber, he was pushed into a bare cell before the padlock was bolted shut.

"Can someone at least let my wife know where I am?" He pleaded.

"You forfeited all rights when you were caught breaking and entering," the smaller of the guards laughed. "Oh, and I wouldn't ask the guards who patrol these dungeons to help you. They don't like people who ask questions. In fact, they don't like people!"

Slumping onto the wet floor, resting his head against the damp brick wall, he prayed for a miracle. Desperate to escape, he resolved that if he were ever set free, he would forget about the boy and return to Ragetta.

Chapter Fourteen: The Feast

After changing into the medieval clothes they perched expectantly on the edge of Daniel's bed. The feast was looming and they had no idea about how to act. They had tried discussing how to broach the subject of their to return to England with the King, but had abandoned it after disagreements had broken out, deciding finally to play it by ear.

It wasn't long before Abednego entered their apartment dressed in a gold and emerald green robe, looking very good for his age. Beckoning them, he led them towards the Great Hall where the feast was being held.

Feeling completely out of their comfort zones, they followed him timidly through a labyrinth of corridors and staircases. All three were determined to memorise the castle's layout but it was so confusing, they gave up.

Huge tapestries were illuminated by candles, creating an aura of magic and mysticism. Exquisite carvings covered virtually every free surface; intricately engraved with life size images of angels, cherubs, unicorns and other mystical creatures, inhabiting fantastic settings.

Dozens of people swarmed through the corridors, from the rich to liveried servants rushing about dusting and polishing. Many stopped chatting as soon as they passed, their eyes following the new additions to the castle. Feeling like the latest attraction at a zoo, they bowed their heads to block out the faces. It hadn't escaped them that everyone, even the servants, were dressed in finely embroidered dresses and robes of silk, satins or velvet, just like medieval times.

Reaching a gigantic, intricately engraved door, they noticed the door knocker was the shape of a trolls face. "We welcome Abednego and our guests of honour for tonight's feast," a loud voice boomed.

"Who said that?" asked Michael.

Abednego laughed, "That was the door knocker. He announces people as they arrive."

Amazed at a talking door knocker, Dan, Michael and Hazel were starting to wonder what kind of country Kilion was, but before they had time to collect their thoughts, Abednego was ushering them into a huge ballroom. Inside was an almost identical troll's face. "The troll on the outside of the door sees whose about to enter. He then informs his other half who announces the person, or persons, to the Great Hall," explained Abdenego.

Nervously they followed Abednego through the rows of guests who had all been eagerly anticipating their arrival. An eerie silence descended as they approached the raised dais at the front.

The King, seated on an ornate throne, proffered a hand to Michael, Dan and Hazel before indicating for them to sit on the the chairs immediately to his left.

The Queen sat to the right of the King; unlike Mazarin who was tall and toned, she was petite and dainty. Her face was pale and her features delicate, like a finely sculptured porcelain doll. Her green eyes stared ahead of her, her lips curled into a smile as she gazed at the rows of tables before her.

Next to her, five meticulously dressed men whispered amongst themselves, their eyes scanning their surroundings, ensuring nobody could overhear their conversation. All appeared to be older and more serious than the King and Queen.

As soon as Michael, Dan and Hazel were seated, everyone, even the five Ministers, ceased their conversations and stared at the newcomers. Embarrassed by the attention, they turned to face the King, smiling awkwardly at their host.

Sensing their fear, the King stood up to raise a toast, "Ladies and gentlemen, it is my pleasure to introduce you to Michael, Hazel and Daniel who will be staying with us. Please make every effort to ensure they feel welcome, showing them the same kindness you bestowed upon me when I came as a stranger to this land. Please join me in raising your glasses to welcome them."

Hundreds of glasses filled the air, then the sound of clinking, laughter and clapping resounded throughout the hall as the buzzing of voices started.

Ensuring no-one was paying attention, Daniel, seated between Michael and Hazel, grabbed their arms and whispered, "What did he mean when he said we were going to be staying here? I thought we'd be leaving soon, tonight even! What are we going to do?"

Michael shrugged.

Placing her hand reassuringly on Dan's arm, Hazel comforted him, "Let's not worry unnecessarily, he was probably referring to us staying tonight and tomorrow. As soon as the feast is over, we'll ask for help."

Unable to shake his pent up frustration, Dan nodded dolefully. It was way past the time he'd told Mary he would be home, and he hated the thought of her worrying. Still, with no other options available, he sat at the table, clicking his thumbs, wondering how long the feast would last.

Once the King had resumed his seat, a band in the corner of the Great Hall struck up a tune. Immediately, cutlery and plates appeared before them, taking the three friends by surprise. These were followed by delicious dishes of food, complete with gold serving utensils. Where it had all come from and how it had appeared, they dared not ask, but they were starting to expect the unexpected.

"Tuck in, you must be starving," King Mazarin, noticing their reticence, picked up a dish of meat, surrounded with brightly coloured vegetables and passed it to Michael.

Not wanting to appear rude by saying they'd already eaten, Michael grasped the dish and ladled some meat and vegetables, or at least that's what they looked like, onto his plate, slightly worried that he had no idea what he was about to consume. Passing the dish to Daniel he tucked in. Chewing the fresh meat heartily, he hadn't realised just how hungry he was.

***

"Remember what I said; smile gracefully, keep your head held high and leave him feeling good about himself. One thing that everyone, male and female has in common is their ego. Take it from me; the surest way to win a man's approval is to feed it. Compliment him, make him feel important. Pay him attention and he'll be yours for the taking my dear." Listening to her mother repeat her earlier advice, Viola crossed her knife and fork on a virtually untouched plate of food. Smiling conspiratorially at her mother, she stood up, squared her shoulders and straightened her back as she contemplated the task ahead.

Disdainfully she stared at the boy she had been instructed to beguile; small and skinny, he looked no older than twelve or thirteen. Facially, he wasn't too bad; in fact, she could imagine he might be quite handsome in a few years. However, he did look rather young which would result in them looking physically, rather odd as a couple. At sixteen, she suspected she was at least three or four inches taller than him and looked at least a couple of years older.

Shifting her gaze to his dark haired friend, she wished she had been asked to prey on him. He was taller and broader, with dark eyes and tanned skin and very much more to her liking! Determined not to prejudice herself against Michael before they'd even spoken, she returned her gaze to the direction of the blond haired boy. She reminded herself that as she had no intention of becoming emotionally attached, his appearance was really inconsequential. More important was his wealth and royal connection.

As the last scraps of food were devoured, the King rose from his throne and clapped his hands; the platters disappeared and the tables and chairs reformed in clusters along the side of the hall. The tempo picked up as Courtiers descended on the newly created dance floor. Within minutes dresses were swirling and colours merged as couple's glided across the floor. Sensing an opportunity, Viola smiled radiantly and glided towards her unsuspecting prey. Sophie watched her elder sister swooping in for the kill, pitying the poor lad who looked too helpless to defend himself.

Dan, Hazel and Michael, having finally managed to monopolise the King's attention, noticed how ill at ease he was in their company. Muttering their thanks for his hospitality, they watched him twist his ring nervously. Unsure if they were worrying unduly Michael, Dan and Hazel had the distinct impression Mazarin's concerned expression was connected to their arrival. Once pleasantries were over, the conversation faltered as none of them found the courage to request directions home; despite being desperate to return, all were struck dumb by the King's presence.

Unaccustomed to conversing with royalty, Viola wondered how best to initiate a conversation. Stopping by their table she coughed politely to gain their attention. The King, glad of a distraction greeted her warmly and introduced her.

With the formal introductions over, Mazarin fell silent, his head throbbing with the unrest caused by their arrival. He needed time to consult Abednego to discover the reason for their unexpected visit, and only then could he work out how to deal with this situation.

His initial instinct had been to keep their stay short, to stop people asking questions. However, since noticing Michael's resemblance to Mathis, he had changed his mind and decided to detain them a while longer in Kilion; were they from the same country Mathis had settled in? If so, how had they managed to get through the porthole, which had been closed, since Mathis death? If they had managed it, did that mean others could? Could citizens from Kilion visit England? And lastly, the question he was most determined to ask was, had Mathis had a son no-one had known about? Eager to have his curiosity satisfied, but unwilling to appear too concerned in front of his Ministers, he decided to leave any questions until the following day; by which time they might feel more comfortable.

Not wanting to appear too forward, Viola shuffled her feet nervously, studying Michael from under hooded eyelids. Looking more uncomfortable then regal, she couldn't help but question her mother's source of information.

As silence descended, Viola smiled at Michael, hoping he might initiate conversation. He didn't. Michael was paralysed with fear, half expecting her to start laughing at him like most other girls his age. But she didn't laugh, instead he found her smile was quite kind.

Realising she would have to take the lead, and hoping he might relax more if he was on his own, she put herself out on a limb. Extending her hand she asked, "Would you like to dance?"

Dumbstruck, Michael had no idea how to respond. He'd never danced with a girl before, especially not anyone posh, and the thought terrified him. He twiddled his fingers nervously, realising the predicament he was in. If he said yes then he'd end up making a fool of himself by tripping over or treading on her foot. If he said no she might take offence and think he was being offish, and what if the King thought his refusal was an affront to his hospitality?

"What an excellent idea! Perhaps she could introduce you to others in the castle, help make your stay more enjoyable," encouraged the King as Michael smiled at the waiting Viola.

"But I...I" Michael stammered.

"Don't worry, she'll teach you the steps, there's no need to be afraid."

Reluctantly, he followed her onto the dance floor and tried to dance. Considering how easily he fell over whilst doing nothing more complicated than walking, he decided it was politer to keep focused on her feet and ignore her than to break her toe or rip her dress.

"Wonder why she asked him to dance?" said Dan thoughtfully as he gazed at an ungraceful Michael.

"Perhaps she's just being friendly."

"Maybe. But what if she's trying to find out about us?"

"Find out? I reckon she probably saw how awkward we felt and thought that asking him to dance was a pleasant thing to do."

"So why ask Michael to dance? Why not start a conversation with all three of us?"

"For goodness sake Dan, stop analysing things! Has it crossed your mind that she may have taken a liking to him?"

"Like Michael! She looks years older than him!" Dan fretted as he inhaled to calm himself down. "I hope you're right. Let's pray she doesn't ask too many questions and that he doesn't say too much."

"It's a dance, not a police investigation. Will you stop being so suspicious." Regretting the harshness of her words, she remembered what Abednego had said about trusting strangers. "I'm sorry for seeming so harsh, but surely a dance can't be too bad."

"Do they dance much where you come from?"

Looking up in surprise and treading on her toes in the process, Michael's face reddened with embarrassment at his clumsiness. He waited for an insult, but it didn't come, instead her smile was kind and understanding. "We do dance, but not like this."

Sensing his discomfort, she felt an emotion she hadn't experienced before. Was it pity perhaps? She smiled at him, this time more naturally. "What type of dancing do you do then?"

He pictured his mum gyrating her hips and knocking over vases, "Sometimes individually… but with a group of friends, often in the shape of a circle, then we move as we want to the beat of the music." His description sounded ridiculous and he wondered what vision he had just conjured for her.

"Perhaps you can show me later?"

"Well, I er…" he stuttered.

"I'm joking. Relax." he smiled, relieved.

Having achieved nothing as the first song ended, she exclaimed how much she liked the next song as soon as the first note was played, "Just one more?" Tightening her grip on his arm, she feared the thought of returning to her mother with no more knowledge than his style of dancing.

Michael couldn't believe she wanted to put either of them through the humiliation of another dance. She must be either mad or desperate.

Dan watched apprehensively fearing that Michael, unused to female attention, would let something slip. Worried, he resorted to trying to catch Michael's attention.

"Dan, are you alright? You look like you've got something in your eye!" Hazel whispered so no-one could hear.

"I'm winking to get his attention."

"Well I'd stop it if I were you. People will either think that you and Michael are more than just friends or that you're trying to crack onto the girl he's dancing with." Dan acknowledged defeat.

On the dance floor, Viola noticed Dan winking in their direction. Was it at her? Her heart fluttered with an unexpected emotion. What a shame it was Michael and not Dan, she thought yet again.

Returning her attention to Michael, she again attempted initiating conversation, "It's always nice to see new faces at Court. It gets a bit boring sometimes; there aren't many teenagers here in the castle."

"I haven't seen many," he replied, not sure how she expected him to respond.

"So are you staying for a while, or is it a flying visit?"

Alarm bells rang! Abednego had told him to say nothing to anybody, and even if he wanted to, he wasn't sure himself.

Noticing his reluctance, she continued, "It's just that if you were staying for a bit, I could introduce you to some of my friends."

"We're not sure when we'll be leaving, we're playing it by ear, but it's likely we'll be here tomorrow morning at least."

"Excellent, you can all join me after breakfast and I'll take you on a tour of the castle and gardens. I'll invite my friends, you'll love them!"

"Sounds great, I'll just check with Dan and Hazel first."

"Of course, just let me know later." Curtseying as the dance ended, she smiled before returning to her table.

Watching her leave, he stood momentarily, deep in thought. Tonight was the first time a female had shown any interest in him and he wasn't sure whether to feel suspicious or happy that finally he'd been noticed. Returning to his friends, who remained close to the King and his Ministers, he grinned.

"So, what did she say?" enquired Dan.

"Nothing much."

"Nothing much? She either said something or she didn't."

Annoyed at Dan's aggressive tone, Michael responded off-handedly, "We talked a bit, that's all.

"Did she try to find anything out?" Pestered Dan, getting agitated by Michael's secretiveness.

"Are you insinuating she only asked me to dance to discover who we are? That's it isn't it? You think no-one would ever ask me to dance simply because they wanted to?" Michael was fuming at the inference. It was the first time anyone other than his mother had asked him to dance and Dan was making it sound like she was an undercover spy, using him to gain knowledge.

Realising how insensitive he sounded, Dan tried to mollify Michael, "Sorry, I'm just nervous after Abednego's warning. I can't help being wary of everyone, you know what a suspicious nature I have. I just think we should be careful."

"Stop bickering! Michael, I'm sure Dan didn't mean it to sound so harsh, he's just concerned; we both are. Now, did she ask any questions?"

"She asked about dancing at home and wanted to know how long we were staying." Dan looked up, alarmed.

Conscious of Dan's not very well hidden jerk of the head, Michael felt the need to justify himself by adding, "she said if we're staying she'd take us all on a tour of the castle with her friends, that's all."

"Did you accept?" Excited by the prospect of touring the ground, Hazel wondered whether it might help them escape. The more they explored, the greater their chance of success.

"I said I'd ask you first."

Satisfied that Viola's motives were innocent, Dan nodded, "tell her we'll go… But only if we haven't already been told how to get home."

"Obviously."

Chapter Fifteen: The King's Men

The King's Ministers who had remained silent throughout the meal, now pretended to be deep in political discussions so as not to attract attention. Sensing an opportunity while Michael was dancing, they had surreptitiously sidled closer to Dan and Hazel, eavesdropping on their conversation to find out what they could about them, all to no avail; nothing.

Later, overhearing the encounter between Dan and Michael, they were disappointed that Viola had discovered so little, though conceded that gentle persuasion was the right course of action. Michael had clearly been flattered by Viola's attention, and that was knowledge they could definitely use to their advantage. Dan seemed more suspicious than the others while the girl was clearly the mediator. Unanimously they decided Viola would be an invaluable ally, for it was more likely the friends would confide in her rather than an older Minister. With money-grabbing Martha as her mother, they didn't think purchasing her loyalty would be too problematic; things were already falling into place.

"I think he's taken a fancy to her," commented Raglin thoughtfully.

"It would certainly help matters."

"It's a good job she danced with Michael rather than Daniel. We definitely need to keep an eye on that one, he could cause trouble," noted Duclem, wiping his bushy beard with his handkerchief to detach any food which had become embedded in it.

"Hargrin, did you get those tablets off of Zawi Chemi?" enquired Raglin as he inspected the youngest and newest member of the group.

"I managed to get three but as they only last 24 hours, we'll need more." Hargrin looked down on the others, his height and good looks clearly intimidating all but Raglin, the oldest, wisest Minister. Despite being one of many junior Court Ministers, his lack of scruples had been immediately apparent to Raglin who was always on the lookout for inexperienced Ministers to exploit for political gain. Taking Hargrin under his wing, he had introduced him to the elite group with whom he now stood. Accepting his company, the others knew Hargrin would undertake any task necessary to gain recognition; tasks they would rather not do.

Hargrin was a willing participant in the game. Hungry for a share of their power and influence, it was a small price to pay to cement the alliance. They all knew where they stood and what each would gain from a successful alliance. With natural self-confidence, charm and charisma, very few ladies, including Zawi Chemi could resist him. He had gained the tablets with ease. With charm to spare came a skill for deception, for Hargrin was an accomplished liar. Even the older Ministers couldn't tell when he was being truthful, which caused them some concern. Yet as their prime objective was to win Michael's friendship, his other qualities made him the best person to achieve this, so these concerns were temporarily swept to the side.

"Can I have two volunteers, someone to divert them and someone to spike their drinks," requested Raglin.

Nervously twiddling his fingers, Tacitus eyed his companions in turn. Unsure of himself, Tacitus constantly feared losing his Ministerial position. Everyone knew it was Raglin rather than King Mazarin who really controlled the council.

Raglan had made each of his 65 years count so that his wealth of experience made him increasingly fearsome. He could go from being kind and amenable to vengeful and unforgiving over actions almost all would fail to notice. Only a handful had dared cross him, and all had been stripped of their office.

"I'll do it," Tacitus offered.

"Excellent. Hargrin, where are the tablets?"

Producing a small ball of tin foil, Hargrin unwrapped the bundle to produce three tiny pink pellets.

Taking the offered pills, Tacitus clutched them, "Someone will have to distract them."

"Leave it to me," Hargrin offered. Conscious of their attention, he strolled towards the King, deliberately stumbling as he walked past Hazel, falling straight into her.

Stumbling, Hazel clasped at Daniel for support, spilling both their drinks. She looked on in horror as bright red liquid cascaded over the polished floorboards.

With a feigned look of mortification masking his inner delight, Hargrin made eye contact with Hazel as his husky voice apologised. With a graceful ease, he slid an arm round her shoulder to steady her before flashing a dazzling smile.

"T… t… that's okay," she stuttered, returning her attention to her cup which had landed by the leg of a table.

"Here, let me." Scooping up the empty cups, he winked across at his accomplices, revelling in how smoothly it had gone. "Tacitus," he called, "will you be kind enough to refill these glasses while I deal with this mess?"

Turning his attention towards them, Hargrin introduced himself. "How nice to make your acquaintance, although I apologise about your drinks, here," he indicated to Michael, "I'll get Tacitus to get you a nice fresh drink as well while he's at it."

Taking his cue, Tacitus carried their cups on a discarded tray to the drinks table. Ladling in the liquid, he checked no-one was watching before slipping a pill into each of the glasses. Bubbles erupted and the frothy liquid climbed up the metal sides until they almost spilled. Just as it reached the brim, the froth subsided, the bubbles burst and the liquid returned to its original state. Sighing, his hands shook as he returned to Hargrin who had them locked deep in conversation.

So engrossed in their banter with Hargrin, they barely acknowledged Tacitus as they took their drinks. After returning to the others, Tacitus watched the scene before him. As he did so, it occurred to him just how young and innocent the visitors were. He felt a stab of guilt at his role, but was too scared to help them. Years of waiting had preceded this moment and he couldn't let doubt cloud his judgement. Aware that backing out was not an option, he resolved that as far as possible he wouldn't be involved in any harm befalling them unless absolutely necessary. Hargrin meanwhile, continued winning them over, with no thought for their safety.

As Hargrin charmed; Michael, Hazel and even Dan relaxed, giggling at his jokes and descriptions of Kilion. He spoke of its wonders and of life at Court. They felt so at ease that soon they were hanging on his every word, and when he sipped his drink, they subconsciously followed suit. Soon their cups were empty and they were left wanting more.

Feeling light headed, Dan casually leaned on the table to prevent himself falling over and looking foolish. He watched mouths open and close but his senses had abandoned him, he couldn't understand anything that was being said. Both Hazel and Michael felt the same, but no-one was prepared to speak of it. Instead they all tried acting normally, praying no-one would notice.

Sensing his work was done; Hargin bowed and excused himself to rejoin his accomplices.

"Well done both of you. It seems the tablets are already taking effect," Raglin rubbed his hands in excitement.

"The wine isn't doing them any favours either, not a great combination. Poor kids can't even string a sentence together."

"Dan can barely stand," grinned Duclem.

"Let's hope they do the trick, I haven't put in this much time and effort for it to fail now," Raglin responded.

"Can you get more tablets for tomorrow Hargrin?"

"How many?"

"About a week's worth. The plan won't work unless they trust us completely and have no recollection of their past. Rushing will only cause mistakes, and I for one do not want to be the one to tell him if that happens!"

Chapter Sixteen: Drugged

Tables spun and his head felt light. Stumbling, Michael slurred, "Don't feel good, gotta sit." Staggering towards the nearest chair, he hoped his legs didn't give way before he reached it.

Dan joined him, taking some comfort from the knowledge that Michael felt as bad as as he did. Leaning his head between his legs, he prayed he wasn't going to vomit in front of everyone.

Aware of how ridiculous they must look after only two glasses of wine, Hazel sat next to Dan. Only sixteen and already regretting drinking too much, she hoped it wasn't a sign of things to come. For some reason she wasn't as badly affected as the other two, who she knew would cringe when she reminded them how drunk they had been after just two glasses.

"How you feeling?" Hazel asked Dan as she steadied him.

"Awful."

"What's time?" Michael groaned.

"Just gone eleven. The night will be over soon enough. Then we can get back to our rooms and get a good night's sleep."

"Hazel," whispered Michael, "she's coming over."

They watched Violas bony frame approaching.

"I apologise, but my mum wants me to introduce her to Michael." For some reason, and she couldn't put her finger on it, Viola, had taken an immediate dislike to Hazel, but knew how important she must be to Michael, so refrained from showing disdain. Dan and Michael, she noticed, looked positively awful.

Hazel eyed Viola suspiciously; unsure why she suddenly felt hostile towards Viola, after all she had done nothing wrong. It was just something about her, something not quite right. Perhaps it was her cold calculating eyes which looked older than her years.

"Hi Michael, have you given tomorrow's tour any thought?"

What tour? Straining his memory, it took a while to click. Yes, he vaguely remembered discussing it, but he couldn't quire remember the outcome. Dan moaned beside him, 'I feel sick!"

"The tour?" Frustrated, Viola wondered if they weren't completely normal. Their faces looked blank and it hadn't even been that long since they had discussed the idea.

"Okay," Michael agreed, hoping it was the right answer.

"And what about meeting my mum?"

"Erm, I'm not…" Irritated, she grabbed his hand and hoisted him from his seat.

"See you… minute," Dan slurred.

Turning to face Hazel, Dan's face took on a bemused expression. "Why are there two of you?" He rubbed his eyes in disbelief.

"Put your head back between your knees. We'll leave as soon as we can," soothed Hazel who hadn't thought about how they were going to return to their rooms.

***

Obediently following Viola, Michael couldn't help thinking that Martha looked surprisingly good considering she had a teenage daughter. Then he noticed a girl about his age whom he assumed was Viola's younger sister.

As Martha turned her attention to him, Michael grinned stupidly, swaying to and fro like a ship in a storm.

"This is Michael who is staying at the castle."

"Nice to meet you."

"Hi."

"So, how long do we have the pleasure of your company Michael?"

"For... Erm..." he thought. How long *was* he staying for? He didn't know, in fact he couldn't even recall why he was even here, "a while," he added in a non-committal manner. Despite his senses being the worse for wear, he could feel her eyes boring into him, assessing him like cattle at a market.

Determined not to be intimidated, he returned her glare and noticed a huge beauty spot pencilled onto her cheek; it looked awful, as though a creature had dug into her face and left a gaping black hole. As images of insects crawling into her cheek filled his imagination, he felt a compulsion to laugh. He tried to control it but it got the better of him. As he opened his mouth to ask a question, instead of words, a torrent of laughter escaped. Not just a giggle, but a resounding laugh. Unable to control himself, he was clutching his side with one hand and wiping tears from his eyes with the other.

A scowl replaced her smile. He could tell she was mad. "I'm so very sorry," he spluttered between breaths of laughter, "it's just I can't remember the last time I had such fun, and I've never had wine before, it seems to have gone to my head." Finally he composed himself as his laughter subsided, "I meant no offence."

"Not at all," her face softened as her jawbones relaxed. "Viola informs me she's taking you and your companions on a tour of the castle tomorrow."

"Yes she is." Once more the sickly feeling started to take hold. Please let her shut up soon, he thought to himself.

"Just make sure you don't go anywhere out of bounds. I'm not so sure the King will be as lenient a second time Viola." Nausea swept over Michael as he started to lose sense of his surroundings.

"It won't happen again. I didn't know it was out of…"

Sophie watched with interest as Michael turned pale green. Although concerned, she had no inclination to arouse her sister or mothers anger by starting a conversation with the stranger Viola was missioned with ensnaring.

Sensing Viola's sister staring at him, he vaguely wondered why they had not been introduced, but as another wave of nausea swept over him he concentrated on inclining his head forwards as they did in films.

Eager to get away he murmured, "It's getting late and I'd better get some sleep. I'll see you tomorrow."

Stumbling to his friends, he collapsed onto an empty chair, told them what he could remember, and then closed his eyes to try and block out everything. "I want to go to bed."

"So do I, but how we gonna get there?" As they contemplated this problem, it was with relief that they saw Abednego approaching.

"Hello," giggled Michael.

"Good evening," replied Abednego. "You all look tired. I think it's best you get a good night's sleep before tomorrow." Proffering his hand to Hazel, she took it even though out of the three, she needed his help the least.

With Abednego's frail body trying to supporting them all, it was some time before they slumped onto their beds. The old man made a mental note to let them have a lie-in, as the wine had obviously affected them more than he had anticipated. At least he had avoided any questions about them returning home, but he knew they would be on the case first thing the next morning. More importantly, how was he going to keep Michael's possession of the ring secret? Everyone would ask how they had entered Kilion; what was he going to say? He knew he wasn't going to get much sleep before his meeting with the King the following morning. He needed to prepare a believable story.

Chapter Seventeen: Reported Missing

The sickening feeling from fourteen years ago returned. Last time her instincts had been proven right, surely it couldn't happen twice? But where was Michael? Why wasn't he here with his friends? Why had the door been left open?

Last time she had waited until morning to report Mathis missing, by which time he'd become a police statistic. This was different, Michael was still a boy and she wasn't going to make the same mistake twice.

Dialling Dan's number, her hand shook. Her hope was that Michael had gone there and lost track of time. But what if he wasn't? What if Dan was missing as well?

"Dan, is that you?" A worried voice answered.

Holding the phone away from her ear, Catherine's heart pounded as her worst fears were realised.

"Dan, is that you? Where are you?"

"It's Catherine, Michael's mum."

"Catherine, thank God, is Dan there? He was supposed to be home ages ago. Is everything okay?" She gabbled, hardly pausing for breath.

"I'm afraid…" she started, but was cut off mid flow.

"Something's happened hasn't it? What's wrong?"

"None of them are here; I returned home to an empty flat. I hoped they'd gone to yours." She trembled, her hand sweating so much the receiver kept slipping.

"I haven't seen Dan since dinner time."

"Is there a note there? Did he mention anything about going somewhere else?"

Catherine asked, knowing she was clutching at straws.

"No, and he's not answering his phone. I've only just found your number and was just about to call when..."

"I think I should call Hazel's Nan, see if she can help."

"Thanks Catherine, let me know how it goes. If it's any consolation, they're sensible kids, I'm sure they'll be fine." Mary attempted to soothe Catherine, only too aware of the past. She couldn't even begin to imagine what the poor woman was going through.

Dropping the receiver to her side, Catherine felt relieved that at least she was dealing with Mary rather than his parents, which would have made the situation, if possible, even worse.

***

Clutching the receiver to her chest, Mary stared at the only picture of Daniel on the wall as the seriousness of the situation sank in. Under her care, Dan had gone missing! She felt sick. Though biologically he wasn't her son, it was her he came to when ill or scared, or needed help with his homework. She was determined to find him.

She scoured through his belongings for an address book or diary she had missed but found nothing.

***

She knew Michael wouldn't be at Hazel's but she needed to see if Hazel at least was home. Her fingers trembled as she dialled the number. "Is that Rose?"

"Who's speaking?" Her old, yet firm voice queried.

"It's Catherine, Michael's mum."

"Hello dear. Is Hazel with you? She's not come home and she was supposed to be helping me sort clothes for a church jumble sale."

"I'm afraid not, that's why I've called. I don't know where she is, or Michael or Dan. They weren't here when I got back from work."

"So, you're saying they're missing?"

"I was hoping you might know something," croaked Catherine.

"No... I don't." There was a pause before Rose added, "were they acting strangely at yours?"

"I don't think so, though I left for work soon after they arrived. Have you tried Hazel's mobile?"

"Several times. I've left messages and texts but can't think of what else to do. We must report them missing immediately."

"Yes, you're right. I feel awful."

"It's no-one's fault, they should take responsibility for their own actions. They're old enough to know better."

Although relieved that neither blamed her, it didn't dull the guilt she felt. If anything happened to them, she would never forgive herself.

"I'll meet you at the police station in half an hour." A strong voiced Rose instructed from the other end of the phone.

Surprised at how formidable the old lady seemed, she informed Mary, then wrapped herself protectively in her second-hand coat and made her way, once more, to report a missing person.

***

A white haired lady was waiting for her, hand outstretched, her smile polite, 'call me Rose," she instructed as she shook Catherine's hand firmly, before walking confidently towards Mary who was approaching.

Expecting a middle-aged spinster in a frumpy dress with a neat bun, Catherine instead faced a young lady no older than thirty-five. Slightly overweight and of medium height, Mary's hair hung loose about her shoulders and her face was sweet rather than attractive. Kind blue eyes met hers as she hugged her close, taking Catherine aback.

"I'm Mary, I'm afraid his parents can't be here…"

"We know, they're away. Now Hurry up dears, the quicker we report them missing, the quicker the police can start looking." Authoritative to a fault, Rose ushered them into the station towards the front desk where a young policeman was filling out forms.

Questions were asked, forms filled in and more details requested. Information was taken, verified and checked again while tears were shed and tissues were used.

Assured by the professionalism of the police, they left the station feeling confident everything in their power would be done to find their children. But would it be enough?

After making a cup of tea, Mary waited by the phone, praying for news. She knew she should inform Dan's parents but as usual, they had left no contact details. In fact, she didn't even have an exact date for their return! She was tempted to stop trying to find a phone number and just hope he showed up before they did. Yet visions of his photo on the front page of a newspaper haunted her. She could just imagine them flitting from one meeting to another, grabbing a paper to keep up with the news and finding a photo of their son with the word 'missing' above it. How would she explain that away? Would she lose her job? Even if she was dismissed, she knew she had to at least try to contact them.

Rummaging through the drawers in the front room, she found an address book, and finding only two long distance numbers, she dialled each but both amounted to nothing. Next she called all their friends and colleagues, working through the alphabet, apologising profusely for disturbing them so late at night.

Responses varied from, "I'm afraid not, sorry," to, "I'm not sure who you're talking about," with a couple shouting obscenities about the lateness of the hour before slamming the receiver down.

An hour later and no better off, her eyes wandered about the room. Despite being physically exhausted she couldn't think about sleep. Perhaps she had missed a vital clue, something that was staring her in the face.

Returning to his room, she decided to search again, every crevice this time. Working methodically round his room, by the time the clock chimed two, she couldn't even think straight. Noticing his unmade bed, she instinctively went to straighten it up, just in case he returned. It was quite by chance that, as she was plumping his pillows, she noticed a scrunched up piece of paper that was caught in his pillowcase. Straightening the creases, she read.

Dear Diary,

I still can't work figure out why the old man wanted Michael to have the ring, but perhaps we'll find out soon. It glowed again today in Science but Hazel and I weren't there. Michael told us about it afterwards. Alvin had tripped him up and then he and Animal had kicked him when he was on the floor, in front of everyone.

The ring glowed when he returned to his desk. Michael thinks it responds to his feelings, as though it knows when he's upset. This time the wind started blowing and the window flew open so hard it hit Alvin and Animal on their head. Unfortunately they weren't hurt too badly. We still can't work out why only Michael, Hazel and I can see it, not even his mum has said anything. We're getting together as soon as possible to try to work out who the old man is. We might need to go back to the shop and find out about this magical ring! So excited, best adventure ever.

Shoving the paper in her pocket, Mary's mind whirled. Had she read it right? A magic ring? Surely the ever rational Dan couldn't have written that? Though it looked like his handwriting and it was under his pillow; a ring affecting the weather? Surely it was coincidence? And people probably had noticed the ring, they just hadn't commented on it.

More worrying was the idea that at 15, Daniel believed in magic! He'd clearly been reading far too much Harry

Potter. And the old man? Who was he? What if they had gone to find him or the shop tonight? Could they be lost? Was he involved in their disappearance!

Blinking away the tiredness, perhaps she was worrying too much? Perhaps this fantasy was their way of escaping; at least it was better than drink or drugs. Perhaps this was their version of an imaginary friend. Hazel had lost her mum, Michael his dad, and Dan virtually never saw his parents. No wonder they had over-active imaginations!

While the niggling feeling persisted, what could she say? The story was ridiculous. Finally, she decided to get some rest and clear her head. She could take it to the police station tomorrow.

On her way to bed, she noticed the door to the Hopkins study was slightly ajar. Despite almost collapsing from exhaustion, she felt an intense desire to peek inside; perhaps she might discover where they were staying. She couldn't think why she hadn't searched there before.

Captivated by the huge table in the centre of the room, she figured it was a perfect place to store important paperwork. Tugging, expecting the drawer to be locked, she was surprised to find it opened easily. Flicking through organised piles of papers, she found bills, quotes and personal correspondence, but no information on their business, not even an address or phone number for their offices. What she did discover to her amazement, were two passports. She stared in disbelief, for if they were abroad on business, as they had led her to believe, how could their passports be here? And if they weren't abroad, why hadn't they left contact details?

Neither passport had expired, both having been issued just three years previously. There were no stamps or any evidence that they had ever left British soil.

Why lie to her?

Her head throbbed; it was all too much. Yesterday everything had seemed perfect. Yet just 24 hours later, Michael, Dan and Hazel had gone missing, Dan seemed to be living in a fantasy world and now she had discovered her employers had been lying to her and Daniel for years. Sleep seemed her only escape.

***

Waking with a start, Rose looked at her watch. It had just turned four and the sun had yet to wake from its slumber.

She had fallen asleep by the phone, waiting for a call. Still half asleep, she stared at the photo of Hazel on the mantelpiece when a thought struck her; she'd forgotten to tell Samuel, Hazel's dad, that his daughter was missing. Guiltily she dialled his number, waiting with baited breath.

Once, twice, three times and, just as she was about to hang up, someone answered; her heart sank. She'd been so sure no-one would wake-up she hadn't planned what to say.

"Hello," a groggy voice answered.

"Sam? It's Rose. I'm sorry for waking you in the middle of the night but..."

"What's wrong?" All traces of grogginess vanished as his tone became insistent.

"It's Hazel. She hasn't come home. She was round a friends and supposed to be back by half eight but hasn't come home. She's not answering her phone…"

"Do we know anything?"

"She was with Dan at Michael's house but when his mum came back from work they were gone and the door was open. That's all we know. I'm so sorry."

"Wait there! I'm coming to collect you. We need to report it to the police immediately."

"We've already been, they were really helpful and promised to start their search immediately. I should have called earlier but it was manic, I wasn't thinking straight."

Samuel sat bolt upright. With the option of going to the police taken from him, he didn't know what to do, or say. His first instinct was to feel angry at not being told earlier. He should have been at the station. But deep down, he knew it hadn't been deliberate.

"Sam, are you still there?"

"Yes, sorry… So what do you suggest we do?" His daughter was missing. The police were involved. He felt lost.

"Stay by your phone. If we've heard nothing by the morning, we'll try the police again."

"I feel so helpless," he whispered as he imagined Hazel, hurt and vulnerable somewhere.

"It's only been a few hours and at least she's with Michael and Daniel. They're all sensible, so hopefully they'll be okay."

"I'm going to go in case she's trying to get through. Night" Hanging up, she wrapped her cardigan tightly around her, for the heat of the evening was failing to offer any comfort.

***

The phone had woken her. Waiting until the call was over, she opened her eyes, glanced at the alarm clock then asked who had called at such an ungodly hour.

Crawling back under the covers, he held his wife's hand before responding, "It was Rose."

"Is everything alright?"

"It's Hazel, she hasn't come home."

She felt helpless, completely out of her depth. What do you say to someone whose daughter has gone missing? Somehow words seemed inadequate.

Thinking he would welcome time by himself, she dragged herself out of bed, gave him a kiss and retreated to the kitchen to make a pot of tea. It was going to be a long night.

Chapter Eighteen: Memory Loss

"Are you awake?" Michael hissed as he peered across at Dan.

"I wasn't until a second ago. What is it?" Rolling over onto his side, it was still too dark to see Michael clearly, although Dan could tell he was wide awake from the clarity of his voice.

"I couldn't sleep."

"So, you thought you'd wake me up too?"

"I need to ask you something."

"In the middle of the night?" Dan mumbled grumpily.

"I've just spend half an hour thinking about yesterday and last night."

"And?" Dan groaned, "I presume there is an 'and'?"

"Firstly, I don't feel ill any more, which is strange considering how awful I felt. So I wondered if you were feeling better as well." Michael's voice was full of excitement.

"That's why you woke me? To see how I'm feeling! How thoughtful!"

Ignoring the obvious sarcasm, Michael persisted, "Are you feeling better or not?"

Rubbing sleep from his eyes, Dan was pleased to realise his head was no longer groggy, he was no longer seeing double and the sickly feeling had vanished. "I'm feeling much better, thanks. I still can't believe I was so bad after just two glasses!"

"How do you suppose we recovered so quickly? I thought alcohol took longer to wear off, which got me thinking that perhaps it was something we ate rather than drank?"

"I hope you're right, otherwise we're going to get a reputation as lightweights."

"So I tried remembering what we ate, but then figured it couldn't have been otherwise others would have been affected as well."

"Yes."

"So maybe it was something we ate during the day."

"Can you get to the point Sherlock, only I'm tired!"

"Nothing." Michael whispered excitedly.

"Nothing!"

"Shhh, you'll wake everyone up!" Michael chided Dan.

"So you've woken me at this ungodly hour to tell me you don't know what caused our sickness?" Unimpressed, Dan relaxed back into his mattress, pulled the covers to his chin and closed his eyes.

"Don't you get it?" Michael continued excitedly.

"If you're referring to sleep, then no, I'm not getting it. Please can we continue this conversation tomorrow, when the sun is shining and my brain is functioning properly?"

"The point I'm trying to make is not that we felt ill. It's that when I tried remembering what we ate and did yesterday, I couldn't remember, not a single thing. Can you?" Michael's excitement at this less than obvious discovery was starting to annoy Dan.

"Can't this wait?"

Exasperated by Dan, Michael hissed, "Just tell me what we did then you can go straight back to sleep."

"We went to a feast, you danced with a skinny girl and after talking to one of the King's Ministers, we felt sick. Now, goodnight."

"That was yesterday evening. What did we do during the day?"

Dan tried to remember but was horrified to discover it was all a blank. Finally the importance of Michael's message dawned on him.

"Bingo! I couldn't remember either and had to find out whether it was just me."

"Do you think Hazel's lost her memory too?"

"Probably."

"But what's happened? Why can't we remember anything?" an agitated Dan asked desperately.

"Before we make any decisions we should wake Hazel and find out for certain."

As Michael felt along the wall for a light switch, Dan hissed, "Don't turn the lights on! We don't want anyone walking outside and knowing we're awake!"

"Good thinking Watson."

Dan smiled, knowing he had deserved it.

Opening the linking door between their apartments, they tiptoed to Hazel's bed.

"Why are we being so careful not to disturb her when the reason we're here is to wake her up?" Dan asked.

"Are you stupid?"

"Can't remember."

"If she wakes up hearing banging, she'll scream, whereas if we rouse her gently, she won't, will she? Come on Watson, use your common."

Michael perched on the side of her bed then tapped Hazel's shoulder.

Unimpressed with the intrusion at such an unreasonable hour, her greeting wasn't particularly friendly, "What you woken me for?"

"It's really important," Michael urged before explaining his discovery.

"So, you want to know if I can remember anything earlier than last night?"

"Exactly."

Considering thoughtfully, her answer was just as expected, she recalled the feast with the King, speaking to Abednego, Michael dancing with the thin girl and feeling ill, oh and the dreamy Minister who chatted to them.

"Yes, and him," Dan sighed.

"It's not all bad. We've got fantastic rooms, are friends with the King and had a feast in our honour. Okay so we can't remember much…"

"Anything," corrected Michael.

"Okay, anything, but I'm sure it's just temporary. What an adventure though!" Hazel concluded that if she had to be anywhere with no memory, it may as well be in a massive castle.

Dan failed to share their optimism but kept quiet, not wanting to dampen the situation.

"Let's explore!" Tumbling out of bed, Hazel glanced at her watch, "it's only half four, we've at least a couple of hours until people start getting up."

"It's too dangerous!" protested Dan.

"Great idea!" enthused Michael, still on a high from his earlier discovery and being asked to dance. "As long as we take a pencil and paper to make a note of the route, we shouldn't get lost." Rummaging through the drawers beside the bed, Michael found what he was looking for and handed them to Dan.

Unable to believe Michael was mad enough to agree to Hazel's crazy idea, Dan eyed him suspiciously. Michael was usually as reticent about exploring places as he was.

Shrugging, Michael stuttered, "Aren't you j… j… just a little bit curious?"

"Not enough to risk my life!"

"Stop worrying and hurry up," commanded an eager Hazel.

Outvoted, Dan pushed his dark and slightly unkempt hair back from his face and followed obediently. Obviously he wasn't going to change their minds so decided it would be best to stick together. There was no alternative but to join them in their quest for trouble.

Creeping along the hallway, carefully recording each turn Michael, Dan and Hazel cautiously wandered through the maze of passages. Doors, wooden and metal, some adorned with name plaques, others with numbers and some simply left blank, lined the hallways on both sides.

"Looks like a glorified hotel if you ask me," Dan moaned, wishing he was still in bed, "this is pointless. We'd be better off trying to figure out what's happened to our memory, oh and trying to get some sleep… you know… the thing most people do at night."

"Stop moaning. We will try to figure out why we've lost our memories, but this is our chance to find out where we are for ourselves. We might even find clues as to why we can't remember anything."

"Of course, how could I have been so stupid? Let's take the next right, then left, and head straight down the corridor to a room where the mysteries of memory loss are revealed by a man who doesn't exist! Why didn't I see it before?"

"Wait!" Hazel hissed.

"What?" Dan sighed.

"I've found something!" Her fingers trembled as her hand rested on a cold, metal statue.

"A statue! Is that it?!" Michael continued, "It's hardly a discovery worth mentioning, the castle's littered with them."

"But this one moves, look!" Leaning on the right ear of the bearded horse, Hazel turned the metal monstrosity in an anti-clockwise direction to reveal an opening where previously there had been a brick wall. Hazel surged forwards, disappearing through the black hole and out of sight. Scared, but not wanting to be separated, Michael and Dan followed.

Within seconds the hole closed. They were trapped.

"So much for that clever idea. What do we do now? Walk through walls?" A grumpy Michael moaned.

"There's a passage leading forwards and candles lighting the way. Watch out though, the floor looks wet and uneven," warned Hazel who'd already begun edging forwards.

"Can you see where it leads?" asked Dan.

"It's too dark, I can only see a couple of metres ahead," her voice echoed in the confines of the narrow walls.

"Great! I feel so much better!" grumbled Dan, slightly unnerved by their confinement and the fear of being caught.

Scuffling along, they dodged rocks jutting out from the walls. Silence encased them, broken only by the irregular drips onto the concrete. Finally they reached the end of the tunnel. Their only option was to descend a staircase into the darkness below. Hazel braced herself, wondering which was worse; falling down the uneven steps, burning herself on the candles which were just inches away from her shivering body, or not knowing what was at the bottom of the stairs.

The lower they descended, the fewer the candles there were and the darker the gloom. Puddles embraced their feet while slippery fungus clung to the steps, waiting to claim their next victim. With the end in sight, Hazel lost her concentration and footing, collapsing onto the stone. Cursing, she rubbed her knee, feeling the warmth of her blood on her palm.

"You alright?" Shouted Dan.

"Just a cut knee," she croaked, shaken and shocked.

Huddled at the bottom, their feeling of confinement disappeared as they stared at the tunnel that extended as far as the eye could see in either direction. The ceiling was much higher, with small lanterns and candles providing light. The rough stone had been replaced by smooth paving slabs, making movement much easier. To their left, a canal ran adjacent to the path. Murky water filled with green algae, housed a dozen or so brightly coloured boats which looked out of place in their dismal surroundings.

"An underground waterway, I've never seen anything like it," mused Hazel, all thoughts of her cut knee swept aside as she stared at the small boats in wonderment.

"Not that you'd be able to remember if you had," added Michael.

"What do you suppose the stream's for? It can't be for show; do you think anyone actually comes down here?"

"I'm not sure we've time to discuss the features. We should really be trying to find a way out," Dan urged.

"Let's see what's down this turning on the right,"

Without even trying to dissuade her, they followed Hazel down the nearest turning and through a huge wooden door, stepping into what looked like a laboratory.

Bottles of all shapes and sizes lined shelves and cabinets on the long wall to the far side of the room. Huge, white tables dominating the centre of the room were cluttered with pestles, test tubes, boxes and strange contraptions containing multi coloured liquids. On the wall to their left, an assortment of machines flashed silently. One rumbled, emitting steam at regular intervals while another had so many tubes jutting from the main bodywork it looked like it had been made from a Locarno set.

"Look over there!" To their right the wall was covered with more shelves, each stacked with dozens of jars. Edging closer, they noticed some bottles contained frothy liquids; others held pills while the smaller jars were filled with powders and granules. Next to them were larger jars containing what they thought were herbs and flowers. Then on the top shelf, they noticed movement; peering closer they were horrified to discover live insects scrambling to escape their glass prisons. Though the movements were easy to detect, it was much harder to distinguish what types of insects they were.

"It must be a laboratory for making medicines," commented Michael.

"What medicines do you know of that contain beetles and butterflies? I bet they make potions here, which means there must be witches and wizards in the castle!"

"What's that?" Michael gasped.

"What's what?"

"That noise," Michael whispered, certain they weren't alone.

Dan grabbed at their arms and pulled them to the floor, underneath a table. "Shhhhhhhh," whispered Dan, "someone's coming." Watching shadows under the laboratory door, they held their breath as the door creaked open.

"How many more do you think you'll need?" An old, female voice enquired.

"A weeks' worth should do the trick," a softer, deeper voice replied.

Focusing, Dan listened intently. The male voice sounded vaguely familiar. He desperately tried to remember where he'd heard it, but he couldn't put a face to the voice.

"I can give you some now, but I don't have many in stock. If I start preparing another batch later this morning,

I should be able to get the rest to you for this evening. Is that okay?"

"Perfect, sorry about the short notice. You really are an asset." His voice, smooth and complimentary was obviously working its charm.

"Just remember that continued use could result in permanent memory loss," she warned.

"No worries, they won't be used for any longer than a week, on that you've my word." A pause followed, during which time they heard the chink of a bottle and the rustling of paper.

"Remember, this arrangement is just between us. Never mention it to the King, for although it's being done on his orders, he specifically requested that no-one utter a word in public, for obvious reasons."

A grunt of agreement followed by the sound of a bottle being replaced on the shelf was the last they heard before the couple exited the room.

Once more alone, Hazel whispered, "What do you make of that?"

"At least that explains why we can't remember anything," mused Dan.

"But why would anyone want us to have no memory? And why for just a week?"

"I'm sure I recognised the man's voice, but I can't think whose it was."

"For the next few days we need to watch everything we eat and drink at all times," said Michael.

"Agreed. And if we see anyone tampering with our food, we discard it without anyone noticing so they don't know we know."

"Remember, when our memories return, we've got to pretend not to remember anything," reasoned Dan.

"Let's go, before we're caught." Rising to her feet, Hazel glanced at her scraped knee, wincing in pain.

Once on the landing, Dan and Michael began retracing their steps to the less than safe staircase.

"Where are you going?" We've loads of time." Leaving them open-mouthed, Hazel sauntered off in the opposite direction, stopping outside another wooden door. Cautiously, she peeked through the crack. Hearing nothing and seeing nobody, she swept inside and her sparkly blue eyes gazed around at the stacks of books lining row after row of shelves.

"This room's got to be less dangerous than the previous one. What could possibly be wrong with a library?"

Wandering round the rows of books, she smiled at some of the titles on display, 'Creatures of Kilion', and 'Witches, Warlocks and Werewolves '. Selecting a couple of the slimmer books with interesting covers, she shoved them under her top and folded her arms across her chest, anxious for the others not to notice.

"What do you make of the titles?" asked Michael, "do you think everyone has magical powers?"

"I don't think so, otherwise that man wouldn't have had to buy those tablets and these books wouldn't be in a secret underground library," reasoned Dan. "Perhaps some people have magical powers but definitely not everyone."

"Let's quickly look in just one more room," pleaded Hazel who was mentally weighing up the excitement of exploring with her fear of being discovered.

Relieved that their dangerous exploits would soon be ending, Dan and Michael readily agreed. Leaving the library, they took the next right, entering a room much smaller than the previous two. The walls were a murky blue and devoid of any tapestries or paintings. Only one small candelabrum, hanging in the centre of the room, provided any light.

As in the other rooms, shelves took up much of the wall space. However, it was human skulls rather than books which adorned them. All three stared in wonderment and foreboding as they faced row upon row of fleshless faces, all detached from their bodies. In front of each skull stood a small plaque with italic writing, which they presumed to be their names.

Shuffling forwards, morbidly curious to discover the reason for the skulls, Hazel read one of the plaques, 'Simone Stanton'. Next to that, another one read 'Delia Spandicus'.

"Where are we?"

"Looks like some kind of mortuary where they just happen to forget to bury the skulls alongside the rest of the body," croaked a disbelieving Michael, who couldn't quite comprehend what he was seeing.

"Look in the corner... there are some... strange implements." Hazel hissed, picking up a brass object which resembled an extremely large pair of tweezers.

"Put them down and wipe your fingerprints off." Dan ordered, desperate to make a quick exit from the less than appealing room.

Wiping the tweezers with her sleeve, she returned it to its original spot then moved away from the table.

"Let's go before we get caught," pleaded Michael, his heart beating so furiously his ribcage felt like it was rattling.

"Yes, let's go, I could do with a bit more sleep." Dan agreed, thankful that at least Michael was seeing sense at last. Departing, they headed towards the staircase when they heard footsteps from one of the side turnings.

"Quick, hide!"

"Where?"

"Jump into one of those boats on the river until they've gone," instructed Dan. They clambered in as quietly as possible and ducked before anyone saw them.

Dressed in red and green, strange creatures appeared from a side turning and stood just yards away from the side of the canal; their long, pointed ears protruding from green metal helmets. As their snouts sniffed the air, their pale green faces sneered. The creature on the right was slightly fatter than his companion, as he examined his watch he rubbed his snout with his hand; a cross between that of a human hand and a pigs trotter, then adjusted his breast plate, "Must have been rats," he snuffled.

They dare not move. They were in a state of shock at the sight of the creatures which were a cross between a pig and a human. Seconds turned to minutes and the two guards showed no sign of moving.

"It's gone five. We need to do something, we could be stuck here forever," whispered Michael.

"Some boats are moving along the stream. We could let the rope off so our boat drifts down, then climb out further on?" suggested Dan.

"Done it!" Hazel informed them.

"For crying out loud," groaned Michael, "it was just a suggestion. Will you calm down and stop trying to get us killed?"

Gulping, she bowed her head in shame at the realisation that their predicament was her fault.

Peering out, Michael was certain the creatures hadn't noticed anything suspicious, but was too scared to try to stop the boat from following the course Hazel had set it on.

Silently they continued, praying their boat would stop soon and that they would be able to find their way back before daylight. Eventually the guards left but their boat kept drifting. Soon, the candles became more infrequent, and then suddenly the path beside the canal ended abruptly and they found themselves floating through a larger tunnel. For a few seconds all was black and deadly quiet, except for the sound of tiny water droplets falling from the archway ceiling.

Seeing only darkness, a sense of foreboding encased Michael, and at that moment his chest started feeling warm. Alarmed, he noticed the ring was glowing, and although unable to remember having seen it before, it felt distinctly familiar.

"That's it, we're in trouble," moaned Michael, who was almost certain they would be caught stuck inside the tunnel.

As the boat drifted to within feet of a locked door, the ring shone even brighter. Within seconds a red glow illuminated the air and the large doors which had previously barricaded their way, slowly creaked open, allowing the boat to lumber through.

The view which greeted them was dark and gloomy, similar to the one they had left behind. The only difference was that this passage was even dirtier and dustier than the previous one, with cobwebs covering cracks in the wall and moths fluttering past any light they could find. Water dripped from the walls onto the uneven floor below, and the acrid smell of damp invaded their nostrils.

The boat, as if responding to the power of the ring, came to a standstill. Certain they were alone, they alighted and stood statue-still on the sidewalk, considering the predicament of returning to their rooms without directions, and more importantly, without being noticed. With no ideas forthcoming, it was a sullen Dan who voiced their thoughts. "Great! We're stuck. What are we going to do now?"

Chapter Nineteen: The Dungeon

All three were filled with trepidation. A huge door blocked their return by boat while a stone wall barred their path on the sidewalk in the same direction. They had contemplated returning to the boat and hoping the ring would once more work its magic, but the current was one way so there was no use even trying. Desperate, they prodded at the wet stone walls; hoping to discover another secret passageway which would allow them to escape the stagnant smelling chamber; nothing happened.

"Who's that?" A tired, voice called from the darkness.

"Oh no, we've been caught! What do we do now?" startled, Michael shook at the thought of being caught by the hog men.

"Shhhhh," ordered Dan.

"Please can I have some water? I'm so thirsty."

They were too frightened to respond.

"Are you guards?" The helpless voice whispered.

"Shouldn't we find out who he is?" Hearing his despair, Hazel knew she'd spend the rest of the night feeling guilty if she didn't try helping.

"Okay, but don't let him see who we are," Dan reasoned.

Readjusting her position to take the pressure off her grazed knee, and to steady the books she was still clutching onto, she nudged Michael, implying he should start interrogating.

"Who are you?" His quiet voice was barely audible where his throat had clammed up.

"Grimbald."

"Why are you here?" Michael continued, unsure about where his questioning was going.

"Who are you first? How do I know I can trust you? It could be a trap to get me to talk." The voice sounded wary.

"I'm Michael and I'm with Daniel and Hazel."

"Where you from?" he queried, his voice a little brighter.

"We're not sure, we seem to have lost our memory," Michael explained.

"Quiet!" Daniel hissed, "how do we know we can trust him?"

"Sorry."

"Was it you I saw walking through the village yesterday evening?" The voice questioned, more animated now.

"We're not sure. We can't remember much about yesterday," Michael admitted as Dan sighed in despair.

"I told you not to give anything away."

"If he did see us yesterday, he might be able to help us."

Almost certain they were the teenagers he'd seen, Grimbald became much more confident. What a coincidence that he should be discovered in the darkest depths of the castle by the very people he'd set out to see!

"I live in the nearby village," he said before pausing, realising if they had no memory, this could take some time.

"Which one is the lad with the blond hair? What's your name?"

Michael looked at his friends, "M... M... Michael." He stammered.

"Please excuse the impertinence of my question, but who is your dad?"

Unable to remember anything other than the feast, Michael replied, "I'm really sorry, I can't remember anything earlier than last night. Why do you ask?" For some reason the question had hit a nerve.

"Do you know if your memory loss is permanent?" asked Grimbald, who was feeling rather agitated at not being able to help. Yet he had to consider that these poor teenagers were stuck in a strange country, full of dangers and were completely defenceless. Rather than finding out nothing, he'd actually discovered quite a lot. After all, why would they be invited to stay at the castle if they weren't important and why would someone drug them if they weren't being used?

"Can you get me out of here?"

Emerging from the gloomy shadows, they tiptoed cautiously in the direction of Grimbalds voice. Soon he was within view and the prognosis looked bleak; metal bars imprisoned him in a space so tiny; there was no room for even the most basic of furniture. They looked in and saw a weary face, wrinkles sagging around his eyes and grey hair streaking from his temples.

"There's a padlock. We just need to get the key." Dan tried twisting and yanking it.

"Quiet, I can hear something."

Retreating into the shadows, they were only just quick enough to avoid being caught by the hog guards who swaggered towards the cell. As they drew closer, Michael could almost taste their stale aroma. One pushed a bowl of slops under the bottom bar of the cell, while the other creature pushed through a similar bowl containing clear liquid.

Without waiting for the implements to be returned, they retreated, laughing at his misfortune.

Remembering Grimbald, Dan said, "We won't forget about you. We promise we'll help you escape."

With the knowledge that their memories were being wiped, Grimbald thought it unlikely they would return; but with no key, they couldn't help now. Resigned to his fate, he watched them depart, his heart sinking.

Tiptoeing forwards, they stayed close to the walls, following the creatures until they stopped near the tunnels entrance.

Watching anxiously, the creatures glanced backwards before the bigger of the two stepped onto the centre of a paving slab. The slab, a slightly paler shade of grey than the others, turned blue. Making a mental note of the square, they watched, astonished as the bricks in the wall disappeared, starting in the middle and working outwards, forming an opening about five foot high by three foot wide.

Grunting, they stepped through the hole before the bricks efficiently reassembled.

Waiting for a few minutes, Michael glanced around, and then stepped onto the slab, waiting expectantly. Nothing happened.

"We're stuck." Michael groaned; his heart thudded as visions of being arrested and joining Grimbald in the dungeon filled his head.

"Your right foot's not on properly." Hazel pointed out.

Readjusting his foot, he held his breath in anticipation. Suddenly the bricks vibrated, starting with the one in the centre and working its way out. Eventually they had all dispersed, creating a much needed escape route.

As the hole closed behind them, they retraced their steps, keeping a watchful eye on the turnings leading off from the main passageway until they reached the staircase.

Climbing carefully, they returned along the passage until they saw a matching statue of the bearded horse where they were almost certain there hadn't been one previously. Pulling its ear clockwise, an opening appeared, allowing them to return to the familiar surroundings of the castle.

Unfolding their list of directions which had been stuffed in Dan's trouser pocket, they used it to retrace their steps. By the time they fell sleepily onto their beds it was nearly six o clock, the sun was rising on the horizon and the birds were already chirping their morning melodies.

Chapter Twenty: Richard's Return to the Castle

Staring in awe at the turreted castle, Richard approached the guards and showed them the royal seal allowing him immediate access.

"Richard, long time, no see! How are you?" Raglin exclaimed, a large but insincere grin stretching across his face. His ageing body was attired in expensive clothes which grated on Richard. Every time Richard compared his sacrifice to the others, anger consumed him, burning deeply into his soul. Whilst he had lost his family and freedom, and then been forced to live a life of seclusion with only a limping fool for company, Raglin and the others lived in luxury and wealth; no wonder Raglin was smiling.

Every step taken deeper into the castle saw his resentment grow. The more he thought about it, the more he regretted his decision fourteen years ago. The only thing preventing him from freeing Mathis just to spite them was how much his sacrifice had cost him. If he pulled out now, the death of his wife and children would have been for nothing; at least now the waiting was nearly over. Soon, he'd be wealthy beyond his wildest dreams and free to start his life again.

The castle was quiet. Many were still asleep or nursing hangovers from the previous night's feast, allowing them to reach Raglin's apartments unnoticed. Hidden deep within these apartments, berobed characters were gathering. To gain entrance Raglin twisted the troll's face anticlockwise, whereupon an opening appeared that was just big enough to allow the men to squeeze through the gap. Richard followed Raglin down through the dark passages until they approached a door in the deepest, darkest depths of the castle.

Knocking, they waited for permission to enter, before sweeping in to present their low bows. A cloaked figure lounged on a chair in the centre of the room, the lower half of his body obscured by a large desk. Around him were gathered old colleagues, Courtiers for whom Richard had once worked. All sat silently, staring at the newcomer. Feeling uneasy in his meagre clothes, he kept his eyes fixed on the floor. He had no inclination to look at them, for he felt out of place and despised their pitiful glances.

Raglin sat between Duclem and Tacitus who was twiddling his fingers, looking as nervous as Richard felt. Noticing a vacant seat, Richard sat between Cornelius who was staring into space and the newcomer, Hargrin who he'd never seen but had heard much about.

The room was deadly silent. All eyes were transfixed on the cloaked figure who was rising to his feet. "What news on the youngsters?" he growled. All except Raglin, who met with him regularly, cowered at his voice. If before, Richard had wondered why so many followed him, the sheer authority he commanded by his very presence dispelled any doubts.

Addressing his audience, Raglin reported that their memories had already been taken from them, Zawi was producing more tablets in order to continue this, and that Hargrin had started winning their trust. As his achievements were recognised by the Master, Hargrin smiled politely, not wanting to appear overly confident.

Richard's resentment continued to swell as his role of prison keeper and abductor of Mathis, remained overlooked. Then, as though he had looked into his soul and read his thoughts, the Master turned his attention to the keeper, "Have you any news to report?"

Michael paled and his mind went blank, he'd not prepared anything to report.

"Well, have you or haven't you? We're busy people, we don't have all day," the impatient voice boomed.

"Sorry. Yes, erm… He remains undiscovered; he's weak, too weak to even walk properly. His will to live has disappeared, he'll be really easy to manipulate, especially with the boy."

From under his hood, his husky voice drooled, "Good. Hargrin, continue drugging them and gaining their confidence. Ensure they do nothing, and I mean nothing, without consulting you first."

Hargrin, who for all his confidence, quaked at being spoken to directly, nodded, aware that failure to fulfil his duty would incur the wrath of the only man Richard had met who had no conscience at all.

"As soon as the boy's confided in Hargrin, Mathis will be putty in my hands." Clasping his hands, his voice had risen excitedly.

Talking broke out between the followers of Azarel, who contented himself with watching their chatter while discretely judging them from behind the hood that hid his facial features.

As the meeting closed, they took their leave and returned to the main area of the castle, which was now buzzing with life. People wandered round excitedly, some talking of the unexpected guests while others nursed aching stomachs and sore heads.

"Would you care to join me for a quick drink before you leave? After all, the journey must have been exhausting."

"Thanks," sighed Richard, knowing only too well it was an order rather than a request.

"Richard," Raglin placed his arm around Richard's shoulder, though the effect was more intimidating than comforting. "We're all aware of the personal sacrifice you've made." Re-entering Raglin's suite, Raglin headed towards the coffee table where the finest china cups were arranged, and poured two cups of liquid.

Taking the proffered cup, he sipped the rich fluid, imported from Zancaster, over the other side of the ocean.

Pleasantries pushed aside, Raglin asked, "Worth the sacrifice?"

"As you know, I've lost a great deal, but I'm certain the end will justify the means."

"What faith! How refreshing. I only wish everyone showed such commitment." He studied the face of the haggard man before him. "By this time next month you'll be restored to your former rank, and I've no doubt you'll be rewarded with prestigious titles and financial security."

"That's my hope!" Richard muttered.

"It had also occurred to me, that having spent so much time with Mathis, you may have built up, shall we say, a rapport with him. So I was wondering whether, during this time, he ever… you know… let anything slip?"

"I'm afraid we hardly speak. I see 'im as little as possible, and virtually never chat if I can 'elp it. After kidnapping and imprisoning him, it's unlikely he'd share any secrets with me!"

"I see. Well, if you don't mind, I've a few questions I'd like to ask anyway?" Raglin stared at Richard, and although his voice was soft, his eyes bore into him with a fierce intensity, daring him to refuse.

"Certainly." Clasping his stubby hands together, Richard felt himself sweating. Like everyone, he was fearful of annoying Raglin, who had such a bad reputation at Court; nobody had crossed him for years, even the King consulted him before changing or passing new laws.

"Has he ever mentioned the existence of a fountain or waterfall?"

Thinking back over their limited conversations, Richard honestly couldn't remember every topic they had discussed, but was certain they'd never mentioned a fountain.

"IT'S A SIMPLE QUESTION. DID HE OR DIDN'T HE?" Raglin roared.

His legs quivering with fear Richard trembled "Not that I remember."

"And he never talked of a family? A wife or child?"

"No. Like I said, we've never really spoken. He refused to answer any questions."

"You'd better not be lying!" Raglin circled the room, agitated by how little Richard had discovered during the 14 years they'd been closeted up together. Taking deep breaths he tried calming himself, knowing that until Mathis was in his possession, he'd at least have to be civil to the idiot before him.

"I've no reason to lie," said Richard.

Raglin stared directly into his frightened misty green eyes and watched Richard's leg twitch nervously. He concluded that although a fool, he wasn't a liar. "I believe you." Watching Richard heave a sigh of relief, Raglin turned his head away, ashamed that his Master had someone as pathetic as this among his core followers.

"Sorry about that. It's all so tense, you understand? Thanks once again for everything. It's been greatly appreciated. Now, if you'll excuse me, I have a meeting with the King and I can't be late."

Placing his cup down, Richard's hand was still shaking from the less than pleasant conversation. He needed to get away from Raglin and the castle. He wanted to be alone.

It wasn't until he was halfway home that he wondered why Raglin had asked about a fountain. Was it important? If so, why? And why, after fourteen years, was he suddenly worrying about whether Mathis had a wife or child? With no way of finding the answers, he shoved them into the recesses of his mind and concentrated on thinking positive thoughts, mainly about life after the forest.

Heading towards the Master's apartments, Raglin was still seething at how little Richard had discovered. Entering, he cast his eyes to the floor to avoid the accusing gaze.

"What troubles you Raglin?" The deep voice enquired as he studied a pile of dusty books.

"Pardon the intrusion Master, but could I clarify a few matters?"

"And they are…?"

"What will we do if the boy doesn't know where the ring is? Or if we discover that Dragon Falls is a myth?"

"Do you think I'd have waited in some grubby hell hole hidden in the middle of a palace that's rightfully mine, if I didn't know the information to be true?" Lifting his eyes to look at Raglin squarely, he allowed his guest a full view of the scars etched across his face.

"My sincerest apologies, I didn't intend to cause offence." His trembling hand clasped at the papers under his cloak, clammy with sweat.

"Anything else?"

"Perhaps we could revisit our plan so I can ensure it's implemented properly."

"Very well. Once Hargrin has the boy's friendship, we'll reunite Mathis with his son in the forest. Mathis will then be provided with a simple choice; he can either inform the boys of the rings location and tell you the secret password to open the gateway to Dragons Falls, or he can watch his son being tortured… My instinct tells me the rings whereabouts will be a secret no more."

"And Abednego?"

"He'll be in the palace, none the wiser"

"But what about their friendship?"

"Hargrin will drive a wedge between them, perhaps give Michael reason to suspect Abdnigo's loyalty. But you must make it clear to Hargrin that no-one should be able to trace the dissent back to him or anyone else in the circle."

"But doesn't the gateway to Dragon Falls need to be opened by the rightful owner of the ring?"

"It does and it will. When Mathis sustains an 'accidental injury,' you and Hargrin will be on hand to offer assistance. By telling Michael about Dragons Falls and helping him open the gateway, you can assist him in bringing back the water of life. Once we have it here, I and not Mathis will be the recipient."

"Excellent."

"Then at last my health will be revived and I shall rule this Kingdom as is my destiny and my right." Looking at his scarred hands, still too sore to write more than a few sentences or to clutch objects for too long, Azarel longed for the healing waters to work their magic on his aching and decrepit body.

"And what will happen to Michael and his friends afterwards?"

"It's imperative that no harm befall Hazel. She'll have all memories of Kilion eradicated and be returned as soon as possible. Dan we will use as a bargaining chip, we can make a fortune from ransoming him. Mathis and the current Queen, I intend to use as a peace offering as a token of our friendship to the Vampires in the woods, thereby making a very useful alliance. The King, as you are aware, will be assassinated in the not too distant future, thereby making my seizure of power so peaceful it's unlikely anyone will wish to attempt to overthrow me."

"An alliance with the vampires, genius! So we'll be disposing of potential opposition whilst allying with potential enemies. But what of Michael?"

"I'm not sure yet. It depends on how much control we have over the ring and whether it will accept me as its new

Master. If it does, he can be disposed of. If not, I may have to keep him safely under my control and use him to command the ring when necessary."

A twinge of pity for the children unexpectedly touched Raglin, as he considered how unfortunate it was they had been caught in the epicentre of this power struggle. Yet he knew it was a small price to pay for the glory that would be theirs.

"I suggest we tell Hargrin everything, including the existence of the fountain. It might help him extract the information we need much more quickly." Suggested Raglin, for although he was worried about losing some control by sharing his knowledge, he thought it a small price to pay for the plan going smoothly.

"You think he can be trusted?" The figure asked, still unsure of the newly admitted member of their circle.

"So far he has proven himself worthy and I can smell the ambition emanating from him. He is desperate for power and knows it is us, not the ineffectual Mazarin, who can offer it to him." Raglin replied, hoping fervently his analysis of his young apprentice was accurate.

"Very well, you've proven yourself a good judge of character. Though warn him, if he lets us down, it will be more than his job on the line."

Smiling to himself, Raglin sensed he was onto a winner. If Hargrin obtained the information, he, could take the credit for suggesting him. However, if it went wrong, it would be Hargrin rather than himself who would pay the price.

"I'll be sure to warn him."

After moments of revelling in their imminent triumph, Raglin returned to his apartments. He needed time to collect his thoughts before his later meeting with the King and Abednego.

Chapter Twenty-one: The Second Ring

Conscious of his approaching meeting with the King and Abednego, Raglin sought out the junior Minister.

"What an unexpected pleasure," Hargrin exclaimed, allowing his guest to enter.

"I've only minutes to spare so I will get straight to the crux of the matter. What I am about to reveal is strictly confidential and must go no further, do you understand?"

Nervous at Raglin's serious tone, Hargrin nodded in agreement, "I understand."

"Good." Raglin took a seat and proffered for Hargrin to do likewise.

Part of Hargrin was nervous at the obvious sensitivity of the information, yet he couldn't help but revel in the knowledge that he was being trusted above the others.

Hargrin learned that years ago Raglin had overheard Abednego talking to his late wife about a child he visited in England, a child he had assumed had been born of Mathis which no-one else knew about, and who might well possess a ring. Hargrin was also surprised by the revelation that there were definitely two rings, and that there was a story behind them which very few people knew about, there was also an idea that both rings could open the gateway to the healing waters of Dragons Falls. Furthermore there was even a rumour that there might, just maybe, be three rings. A knowing smile spread across Hargrin's face as his eyes glistened with ambition.

"As Mathis was found with no ring," Raglin continued "we believe he either hid it somewhere or left it to a wife or child, who no-one here knows existed."

Comprehending the enormity of his role Hargrin's smile beamed. Relishing his importance in this operation, he ignored the potential dangers ahead.

"Find out as much as you can about the ring, its powers and whether it's in Michael's possession."

"What if he doesn't have it or know where it is?"

"Then we'll reunite him with Mathis who will have to either tell us where the ring is, or watch his son die."

"And once we have the ring and password?"

"Azarel can use its waters to recuperate and take over Kilion," Raglin continued.

"If the ring's so powerful, why haven't people looked for it sooner?" Hargrin queried.

Aware of time ticking away, Raglin replied, "Like you, most people thought the ring a myth, and others have searched for years, some near the battlefield where the old King fell, others across Kilion. Yet neither ring has been found. Now we have Michael, Mathis will no longer be able to keep the information to himself."

Stroking his neatly trimmed beard, Hargrin confirmed, "So we need Mathis for the ring and password and Michael for the bait? What about Mazarin?"

"Until we have the water, Kilion will function as normal, Mazarin and Jeanne running the country with Abednego helping. We can't do anything until Azarel has healed. Now I really must depart. Mention it to no-one, we can't afford any gossip."

"Can I enlist Viola's help?"

"I'll leave it to your discretion, as long as the subject of our conversation remains a secret."

Pleased with his mornings work, Raglin left Hargrin and headed straight for the King's apartment. Arriving slightly early, he settled himself down before Abednego arrived.

***

Abednego bowed dutifully to Mazarin who sat on his throne, his dark chestnut hair slicked back beneath his crown. His wife, the dainty Jeanne was perched beside him, her pale features emphasized by her emerald green gown.

Abednego took his usual place between the King and Raglin, who was stroking his moustache, with an amused expression adorning his face. Eager to commence their discussion, Mazarin waved a parchment before Abednigo indignantly.

Still sleepy, Abednego reluctantly took the parchment, unrolled it and read the first two agenda items: 1. The ring. 2. Michael. Cringing, it wasn't the first time Abednego had wished the rings had never existed. He regretted ever making the promise to his now deceased nephew, for it had caused him nothing but pain; from watching helplessly as Mathis had been killed in the alley, to sleepless nights over Michael's inheritance and the danger he faced as a consequence. Ever since Michael's arrival, Abednego's heart had lurched when he thought of the awful consequences of the ring for Mathis. Even now, he wondered whether Mathis would still be alive if he hadn't taken the ring when he'd left Kilion. His sole consolation was that for better or worse, he had passed the ring on to its rightful owner and prevented it falling into the wrong hands.

Clearing his throat, Mazarin began, "I have called this meeting at such short notice to seek advice on a recently discovered document, which seems to be even more important than the visit of Michael." Extracting a torn piece of parchment from under his doublet, Mazarin glanced at his wife whose smile offered reassurance.

"The document I hold was penned by Melchior prior to his last battle, God rest his soul."

Sorrow filled Abednego as he was reminded that not only had he outlived Balthazar, his older brother, but both his nephews, Mathis and Melchior.

"Since its discovery a few months ago, I have been forced to conclude that there are, in fact, two rings and not just the one as previously presumed. Further enquiries have revealed that Balthazar gave a ring to both Melchior and Mathis on their fifteenth birthdays."

Mortified at this discovery, Abednego coughed, playing for time while he considered his response.

"May I read?" Raglin asked. Like Abednigo, he had hoped Mazarin would remain unaware of the existence of the second ring.

As Abednego passed the parchment to Raglin, Mazarin explained, "It seems Melchior wrote this just before his death. It states that he received the ring on his fifteenth birthday, but although he chose never to use it to rule, he kept it safe to ensure its powers never fell into the wrong hands. It seems Melchior anticipated defeat, and so as a precaution, was going to hide the ring to ensure it would never be used for evil. Unfortunately he doesn't state where he intended to dispose of it."

Casting his eye over the faded scrawl, Raglin read the letter, unable to think of a worse time for it to have been found.

Rising from his seat and walking towards the window, Mazarin asked, "I don't suppose either of you know where Melchior's ring is do you?"

Abednego swallowed hard, his throat dry from anxiety. He didn't want to lie to the King, but he felt compelled to, for the sake of the Kingdom. Years ago he had decided never to tell anyone, other than the rightful owner, the whereabouts of either ring, and it was a policy he wasn't going to abandon.

"No," Abednego replied bluntly.

"No idea," Raglin responded.

"You're sure? Neither of you have any idea at all?

Again there was silence.

Determined, Mazarin continued, "As Melchior's Uncle, did he ever indicate at any point, what he intended doing with it? Who he might give it to?" His expression was earnest. So too was Raglin's.

Again he lied, "Like you, I thought only one ring existed, that Melchior had decided to rule without it and passed it to Mathis as his heir. I assumed it was in England. Sorry I can't be of more assistance."

Abe wished the parchment had never been found. He couldn't recall Mazarin ever being this pushy. Despite this increased desire, Abednego would make sure Mazarin never gained possession of either ring. It wasn't that he didn't like Mazarin, he did; it was simply that history had proven on numerous occasions, that whenever either ring had been worn by someone other than the direct descendant of the original owner, it had corrupted them, often leading to civil wars. Yet more than misuse by Mazarin, Abednego was concerned that greedy, power-hungry Ministers such as Raglin would influence the King and ultimately gain control of it themselves. If they discovered that two rings, once combined, could change the order of life, Kilion would be subject to chaos and destruction. This thought alone had driven Abednego to spend his life protecting Michael's inheritance, for the thought of Kilion being pulled apart filled him with dread. As far as he was concerned, only Michael, the rightful heir, would ever possess a ring and Abednego would dedicate himself to ensuring it was only ever used for good.

"So are we assuming Mathis' ring is still in England?" Mazarin continued, unwilling to let the subject drop.

Already weary, Abednego's leaned back in his chair, "I've no doubt he took it with him."

"So where is it now?"

"I presume he was wearing it when attacked so I reckon whoever killed him took the ring."

"He wasn't wearing the ring when he was attacked!" Raglin retorted, knowing full well that when Richard had brought Mathis to him, no ring had been found.

"And how do you know?" Abednego's eyes were accusing, daring Raglin to incriminate himself. Abednego was certain Raglin had been involved in Mathis death, though he'd never been able to prove his theory. For years he had waited for Raglin to slip up, and if that were to happen now in front of the King, even better.

"The Gate Keeper who attended his funeral said there was no ring on the body at the mortuary." Raglin replied, hoping the interfering old man would let the matter drop. Kicking himself for his impetuousness, he made a mental note to be more careful in future. He couldn't afford to make too many mistakes around Abednego.

"But that doesn't exclude the possibility that the attacker removed the ring at the time. With no established motive for the murder, I assume it was a mugging that went wrong. That being the case, the ring would be the first thing he'd remove, don't you agree?" Abednego stared Raglin down, daring him to disagree.

Mazarin nodded in agreement. "Makes sense."

"It's a possibility," Raglin reticently agreed, despite his knowledge to the contrary.

"Anyway, I called you here to inform you that I am officially re-opening the search, this time for both rings with substantial rewards offered for any information which leads to their discovery." Determined more than ever to possess at least one, Mazarin was so enthused he didn't notice either of his Ministers looking uncomfortable.

"One word of warning," Abednigo said, "this must be done secretly, for most of Kilion and those locally in the Marshaland probably think that you have a ring already. If they were ever to discover that you didn't, they could try to take your power, search for the ring themselves and even worse, some might start to worry that without it, the creatures from the other side of the stream might well start their attacks."

Mazarin gulped. He had considered none of this, only how to get the ring. Understanding the importance of the counsel, he agreed immediately, which at least gave Abednigo some breathing space.

"Now to Michael. Abednego, did Mathis have a son? How did he get here?" After a brief pause his face lit up "Could he have the ring?"

Having spent much of the night perfecting his story, Abednego regaled it with ease. "Michael is my great nephew on my dearly departed wife's side. You may recall that my wife, God rest her soul, had a younger sister Jennifer who found coping with life extremely difficult. Just after Mathis left for England, Jennifer lost both her daughter and son-in-law. In no fit state to care for her six month old grandson and afraid of bringing him to Court due to the on-going civil wars..., you remember..." He paused, looking at the King and Queen to assess their reactions before continuing, "she decided, after some consideration, to ask Mathis to find a suitable family for him in England, away from Court life . With Mathis close by he could help look after Michael and maintain a link with Kilion. Mathis found a loving family and my wife and I visited through the portal regularly. Unfortunately just months later, as you know, Mathis was brutally murdered… Since then I have managed to make occasional trips to England, partly to continue my search for the ring as requested, and partly to visit my great nephew. A couple of week's back he turned 15 and asked to visit, he said he wanted to see the places I had told him of; how could I refuse? So yesterday I visited him and left the gateway open so he could follow. I hope you don't mind, but as he's so shy I suggested he bring some friends..."

Infuriated, Raglin demanded, "How did you leave and he enter? The doorway has been closed for years."

Abe's response was firm and authoritive, "One of the witches has been making potions, allowing me to open the doorway to England, Michael simply followed me back."

It all seemed so plausible and Abednego spoke so calmly, Raglin wondered whether he could, in reality, be telling the truth.

Mazarin interceded, "Could Mathis have left the ring to him. After all they would have been cousins of sorts."

"Unlikely. He was only a baby, maybe if he'd been older." Abe hoped he might just have managed to save Michael from an inquisition at best, and from complete immersion in Court intrigue at worst.

Raglin felt sick. What if he'd misheard the conversation between Abednego and his wife all those years ago? When he'd heard them discussing a boy and bringing him back to Kilion when he was 15, Raglin had assumed Mathis had become a father and the boy would have the ring. Now an awful feeling descended into the pit of his stomach, for it seemed Abednego had been discussing his great nephew, a boy with no claim to the ring or Mathis' emotions. No longer could Michael be used as bait; ultimately the ring was as lost as it had ever been. How was he going to tell the Master?

"Yet his resemblance to Mathis is uncanny. Are you sure he's not related?" Raglin clutched at straws, though they were weak and he could feel they were about to snap in his hands. Beads of sweat formed as he waited for Abednego's answer.

"I can assure you both that when visiting Michael, not once did Mathis mention anyone special. We have to accept he left no relations."

While Mazarin was disappointed that he was no nearer to possessing the ring, at least Michael wasn't a claimant to the throne! "They're free to come and go as they please. I hope they enjoy their stay here with you. Abe, why don't you bring Michael and his friends to watch the match later? They can join me in the box." Now he knew he faced no threat, the least he could do for his loyal servant was to make his nephew's visit as enjoyable as possible.

"Thank you." Abe answered, guilty at his duplicity. Bowing low, he retired from the rooms, with many tasks to perform prior to the game.

Mulling over these developments, Raglin wondered how to broach this subject with the Master. After much reflection, he decided to act as though the meeting had never happened. Let the Master continue to pursue their agreed course of action, at least it would allow him time to devise an alternative plan.

Chapter Twenty-two: Sisterly Love

Knocking on Martha Malovski's door, Hargrin grinned into his pocket mirror one last time, admiring the whiteness of his perfectly straight teeth.

"Hargrin," a surprised Martha gasped, "and to what do I owe this pleasure?" Turning to hide her flushed face; she left the door open behind her as she nervously glided into the front room.

Once composed, she turned to face her visitor and swept her long, silky blonde hair back from her face while smiling provocatively. "Do take a seat. Would you like some refreshments?"

Noticing his effect on her, he shot her a gleaming grin, "Your company is refreshment enough."

Blushing again, Martha's mind began plotting ways to ensnare him. He would be a prize indeed.

"Ms Malovski, or may I call you Martha?"

"Martha, please, " she responded; her expression much softer than usual.

Taking a seat, he cast his chocolate brown eyes around the room, immediately judging that what she had in wealth, she lacked in taste. "I'll not waste your precious time with idle talk; if it's alright with you, I'll get straight to the point."

"Please do."

"King Mazarin has entrusted me with a special task." Pausing for effect, he watched her gulp, her hand involuntarily clasping her throat, "but before I continue, I must make it absolutely clear that what I'm about to divulge must be kept in the strictest of confidence, you mustn't even mention it to the King. You must speak only to me."

"Not a single word will cross my lips," she replied huskily as her throat tightened with excitement.

Motivated by the ease of duping her, he began, "As you may be aware, Michael is an important guest. However, he doesn't really know anyone at Court except his two companions. To put them at ease, King Mazarin thinks he might feel better if he made some friends within the castle during his stay. Last night we noticed how kind and hospitable Viola was to him and thought her an obvious choice of companion."

Astounded that a simple ploy to gain a suitable match for her daughter had already received the blessing of the King, Martha was keen to emphasise that Viola would be more than willing to serve Mazarin in this matter.

As his gaze once more fixed on her, a shiver shot through her spine and a tingling sensation attacked her whole being. All embarrassment had disappeared, replaced by a warm feeling in the pit of her stomach.

"Michael's had a rough time recently, so is visiting Kilion to help him take his mind off it. As a result, Mazarin would prefer it if Viola and her friends refrained from mentioning the past or questioning his arrival at the Castle." Starting to feel uncomfortable under her obvious scrutiny, Hargrin sauntered to the bookshelf, which all Courtiers displayed as a sign of intellectual achievement.

"Of course," she agreed, unashamedly studying his muscular physique as his hands skimmed the books on the top shelf.

"Michael mustn't know of our conversation. He's had his confidence knocked recently and if he thinks we've asked Viola to befriend him, it will shatter what is left of it. It could…" Spying a book on witchcraft, he stared at the title for a while, wondering how she had acquired this limited edition copy. Melchior had forbidden witchcraft during his reign and the number allowed to practice magic and the dark arts had been limited to the remaining fourteen members of the round circle, since the fifteenth member had disappeared years ago, taking some potions with her .

Seeing his shoulders stiffen, she became anxious, "Is everything okay?"

"Oh yes." Determined to remain focused, he returned his gaze to hers, though made certain he was out of reach.

"He's a lucky boy, to have so many looking out for him." Resisting the temptation to get closer to him, she watched him return to his seat.

"While I will be doing all I can to guide him, he's more likely to confide in someone of his own age."

"Naturally."

"Viola is to report everything he says back to me. We have a feeling he may be receiving some important news soon and feel he may need to talk to someone about it."

"You can count on us." Edging towards her visitor, she inhaled the sweet aroma of his aftershave and pondered how to win his heart as her daughter was trying to win Michael's.

"Finally, and I apologise for bombarding you with so much information, the doctor has prescribed Michael, Dan and Hazel some anti-depressants in the form of tablets to help them. Knowing how stubborn they can be, King Mazarin considers it would be better for them if they weren't aware, just so they don't become dependent on them. With this in mind, we would be grateful if you could ask your charming daughter to slip a tablet into each of their drinks tonight so they won't notice, you know, just to help them enjoy themselves."

"And if she gets caught?"

"I'm sure with a mother as clever as you, she'll do herself justice. The King and I are aware of the situation so nothing can go wrong. You do understand it's for their well-being. She'd be like their guardian angel, helping them through this time of crisis." Oh, he was good; he was even impressing himself.

"You're right, I'm sure she will do herself justice. Leave it to me."

Dispensing three tablets into her grasping claws, he quickly withdrew his hand and threw her another of his charming smiles as he sidled towards the door. Tensing as she tried invading his personal space, he suddenly felt ill at ease. Known throughout Court for her gold digging ways, he could feel her eyes boring into him, assessing how good a match he would be and how much money marriage to him would add to the income left by the latest of her deceased husbands. "Please excuse me, I've a meeting to attend," he said, "just one last thing though."

"Yes?"

"No mention of our meeting or Michael's needs should be made to any other Minister or indeed, the King. It is I who has been charged with relaying any relevant information to him. Mazarin is anxious no-one suspects anything, it would only cause further distress to Michael. If this isn't adhered to then things could get awkward."

"Your wish is my command," she winked conspiratorially.

"I will call daily for your invaluable assistance in this most delicate matter, during which time your daughter will brief me on what confidences have been divulged."

Listening intently, Martha's mind imagined their future together. She knew dominating him would prove difficult, but the challenge could prove entertaining and the prize worthwhile. To tame a pussy cat was nothing, to tame a tiger was so much more rewarding.

***

Pulling back from the door, Sophie pondered the conversation she had just overheard, worrying at the promises her mother had so easily made on Viola's behalf.

Recalling the feast, Sophie remembered Michael's initial shyness as well as his almost hysterical laughter, not the reaction of a depressed teenager. Also, with two friends to confide in, she found it odd he would need more people, especially virtual strangers. She understood how Viola could keep them entertained, but no more than that.

She wrote down what she remembered of the conversation. Something wasn't right and she was determined to discover what it was before someone, probably Michael, got hurt. She doubted Mazarin even knew of this enterprise, for there was nothing to indicate his involvement, they weren't even to approach him in private. Perhaps it was Hargrin's plan. However, she dare not mention her suspicions to her mother, for like a silly schoolgirl, she had been completely taken in by his charm and praise. Sophie knew that first she would be told off for eavesdropping, and then she would be accused of jealousy.

Believing the only way to help Michael was to persuade her sister not to help; she wondered how she could win her over after years of distance between them.

As Viola came out of the bathroom, Sophie began her offensive. "That dress suits you, the blue brings out the colour of your eyes." Trying to look genuine, Sophie continued, "have you thought about how you might wear your hair tonight?"

Startled by Sophie's compliment, Viola shifted uncomfortably, "Do you really think blue suits me?" She asked.

"I've always felt that bright, vibrant colours suit your complexion and reflect your personality," Sophie continued, hoping she hadn't overplayed her hand with compliments which were so obviously untrue. "I'd wear your hair loose, it makes your face look softer."

"I have been told my hair frames my face to perfection." Striking a pose for the mirror, her lips slightly parted and her red hair flowing down her back, Viola turned to face her sister, her mind suddenly suspicious.

Sensing a need to justify her kindness Sophie explained, "It's my way of saying sorry," the words caught in her throat. The idea of apologising made her feel nauseous. "I know I have never shown it, but I have always admired you. I admit I've been prone to jealously on occasions, but recently I've started to realise just how destructive it's been to our relationship."

Responding more positively than Sophie had expected, Viola moved closer to her younger sister, her face softer and her smile more genuine than Sophie had ever seen.

"They say the first step to recovery is admitting your problem. It would be cruel of me to spurn your advances of friendship." Swivelling around, her face glowing, the thought that she had another admirer, even if only her younger sister, fuelled her already large ego, so much so that she was contemplating allowing her sister to spend time with her. "As your older and wiser sibling, I'm going to take you under my wing and teach you the ways of Court so you can be just like me."

"I'm overwhelmed." Hanging her head into her chest, Sophie had to try really hard to stifle a giggle.

Despite wondering at her sister's complete turnaround, she didn't concern herself overly at its cause. "I'm taking Michael and his friends on a tour of the castle in a while. Would you like to accompany us?"

"That would be wonderful," she responded eagerly, glad the grovelling could stop. While getting ready, she started planning how to gain Michael's confidence and inform him of her suspicions without her sister or mother suspecting. Care was needed.

"We've got an hour until we meet. Why don't you try my silver dress with the slightly ruffed sleeves and black belt if you've nothing of your own?"

Feeling more alive than she had done in ages, Sophie thanked Viola and rummaged for the dress. For some reason she really wanted to make an effort and look nice.

Chapter Twenty-three: Breakfast

While the castle slumbered, servants had been busy preparing the stadium. Awake since dawn, Abe had devoured his breakfast, then headed for the kitchens as he contemplated the state he had left Michael and his friends in the previous evening.

Entering the steam filled room; his visibility was clouded by the swirls of vapour, "Flora? Margery?" He shouted, hoping he could be heard above the noise of cooks chatting, pans spitting and timers sounding.

A large woman in her late forties appeared from the mist, her hand outstretched. "Abednego! We don't see you for weeks and now it's been twice in two days! These visitors must be very special."

"He's my great nephew." His steady hand clasped hers as he looked at the ever growing collection of tyres around her once sleek waist.

"How sweet! I suppose you're here to collect those breakfasts you ordered." Returning with a tray of treats, she winked at him, still trying her luck after years of failed flirting.

"They seemed so poorly last night, I didn't want to disturb them too early." Already he was feeling a protective, nurturing streak he hadn't felt for years and he liked the feeling.

Thanking Flora for the food, he strolled along the labyrinth of corridors before knocking and waiting patiently outside. After a few seconds, he heard Michael's groggy voice so took it upon himself to enter. "I thought I'd bring you some food to help settle your stomach."

Michael watched the old man steadily place a tray on the table.

"Who's that?" Hazel shouted through the partially opened door separating their rooms.

"Abednego's brought us some breakfast," replied Dan as she waltzed into the room and examined the tray.

"Oh good, I'm starving!" Abednego stared in amazement, scarcely able to believe these were the same three youngsters who, just hours earlier had been lolling over chairs with their heads hanging between their legs.

"Glad you've all recovered so quickly," a pleased but slightly confused Abednego picked up the pot from the tray and poured chocolate coloured liquid into three dainty china cups.

"I'm feeling surprisingly well considering that last night I felt like I'd been hit over the head with a lump of wood," said Dan.

"King Mazarin asked if we would like to join him in the Royal Box for the match this afternoon, shall I confirm on your behalf?" Expecting them to start questioning him about returning to Grays, he was taken aback when Dan immediately replied they would love to attend, and with Hazel's excitement at spending time with the King, and then Michael in agreement, Abednego was starting to suspect something was amiss.

"Excellent. I'll meet you in the Great Hall at one o'clock. Until then, enjoy breakfast and your tour of the castle! If you've any questions, please feel free to ask me, and remember, trust no-one"

As soon as Abednego departed, Michael poured some milk into his cup, only to be halted. "What are you doing?" shrieked Dan.

"Pouring milk," replied Michael, "What does it look like I'm doing?" Stirring the frothy liquid, he picked up his cup and squeezed his fingers through the tiny handle.

"Don't!"

"Why?"

Dan's face turned a pale shade of red as he snatched the cup from Michael's hand so quickly he didn't stand a chance. Michael watched in horror as Dan proceeded to pour the liquid down the bathroom sink.

"Why are you tipping away a perfectly good drink?" Frustrated, Michael picked up another cup and this time sipped it without adding any milk.

"STOP!" Dan raised his hand like a traffic warden, his fingers twitching nervously.

"What's your problem?" snapped Michael, facing Dan squarely.

"Last night someone drugged either our food or drink. This being the case, don't you think we should be a little more cautious about what we consume?"

"I understand what you're saying and I can assure you that being drugged and losing my memory isn't high on my agenda of things to do. However, dying of dehydration doesn't figure on that list either." Taking another sip, Michael secretly enjoyed defying Dan, "and she said that the new tablets wouldn't be ready until this evening."

Feeling the need to intercede, Hazel added, "We're all worried Dan, but I honestly think we can trust Abednego." Reaching for a plate of food, her stomach growling, Hazel contemplated the assortment of strange delicacies before her.

Mollified, Dan responded, "I guess we could have a bite to eat, after all, we need to maintain our energy." Nibbling on a pink, chewy ball, Dan had no idea what he was eating or whether he even liked it. "But we do need to have a plan of action for later."

"Let's watch everyone, pour our own drinks and make sure no-one tampers with our food. It's important we make sure no-one suspects we know. We can't trust anyone." Looking at Michael she added, "including Viola."

Offended they would suspect her, but not wanting to start an argument, Michael agreed. "Quite right."

"I'm going to write down all that's happened and keep a note of it in my pocket," suggested Dan, "so if we get drugged again, we can read what we've found out and continue trying to stop it. We were incredibly fortunate to find out what we did last night; we can't rely on it happening a second time."

"Let's start writing," instructed Hazel.

After making his finishing touches, Dan hid his notes in his pocket. Noticing it was nearly ten o clock, they devoured as much food as they could before making their way to the Great Hall.

Chapter Twenty-four: Valkyrites

"Ouch."

"What are you moaning about now?"

"You, you idiot. Next time you walk through nettles, can you hold them back until I've passed through, instead of letting them go so they scratch my legs! They're being cut to pieces!" Watching yet another drop of blood escape from the third cut she'd acquired that morning, Mrs Hopkins was ruing the day she had ever agreed to visit this godforsaken land.

"Stop moaning dear, you're starting to sound like your mother."

"My mother! Never, ever compare me to her! And how you have the audacity to say that about my mother, when yours scolds anyone who dares to hold an opinion that differs from her own, I don't know!" Angry, tired and frustrated, they'd been niggling at each other ever since they'd arrived.

Turning to face his wife, who after weeks of trekking through this strange land, was now even skinnier than usual, he saw blood and instantly felt a pang of guilt; "I'm sorry." With his slimmer than usual frame, through the same deprivation of food and creature comforts, he approached his wife and hugged her.

"That's okay," her weary voice replied, "just think in future."

"Intuition tells me it's just through here." Pointing in the direction of yet more trees, he sat on a rock and reached into his rucksack.

Staring at row upon row of thick trees, some with trunks so wide you could almost make a home in them, Yvonne Hopkins sighed. Despite being morning, the leaves were so dense they blocked out almost all of the sunlight, giving the impression of a constant dusk. The chirping of birds which had initially irritated them had ceased after a couple of days, the grass was a dull yellow, interspersed with weeds and nettles which stung their feet and legs, and then for two weeks they had neither seen nor heard another living creature.

"It's gone!" Her husband's gruff voice shouted in consternation. Rummaging frantically through his half empty rucksack, he flung what was left of their food supplies on the floor, followed by their compass and a blanket.

"What's gone?" Dropping to her knees beside her husband, she snatched his bag, and then turning it upside down she made sure there was nothing left in there.

"Where's the map?" His frightened voice quivered.

"How should I know? You had it last!"

Both emptied their pockets and Yvonne hunted through her scratched handbag where she kept all her personal belongings.

Ralph started to panic. His breathing quickened and soon he was hyperventilating. His face turned red as his hand scoured the floor for his asthma pump. Craning her long neck round, she noticed his pump peeping out from under their blanket. Retrieving it, she shoved it into her husband's mouth and soothed him.

Inhaling and exhaling a few times, gradually his breathing stabilised. Once more he searched the undergrowth; he couldn't look at his wife, knowing how badly he had let her down.

"Found it?" she enquired, her greasy hair clinging to her face. Despite their dilemma, Ralph suppressed a smile, thinking to himself that it was just as well his proud wife couldn't see herself now, her reflection would probably have annoyed her more than the lost map.

"Afraid not." Avoiding her accusing gaze, he busied himself re-packing their bag in as an orderly a fashion as possible.

"Well, that's just great!" Her face turned almost as red as his had been moments earlier. Her pupils dilated so much her iris' seemed to merge into the blackness which had become her eyes, while her lips pouted like those of a disapproving headmistress. "We're stuck in the deepest depths of a grotty, dangerous forest, we've no idea where we're going, and to top it all off, there's not a person in the world who can help us." Fists clenched, she rose to her feet and paced the ground, her anger consuming her.

"Sorry." He mumbled, aware of how inadequate it sounded under the circumstances.

"SORRY! YOU'RE SORRY ARE YOU?" She screamed like a banshee; she wanted to hit him, to throttle his fat neck. Striding away from him, tears of frustration rolled down her cheeks. They were lost and there was no way they could get out of there before their food supplies run out.

"If we try to figure it out logically, perhaps we've a chance." Ralph suggested, although he knew she was unlikely to listen to reason. Instead he resigned himself to absorbing all the verbal abuse she was likely to throw at him, as graciously as possible.

Anxious to escape their prison of trees and shrubbery, she surged forwards. Branches scraped her and thorns pricked her, but her adrenaline was pumping and all she could think of was finding what they were looking for, swiftly followed by returning home as soon as possible.

Zipping up the bag, he ran after her, tripping and stumbling as he went. With only the occasional rays of sunlight peeping through the dense foliage, water droplets fell on them, reminding them that it had been hours since they had last eaten or drunk. His stomach rumbled but he was too afraid to talk of eating, knowing their food supplies were dwindling and they had no idea how much longer their limited rations would have to last.

"Shhhhh," she whispered, halting abruptly.

"What?" Standing close behind her, sensing her body was still taut with rage, he remained quiet, his breathing barely audible.

After seconds of standing like statues, she let out a sigh. "Thought I heard something, that's all." Relaxing her guard, she wiped a drop of water from her face before pushing another branch out of the way.

Crashing through the trees, seemingly from nowhere, four huge creatures descended; their bodies swooping at them like an oncoming train. Panic stricken, they stumbled frantically through the undergrowth back the way they had come; their faces and limbs battered by the nettles and branches blocking their pathway. Shrieking shrilly, wings beating in the wind, their bulky frames soared towards the petrified couple; their eyes burning as bright as coals on fire, their beaks opened wide as their screams reverberated through the forest.

Banging her bony knee on a broken trunk, Yvonne Hopkins gasped in pain as yet more blood poured down her leg, running over recently healed scabs. "Ralph, wait!"

"Come on, hurry!" Turning round, sweat dripping from his forehead, he knew he couldn't run much longer. His breathing was already heavy and his legs trembled beneath him.

Watching the scene behind him, his throat clammed up as he witnessed one of the huge beasts destroy the trees as it swooped down towards his wife. Its huge beak was opened wide and its claws were poised to grip. Sweeping forwards, it clutched his wife around her dainty waist and soared into the sky. Her handbag had fallen from her grasp and landed close to him.

Shocked, Ralph froze as another of the ghastly creatures headed in his direction. His legs shook so violently he could barely stand straight. Grabbing his inhaler from his pocket, he inhaled, then clutched onto it as he awaited his fate.

Closing his eyes he stood, waiting to be taken. As they wrapped themselves around his thick frame, the pinnacles of the claws digging in his flesh, all he could do was pray that both he and his wife would survive.

Chapter Twenty-five: The Forest

Stretching out his almost translucent hand, Mathis grabbed the food Siddons offered and chomped noisily.

"I take it you're getting your appetite back?"

"It's delicious; I'm not used to eating so much." Mathis mumbled; his mouth still full. "When all you've had for years is plain porridge, anything different's a feast."

With more colour in his face and hope in his eyes, Siddons felt pleased at his achievement.

"How's the plan coming on?" Mathis asked as he wiped some juice from his lips. Whilst exercising, Mathis dreamed of freedom, of watching the sun rise and set, of walking in open fields and seeing his family again; things he had taken for granted.

"I haven't put the finishing touches on it yet, but it's getting there."

Mathis considered the strange creature before him and not for the first time, wondered how it was that a Royal Prince, once so rich and powerful, was relying on such a tiny animal for his freedom. "Can I help at all? Once I'm free I guarantee you'll be richly rewarded," he promised before resting his throat.

Preening his wings, Siddons deliberately avoided Mathis' gaze. His initial elation at finding Mathis had subsided as he troubled over the escape plan. Ideas eluded him and he had no idea how to tell Mathis.

Uncomfortable with the silence, Mathis mumbled, "I hope the food you bring tomorrow is as nice as today's selection. It was delicious."

Suddenly Siddons felt the urge to be alone, to contemplate his dilemma.

"You'd better be going. They'll be here soon, delivering my mud flavoured porridge. Can't wait!" Trying to inject some humour into the conversation, Mathis bid Siddons farewell.

As he watched his friend leave, Mathis settled himself in a corner. Closing his eyes, he pictured his reunion with his wife and son. The idea they had moved on hadn't even occurred to him.

Entering the cell, Richard sneered. In response, Mathis stared back, his eyes defiantly holding those of his captor.

"Got yourself some spirit at last?" Richard scowled. Pushing a bowl of slops under the bars, "I'd make the most of it if I were you."

Confused, Mathis clasped the bowl, anxious to consume its unsavoury contents in order to build up his energy.

"Don't look so astounded," Richard drooled, "you must have known this captivity couldn't have lasted forever. In fact, it's a wonder I've had to keep you so long!"

Mathis heart pounded and his hands trembled. "You're setting me free?"

"Free!" Richard repeated. "That's one way of describing it." Chuckling, Richard returned to his study, where he had already started planning his own escape from this godforsaken place.

***

Flying back to his tiny village on the outskirts of the forest, Siddons landed next to his favourite tree trunk.

Picking one of his favourites flowers, he sniffed the perfume of the herytrebs petals and closed his eyes. His heavy heart was weighed down with the worry of Mathis' escape. For so long he had fantasised over finding the Prince and not once had he considered what he would do once it had happened.

Nearby the stream gently lapped against the cave walls. He was tempted to stay there the night, knowing he wouldn't be missed; perhaps the sound of ripples splashing against the rocks would inspire him.

"Sidds, what are you doing here? Have you forgotten about the village meeting?" Ezra, his junior by a few years, startled him by appearing from behind the tree trunk.

"You go, let me know what's decided," he replied to the red, furry Snufflepug who followed him round like a lost puppy.

"Surely you want to voice your opinions?" she pleaded, her pink eyes gazing at her hero adoringly.

"My opinions are of little worth," he scoffed, knowing his reputation as an idle dreamer, without a proper job, meant nothing he said would be taken seriously.

"Of course they are. Anyway, you really should attend; the future of the whole village is under threat."

"Alright, stop moaning." Pushing himself off the trunk, he strolled alongside her to the council meeting.

"Where have you been?" she enquired.

"Just sitting, thinking," he replied defensively.

"So where were you when I walked past half an hour ago?" Her eyes fixed on him. He felt awkward.

"I went into the cave for a while and took a walk nearby." Thrown off guard, he felt uncomfortable lying so tried changing topic. "What a pretty, erm," he scrutinised her for something to compliment, "flower you're wearing."

"Thanks," she blushed, "but I know you're hiding something and I promise," she crossed her fluffy chest, "that if you tell me, I won't tell a living soul." Sensing his determination to remain silent, she continued, "but if I happen to follow you and find out by myself, well, that would be another matter now, wouldn't it?"

Frustrated, he decided to tell her. He couldn't risk her telling others in case it ended Mathis' chance of escape. "Okay, but promise you wont tell anyone."

"Promise," she whispered, surprised at this new side to Siddons.

"Remember Mathis, Prince of Kilion? About seventeen years ago, he went to a place called England and for a while, no-one heard of him. A couple of years later, after his brother, King Melchior was killed in battle, Mathis was attacked and declared dead. Ring any bells?"

"I've heard people talk of him."

"Well, I've found him. He's being kept prisoner and I'm helping him escape." There, he thought, I've said it, although he resented being forced to share his secret.

"You mean the Prince they buried years ago shortly after the war?"

"That's the one." Wearily he trudged onwards.

"Why have you been looking for a corpse? And why move his body?" Her face was serious; she had clearly missed his point.

"He's not a corpse, he's alive!" Siddons raised his voice in frustration.

"Of course... he's not dead. They all imagined it! So did they bury the wrong person?" she chuckled. "Honestly, you want me to believe that Prince Mathis is really your friend who you're helping escape?" Sauntering alongside him she giggled, "Siddons, just admit it, you're seeing someone and you don't want anyone to know. Bless you for trying to save my feelings but I'm okay; I've been over you for ages."

Stunned, he wasn't sure whether to feel relieved she hadn't believed him or worried that even a giggling teenager couldn't take him seriously. "Thanks," he replied, though he wasn't sure why he was acting grateful after she'd blackmailed him into divulging his secret, then laughed in his face when he had.

"You're such a dreamer," she sighed, "that's why everyone likes you." Despite her attempt at consoling him, he felt depressed.

Reaching the village, they sat near the back of the crowd and waited patiently for order to be called. Discussions began on the new vampire colony on the other side of the mountains. It was considered only a matter of time before their clan was discovered by the blood suckers and sealed their fate.

Siddons remained silent; mentally rescheduling his day's activities, for it looked like it was going to be a long meeting.

***

Pacing the floor, Ragetta ran her hands through her shoulder length hair. Where was he? He would never stay out all night without informing her. Something was wrong.

She prayed he hadn't been foolish enough to follow the boy into the castle; especially given the circumstances under which they had been forced to leave and yet it was the only explanation. He must have been caught trespassing and imprisoned!

Studying her weary face in the mirror, her attention was drawn to the bags under her eyes. Her concentration was waning and she was constantly yawning, yet she couldn't sleep. She needed to focus. She couldn't simply wait for him, and if he was behind bars, she needed to help him escape.

If he had been imprisoned because of the boy, did it mean the boy really was important? What if they needed to keep Grimbald quiet? Her mind flitted from one scenario to another. Perhaps he was Mathis' son and rightful heir? What if they thought Grimbald planned to put the boy on the throne? That would be treason and punishable by death! With every new thought, her anxiety grew.

Scribbling a quick note to explain her absence to Grimbald in case he returned, she grabbed some food and her coat before slamming the door behind her and heading for the castle. Pulling her collar closely around her neck, she was halfway there when doubts crept in. If she went to the castle, would she end up being locked in a cell with

Grimbald? What good would that do? Rooted to the spot, she weighed up her options.

After careful consideration, she retraced her steps and walked back through the village, this time in the direction of the forest and stream.

The only way she could gain access to the castle without being caught was by using an invisibility potion, and the only person in Kilion with magic powers who didn't reside at Court was the wise woman of the woods. No one had seen her for years and some claimed her existence was mythical, or that she had died, but with her husband's life at stake, Ragetta was prepared to risk it.

Passing through the streets into open fields and towards the forest, her pace quickened the closer she got. Part of the reason very few, if any, had ventured to find the witch was the distance; it was a few hours walk to the forest. More important was the fact that the forest was populated with dangerous creatures. Scared but desperate, Ragetta kept a constant vigil for strange, blood sucking animals and beasts as she entered, praying her instincts about the witch were right.

Chapter Twenty-six: Tour of the Castle

"Viola dear, a little word before you meet with Michael?" Martha patted the settee next to her.

"Will it take long?" she sighed, not interested in her mother's constant advice.

"Hargrin visited earlier, you know who he is?" Viola nodded silently.

"Turns out the King and I are on the same wavelength." Settling back into the leather sofa, Martha explained the situation, the task of gaining Michael's trust, Hargrin's warning not to mention his past and the reason for their visit.

Listening intently, Viola nodded approvingly. That was until her mother landed the biggest surprise upon her, "he's requested that you slip tablets into their drinks to help them relax," she continued quickly to prevent Viola from interjecting, "of course, I said you'd be delighted to help the King out in this matter." She paused, her expression eager.

"You mean, without my permission, you've agreed to me spiking their drinks?"

"Only to help them relax dear."

"And you don't find it strange that the King would need to spike their drinks to help them relax? Didn't it occur to you that they might be something else?"

Startled at this suggestion, Martha rose from the settee and began pacing the floor. "My darling, are you doubting that both the King and Hargrin have Michael's best interests at heart? They simply want him and his friends to be happy, to put the past behind them and enjoy their time here. Surely you want to help them with that?"

Viola sighed. She didn't like the sound of it but clearly Hargrin had taken her mother in and she knew better than to defy her mother's wishes. "Okay, I'll do as you say, but I'm not happy."

"Just so long as you do as I ask."

"I'll win him over for you, but I'm going to do it my way. Interfere and I'll refuse to co-operate, do I make myself clear?"

Prepared to lose the battle to win the war, Martha nodded gracefully, "Just adhere to the King's instructions."

Satisfied, but scared by the task thrust upon her, Viola nodded, all the while thinking she was far too young to be embroiled in such intrigue.

***

Retreating from behind the door, Sophie sat behind her desk, her head buried in a book as Viola entered; her face was ashen.

"Everything okay?" Sophie queried.

"Fine," Viola responded, her mind distracted.

Sophie smirked. It seemed that because her mother didn't allow her to voice her opinions, Martha and Viola naturally assumed she didn't have ears either. So, while Viola prettied herself for the tour, Sophie sat just feet away, composing a note of warning about her own family.

Michael,

Make sure no-one sees this note; hide it as soon as you've read it. There are people in the castle plotting against you. They're trying to spike your drink with tablets. Please be careful. I need to talk to you in person. Meet me by the Castle Library tomorrow at 1pm. Most people will be at worship so we shouldn't be disturbed. It is down the corridor from the Hall. Please come, it's urgent.

Leaving the note unsigned in case it fell into the wrong hands, she folded it up and shoved it into her small bag. If possible, she intended to pass it surreptitiously to one of them during their tour. If not, she'd hide it under their napkin in the Great Hall for them to find at dinner.

***

"Ready to go?" Viola enquired.

"Yes, and I'm so excited, I really appreciate being invited."

"May I ask a favour?" Viola asked.

"Certainly, what is it?"

Unused to asking her younger sister for anything, Viola was finding all this niceness strange. "Could you keep Hazel occupied while I talk to Michael, and perhaps, discreetly enquire as to the nature of their relationship? Only I get the impression she has quite some influence with him."

"Absolutely, I'll find out how things stand between all three of them if that's any help?"

"It is... thanks." Looking at her sister properly for the first time in ages, it dawned on Viola that Sophie was no longer a child, in fact she was showing herself to be really quite mature."

"Isn't it nice that we're no longer at each other's throats?" observed an unexpectedly emotional Sophie.

"I suppose." Glancing in the mirror once more, Viola straightened her dress, wiped away a few loose strands of shimmery red hair from her face and then smoothly replenished her understated lipstick.

Appraising herself one last time, Sophie admired her reflection.

Waving her daughters off, Martha smiled, leaving Sophie to wonder if she had any idea of the trouble she could be causing Viola. Sophie was also annoyed that their mother had unknowingly placed her in an awkward situation. Morally she felt compelled to warn Michael of the plot against him, but by doing so, she was risking getting caught and was reticent about revealing her families role in the plot.

Entering the Great Hall Michael, Daniel and Hazel were already waiting, their faces flushed with excitement.

Once assembled, Viola carried out the introductions. First she introduced Zoe, a shy teenager who hated attention for fear of being teased over her excess weight; self-conscious, she consoled herself in the arms of food, worsening her insecurities. With Viola as a best friend, looking all slim and fit, it was hardly surprising she felt inadequate, and yet, Sophie thought, her smile was sweet and knew her nature to be kind. Eager to please, Sophie wondered how far Viola abused this attribute for her own gain. Extending her chubby hand to the visitors, Zoe lowered her gaze, worried she would be greeted with looks of disgust or pity, like those she received from her parents and their friends. Sophie watched as Hazel shook Zoe's hand and smiled. Michael took it next, too shy to say much, and then Dan who, like Hazel, was aware of how awkward Zoe felt and was extra friendly in his greeting.

Next to be introduced was Cynthia, plain but outgoing. All three from their greeting, obviously took an instant liking to her. Cynthia's smile illuminated her face as she gabbled with excitement.

Finally, it was Sophie's turn. Michael remembered her from the previous evening and shook her hand; Dan inclined his head in her direction, noticing a vague similarity between her and her elder sister, but instinctively liking the younger sister much better; Hazel smiled warmly at her, and like Dan, knew instantaneously that she preferred Sophie to Viola.

Introductions over, Viola was eager to begin the tour of discovery. Grabbing Michael's arm, she propelled him out the Great Hall and through a labyrinth of corridors. Cynthia, acknowledging Viola's claim to Michael, considered Dan a more than adequate substitute and monopolised his attention, chatting animatedly as they toured the castle, pointing out rooms and pictures of interest while flashing him her winning smile.

Meanwhile Hazel, Zoe and Sophie fell to the back of the group, taking their time viewing the wonders around them while making sure they didn't lose sight of the others. Zoe said very little, worried about making a fool of herself, and content to amble beside them, her only contribution was to answer a question from Hazel. It was left to Sophie to explain about the castle, the permanent residents, the Court hierarchy and the governing of the country. Intrigued, Hazel lapped it up.

Finally, after visiting the kitchens, taking a tour of the library and showing them the location of the King's apartments, Viola led them to a huge expanse of luscious castle gardens. Feeling sufficiently confident by this point, Sophie asked Hazel how she knew Michael and Daniel.

"They're my best friends," Hazel replied, "we can talk about anything and we do everything together."

"So, you're not dating either of them?" Feeling awkward at asking something so intimate, Sophie hurriedly added, "not that you have to answer, I mean, it's none of my business."

Amused at Sophie's sensitivity, Hazel responded, "No, we're just good friends. We know each other far too well. Why, got your eye on one of them?" Hazel teased, thinking the question would have been better suited to Viola.

Blushing, her movements became bashful. "Ab… ab... absolutely not," she muttered, the thought had not even crossed her mind.

"I was just teasing," Hazel soothed, realising Sophie wasn't as forthright as Viola, or indeed anything like her.

"Don't worry," murmured an embarrassed Sophie, though it hadn't escaped her notice that Daniel was very easy on the eye.

As people buzzed around outside, talking about the afternoon game between the King's Men and the Mountain Leopards, they could barely hear each other speak. Men were jeering; glasses were clinking, women giggled as they drank too much and children played games as the band played. There was already a jovial atmosphere in readiness for the match only a couple of hours away.

"It's only midday, the match hasn't even started and people are already drinking! They'll be some sore heads tomorrow!" Zoe observed.

"I think you may be right," Hazel grinned, recalling the previous night and how she had felt.

Ahead, Viola halted and whispered to Cynthia who nodded in agreement. "What a great idea!"

Sophie's heart sank, what was her sister planning now?

Escaping the crowds, they circumnavigated the grounds, along a narrow path and away from the building. "Where are we going?" enquired the ever cautious Dan.

"Somewhere interesting," Viola responded, her face jubilant.

"We're not going to...?" Sophie stammered, but was cut short by Viola's brisk reply.

"Don't worry. I'm just showing them where the secret garden passage lies. Michael knows this place is riddled with secret corridors, doors and escape routes and that unless you know the secret, which very few do, they remain barred to people like us.

"But remember…"

"I'm not going to try to open anything, and if you keep your mouth shut, mother need never find out… agreed?" Her face smiled, her voice threatened.

"No reason she should," Sophie responded. She didn't know why but she was nervous. Perhaps it was their isolation from the rest of the castle, with so many strangers roaming the grounds to watch the game, there was no knowing who they might meet. She was also worried about skulking around off limit areas. She hated getting in trouble, and the thought of being caught made her feel physically sick.

"Don't worry sis," Viola played her part of reassuring, older sister well. "we'll head back as soon as I've shown them round."

Slightly reassured, Sophie followed Viola who was still chatting to Hazel and Zoe. Ducking under branches and dodging blooming flowers, they weaved their way through the gardens until they reached what looked like a tombstone, although the writing was illegible. "Here it is," announced Viola, pointing to the slab of marble.

"What is it?" Dan enquired.

"Not many people know this, but I overheard some guards saying that whoever opens this passageway will be offered sanctuary in a place so safe, not even the witches in the coven will be able to find them."

"Is it still in use?" questioned Dan.

"I don't think anyone knows how to use it. The secret's been lost."

Michael could feel his leg getting warm. Shoving his hand in his trouser pocket, he clasped the ring to stop people noticing its glow. He needed to escape before it shone any brighter. "I need a bit of time to myself. I'm just going for a walk, if that's okay?"

Shocked by his lack of interest, Viola was unsure how to react, that was until Dan asked, "So, has no-one tried to figure out how it works?"

Surprised, Viola wasn't sure. "Not that I'm aware of, perhaps the witches are trying to figure it out, but to be honest, it isn't needed anymore, at least not since Mazarin became King. The previous King, Melchior, was frequently attacked by a distant cousin and so the tunnels were often used. His brother, Mathis, had left Kilion, perhaps through these very tunnels. Melchior was desperate to keep his throne, but he was unfortunately killed in the Final Battle, as we call it. Despite fighting bravely, he was betrayed and slain on the field, but the most curious part of the whole story was that despite trying to claim the throne for months, and despite winning, Azarel, his distant cousin, just disappeared. His body was never found and not once since then has he tried claiming the Kingdom. Not long after that, reports were circulated that Mathis had been killed in a place called England. That meant the throne was inherited by their second cousin, King Mazarin. We've had peace ever since and the tunnels haven't been used in that time."

Hazel and Dan had listened silently, engrossed. At the tale of Mathis, a shiver shot through Dan's spine. He had no idea why, but it had hit a nerve. Spying Michael in the distance, he made a mental note to fill him in. For some reason, this information seemed crucial.

"Shall we leave?" asked Viola, who was upset by Michael's lack of interest. Not for the first time she wished Dan had been her intended target. Pivoting round, she caught up with Michael, whose ring had ceased glowing, and led them back to the castle. The sun was now high in the sky and there was only a light breeze to protect them from the full heat of the day.

Zoe joined Viola and Michael while the rest strolled nonchalantly behind at a slower pace. Dan remained silent as did Sophie, who still hadn't passed on her note for fear of being noticed. Hazel, meanwhile, chatted to Cynthia who had decided the best way to win over Dan was to ingratiate herself with his friends, starting with Hazel.

Just before reaching their rooms to prepare for the match, Sophie tugged at Hazel's sleeve to keep her back from the others. Handing over the note, she whispered for Hazel to hide it. "Read it urgently, as soon as you're in your room."

"What is it?" Hazel asked suspiciously.

"It's not safe to talk now. Just read it and meet me when and where it says." Anxious not to arouse suspicion, she said goodbye to Hazel and the others, and then left with Viola who had arranged to speak to Michael at the feast later.

Excited about the game Michael, Dan and Hazel entered their rooms and were finally alone. Michael told them of the rings reaction at the passageway, while Dan regaled the tale of King Melchior and Prince Mathis, along with the mysterious relative. Waiting patiently for them to settle, Hazel produced Sophie's note and read it to them. As usual, Dan wrote everything down underneath the information on their meeting with Grimbald.

Meanwhile, as Viola and Sophie got ready for the match, Sophie was pleased to report that Hazel and Michael were no more than friends. Generally pleased with the morning's progress and Sophie's help, Viola extracted a beautiful Bordeaux dress with crystals nipping the waist in from her wardrobe and passed it to her sister. "In case I forget, I think you should wear this for the feast tonight, you'll look really pretty in it."

Gobsmacked, Sophie held the dress up to the light and admired the diamonds glittering in the light, and imagined herself swirling to the music. It was a shame, thought Sophie, that just as she was building a relationship with Viola, she would have to ruin it by telling the visitors what was happening. Maybe she could inform them without implicating her sister?

Spectators filled every crevice of the castle and its grounds as preparations for the most awaited event of the year were finalised. Organisers ran in all directions, ensuring everything was in place for the spectacle. Abednego weaved through the chattering groups until he finally reached the Great Hall where he met Michael, Dan and Hazel. Excited, Hazel was desperate to know the rules so Abednigo explained the regulations as simply as he could. By this point, even Michael was enthusiastic about watching the King's Men play in the final match of the year which would determine the League Champions.

Queues wound round the outbuildings and into the distance. Even the sun seemed to be smiling, its heat intense and the atmosphere intoxicating. In the midst of the grounds a huge stadium had appeared, ovular in shape, over a hundred metres long and taller than the castle. Shocked at the sudden emergence of such a gigantic structure,

Abednego explained that for the most part of the year, it remained invisible for security purposes.

"Hadn't we better start lining up?" Queried Michael, noticing that the queue was already ridiculously long, and that people hadn't yet started being admitted.

"We're sitting with the King and Queen so we can use the special entrance at the side of the stadium." Grinning at their awestruck faces, Abe led them through their entrance and purchased some refreshments which they readily accepted, knowing there was no way anyone could have tampered with them.

As well as having to remember the rules of the game, they were introduced to numerous Courtiers. Forced into making polite conversation, they smiled sweetly while trying to remember their political positions and connections. Before long they had spoken to so many people, their heads were swimming with the information and all they wanted to do was to get to the Royal Box; eat, drink and watch the match.

Finally and to their relief, Abednego led them past security and up the stairs to the top of the stadium. Entering a glass encased pod, they gazed around in wonderment. Through the glass floor, they saw hordes of people clambering up the aisles, with attendants busily showing ticket holders to their seats and programmes being bought, allowing people to pour over team and player statistics.

"This is amazing!" a wonderstruck Dan breathed.

Smiling, the King extended his hand and once more introduced his wife, Queen Jeanne. As they took their seats, he explained that as much of the game took place in the air, and that they were in the prime location to see the best of the game.

Relaxing deep into their cushioned chairs, swivelling round so they could see a full 360 degrees, they enquired about the game, fascinated by such a huge event.

Finally, a huge horn sounded and a voice boomed throughout the stadium asking people to take their seats. As two teams assembled onto the pitch, screams and cheers permeated the air. Taking their positions, poised to begin, the whistle sounded and the game started.

***

Glancing from side to side, worried about being seen, Raglin swept along the side of the building, away from the stadium until he reached the royal stables; the pre-arranged meeting place. With relief he spied the lone figure already there, glancing at his wrist.

Not until he was almost upon him did Raglin speak; his voice a whisper. "I'm glad you could make it." Extending his hand, he examined the figure's coal black eyes, dark stubble and slim physique, it was lithe and yet with an aura of strength.

"Once given, my word is never broken." Giving nothing away, especially his contempt for the velvet cloaked, jewel encrusted individual before him, his face remained expressionless, ready to conclude their business as quickly as possible.

"Glad to hear it." Patting the figure on the shoulder, Raglin felt him recoil and withdrew his hand quickly, a little annoyed at the unintentional rebuff.

"Who do you want me to kill?"

Raglin was impressed by his no nonsense attitude and relaxed a little. "You have a month to prepare as there are still some aspects of the plan I need to consider prior to the… assassination."

A thoughtful look crossed the stranger's face, a month was certainly long enough to gather the required information, and he wanted to make sure the murder was done in such a way as to appear accidental. He had no doubt it was a political assassination, which meant castle security could cause a problem, making this murder more difficult than most. "A month is sufficient."

"How much?" Ready to barter, Raglin knew the price would be high.

"You've yet to tell me who I'm killing." His expressionless face stared at the Courtier, nothing of his thoughts showing, not even in his eyes.

Inhaling deeply, worried about the assassin's reaction, Raglin paused, aware of the seriousness of his next words. They were treasonable, and if discovered, would be punishable by death. Could Raglin trust him? What if the assassin recoiled? What if he reported Raglin to the King? This answer would determine his whole future; he was placing his trust in an unknown quantity, handing this killer the ammunition to bring him down.

"The name of the man I'm to kill?" He repeated. He could see the older man thinking, watched as his eyes scrunched slightly, his forehead creased, deep in thought. He waited.

"The King. I want you to kill the King."

Nothing he could remember had affected him quite so dramatically. The assassin stumbled backwards, reeling from a blow that had felt almost physical. "The King?" he whispered, wanting confirmation he had heard right.

"The King," Raglin repeated, his heart thumping.

There was silence. Nothing was said for a while as both men considered their position. Staring at Raglin, he wondered what the Courtier stood to gain from the King's death. Everyone knew Raglin was at the apogee of his powers, enjoying a life of enviable riches, a position of prominence and with no potential rival for power. With the King gone, and his heir a distant cousin from another country, Raglin's power would surely be uncertain. Something wasn't right, there were forces at work here and he had no idea what they were. What would it mean for Kilion? His head was pounding with the potential consequences of his actions.

"Well?" Raglin's nerves were on edge and his patience was starting to wane. The longer he took to answer, the more likely he thought that he would refuse the commission.

Seeing Raglin in a new light, as a man with less integrity than he, a paid killer, he had to think quickly. "I have a month to work out how to kill the King?"

Relieved the venture hadn't been dismissed completely, Raglin smiled, "A month."

"And what would be my reward? It's going to be the biggest job I've ever undertaken. If I'm caught, my life will certainly be forfeit."

"I've done my research; I know your reputation enough to be certain you'll be successful."

"You're right, I've been successful so far, but never before have I undertaken such a dangerous task. But if it's not that important that you can't find suitable compensation for my efforts, I'm afraid you're wasting my time."

Grabbing his sleeve as he turned to leave, Raglin whispered, "It'll be worth your while. You'll be given enough money to keep you for life, a place wherever you want and a position at Court, of course that would only be after a respectable period of time and if no-one suspects foul play."

A place of his own, a job at Court, no more murders. It sounded appealing. "I'll do it. But first I'll need some information."

A huge weight had been lifted from his shoulders. Raglin was ready to agree to anything to fulfil their plan.

Discussions continued, questions were answered and plans were made. The assassin gathered information, all the while wondering if he would have the courage to go through with it. All he knew was that at the moment, he was not prepared to risk his position by turning down someone so powerful.

Chapter Twenty-seven: Relocation

"What do you make of that?" Ezra asked.

"Of what?" Siddons replied, his mind focused on helping Mathis escape.

"Relocating the village."

"Relocating! Is that what's happening?"

"Were you just at the same meeting as me?"

"Yes, but I, erm..."

"Your mind was elsewhere. You were thinking of your secret jaunts weren't you?" She stared into his eyes as though she could read his thoughts. Siddons, finding the intimacy disconcerting, squirmed.

"When are we moving?" he asked, worried that any plans he might conjure up, would be ruined. Finding Mathis would mean nothing if he couldn't get the Prince out of his cell.

"Did you pay attention to anything? We're starting to pack up tomorrow with a view to moving within the week." She sighed, concerned that even with something as important as saving the village and its inhabitants, Siddons was still daydreaming. For the first time she understood his parent's frustration as they despaired of him ever acting responsibly. Despite being a couple of years younger, Ezra often felt older. Watching the other Snufflepugs scurrying around with determination; the enormity of the situation hit her. They were moving! The whole village was being forced to run away from their enemy. With no idea of where they were to settle or find food, the whole situation was scary.

Scrutinising the village before her, for the first time she appreciated the real beauty of her home.

"Immediately! But we can't leave! I need to stay." Springing to his feet indignantly, Siddons paced the floor, his hands clasping and unclasping with frustration. He felt like he was drowning. He hated that the situation was out of his control, that he was caught up in a whirlpool of activity which was threatening to drag him under. It seemed that fortunes tide was not in his favour. He felt so close to helping Mathis and now they had to move. He loved his village and wanted them to be safe, and yet for some reason, more important to him was the thought of saving the life of the Prince the country had adored, to rescue him from his life in captivity, to release him, like a broken bird back into his natural habitat.

"What is it?" Ezra asked, curious as to why the move was affecting him so badly."

Turning his back on her, he made his way to where their chief was still discussing the situation with worried Snufflepugs. He waited in silence until they finished and the chief was able to give Siddons his full attention.

"Siddons isn't it? You're one of our villagers without a job aren't you?"

"Well... the..." Siddons stammered, but was stopped short by the chief who was determined not to be interrupted.

"You can keep watch as we pack up. The vampires are getting closer and it's only a matter of time before they discover our community. As you've no family commitments, you could take on the night watch."

"Night duty!" Siddons squeaked. He couldn't think of anything worse and wished he had kept a low profile.

"Most of the others will be working or packing, so I'm entrusting you with the vital job of ensuring the safety of the village, starting tonight."

"I can't do it!" Siddons protested. I've important things to do," he blurted out, regretting it immediately.

"So despite having no job and being kept by the community all your life, you're refusing to donate your time to help save your village?" His eyes glared like thunder as he leaned forwards.

"I love this village, I do. But I need to have at least a couple of hours off tonight. I can't tell you why, but it is vital. I promise what I'm doing could bring long term benefits to everyone here."

"More important than saving our lives?" His coal black eyes bore into Siddons, making his fur and feathers stand on end. Siddons lowered his eyes, suitably chastised, "Well, what is it?"

"I wish I could tell you… but I can promise you it's important."

"If it is more important than the village, your family which has brought you up and provided for you, then you're not the Snufflepug I thought you were. Perhaps you should leave and work out what's important to you."

"But I didn't say..."

"Just pack and go. We'll be leaving at the end of the week. If by then you've changed your priorities, you may return and prove yourself. If however, this other thing still takes priority, I think it's best you don't return."

Desperate to explain his predicament but unwilling to risk Mathis safety, Siddons' voice deserted him and he retreated from the chief, his heart downtrodden; everything seemed bleak. He had chosen Mathis above the village, and now he would have to leave his loved ones behind. He couldn't help but wonder whether he had made the right decision. Should he abandon Mathis and agree to do the watch? That would be the easiest option, and yet in his heart he knew he couldn't do it. What if they decided to kill him? Mathis couldn't defend himself. At least in the village there were hundreds of Snufflepugs; Mathis was all alone. For that reason, Siddons knew what he had to do.

He couldn't bring himself to say goodbye to Ezra or to explain to his parents how he had been banished; he didn't know how to justify his decision. Instead he left quietly, with no fuss, no scenes and no arguments.

***

Nestling back into his chair with his pen poised to write, the scarred face, gargoyle-like in its grotesqueness, studied his reflection, imagining what he would look like with his health restored.

Wiping dust from the oak table, he produced some parchment from the bottom drawer and dipped his nib into the nearby inkpot. Gazing at his bleak surroundings, and imagining the day he would no longer have to hide from society, he considered what he would write in the letter she had waited so patiently for.

Mother,

All is going to plan. The boy, Michael, is here with Hazel and Daniel - as you predicted. There's no sign of the ring yet but I'll have it soon enough. Abednego has the King convinced Michael is a relation of his, and I think he's also convinced Raglin. Yet the old man doesn't deceive me. I have no doubt the boy is Mathis' son, just like you said. You won't know him but a new Courtier, Hargrin, has befriended the boy and is trying to gain his trust. The memory tablets have been successful, just as you predicted. None of them can remember anything before their entry to Kilion.

We're being helped by a teenage girl who is also trying to gather information from them. It all seems to be going well so far, and I'm hoping our plan will be accomplished earlier and easier than expected. Arrangements have been made for the King's assassination, so his death will look accidental. This will mean no suspicious circumstances will cloud my ascent to the throne once they realise I am still alive.

I will write to you when Michael has been has been reunited with his long lost father. As soon as Mathis has divulged the whereabouts of the ring and the secret password, I'll call for your assistance. Once I access Dragon Falls, rejuvenate myself and claim what is rightfully mine, we can start working for what you most desire.

I hope to have much of this achieved by the end of the month. I look forward to seeing you when the time is right. You have my word that no harm shall befall either Hazel or Daniel as requested.

Your loving son,
Azarel

Rolling the parchment up tightly, he dripped some wax from his candle into a pot then sealed the message. Whistling, he beckoned his hunting hawk, threw it a crust of bread then attached the parchment to a loop around his leg. Whispering instructions in his birds' ear, he watched as it soared out through the small opening in the wall, along a narrow secret passageway and out through the window the other side.

Leaning back in his chair contentedly, he opened a restricted book of magic in preparation for his Kingship.

Chapter Twenty-eight: The Forest

After hours of wading through overgrown foliage, scraping herself on bushes and trying to recall the direction she used to go in as a child, Ragetta headed deeper into the forest in the hope that her journey wasn't in vain. As dusk closed in, she spied a strange looking bag sprawled amongst the nettles. Intrigued, she picked it up and peeked inside to find the remnants of food and a material pouch containing strange coins, pieces of paper and plastic. Flicking through the plastic cards, she noticed one had a picture of a woman in the corner, a Mrs. Yvonne Hopkins. Scanning the text, she was horrified to discover that the woman came from Great Britain. Alarm bells rang; that was where Mathis had gone. Unnerved by the strange events occurring, she clutched the bag to her chest and hurried in the direction of the witch.

Within minutes a bright green pixie jumped out from the foliage, attacked her calf, sunk its teeth into her flesh and drew a trickle of crimson blood before scurrying off. With aching limbs and a gnawed leg, Ragetta tried to be as quiet as possible, especially as the moons and stars would soon replace the last of the sun's rays. It was well known that as the stars woke from their slumber, so too did the darker world which had its heart in the forest. Vampires, werewolves and other bloodthirsty creatures of the night began their search for food and survival. It would be minutes, rather than hours before they would start prowling their turf; searching for their next victim and Ragetta knew her sturdy physique would provide quite a feast.

Chapter Twenty-nine: Dinner

Once more, Daniel, Hazel and Michael found themselves seated at the top of the Great Hall with the King, Queen Jeanne, Abednego and his five Ministers. Still overwhelmed by the situation, they studied everybody's movements, hoping to discover who was drugging them. Again they were faced with a multitude of courses, each containing dishes so beautifully presented it was a shame they had to be eaten. Conscious of the danger, they waited patiently until each dish had been picked at before indulging their appetites. They declined any drinks, instead pouring their own from the communal jug which even the King was using.

Avoiding all alcohol, they sipped warily, remaining silent for most of the meal. For despite spending most of the afternoon in the company of the King and Queen, they still felt too nervous to talk to them in front of so many people. They also avoided contact with the King's Ministers in case they were involved in the plot; although this did not stop Hazel from glancing in Hargrin's direction on more than one occasion.

Left to their own devices Michael, Dan and Hazel spent the majority of the meal people watching or making small talk, commenting on the different foods and the extravagant dress of the Courtiers.

"How long do you think we'll be expected to stay tonight?" Queried Dan, who wanted nothing more than to leave the feast and curl up safely in bed, away from any enemies.

"Probably 'till the end," commented Michael, just as eager as Dan to escape.

Just like the previous evening, once the meal had ended, the King rose from his seat, thanked everyone for attending and indicated for the musicians to commence playing. Tables disappeared and chairs readjusted so the centre of the hall was free for dancing.

As expected, it was not long before Viola approached. "How's the rest of your day been?" she asked. "Did you enjoy watching the match in the royal pod?" Her eyes glistened excitedly and Hazel detected a faint undertone of jealousy at the privileges they'd enjoyed.

"It was amazing," enthused Michael who had loved every minute.

Hazel agreed, her eyes glinting with excitement as she recalled how the striker from the King's Men had, at one point, flown so close to their pod, she was sure that if the glass hadn't been a barrier, she would literally have been able to reach out and touch him.

While Dan had also enjoyed the game, he still doubted Viola's intentions, so refrained from commenting and silence descended.

Feeling uncomfortable, Michael broke the silence by asking, "So, much on tomorrow?" Michael had intended it as a simple question, not realising that it could have been, and was, mistaken for an invitation.

"Nothing really," she replied immediately, "why? Would you like to meet up again? I could show you more of the castle."

"Great idea!" a voice boomed from behind. Swivelling round, Michael was perturbed to discover that Hargrin had been listening in. "Why don't I take the four of you out in my carriage tomorrow morning after breakfast? It's a great way to see the castle grounds without putting too much strain on the old legs." Hargrin winked in Hazel's direction.

"What an excellent idea," Hazel agreed, just as Hargrin had expected.

"Well... I... I'm not so sure it is," Dan responded quickly, worried about his trustworthiness, though some may have mistaken it for jealousy.

"Why not?" Hazel replied, anxious not to let the ever cautious Dan put a dampener on the invitation.

"We don't know what we're doing yet and the King might want us elsewhere," Dan retorted, not trusting the Minister even a fraction. He'd had a bad feeling about Hargrin all night. For some reason, he suspected Hargrin was involved in the plot, though he couldn't put his finger on why.

"There's no need to worry Daniel." Hargrin rested his hand on Dan's shoulder reassuringly, "I've already got the King's approval, as long as I get you back before lunch."

"That's settled then," Viola sealed the deal, grateful for Hargrin's suggestion.

"So it would seem," Hazel smiled to herself, unable to think of a better way to start the day.

Hargrin departed, pleased at his progress with the teenagers except for Dan, who was incredibly suspicious for a teenager. Meanwhile Viola used this opportunity to offer herself to get their drinks for them, and fulfil her duty to her mother.

Not wanting to appear rude, it was difficult to refuse. So reluctantly they accepted, though Dan glanced at Hazel, a worried expression on his face.

Guilt stricken, Viola couldn't bear to watch them drink, so she excused herself and hurried back to where Martha and Sophie sat watching.

"Do you think Violas' responsible?" Daniel asked, peering at his drink suspiciously.

"I don't know," replied Hazel, "but I can't recall her being anywhere near our drinks last night. Then again, I wasn't looking out for anything strange."

"I'm certain she wouldn't try to harm us," defended Michael who was determined to believe the best in the one person who had shown him any friendship other than Daniel and Hazel.

"Even so, it's best if we stick to our original plans," suggested Dan. "One at a time, we'll go on a walk or visit the toilet and refill our cups from jugs we know to be safe."

Dan went first, smiling at those he'd been introduced to at the match. Ensuring no one was watching, he tipped the liquid into a plant pot in the corner of the Hall, and then picking up an empty cup, he found a jug, poured himself a drink and then returned to where the other two sat. One by one Michael and Hazel followed suit.

Remembering how they had been affected the previous evening, they gradually began acting more and more inebriated, speaking slowly and slurring their words. Again, they sat down and pretended to rest their heads in their hands, all the while glancing around the hall to ascertain whether anyone was taking any notice. This was harder than they had imagined for the room was filled with laughter, chatting and dancing bodies which made any detective work almost impossible. Wearied by the day's events and by trying to act drunk, they eventually resorted to slouching at the table waiting for the end of the night.

"I wish we knew who to avoid," mumbled Hazel.

"Maybe Sophie will be able to shed some light on the situation," a hopeful Dan suggested.

"I hope you're right. What was she like Hazel? You talked to her more than either of us two," asked Michael.

"She seemed really nice and normal really. I think we can trust her; I can't see why she would make anything up." Hazel wiped her hair from her face and threw a glance at Sophie who was looking in their direction with a look of pity. Viola meanwhile, was chatting to Zoe, paying them no attention at all.

They waited patiently until the end of the evening for Abednigo to escort them back. They had decided to tell him everything and only hoped their trust wasn't misplaced.

***

"It seems Viola is proving a most capable accomplice," Raglin whispered to his advisors who were once more huddled in the corner of the Hall. He himself was beside himself with pleasure at the thought of finally arranging for the King's untimely death. The fact that Hargrin and Viola were gaining Michael's trust and that the memory tablets had again been administered successfully was the icing on the cake so to speak. He couldn't wait to report back to their Master.

Only Tacitus felt guilty as he watched Michael, Dan and Hazel slouching and wondered whether he was doing the right thing.

***

Having spent much of the evening with the King, Abednego ventured over to his guests and was once more perplexed at the state in which he found them. Listening to their slurred conversation, he approached, taking them by surprise.

Once in their rooms, away from the din of the hall and prying eyes, they felt safe to speak freely. Taken aback by the way they suddenly discarded their drunken behaviour, Abednego perched his old body on a bed.

He listened intently as they described how Michael had woken them up the previous night for them to discover how much better they felt. He was shocked at how easily they had uncovered the secret passageways, and was mortified to find out that someone was imprisoned in the secret dungeons. He had thought they were no longer used. As the name Grimbald was mentioned, he wondered if it were Mathis' faithful servant, and if so, then why after years of having left the castle, was he now prisoner? He knew Grimbald had been a a firm supporter of Mathis and that he had never been one to hold his tongue or curb his actions, yet that didn't explain why he was imprisoned now.

This worried Abednigo. He was certain Mazarin had no knowledge of this. He would never detain anyone without a trial, but most worrying was the conversation they'd overheard about the selling of memory loss tables to a non-magical person. Not only was it against Court rules, it was only for those in the coven to have access to the magical products unless otherwise under specific orders from the King by a royal written order, but it also clearly meant Michael and his friends were in danger and his story wasn't believed. A sickly feeling settled in his stomach, for if Michael's real identity were to be discovered, he could be in the utmost danger. Abednego saw no alternative but to tell them the truth about Michael's ancestry.

Bewildered, they heard how Mathis had been attacked in the alley and how Abednego acquired the ring that Michael now possessed. They were astounded to learn that Michael was heir to Kilion and that he could, if he wanted, claim the throne as his own. Speechless, Michael opened and closed his mouth like a goldfish, but nothing came out. Dan and Hazel stared at him incredulously, hardly able to comprehend this new added complication.

Once the news had been digested they discussed their options, for what felt like hours. Eventually they agreed that for the moment they should carry on pretending that Michael was Abednego's great nephew through his wife. No-one else, not Viola, Sophie, or Hargrin, were to be allowed to find out Michael's birthright. They would wait to see if anyone else would make the first move.

Finally Abednego left, and yet despite the lateness of the hour they couldn't sleep. Not only were they contemplating

Michael's new status, but more importantly, the very real dangers which now faced them.

Chapter Thirty: The Witch

It was past midnight when Regatta found herself standing beside the large, 'Tingle Tree' stump she remembered so fondly from her childhood. But that had been years ago when her family had spent days camping in the forest, enjoying Mother Nature's beauty. Since then King Melchior had been slain and Mazarin had, through his weakness, allowed creatures of the night to take up residence in this once stunning setting.

Tugging at the sole branch near the roots, and then straining to press the knot underneath for a full three seconds, she waited for the top of the stump to open. Clambering into the dark opening, she descended the ladder as she had done all those years ago, though not nearly as elegantly. As the wood reformed above her, obscuring this secret hideaway, a light automatically switched on, allowing Ragetta to familiarise herself with the unchanged surroundings.

The furniture was wooden, nicely crafted and very homely. Turning left, then right then left again, she trod carefully along underground passages until she encountered a large open space. There she was faced with different sized doors, each leading to their own secret destination. Standing amidst the five entrances, she prayed her memory was right and chose the middle door. Knocking twice, she waited with baited breath. Had she made the right decision in coming here?

Slowly, the door creaked open, revealing only darkness. "Come in."

She tip-toed over the mud encrusted floor and headed into the underground lounge where an old woman sat silently meditating.

Opening her blooedshot eyes, the old witch studied the woman before her carefully, assessing her windswept hair and the pain in her eyes. "Is it really you?"

"It is!... I can't believe you've been here all this time on your own. How have you been?"

"Not bad under the circumstances. As you can see I'm still alive, which is always a blessing. Yourself?" Her voice croaked.

"Not good, I've come here in the hope you can help me." Sitting beside the old woman, she studied the room, liking what had been done with it.

"Did anyone see you come in?"

"No-one. In fact, I've not come across a single person."

"You do realise that by coming here you've risked both our lives?"

"I know and for that I'm truly sorry, but I had no-one else to turn to."

"Sit down. You must be weary." As Ragetta sat on the proffered seat, the witch continued, "so, what's the problem then dear?"

"Grimbald. He's gone missing and I need an invisibility potion to find him."

"An invisibility potion! I can't make that, it's illegal."

"I know and I'd never dream of asking but I can't think of any other solution, I'm desperate."

The old woman stared at Ragetta, studying her face, reading her soul. "I'll do anything I can, within reason, to help you, but first of all sit down and tell me what's happened."

Reliving the last 36 hours in her mind, she began to fill the witch in. "It all started yesterday when Grimbald saw three youths wearing strange clothes. He was on his way home from work. One of them bore a strong resemblance to Prince Mathis."

"Go on."

"I think he thought the boy was related to Mathis, especially as he clearly wasn't from around here. He just wanted to make sure the boy was okay, that he and his friends weren't lost and they had somewhere to stay."

"Was the boy related?"

"I don't know. He left the house before dinner last night in the direction of the castle and I haven't seen him since. He hasn't come home or sent any word and I'm frantic with worry." Ragetta's breathing became erratic as panic once more engulfed her.

"Calm down, take some deep breaths."

"I can't bear it; he left the castle under such bad circumstances; what if he were caught trying to find the boy? What if they've tortured or imprisoned him for information?" I was awake all last night waiting for him, but today I had to act. I couldn't just stay at home and wait. I have to know he's alright, and I couldn't think of anyone else who could help me."

"And once you've got the potion?"

"I'll gain access to the castle and search for him."

"You realise that the penalty for using unauthorised magic outside the castle grounds is death? And they'll know you couldn't have cast the spell yourself. They'll work out you've seen me, extract my whereabouts from you, using force if necessary, then hunt me down. I'd have to leave everything I've worked for and I don't think I can take it again. Last time I was on the run for over a year; my life was constantly in danger. Do you realise how awful it is? Not knowing whether each day will be your last.

"I'm sorry. You're right. It was wrong of me to ask! I could never put you through that!" Cradling her head in her hands, Ragetta felt ashamed. "What should I do? I can't just do nothing, not while my husband's probably languishing in prison." Clasping her hands tightly, Ragetta felt forlorn and empty, as though all hope had dissipated.

"Keep focused and remember that whatever his faults, Mazarin is a kind man. In all his time as King, no-one has ever been put to death, and people have committed worse crimes than Grimbald could have done." Placing her arm around Ragetta's shoulder, the old witch puller her close.

"So we can't use any magic?" Ragetta sobbed, exhausted from her sleepless night and dangerous journey. Finding it all too much, she began to sob.

Uncomfortable at watching such raw emotion after years of isolation, the old woman croaked, "It's gone midnight. I imagine you're starving. I'll put something on which will make you feel better, and then I'll make up the bed in the spare room so you can get some decent sleep. Tomorrow morning, when our heads are clearer and you're refreshed, we'll think of a way to save that husband of yours without endangering our own lives."

Ragetta nodded gratefully and lay her head on the arm of the chair, gazing at the underground hideout which had provided her with so many memories.

Adding fuel to the fire to renew its zest for life, the witch then placed some meat in a pan and adjusted it so it sat nicely above the dancing flames. Once accomplished, she stood in the kitchen doorway and watched Ragetta appraise her surroundings.

With the meat cooked, the witch poured a glass of water and took the refreshments through. Unexpectedly, feeling compelled to do something she hadn't done in years; the old witch produced her dusty, glass ball. Perhaps she could put Ragetta's mind at rest before bed by finding out for certain that Grimbald was alright.

Settling herself beside Ragetta, the old woman wiped the dust from her ball, and then placed it in a delicate crystal holder modelled in the shape of a hand. There it sat; resting in the palm while strategically bent fingers guaranteed its safety in their firm clasp.

"I can try to find out where Grimbald is, if you'd like? It's never let me down in the past but I must warn you, I haven't done it in years."

"I just want to know he's alive and safe."

Closing her eyes, the wrinkled face concentrated. Slowly rocking backwards and forwards, she rested her fingertips on the ball. Within seconds, the ball clouded up, different colour mists swirling and dancing in crazed confusion.

A satisfied smile spread across the old face as she leaned back and the swirling mists evaporated, leaving a once more translucent ball. "You needn't fear, he's alive. He's in a dark place at the moment but he's safe, as is the boy. Both are at the castle. I'm not quite sure how, but they'll escape without our help. You will see him again, and I have a feeling it won't be long."

"You're not just saying that to stop me going, are you?" Ragetta eyed her suspiciously, wondering how all that had been deduced from coloured smoke.

"You know I wouldn't do that! Strangely, I also got the impression, although I could be wrong, that you're right about the boy, for I sensed something of Prince Mathis, but as he is dead, it must have been the boy I felt. There's a definite connection."

"Should I go back to our house and wait for him?"

"No. You won't be safe. If they think Grimbald knows, it's obvious that you would also be suspect. They might be looking for you even as we speak and the first place they'll look is your house." Stay here and we'll work out what to do tomorrow."

"Thanks mum."

"Did you honestly think I'd turn my own daughter away in her time of need? You know I would have told you where I was before, but I couldn't put your life in danger. Not only would my life be forfeit, but so too would the life of anyone found contacting me. I couldn't live with myself if that happened."

Emotionally drained, silent tears fell of both sorrow and joy. "I've missed you so much." Hugging her mother tight, Ragetta gave silent thanks that she had made the right choice in risking this trip. She could always remember her mum knowing what to do for the best, and now she was older she was glad she could still count on her.

***

"Good morning." From the shadows under Abednego's eyes, they assumed he'd slept as little as they had. "Sleep well?"

"Not really, although the fact we remember what happened yesterday is something!" Pausing, Michael took a breath before continuing, "Can I just clarify… I didn't just imagine I'm King, did I? Only I can't get my head around it."

"I can't believe I'm been best friends with a real life King!" squealed an excited Hazel.

"Ssssshhhh….." Abednego commanded, "If we're overheard, the consequences could be dire. Remember what we discussed last night; nobody must know anything until we've planned what to do. For your own safety, nothing I've said can be repeated until we know you're out of danger." Abednego's caution silenced them.

Going over the tale they had concocted on their backgrounds, they made certain there were no discrepancies which could arouse suspicion. Abednego recited his family tree so they knew the different relationships and the fates of those who had died, leading to Michael's supposed orphanage. "Keep lies to a minimum, though it's unlikely you'll be asked much if they're trying to take your memories. I've told the King and others that you've recently suffered a loss and asked that no-one speak of your past. So hopefully, we'll be okay on that front, at least."

"But it's not much of a lie, is it?" Commented Michael, "for you really are my great Uncle, aren't you?"

"Yes." The wrinkled face smiled for the first time that morning, "and as such, it makes me responsible for your safety."

"Thanks."

"Despite the circumstances, I'm glad you're here." Abednego was determined to make spending time with Michael a priority; he needed to make up for lost time.

Unable to resist the urge, Michael threw his arms around the old man in a hug so heartfelt Hazel thought she was going to cry.

"This may seem a stupid question, but why did you help the ring bring me here with all this danger about?" His pale blue eyes watched Abednego intently. He didn't mean to seem accusing, but he needed an answer.

It took a while for Abednego to gather his thoughts, then he said, "I can see that my decision to bring you here could appear rash, even dangerous. Yet I promise you that when I first gave the ring to your friends, I had no idea of the dangers you would face." Looking his great-nephew in the eye, his voice apologetic, he continued, "hand on heart, I didn't think anyone would suspect a connection between you and Mathis. I thought by bringing you here at fifteen, as my relation, I could at least get to know you and see you grow to adulthood. I hoped that by coming to Court, you could get to know and love the people and country. I wrongly assumed that by the time I revealed your true identity; everyone would love you and accept you as King. I had no idea there would be so much intrigue and that your presence would cause so much curiosity! Perhaps I should have given the matter deeper consideration, but I was convinced you had a right to know your inheritance and be able to understand your history; to know who your father was and why he was so cruelly taken from us at such a young age."

Michael nodded silently. "Do you think they want to kill me?"

"I don't know," Abednego replied, wishing his response could have been more positive. "Honestly, I think their main concern is whether you possess the ring for which they've been searching for years."

"They want its power?" Hazel enquired. "But what about the magic already in the castle? The witch's coven? Can't the King use their magic?"

"Good thinking young lady." Abednego threw a smile in her direction. "But the ring is more powerful than any witch or warlock. The powers you've witnessed are only the tip of the iceberg. You see, it's more than just a magic ring; it's a Key."

"A key to what?" an excited Michael asked.

Abednego inhaled deeply before explaining, "The owner of the ring can defend themselves against others; unlock secret passageways and gain some semblance of control over their surroundings, but more than that, with the password it opens the Gateway to Dragon Falls. There you can access healing waters which can cure any disease, illness or injury. As you may imagine, it makes the ring a very valuable object."

"So not only am I really a King, but I own a ring which can cure illness? This is why they want it, isn't it? So they can live forever?" Michael stammered, barely believing what he was hearing.

"Exactly. Imagine the power the wearer of the ring could have! Now, there's something else you need to know. There are, in fact, two rings. Mathis had one, which you now possess. The other was held by King Melchior, your dad's elder brother who was killed in battle just weeks before your father. It was for Melchior's ring and crown that his cousin, Azarel, attacked Kilion. At the end of the last, treacherous battle, when many of Melchior's supporters abandoned him in search of greater power, he was cruelly slain. His mutilated body was searched but no ring was found. Since then its whereabouts has been a mystery. Most believe he predicted his defeat, and so before the battle he arranged for it to be hidden in order that no-one could use its powers for evil."

"It's like something out of a fairy tale!" Hazel exclaimed. "But if Melchior died, why is Mazarin and not Azarel King?"

"That's even stranger than the disappearing ring! At the same battle, despite leading his side to victory, Azarel disappeared. His body wasn't found among the dead, yet no-one has seen him since, and no further claim to the throne has he ever made."

"How odd," mused Michael.

"Isn't it?" Responded Abednego. "Some think he's still alive but I have my doubts. If he is, why hasn't he tried to take the throne? He was so determined before he caused Civil War. Why would he just give it up when Melchior died?"

"Why didn't my dad become King?" Michael asked expectantly.

"He left Kilion to escape the responsibilities of Kingship. He wanted an ordinary life, a wife and children and to live in peace without interference. When he left he renounced his claim to the throne, which is why it passed to their cousin Mazarin."

"Can you tell me anything else about my dad?"

"Just like his brother, when he turned 15, he was given a ring just as powerful as Melchior's. He was a smart lad and inspired loyalty, yet he hated the politics of Court and the fighting for control. So, one day, out of the blue, he announced he was leaving and taking the ring with him."

"But how come you had it?" asked Michael.

"I was there the night your dad was attacked. I watched helplessly as he was beaten. I couldn't hear what the attacker said that night but your father must have thought he wanted the ring, for as they struggled in the rain, he managed to take it off and let it slip unnoticed into a puddle. Once his body had been dragged away, I scoured the puddles until I found it. It was the only thing I could do to try to put things right."

Michael's eyes glistened with tears as he listened.

"Ever since I've kept the ring, hoping to find you and pass on your rightful inheritance. Now I've fulfilled that, I must beg you to use its powers wisely, for it gives you ascendancy over others and powers even the King craves."

"But if it's my ring they want, how will making me lose my memory benefit them?"

"Perhaps they think that without your memory, you won't remember why you have the ring or how powerful it is, if you have it. Maybe they think it will make it easier to win your trust, get you to tell them what you know."

"Do you think they know I've got it?" His hands were shaking with nerves as he considered the power he held and the consequences of that for him and his friends.

Recalling his conversation with Raglin and the King, Abednego was certain it was no more than a hunch. "No, I think they hope you know where it is, nothing more."

"So all we need to do is not mention Mathis or the ring?" Dan suggested.

"That might be enough to persuade them that their suspicions are unfounded. Look, we'd better get going before breakfast is over," Abednego said, eager to end the discussion which was starting to upset him.

The three teenagers sat silently, readying themselves for the task and day ahead. They were scared, and worried for their own self-preservation.

Sensing their fear, but unable to help, Abednego instead considered the rest of his day. He was exhausted, worried and he knew he had to face the King despite lying to him and he hated that idea, and yet even more worrying were the startled expressions on their faces. As creases of worry formed round their young eyes, he wondered if he had burdened them with too much information too soon.

Heading for the door, he straightened his clothes, and then indicated for them to follow. "You've a busy day with the coach ride and meeting with Sophie. Perhaps we should leave catching up until later. I'll come to collect you a little earlier than normal tonight so we can plan this evening, share further news and decide on a course of action."

"Do we have to go on the tour with Hargrin today?" Dan asked, sure he wouldn't be able to conceal his dislike and suspicions of the Minister.

"Unfortunately yes. I think it would arouse too much suspicion if you were to pull out now with no reasonable excuse. We must act as normal as possible."

"We can use it as an opportunity to learn more of the castle and grounds than we did yesterday," suggested Michael who was eager to see Viola again.

"And, we've nothing other than your instincts linking Hargrin to the plot, and certainly in England the law clearly states a person is innocent until proven guilty," an unusually stern Hazel retorted.

"Just because you think he's good looking," Dan mumbled under his breath. "I just think it's odd how he's showing such an interest in us, that's all."

"Let's not argue about it," Michael interjected. "We'll keep the conversation light hearted and ask questions which could help us later."

Chapter Thirty-one: Regrets

It had been two days since Mary had last seen her Daniel, and the police were no nearer to discovering his whereabouts. She had called all the numbers in her employer's phone book, scoured bookcases, and even the shelves in their study, but she had found nothing; she felt alone and helpless.

Her sleep was disturbed by nightmares and her days fraught with worry. If anything happened to Dan she didn't think she could live with herself.

***

Since that dreadful phone call, Samuel had refused to leave the house, even to go to work, just in case she came home and he wasn't there to hear the news. Guilt wracked him as he acknowledged how bad he had been as a parent since her mother's death. He had loved her mother so tenderly and for so long, so that when she had died, it had ripped his heart apart. The thought of living without Lily who had been his rock, filled him with dread. For weeks he had locked himself in his room, inconsolable, and refusing to communicate with anyone. Even Hazel had been unable to crack the barriers he'd built.

After a couple of months, when Hazel must have thought she had lost her dad as well as her mum, his mother-in-law Rose, suggested Hazel move in with her for a while. Aware only of his own grief, Samuel had agreed, thinking it best for all concerned. Rose would nurture

Hazel; provide the love, support and security she needed, that he was unable to give. With his head all over the place and his heart empty, he'd accepted her solution and allowed a physical as well as emotional barrier to develop between him and his only daughter.

In the following weeks, self-pity had been his constant companion. Making only a token weekly call to Hazel and allowing her to visit just a few times, he allowed their previous closeness to fade to nothing.

Pressurised, after a few months he returned to work. They threatened action if he didn't return soon, and with bills to pay, he saw no alternative. There he found solace in his desk and discovered that at work, his mind was no longer focused on the isolation he felt. His days at work grew longer as he used it to eradicate his pain.

Then like a bolt from the blue he'd met her, and within weeks she began to make life bearable. Around her his heart felt lighter and he felt he could once more, face reality. Deep down, he knew people would say it was too soon, and perhaps they were right, but she brought a smile to his face and took his mind off his problems. Her boundless energy and love of life infected him, weaving through his veins, infiltrating every part of him and like antibiotics, her vitality gradually gave him strength, and replaced his grief with hope. She listened to him, consoled him and told funny anecdotes. She made him go out to places; encouraged him to do things he'd never done and experience a life he'd never known. She intoxicated him like an alcoholic drink and he had become addicted to the feeling she created. He knew it was wrong, knew how much it was upsetting his daughter and how it must have looked to his mother-in-law, but he was addicted to her.

Less than a year after Lily's death he proposed. She immediately accepted. Their wedding was arranged within a matter of a few weeks, a small intimate affair which Hazel and Rose had both grudgingly attended.

Civility on the surface, with burning tensions underneath, he now realised he could have waited, consulted Hazel first before plunging into his second marriage. Maybe if he had considered Hazel's feelings, her relationship with Diane would have been better. Not surprisingly, Hazel considered her an intruder. He couldn't blame her for feeling as she did, and upon reflection, realised he hated the man he had become; a man so absorbed in his own happiness and life that he had forgotten about the person who should have been the centre of his world.

Head in his hands, he once more felt the acute pain that had encased him when Lily passed away, this time caused by the loss of his daughter. Hazel was gone and he didn't even know if he would ever see her again. He wanted to tell her he was sorry for his neglect when she had needed him most. He would apologise for not being there for her when her mother had died. He would clutch her so tightly and tell her she was more important than everyone else, and that no one could take her place in his heart. Regret stabbed at his heart like a sharp blade. He didn't know if he could cope with the loss of his daughter as well as his wife.

Once more he became a recluse, only talking to Rose to find out what progress, if any, had been made. He cut off

Diane, resenting that she had never really known Hazel and couldn't understand his sorrow. She had tried comforting him as she had before, but this time faced rejection instead of gratitude. He couldn't help treating Diane the same way he had treated Hazel when he had lost her mother. Perhaps subconsciously he blamed her for his estrangement from a daughter most people would have been grateful for. If she returned, he promised he would try again, try to win back the love, respect and friendship they had shared for most of their lives.

Chapter Thirty-two: The Carriage Ride

As soon as Hargrin saw Michael, Daniel and Hazel, he stopped conversing with Viola. Approaching them, he threw them a Cheshire cat grin and indicated for them to begin their journey.

As they strolled along, Dan hadn't even been in Hargrin's presence five minutes and already he felt antagonised by the Ministers cocky walk and cheesy smile which had taken up permanent residence on his face.

Heading towards the castle stables, they stopped as the large gates revealed at least a dozen carriages and even more horses. Each dripped in jewels which glittered under the suns warm rays.

The vehicle Hargrin walked towards was breath-taking. As they alighted he offered Hazel assistance and winked conspiratorially at her, leaving her flustered. As a result, her usually graceful movements became ungainly as she clambered inside, followed by a much more elegant Viola. Stroking the ruby red velvet seat, Viola plumped herself opposite Hazel and indicated for Michael to sit beside her.

Determined to disengage himself from Hargrin, who continued to prattle on, Dan showed no sign of the agility he had acquired in the many sports he took part in, dragging himself up and flopping down next to Hazel.

Lastly Hargrin hauled himself into the driver's seat with such ease it made Dan feel sick. Patting the flaxen horses, he grabbed their reigns and guided them expertly; his pressure so slight, their actions so smooth, Dan felt his fist clench and imagined it connecting with the Ministers jaw.

Typical, thought Dan sardonically, even animals were putty in his hands.

As the carriage trundled further from the castle, the shrubbery, flowers and trees increased in density. They travelled to the west of the castle, and where before there had been acres of soft grass, now nature showed off her full range of merchandise; leaves rustled and ripe fruit hung from branches, ready for picking. While remnants of blossom clung to the trees, the majority carpeted the grass creating a harmony of pastel colours.

When the path ended, the carriage continued gliding through the orchard. "It's stunning!" Hazel exclaimed.

Hargrin agreed, determined to prove himself agreeable, particularly to the girl who he felt was more headstrong than the boys, and so more likely to get her way.

"So romantic," sighed Viola who, despite her cold hearted nature, felt oddly warm inside.

Soon the castle was obscured from view. The trees thinned out as they approached a moat protected by a thick, stone wall which was designed to keep intruders out and people in, thought a wary Dan. Riding over the bridge, they came to a barred gate. The West Entrance was guarded by two armoured men; Hargrin nodded and they unbolted the lock. As the gates creaked behind him, Dan glanced at Hazel and Michael, a worried expression clouding his face as he wondered where they were being taken. Afraid to voice his concerns, he stared ahead and prayed silently.

As though he had delved into Dan's thoughts, Hargrin halted the vehicle and then turned to face his companions. "The castle grounds are amazing don't you think?"

Dan nodded mutely.

"Mazarin asked me to show you the locality to help you understand a little of Kilion's culture. So, I shall fill you in on some of our history, and then allow you some time to explore outside the castle. I presume that's okay with you?"

Hoping it might provide an opportunity to discover an escape route, Dan decided it wasn't such a bad idea. What harm could it do? For the first time that morning, Dan's lip quivered into what could only be considered as the beginnings of a smile.

It wasn't much, but Hargrin hoped it was the first sign of a breakthrough and turned his attention once more to guiding the horses. "Promise I'll get you back for lunch," he added to allay any doubts they might still have.

"It's a wonderful idea!" Hazel exclaimed, vaguely remembering their encounter with the man and the boy in village. Now that their memories were beginning to return, she was curious about life outside of Court.

Down the hill the carriage trundled, heading towards another village.

Inside a couple of the quaint houses, Hazel noticed some busy inhabitants scuttling around, while others sat on stools relaxing away from the sun's glare. Small children played in front gardens, many little older than toddlers. Many stopped and stared at the magnificent carriage as it passed, rarely glimpsing such luxury. Hargrin, ever the crowd pleaser, waved at the children who beamed back at him, raising their tiny hands in salutes, clearly awestruck at such a rare occasion. That they seemed so startled made Michael wonder how often anyone came from the castle, least of all the King, and showed their faces to citizens of the locality. If and when I'm King, Michael thought to himself, I'll make sure I'm not a stranger to my people.

Passing out of the village, and riding further into the distance, they watched the fast, flowing stream jump over small rocks, splashing white foam onto its banks. The trees on the other side were skeletal, causing Hazel a sensation of unease. "Why don't the trees over the other side of the stream have leaves despite being so close to water?"

"Good question," Hargrin replied, impressed with her inquisitiveness. "Hundreds of years ago a magical creature, Zindegrot, dwelt in the mountains you see in the distance. He refused to acknowledge anyone else as King, despite having no real claim himself. To bolster his control he surrounded himself with magical and mystical creatures, all intent on acquiring power and sating their greed. For decades he and his creatures would venture from the confines of the mountain for prey, and every so often a citizen of Kilion would go missing. Everyone knew what was happening, Knights went to the mountains to avenge the deaths but none returned. For years this continued, with citizens from Kilion, and particularly this village of Armonia, fearing for their lives." Halting the carriage once more, Hargin revelled in the attention from his enraptured audience, who hung on to his every word.

"And..." Michael encouraged, eager to find out more of the history of the country which might well be his one day.

"And," Hargrin continued, "this continued until just over two centuries ago. When King Josiah died without an heir, Kilion degenerated into chaos and civil war threatened to destroy the land. That was until a single leader emerged triumphant. Through his superior battle skills, integrity and leadership qualities, Marshall gained control of the crown and restored peace. Once harmony had been restored, he set his sights on stopping Zindegrot. He made the area of Armonia the new capital of Kilion, changed its name to Marshaland and built the castle to protect them. These actions showed Kilonians how much he cared for them and cemented their loyalty to him." Glancing up at the mountains in the distance, Hargrin's face, cleared of his slimy grin, became serene and thoughtful. "Many consider Marshall the most honourable and skilled King ever to rule Kilion."

"What did he do?" Hazel urged, not clear on how all this related to the trees having no leaves.

"Rather than send more knights to their end, he threw down his gauntlet and insisted on a duel to the death with Zindegrot, implying that if he failed to take up this request, he would reveal his weakness and incompetence to all in the realm. Zindegrot, anxious to prove his skills, greeted the offer enthusiastically and so the date was set and conditions drawn up. No-one but the two of them were to attend. Marshall demanded that if he were to win, Zindegrot was to promise never to invade Kilion or take any of its inhabitants again. If Zindegrot were to win, Marshall would provide one sacrifice per week from his country as a gift for the rest of his lifetime."

Hazel held her breath, so engrossed in the tale that anxiety for the safety of the inhabitants and Marshal cascaded through her. "What happened?"

"On the date set, Marshall, clad in armour, mounted his stallion with a satchel over his shoulder and rode off to meet Zindegrot at the allocated time. Chronicles by villagers at the time speak of the panic in the village, with many packing to leave, fearful that if he lost, they would be forced to be human sacrifices."

"I'm not sure I'd have been too happy with his promise," muttered Dan.

"For hours no-one heard anything. The village remained silent as its inhabitants contemplated their future if their new King were to lose. You must remember of course, that not one person, not even their greatest Knights, had ever returned from the mountains. As far as the people were concerned, they had lost their King."

"Go on," Viola urged, anxious to hear the conclusion, knowing full well Hargrin was stringing it out for dramatic effect.

"Hours passed and twilight was upon them when his stallion was seen riding out of the forest, over the stream and in the direction of the village."

"He won!" exclaimed an exuberant Hazel.

"He did!" Hargrin confirmed.

"How?" Dan asked, amazed at such a feat.

"He never revealed what happened," Hargrin answered, "but he arrived back exhausted. It was written that his eyes were full of sorrow and that he was so tired he fell off his horse so that one of the villagers had to take him to their house. There he fell into a fever, muttering in his sleep, sweat dripping down his face. Many thought he might die, and for a few days, it seemed they would be proved right."

"But he lived?" asked a mortified Hazel who didn't want to imagine the gallant, handsome King, or at least that's how she pictured him, dying after risking his life for his countrymen.

"After a few days, during which he was tended by the wise women of the village, the fever broke and he regained his strength. When asked by the locals what had happened, he refused to talk. A week later, he had it proclaimed in every town and village that he had been victorious and the terms of the treaty were published. No forest creatures were to forage for human food in Kilion. They were confined to the mountains and were only allowed to hunt their prey in the caves and forest. To ensure the terms were adhered to, the stream surrounding the mountains and forest were saturated with a chemical, poisonous to all but pure humans. That way we could, if we wished, cross over the stream into the forest, but any creature not of human descent would perish if they stepped past the demarcation line drawn at the lake."

"And the trees?" asked Hazel.

"They take in the water with the poisons and while it is not strong enough to destroy the work of Mother Nature, the water is contaminated enough to ensure they remain so weak they have no resources left to produce leaves or fruit. Lastly, to ensure their continued goodwill, because some of the creatures like the vampires and valkyrites can fly, Marshall gained possession of two rings which have significant powers and can help protect Kilion in times of need.

Michael gulped, trying hard to act normal. He dared not ask any more questions for fear of seeming suspect.

Hargrin paused to assess their reactions and was surprised and slightly perturbed to detect no reaction at all, not even a question. This was not a good sign for Raglin had clearly implied he thought Michael had one of the rings.

"Apparently the rings possess magical powers, they can change the weather, control peoples actions, that kind of thing…" Still no reaction. "And if used with the password can access healing waters." Nothing.

"Does Mazarin have them both then?" Hazel asked, attempting to ask what she considered a reasonable question.

"Nobody knows who has them or knows where they are. It was thought that old King Melchior had one, but it was never found. Some think the other ring was given to Mathis, his younger brother but again, if it was, it's been lost."

"What a shame!" Mused Dan, trying not to smirk.

"Indeed!" retorted Hargrin, annoyed at having discovered nothing.

"Why?" asked Viola, "do you need to heal yourself then?"

Hargrin chuckled in a bid to lighten the conversation. "Not at all, but whoever is descended from Zindegrot must be wondering whether they are lost, and if they are, they will know that we only have limited means to defend ourselves. Since Melchior's death, the forest creatures have been steadily gaining confidence, moving from the mountains and gradually pushing nearer and nearer towards the stream."

Dan, Michael and Hazel gasped, shocked at the implication of the disappearance of the rings.

"It is said that it's only a matter of time before they are confident enough to take the final step and cross the barrier. They must be questioning whey their movements haven't been curtailed. Once they discover we have nothing other than the water protecting us, who knows what they'll do to the village," Hargrin whispered; his voice full of foreboding. It had the desired effect for a shiver wove its way down Hazel's spine making the hairs on the back of her neck prickle.

"Have they not looked for them?" Michael asked innocently.

"Sure they have," Hargrin answered, "but it's been in vain. It seems they are lost to time and space, which could ultimately mean the people of Kilion, and especially Marshalland, will be lost to the desires of those in the mountains.

"Could they have the rings?" Hazel enquired.

Hargrin contemplated Hazel, Michael and Dan thoughtfully. "Not a chance. They would have acted by now if they did. Some also believe, though no proof has ever been forthcoming, that there was a third ring held by those in the forest. If all three rings were to come together, whoever possesses them will have control over life and death, of hearts, minds and souls. If this were to happen, both good and evil would rise up against the wearer to prevent this ultimate power. All three rings can unlock the source of all knowledge and use it to overthrow their creators, both good and bad. If a creature as inherently evil as Zindegrot had united them, a battle so mighty, involving all the forces of nature would have already ensued. This must be prevented, for unless good prevails, life as we know it will end."

Terrified, Michael's face paled as he felt the ring on his finger, hidden in his pocket.

Hoping he had dispensed enough fear into them, Hargrin swiftly changed the conversation back to a more cheerful subject. "Perhaps we should take a break here and rest a while."

They nodded silently to indicate their agreement.

"Before we eat, I must request you tell no-one the story. It would only create unnecessary fear. People would panic if they thought their lives in danger."

Again they nodded.

"After all, it could all be conjecture, it might take decades for them to realise we have no rings, if ever."

"Of course," muttered Viola.

"That's one reason we've never held a formal search. If their disappearance were common knowledge, not only would it create fear, but everyone would be searching for them, and who knows into whose hands they might fall?"

With their promises procured and the seed sown, Hargrin manoeuvred the carriage and headed to a smaller stream for them to dismount. So he had manipulated the truth slightly, but it had been a necessary evil to make them fear ownership of the ring. He hoped the story had scared Michael sufficiently to divulge, sooner rather than later, the whereabouts of the ring knowing it could help save the Kingdom, and who else would he turn to but the person who had befriended him and told him of the tale in the first place?

Steadying the horses, Hargrin dismounted gracefully before holding out his hand to assist the others. "I've brought snacks if you're hungry."

After tethering the horses, he produced a wicker hamper from the seat next to his. Laying a huge blanket on the ground, he indicated for them to sit then unpacked the hamper and arranged the contents before them; cups, plates, eating utensils and finally, cakes and a bottled drink.

Michael's mouth watered as he dived in, while Dan, as always, was reticent about eating or drinking anything. However, as Hargrin and Viola devoured the food, he decided it was clearly safe enough to eat and was soon enjoying the delicacies before him.

After demolishing the lot, despite having eaten breakfast not two hours earlier, they relaxed back, all thoughts of rings and monsters having evaporated. Content, they chatted, basking in the sun, listening to the birds chirping and the ripples of the stream. It seemed like heaven.

"So how are you enjoying Court life?" Hargrin enquired.

Worried that Daniel might antagonise the situation, Hazel was quick to respond. "We're having a great time, everyone's being so kind." She saw Dan struggle to hold his tongue but he managed it. There was nothing wrong with letting Hargrin assume they were at ease and suspected nothing.

"Michael, how you finding it in Kilion?" continued Hargrin, his voice nonchalant.

Michael hesitated, choosing his words carefully. "It's an amazing place and everyone is really friendly." His voice was calm, betraying none of his anxieties.

"I suspect," Hargrin continued, "that you're enjoying spending time with your great Uncle Abednego?"

Michael felt Dan tense beside him but he carried on normally. "I am indeed. He's been so kind and attentive. He's really made us feel comfortable despite being so busy. I'm not spending as much time with him as I had hoped but fortunately I came with Hazel and Dan so I haven't been bored."

Beside him Dan exhaled deeply, suitably satisfied with Michael's response and hoping it would quell Hargrin's obvious suspicions.

"It can't be easy for him, what with his age. It's amazing that he still carries out so many duties and responsibilities so well!" Hargrin mused.

Michael remained silent, not sure how to respond for he wasn't certain what point Hargrin was trying to make.

Eager to press the point Hargrin continued. "He's quite a few years older than my father who's already started losing some of his faculties. His mind wanders a little, you know, and it's really rather hard to talk to him. Seeing him like that upsets me, especially when I remember the youth and vitality he once possessed." Shifting his gaze, he focused his attention on the stream.

"Fortunately Abednego has all his senses intact," Dan retorted slightly more sharply than he had intended.

Detecting the animosity in Dan's tone, Hargrin was once more reminded of how hostile Dan was and reminded himself he would have to tread carefully. The last thing he wanted to do was negate the inroads he was making with the other two. "I completely agree. Abednego's an amazing man who, as you say, is in complete control of all of his senses; I didn't intend to imply otherwise. I was simply stating how lucky Michael is to spend such quality time with him. Sometimes I wish I had the same with my dad, more and more I'm regretting how much I took his company for granted when I was younger." As he thought of his father's failing health, a feeling of sadness enveloped him, for his dad had been the one person he had always respected. "Michael, make the most of Abednego, make the most of everyone, for we never know when we'll no longer be able to." Hargrin's voice was low and croaky, as though he was trying to suppress his emotions.

Sensing his honesty, Dan felt a twang of guilt. "Sorry for sounding so sharp... and about your dad," he mumbled, in way of an apology.

The next hour was spent pleasantly; they finished off the cream cakes as Hargrin regaled them with tales of King Melchior and all the changes he had brought to Kilion. He talked about his deeds in battle, his skill as a commander and his greatness as King. They learned of the battles during the last couple of years of his reign, and how he had been slain through treachery. Despite having heard some of it before, Michael, Dan and Hazel, in accordance with their discussions with Abednego, acted ignorant as they listened. Even Viola was enthralled, lapping up the information just as enthusiastically as Michael, finding the whole story fascinating. And so, they learned a lot more new information about their new home.

Still trying to gauge the true nature of Michael's relationship with Abednego and Mathis, Hargrin went on to describe Mathis in his youth, and was pleased to notice that Michael seemed particularly interested. As he waffled on, dredging up anything he could remember, the one question he couldn't get out of his mind was whether Michael really was Mathis' son, and the rightful King of Kilion. It was a hard one to call, for Raglin had told him how, at the meeting with Abednego and the King, the old man had insisted Michael was his great nephew on his wife's side. Hargrin wasn't sure whether he believed the old man, but he was not about to question Michael's background now, especially knowing that whatever the answer was, with his memory wiped, Michael wouldn't be able to tell him anyway.

Determined to win their trust, he moved onto King Mazarin's reign and life under him. Every so often, Viola added her own a snippet of information, each time looking at Michael to make sure he acknowledged it. She told them of the pixies and their penchant for biting peoples ankles. She mentioned the fairies that lived in the outskirts of the woods and surrounding areas, but had been seen less frequently in recent times. They heard how fairies could grant one wish to anyone who caught them, but that it had been so long since one had been caught, or even seen, many were uncertain as to whether they were extinct.

It wasn't long before the sun was in the centre of the sky, bringing with it midday heat and beads of sweat which dripped down their faces. Realising the time, Hargrin informed them it was time to return as he didn't want to be late for Mass. He knew if he were to succeed with his plan, it was imperative God was on his side.

Collecting up the empty utensils, he shoved them and the blanket into the hamper and perched it on the front passenger seat. Once more helping them into the carriage, he untied the horse's reigns, stroked them gently then climbed into the driver's seat.

Very little was said on the return journey, they were each contemplating what they had learned. Michael and Hazel were both wondering whether they had been wrong to suspect Hargrin who was not only attempting to make them feel at ease, but had done nothing to incur their suspicion throughout the trip. Even Viola had acted at ease and given them little cause to suspect her. Perhaps they were focusing on the wrong people, what if they were just being nice? Whatever the case, they remained determined to let nothing slip to anyone other than Abednego.

As the carriage entered the royal stable, the four teenagers clambered from their seats and took their leave. Michael, Dan and Hazel walked Viola back to her rooms, leaving Hargrin to deal with the horses and carriage.

Upon reaching Violas room, they waited as she knocked. Sophie opened the door, stepping back to allow her sister entry. Feet hurting from wearing such high heels, Viola waved goodbye before limping to the bathroom to look at her toes.

At the doorway, Sophie inclined her head in the direction of the library to indicate that they should still meet her there, at one o clock, just twenty minutes later. By this time most people would be heading to Mass in the chapel so the castle and especially the library should be empty, allowing secrets to be shared.

Chapter Thirty-three: The Library

Sophie was already in the library waiting, her knees twitching in agitation as she chewed on her fingernails, glancing from side to side to make sure no one was watching.

"Quick, come inside," Sophie whispered. She led them to the back of the huge library. Row upon row of bookcases protruded from the walls, creating countless aisles, each providing the necessary privacy. Walking the length of the library, Hazel scanned some of the thousands of books, reading their titles. There were sections on History, Geography and even transport, but she couldn't see anything on magic or strange creatures, not like she had seen on their first night.

At the back they found a small round table in the corner, accompanied by four blue cushioned chairs. Each took a seat then huddled forwards to obscure their faces from view in the unlikely event that someone else had decided to use the library during the weekly service.

Avoiding their gazes, Sophie took a deep breath and twiddled her fingers. Her honey blonde hair, Dan noticed, was tinged with light ginger highlights which, when caught in the light, looked rather pretty. Her pale green eyes, almost cat like, had a quality of kindness that made him feel at ease. They also seemed to sparkle when she smiled. Feeling a gentle nudge on his elbow from Hazel, he realised he'd been staring and blushed, tearing his eyes away. Yet his thoughts remained on her for she seemed much nicer than her elder sister, her features were softer and her demeanour was gentle. Not that looks alone would win him over, he was far too sensible for that. But the worried expression her smile couldn't hide, and the way she twiddled her fingers showed how nervous she was, and it was really rather endearing.

"I.. I'm n... not quite s... sure how to s... say this, or whether I should even be s... saying it at all," she stammered, her eyes downcast.

"It's okay," Hazel said. Resting her hand on Sophie's arm comfortingly, her sparkling blue eyes showed concern for the younger girl's plight.

Buoyed by this show of empathy, Sophie returned her smile, dimples embedding themselves in her cheeks as her face brightened. "If I tell you what I overheard, please promise my sister won't get in trouble?" Her thoughts flitted to Viola who, despite being greedy and vain, had recently shown signs that beneath her tough exterior, she could be kind. She remembered how quickly Viola had taken her under her wing, invited her on the tour and lent her nice dresses. She had even baulked at the task of slipping tablets into their drinks.

Michael inhaled sharply for the implication was clear. Somehow, Viola was involved in the plot. Despite being upset, he remained silent, feeling foolish; although he hadn't fallen for her, he had enjoyed her attention and had convinced himself she had been interested in him. He'd defended her motives for befriending them and stuck up for her when her intentions had been questioned. Why had he been so stupid?

Hazel wanted to comfort Michael, but that would only confirm that she was thinking the same, which would make him feel worse. Dan, as always, was deep in thought while Michael prepared himself for the worst. Hazel alone answered. "Tell us what you know and we'll promise to do everything we can to keep Viola out of trouble."

Clearing her throat, she related what she had heard as simply as possible. She started with Hargrin's visit to her mother, recounting how he had charmed her into promising Viola would befriend Michael, Dan and Hazel. Noticing Michael's grimace, she quickly added he'd only suggested this after noticing the interest she had shown in Michael the previous evening.

This at least went some way to cheering him, for he visibly relaxed. Sophie's quick reactions to Michael's feelings and the way she had rushed to assuage his fears endeared her to Hazel who was beginning to think Sophie could be a real ally.

"The reason," she said, "Hargrin wanted Viola to befriend Michael, was so she could find out information about you and pass it straight back to him. Not surprisingly my mum agreed immediately, much to my shame." She paused as they heard footsteps outside. Each held their breath in anticipation, but fortunately the footsteps walked on by. "He also asked if Viola would slip tablets into your drinks during the feast. Again, it didn't take much persuading for my mother to agree... but only because he told her they were to help you relax and that King Mazarin had ordered it."

Michael spluttered, his mind wandering back to the previous evening when Viola had offered to get their drinks. Fortunately, they hadn't drunk them; yet the knowledge that she was actively involved in the conspiracy hurt him more than he expected. He felt miserable; the only female ever to have noticed him was doing so at the request of the King and Ministers.

"So... Hargrin's trying to drug us and he's using Viola to achieve this?" Dan questioned, pleased his suspicions of the smarmy Minister had been proven right.

"Didn't you say it was the King's orders?" queried Michael, unable to believe the King's complicity, but hoping it would at least make him feel better about Viola. He cast his mind back over the last two days; at the way Mazarin had befriended them, even inviting them to watch the match from his royal box. He had been so nice, why would he want them drugged?

"That's what he told her, but at the end of their meeting, he made a big deal about her mentioning nothing to the King. If you want my opinion, it all sounded a little too suspicious," Sophie concluded, glad that so much of the blame was falling onto the ambitions of the man her mother was trying to get her claws into. "Personally, I don't think the King knows anything about it. I think Hargrin's saying it to make sure my mum and Viola do as he asks!"

With every piece of information, the jigsaw started to fall into place. "So Viola genuinely thought she was following the King's command?" Michael asked, feeling much better about Viola's role, which seemed more helpful than conspiratorial.

"Yes," Sophie replied, "and what's more, when mum told Viola what was expected of her, she tried arguing against it, even refusing initially. It was only when our mother told her it was the King's wishes and for your benefit she eventually capitulated. After all, Hargrin's an important Minister, why would he not be following the King's orders? But I could tell when I next saw her, and she has no idea I overheard, that she didn't feel at ease with what she'd been asked to do; her expression was very troubled." Fidgeting in her seat, Sophie now fully comprehended the difficult position in which her sister had been placed. Dislike turned to pity as she hoped her sister would emerge from this unscathed.

Hazel placed her hands on Michael's arm. She said nothing but he knew what she meant and understood that neither Hazel nor Dan blamed Viola for what she had tried to do.

Watching Hazel comfort Michael, Dan felt a twinge of guilt at having questioned Viola's reasons for befriending him. Meanwhile Sophie watched sympathetically, unable to bring herself to tell him that the real reason for Viola's kindness was his supposed wealth and royal connections.

Although pleased that Viola had been an innocent accomplice, Hazel felt somewhat bemused by Hargrin's role. How could she have been taken in so easily? Never again would she be won over by a friendly smile. Michael and Dan were thinking exactly the same, though neither were as shocked by the revelation.

"Oh, and another thing," Sophie continued, "I'm not sure the tablets are relaxants, he placed so much emphasis on them, I get the impression they are far more sinister!"

This revelation didn't evoke the reaction Sophie had imagined and she wondered if they already knew something.

Glancing at Michael then Dan, Hazel wondered whether they should tell Sophie what they already knew. It was clear she was on their side, but telling her might put Sophie in an even more difficult position with her family. She decided to say nothing.

Breaking his silence, Dan mused, "Clearly we can't trust him or Viola, but we must act normal. They can't suspect we know anything." His logical thinking was reassuring and Sophie relaxed, glad that no repercussions would befall Viola.

"What do you think the tablets could be?" Sophie asked, worried about their well-being.

"You're right, they aren't relaxants," Michael answered, "we think they cause memory loss and they are being used to prevent us from remembering our past." He left it at that, not wanting to give too much away, but sensing the need to give her something. After all, she was risking a lot by telling them what she knew.

Under the table Dan kicked him, concerned that even that snippet of information had been too much.

"So why are you here? In Kilion I mean?" Sophie asked, feeling more confident.

Michael explained the reason for their visit as agreed with Abednego. He spoke of being orphaned and how

Abednego, his great Uncle, had agreed to look after him at Court for a while."

"That might explain why my mother believed the story about the relaxants..." As she said it, pieces of the puzzle started falling into place. "And why he instructed her that they shouldn't mention your past; he talked of some family tragedy. Do you think he's using the tablets to help you forget?"

Realising this plausible explanation could stop Sophie probing further, Hazel and Michael nodded, "Probably," Michael answered. "But we're fine and would rather not forget everything!"

"I could always try to hide them?" Sophie suggested.

"That would put Viola in an awkward position," Dan reasoned. "Or Hargrin could just get more."

"Or I could smuggle some empty bottles and jars for you to tip any suspicious drinks in without people noticing?"

"Not a bad idea," agreed Hazel.

"Then you can keep them as evidence if you need to prove anything later on."

"Good thinking," replied Dan, impressed.

"Mass will be finishing soon and I told them I wasn't feeling well so I could miss it. If I'm not back before then I'll be in serious trouble."

Reminded of the danger she had placed herself in, they thanked her profusely and watched her leave.

"Take your eyes off her!" Hazel whispered smugly, unused to seeing Dan showing interest in anyone.

Embarrassed, Dan followed the others back to their rooms, anxious for a rest and time to think before yet another meal in a crowded room full of strange people.

Chapter Thirty-four: The Cave

Darkness had surrounded Yvonne and Ralph Hopkins since being hurled into the cave which had become their prison. Their exit was barred by a huge, jagged rock while small chinks of light from the tiny gaps were the only way they could discern night from day. Now the beams were starting to fade, indicating that dusk was falling.

The boulder refused to budge, not even slightly; it was wedged tight. Perhaps that was just as well, an exasperated Yvonne thought, for the perpetual snorts and grunts from outside the cave indicated they were being guarded, probably by the huge creatures which had detained them in the first place. She couldn't help but wonder why guards had been placed at the front; for anyone with any sense would realise that neither her skinny frame, nor the hunk of meat that was her husband, would have any chance of ever being able to move the gigantic rock in the doorway.

The last twenty-four hours hadn't been easy; their bodies were bruised, scratched and torn from their journey and flight through the forest. Claws had pierced Yvonne's side, leaving her once pale flesh tender and raw around the puncture, and she could only imagine the angry bruises which had developed around her waist. Fortunately, she was unable to see her wounds in the darkness, which was just as well, for even the thought her body being less than perfect made her feel physically sick. At least the scabs on her legs were healing.

Ralph had sustained fewer cuts and bruises, but Yvonne had felt nauseous as her hands had felt the deep gash in his waist. With the minimal light available, she had tended his wound and bandaged it using torn material from his shirt to stem the bleeding and prevent infections from setting in. Despite their pain, both had stopped complaining, for both knew it wouldn't help solve the mess they found themselves in.

    Puddles lined the cave floor, leaving their feet in a perpetual state of sogginess. Initially Ralph and Yvonne had sat on sharp rocks, avoiding the wet floor and bemoaning their situation. Curses and expletives had littered their discussion as they had lamented ever having entered this godforsaken land, and they had regretted their insatiable greed which had ultimately led them there. Hours had been spent wishing that they could turn back the clock and refuse the offer that had seemed so profitable. If only they had been happy with what they'd had; a healthy bank balance, living in a luxurious house, driving sports cars and dining at the finest restaurants. Frequently they had mixed within the upper echelons' of society and they had never had to save for anything, and yet it all seemed a lifetime ago as they mulled over their losses! Only in this prison did they reflect on how foolish they had been; they should have known something wrong with the plan, but at the time neither had questioned the proposition that had been made. Now it was obvious that it was too good to be true, but greed had reared its ugly head and devoured their common sense, feasting on their usual good business acumen, leaving only a lust for money on the plate. As a result now, barely a month after the proposition, they were exhausted, injured and captive to beasts they hadn't even known existed in a country they'd never heard of! Wearily they had resigned themselves to a lifetime of captivity and the probably they would perish in this hell hole! How their fortunes had changed!

Hours had passed before they stopped moaning. At that point they had decided to concentrate on finding an escape. With few ideas and no knowledge of where they were, their suggestions had been feeble and amounted to little more than poking and prodding the cave walls in a futile hope of discovering loose rocks which they could pull down. They knew it was unlikely, but it was no less unlikely than being hurtled through the air by flying beasts.

And so, Ralph Hopkins felt his way along the rough, damp walls, treading cautiously for fear of slipping on the slimy algae which clung to the rocks like limpets. As his foot slipped once more into a puddle which seemed even deeper than the ones his feet had previously graced, he cursed, pulled his foot from the water then paused in thought before asking, "Why do you think they're keeping us here? If they were going to eat us, why haven't they done so already?"

Yvonne mulled over Ralph's observation and couldn't think of a plausible answer, so plumped for the first thing that had entered her head, "Perhaps they're waiting for a special occasion or for someone to come back."

"Perhaps," he mused, more to himself than his wife, "but if they were going to eat us, wouldn't it be simpler to have killed us then eat us later? Doesn't it seem odd that beasts, which in my experience don't have the highest intelligence, are taking the time to imprison us and surround us with guards to make a decision."

"I suppose it's a little weird." Yvonne stopped feeling the wall and turned inwards to face her husband, although she was barely able to see more than the faint shadows of a silhouette. "Are you suggesting they might want to use us as something other than food?" she asked hopefully, figuring that anything was preferable to being eaten.

"Maybe, but I can't imagine what." Again he paused, and aware of his restricted breathing, Yvonne didn't push him; "but then, until a day or two ago, I didn't even know creatures like those existed. So nothing would surprise me now."

Feeling slightly uplifted by the thought that they might not find themselves served on a platter, Yvonne said, "Let's stop wasting precious time and concentrate on escape. We can safely say our plan of finding loose rocks is little better than useless. Have you any other suggestions?"

"I've got it!" Ralph exclaimed excitedly. "What have we been standing in ever since we got here?"

Yvonne sensed the excitement in his voice, but had no idea what he was talking about. "A cave?" she replied, thinking the answer was either really obvious or incredibly obscure.

"But what's in the cave?" he prompted, eager for her to answer correctly.

"A whole load of puddles which have soaked my shoes and are going to give me trench foot," she complained.

"Exactly, we're standing in puddles. And where's the water coming from?" he rasped.

"Just tell me what you're getting at and don't get over excited, the last thing we need is for you to have an asthma attack and put your health at risk!"

Taking deep breaths, he waited until his breathing had stabilised before saying, 'Please answer my question."

Once she was certain he wasn't going to have one of his episodes, the importance of what he was trying to say struck her. Why hadn't they thought of it before? Clearly the water was coming from somewhere, and it definitely wasn't the front of the cave. "You think the water is coming from deep inside the cave?" she asked.

"I think if we work our way deeper into the cave, it might lead us to an opening on the other side!"

In any other circumstances she would have flung her arms around her husband, but as it was, it was so dark he was barely distinguishable and she certainly didn't want to slip on the wet algae infested rocks beneath her. Instead, she settled for pronouncing her delight and suggesting they start their search immediately.

Both imbued with a new lease of life, Yvonne and Ralph carefully manoeuvred their way along the cave, taking care not to slip. This became increasingly difficult as the gaps between the rocks got progressively bigger and the walls increasingly slippery. For the first time since arriving, they were doing something positive to help themselves. The deeper they reached, the more water they faced, which was surely an indicator that they were getting closer to their potential escape route.

Years of water dribbling down the walls had caused erosion of the rocks, making them smoother and harder to grip as they ventured inwards. Yvette, with her calm nature and athletic build was able to manoeuvre herself without too many problems; Ralph, however, was proving less adept. The further he went, the more excitable his overweight frame became and as a result, the more mistakes he made. The third time he misplaced his foot, it slid off a rock and became entrenched in a small hole, his foot at an awkward angle. Yvonne heard the crack of his bone as his outline slumped to the floor. Wincing, she made her way to him to offer comfort and help.

Ralph rested an elbow on the rocky ground to take some of the pressure off his ankle. His body was shaking with pain; his right leg remained outstretched while his left leg was bent to his side.Shivering, pain surged from his ankle up his body, causing tears of frustration.

Maneovering her way towards her husband carefully, she lowered herself onto the stones next to him; ignoring the discomfort it caused her skinny frame. Reaching towards his trapped leg, she started heaving it free from the hole. "I'm so sorry, it's going to really hurt."

Ralph's screams were spine tingling. Tears sprung to her eyes as she saw him writhe in agony, "Sorry," she whispered again.

After much straining, his foot loosened and she lifted it from the crevice. Positioning it in front of her, she helped him move his body into a more comfortable position. Gathering him in her arms, she could just about make out the pain etched across his face. Using her top, she wiped the sweat from his forehead then ran her hands through his hair. Gently massaging his scalp, she whispered soothing words to distract him from his discomfort.

Cradling him, she wondered what their future would bring. He couldn't move and she was torn between staying to comfort him, or continuing the search for an exit. If she stayed here, there was every chance they would starve to death or be eaten by the creatures outside. If she continued searching she faced the possibility of injuring herself also. Yet if she did manage to escape, what then? Would she be caught by the creatures that were bound to find her? Would she simply wander lonely and aimlessly for days until she was too hungry and exhausted to continue? They had already walked for days and not encountered a single soul, why would it be different now?

Her clothes were sodden, her feet were sore from blisters, her head itched and her waist caused her constant pain. She felt wretched, but surely not as awful as her poor husband who lay, head resting in her lap, murmuring and moaning to himself, fidgeting to get comfortable but unable to move his broken ankle.

Too weary to move, she resigned herself to their fate and closed her eyes, waiting for it to be over.

Chapter Thirty-five: Knowledge of the Rings

As arranged, Abednego appeared at their room early to discuss progress and agree strategies. Opening the door eagerly, Dan, already dressed for dinner stood aside, knowing how weary the old man must be, for he looked dead on his feet.

Perching himself on a chair by the small coffee table, Abednego took the weight off his feet and leaned back into the cushions, wishing it was time for bed.

"You'll never guess what we learned today," enthused Michael.

"Well, go on, get it off your chest lad," Abednego instructed, hoping it might help him keep his guests safe from harm.

Looking at the others first for confirmation, Michael ran his hand through his blonde hair before relating their conversation with Sophie to him, from Hargrin's duplicity to Viola's forced promise. When he mentioned Mazarin's supposed role, Abednego opened his mouth to defend the King, but was cut off by Dan. "We know he's not involved, or why else would he forbid any mention of it to him?"

At this Abednego smiled, not just because they had reached the same conclusion as him, but because they were using their initiative and working things out for themselves, unlike Martha who clearly accepted things unquestioningly.

Anyone who knew the King would, he thought, surely realise he would never instruct teenagers to spike drinks with drugs. It was as clear to him as it had been to Michael,

Dan and Hazel, that Mazarin was innocent and that Hargrin was wrongly implicating the King.

Once finished, Abednego raised his right hand to his slightly pursed lips and ran his fingers along them gently, contemplating this new evidence. After a while he muttered, "Hargrin's not working alone, in fact, I'm fairly certain he's being used by my dear friend... Raglin."

"Raglin?" repeated Hazel, unable to place a face to the name.

"The King's Chief Minister after myself. He's theoldest of those who sit at the top table with us, on the other side of the Queen."

Casting her mind back, Hazel vaguely remembered who he was talking about and made a mental note to search him out later that night.

"Raglin definitely suspects your knowledge of the ring." He paused as Michael gasped, his pale face clearly worried.

"So they know he's got the ring?" Dan asked, his face horrified.

"Not 'know', but suspect. I think I've managed to convince Raglin of our story this morning which is at least making him question his belief." He paused before asking, "has Hargrin referred to the ring at all?"

As soon as the question left Abednego's lips, Dan's dark brown eyes lit up. "He spoke of it today, didn't he?" He answered as he stretched his athletic arms above his head, his muscles flexing as he yawned.

"What did he say?" Abdnigo enquired, hoping no-one could hear outside. His weary eyes opened wide in speculation, wondering what he could possibly know.

Unable to contain herself, Hazel regaled the story; her arms flailing as she became engrossed in the tale of the civil war; Marshall's claiming of the throne, his bringing of peace, the combat with Zindegrot; the poisoned stream and finally the magical rings to confine the evil creatures beyond the water. As she spoke, her bright blue eyes sparkled with excitement. Talk of medieval chivalry and battles had captured her vivid imagination, so similar did they seem to the Wars of the Roses when Henry Tudor had dethroned Richard III. Learning about these battles at school had been fascinating, but talking about battles where Michael's Uncle had been a victim so recently well, it was impossible not to be completely overawed.

Once Hazel had finished, Dan added, "Hargrin said that with both rings lost, the creatures could cross the river and threaten Kilion. He implied that with no power preventing them it was only a matter of time. Is that true?"

Abednego was horrified by Hazel's account and Dan's question, for he had no idea that anyone other than himself and the King knew about Kilions complicated history. The Scriptures and the Chronicles carrying this information had been hidden in the Castle archives for decades, and everyone except royalty was denied access. That Hargrin knew the story implied he must have learned it from Raglin, but how had Raglin found out? And who else knew?

"Is it that bad?" a worried Michael asked.

"I'm afraid it is... potentially," Abednego admitted. "Firstly, anyone with even an iota of ambition will search for the ring to gain its magic powers, which will make your position incredibly dangerous. Then, if anyone takes it from you, or finds the second ring, they could try usurping the throne or lead Kilion once more into the depths of Civil War. Even worse, if they were to be victorious, who knows what they'll use the magic for? Even if the ring isn't found, if rumours spread about the possible implications of their loss, people will worry that their lives are in danger from the evil creatures across the stream; I'll let you work out the potential repercussions!" His old voice, usually so soft and calming, quickened as he rose from his seat and paced the floor in agitation, his earlier weariness having evaporated.

"If it makes you feel any better, he made us promise not to tell a living soul and said it was a secret," Dan said to reassure the old man, who seemed to have visibly aged in the last 24 hours.

Abednego didn't respond, his thoughts still on the potential impact for the locals. For a few years and even more so recently, he had heard rumblings of discontent in the village about the weakness of Mazarin's reign, some going so far as to fear for their safety. But as yet no-one knew the reason for his apparent weakness was, that unlike previous King's, Mazarin hadn't the power of the ring to help him control the darker forces.

Returning to the matter at hand, Abednego abandoned his thoughts and looked at them sternly, not because they had done anything wrong, but because of the seriousness of the information Hargrin had divulged. Moving closer to where they stood, he leaned forward and whispered, "No-one is to mention a word of this, do you understand?" His voice was once more calm, but the tone very much indicated the importance of what he was saying.

All three nodded mutely, part of them wishing they hadn't said anything, for it had affected him more than they had predicted.

Stroking the back of his neck that was stiff with tension, Abednego winced at the dull throbbing sensation attacking his temples, an increasingly frequent problem the older he was getting. Sitting himself back down, he whispered, "Nobody's supposed to know that part of our history. All documents relating to it were hidden by Melchior's father, my brother, Balthazar, to stop people finding out too much. You see early in his reign, too many princes and magnates attempted to steal the rings because of their power. So Balthazar split the rings up, secretly giving one to each of his sons. Melchior was never to use his, so many naturally forgot about the ring. Mathis later on meanwhile, used his to go to England. Many thought he had taken it with him and that whoever attacked him took the ring which has never been seen again. For the majority of your grandfather's rule, peace and tranquillity settled on Kilion with no thought given to the rings. When Melchior came to the throne, his father's policy seemed to have been firmly embedded, for again, there were no threats to the peace or attempts to find any rings. This meant he was able to pursue his policy of ruling without the ring." His mind relived his earlier days, when his eldest nephew, so regal and kind, had sat proudly on the throne, ruling as a fair and strong King should.

"But didn't you say there were lots of wars during his reign? I mean, he even died in battle, didn't he?" Dan recalled.

"I did say that, but the battles only occurred near the end; for the first 15 years he ruled in peace with no disturbances. It was only when a distant relative, Azarel, who felt he had a better claim to the throne, reared his ugly head that fighting commenced. It was generally believed, and still is, that he was simply fighting for the throne and not the ring. He just wanted to be a King." Looking at his watch, shocked at how quickly time had disappeared, he saw it was time to leave. "We had better get going, but remember, say nothing," Abednego warned them again.

Chapter Thirty-six: Freedom

In the night sky, hundreds of stars twinkled brightly, like tiny lightbulbs, illuminating the ground below. The two moons, rarely seen, had tonight made an appearance, despite being partly veiled by a hazy red mist which cloaked them protectively from the evils of the night. Those noticing this unusual colouring would be forgiven for taking it as an omen, but for Siddons, who had decided tonight would see him attempt to free Mathis, it remained to be seen whether the omen would be good or bad.

Wings beat rapidly as Siddons manoeuvred himself carefully, evading the dangers of the woods, relying on his size to aid him. His watchful eyes skimmed the trees, careful to avoid creatures of the witching hour. Landing on the branch he had made his resting place, he scoured his surroundings carefully before undertaking his final journey to the obscured building Mathis called home.

Landing on the windowsill, Siddons peered inside to find Mathis standing, slightly awkwardly, one arm propping himself up by the cell wall, the other holding his right leg in a calf stretch. Siddons smiled at the look of determination in Mathis' eyes, which were still little more than faint blue islands swimming in the hollows of skin, but which were at least starting to look healthier. Swooping down, Siddons perched on the mattress, avoiding the protruding springs.

Startled, Mathis lowered his leg and turned to see his furry friend. His eyes lit up with joy as a smile erupted on Siddons face.

"You've made amazing progress!" Siddons chirruped.

"It's amazing what a little hope can do," Mathis responded, stroking his long beard and not for the first time, wishing he looked more presentable.

"I've not brought as much food as I had hoped," Siddons muttered, his head bowed to avoid recriminations, "our village had a meeting today and it was agreed we would relocate at the end of the week." His wings twitched nervously as his eyes fought back tears at the events of only hours ago.

"That's terrible. Why are you moving?" asked Mathis.

"Vampires. Moving's our only real option." Unwilling to discuss it further, Siddons placed the food he had bought next to Mathis on the dirty mattress. "Anyway, our main priority's getting you out of here!" Siddons voice, Mathis could tell, was forcefully jovial, though not very convincing.

"Does that affect..?"

"No, it doesn't. I'm staying to help you. I'll re-join them after." Pushing the food in Mathis' direction, he commanded, "Now eat up quickly."

Mathis could feel tears forming; no-one had ever sacrificed so much for him. After fourteen years alone, he didn't know how to respond to such kindness. Too choked to talk, he felt the tears trickle silently down his translucent skin.

"Don't be so soppy, we can't lose focus," Siddons scolded, unable to watch him cry. He knew it would only bring back his own sorrows. Regret at his earlier rashness was eating at him. He'd never been on his own with no family and no home. All he had was a branch, surrounded by the elements and the fear that some beast might find him. Yet despite this, he knew he had made the right decision. He couldn't turn his back on Mathis now, whatever the cost.

Finding his voice, Mathis whispered, "I can't believe what you've risked for me... I'm so..." he croaked. Unable to find the right words, he left the sentence unfinished.

Changing the subject, Siddons chastised, "Eat up! I know it's not much, but I assure you it's delicious!" Inclining his head towards the few scraps he'd scraped together, he watched Mathis pick it up, inspect it, then devour it ravenously.

Chomping gratefully, Mathis mumbled, "Any ideas on how to get out of here?"

On his flight there, Siddons had instinctively felt that tonight would be a good night for escape; the forest seemed unusually quiet and the sky was brighter than usual, which would light the way. Hoping the appearance of the two moons would prove a good omen, he was determined to use this to their advantage. The only problem was, he had no idea how he was going to make it happen. "Well," he replied, "although the omens are good, my mind's been on other things today," he mumbled, adding quickly, "but I could take a look around the building to gauge its' layout; you never know, I might figure out a plan on my travels."

"Good idea." Mathis agreed, before adding, "you could always just search for the key to my cell while they're asleep? You can fly, and you're small enough to hide if they wake so they won't see you. Once you've found the keys, you could simply unlock the cell door." He'd spent all day mulling it over, and as far as he could see, there should be very few problems, especially if Siddons was careful.

Siddons face lit with joy, "What a wonderful idea!" he beamed, only slightly annoyed that he hadn't thought of this beautifully simple plan himself. "I'll be back as soon as I find out any information or...," he said excitedly, "the keys!"

Fluttering out through the bars into the night's sky, he glanced round carefully, making sure nothing was lurking nearby, then kept close to the wall, flying low to the ground near the dark shadows. Peering round another corner, his whole body was tight with anxiety. Just to the side, a huge gate protruded from the wall, enclosing what Siddons could only presume to be a back garden.

Soaring higher in the air and peering over a wooden blockade, he noticed to his astonishment and delight, that the back door had been left slightly ajar. His eyes followed the contours of the garden attentively, scouring the equipment and shrubbery. Squinting, his vision finally settled on the smallest glimmer of light at the back of the garden. Peering closer, he could just about detect the silhouette of a figure, crouched down, digging at the dirt. Barely discernible, next to him, was a large basket which Siddons thought might contain newly picked vegetables. The basket already appeared quite full, which meant there wouldn't be much time before the crouched figure would return indoors.

Studying the potential obstacles, he wondered why anyone would be gardening at this late hour. However, rather than spend too much time wondering at this unusual behaviour, he decided to take this opportunity to enter the house.

Silently, he flew over the gate, swooped to just above floor level and then stayed close to the wall before reaching the slightly open door. Peering inside at the bleak hallway lit by red wax candles, his heart pounded uncontrollably as he contemplated the danger he was in. Steadying himself, he landed on the floor before edging his way along the stained wall, and towards the staircase where the carpet was frayed at the corners. Clearly neither man took any pride in their home, for dust was scattered liberally on all wooden surfaces and the wall was devoid of paintings and tapestries which would have given it a more homely feel.

Hovering up each stair individually, he cowered in the shadows while making sure the way was clear. At the top, he surveyed his surroundings. There were two closed doors to his left, a large window to his right and yes, there at the end, as if God was on his side stood a door, wide open and revealing to his amazement a thick-set body slumped on a desk, head on hands, snoring. His heart raced. Buoyed on, recalling the omen of the two moons, he knew it was fate. Leaving nothing to chance, he edged into the room, towards the table and could hardly believe his eyes when, beside the snoring head, he saw a set of keys!

His nerves were starting to fray and he prayed he could at least keep calm for the next few minutes, the most important of his life so far. All he had to do was quietly remove them without waking the man from his slumber.

Edging nearer, within seconds he stood beside the keys which would end Mathis' captivity. Rising from the table, just enough to hover directly above them, he dipped and used his feet to grasp onto the key ring. Clutching it, he flew into the air, wincing as the metal clanked together. Sweat poured down his small furry features as the face on the table grunted, stirred slightly and moved his arms to a different position. His tiny heart in his mouth, the little creature expected the captor's eyes to open at any moment but instead, he moved his head to a more comfortable position and relaxed as his snoring resumed.

As quietly as possible, Siddons flew out of the room, across the hallway and down the stairs, all the while remaining as rigid as possible to stop the keys from clattering. With each movement forwards, his big round eyes flitted from side to side, hoping this would suffice to spot any danger, as he couldn't turn his head for fear of disturbing his prize.

Reaching the bottom, his legs started aching with the weight they were carrying, but adrenaline kept him going. Once out of the house, he glanced to the back of the garden and was relieved to find the older man still pruning his vegetables. Transferring the keys to his hands, he made his way back to the cell and dropped the keys noiselessly on Mathis mattress.

Fearing Siddons capture, Mathis face was a picture of pure joy as he touched the keys sprawled next to him. Unable to fully comprehend his furry friend's achievement, he caught his breath and for the second time that evening was lost for words.

"Looks like escape's in the air tonight!" Siddons exclaimed. His heart had finally stopped pounding so furiously, allowing him to concentrate on the enormity of what had just happened.

Stunned, Mathis clutched the keys to his chest. He couldn't believe he would finally be free! An expression of pure joy formed on his face as he considered the implications. The coldness of the keys sent a shiver through him, sparking a vigour he hadn't felt for years. Surging forwards towards the cell door, he was just about to try a key in the lock when Siddons whispered urgently, "Stop!"

Halting abruptly, Mathis turned to face Siddons, a questioning look on his face. "Why?" His scrawny hands trembled, still clutching at the keys which were anxious to be used.

"The servant," mumbled Siddons, "he's still awake. If you leave now, he might catch you! We need to leave it a couple of hours until they're both asleep before making your move."

Accepting the sense of Siddons suggestion, Mathis relaxed back against the crumbling brick wall and hid the keys under the mattress. Sliding onto the cold floor, he wrapped his arms about his knees, leant his head into them and imagined all the things he would do once he was out of there. True, the dangers of the forest scared him, like the vampires Siddons village was hiding from, but as soon as these dark thought had clouded his mind, he thrust them aside, for tonight was to be a night of cheer.

As the minutes passed even slower than usual, they spent their time discussing Mathis future; his return to

Court and being reunited with all those he'd left behind. He couldn't wait to see his faithful Gentleman of the Chamber, Grimbald along with other good friends he'd missed; Tacitus, Cornelius and Robespierre. He would reassure the new King, whoever it was, that he had no intention of trying to take the throne, and then when the time was right, he'd ask to use his brother's ring to return to England and find Catherine and Michael.

Siddons nodded, feigning happiness as Mathis rambled on. Inwardly, he wondered how far it would turn out as he hoped, for if Siddons had learned one thing, it was that very little goes as planned, especially when the equation is littered with so many variables. Yet overjoyed at seeing Mathis in such high spirits, he had neither the heart nor the inclination to put a dampener on it; so instead he listened and nodded in agreement, saying nothing. Finally, after what seemed an eternity, Jasper made his last check.

Sometime later, Mathis tried the keys until he found the right one, and then opened the metal door. Staying close, Siddons flew just slightly ahead, checking the coast was clear before steering Mathis through the house and out of the front door. Quietly closing it behind him, triumph invaded every part of his body as he stood still, taking in the view.

"Quick," Siddons nudged him forwards, thinking they had come too far to get caught now.

Stumbling forwards, stopping frequently for short breaks, Mathis ploughed through the forest, following Siddons who was still flying ahead to keep watch out. After an hour of stopping and starting, for the first time Mathis felt secure in his new found freedom and slumped to the floor, his head resting against the side of a tree. Physically and mentally exhausted, he needed a few minutes to re-energise but it wasn't long before his head drooped onto his chest, his eyes closed and he was sound asleep.

Anxious, but understanding just how exhausted Mathis must be, Siddons waited until he was sound asleep, then made little trips into the surrounding areas to check for signs of danger and to forage for food to help Mathis keep up his strength. And so, for the third time, wings opened wide, he went out, searching for the safest route out of the forest.

Chapter Thirty-seven: Deception

To the chagrin of Michael, Dan and Hazel, there was over an hour until the end of the feast, they were exhausted from the previous night and were tired of pretending to act drunk to convince people the tablets were working. Glancing at her watch for the third time in as many minutes, Hazel heaved a heavy sigh then resumed watching Viola talk conspiratorially with her mother; admitting grudgingly that whatever was being said, Viola wasn't happy. Beside Hazel, Michael was thinking the same, but neither felt inclined to start a conversation.

Desperate to consult with Michael, but fearful of incurring suspicion, Sophie sat quietly people watching at the side of the Hall. In the corner, Hargrin chatted animatedly to Raglin, showing no concern for the effect the drugs were supposedly having on her new friends.

***

"Well done Hargrin," Raglin patted the younger man on the back, "the drugs are clearly working." Hargrin still couldn't believe how well the plan was working; if only the boy had been related to Mathis as first believed; rather than Abednego's great-nephew through his late wife. Either way, his resemblance to Mathis was obvious; Mathis might be led to believe he had a son.

Hargrin beamed with pleasure, once more feeling a growing sense of importance; for while the other Ministers were being left on the sidelines, he had found himself positioned in the centre of this intrigue and he was loving every minute.

His mind wandering, Raglin had initially been unsettled by Abednego's story, but after due consideration had concluded that perhaps it didn't have to cause any problems. For Michael looked sufficiently similar to Mathis to show him to the Prince and declare him his son anyway. His age and looks, as well as his knowledge of Abednego and the Court, should certainly be enough to convince Mathis he'd unknowingly had a son. After all, it wouldn't be the first time such a thing had happened, and following fourteen years of loneliness, Raglin suspected Mathis would be willing to believe almost anything. So as far as he was concerned the outcome would be the same; their possession of the ring and the password.

"My pleasure," Hargrin replied, pleased with the compliment. He sensed however, that the elder man's thoughts were elsewhere. Probably planning their next moves, Hargrin thought, and wondered what he'd be required to do next.

Neither Hargrin or Raglin suspected they were being watched by more than one person. Sophie had been surveilling them most of the evening too, wishing she knew what they were saying. Martha had glimpsed over on more than one occasion; hoping to attract the attention of Hargrin, eager to make herself even more indispensable, but not once had she managed to catch his eye. Michael, Dan and Hazel had also spent a great deal of the evening, watching their conspiratorial conversations; confirming Abednego's belief that Hargrin was working on behalf of

Raglin who was obviously the leader and showing Hargrin much favour. As Hargrin had spent most of the evening beaming with pleasure, laughing and smiling graciously at Raglin like a besotted teenager, anger had surged inside of Hazel, who found it difficult to understand how his actions towards them could cause him so little regret. In fact, the more she watched him, the more obvious it became that far from regretting his actions, he was in fact, enjoying the whole scenario. Lastly, they were being watched by a tired Abednego, determined to protect the three charges in his care from any harm.

Finally, as Raglin patted Hargrin on the back like a pet, the old man snapped, he knew he had to act quickly to help them. His mind flitted across numerous options until it finally rested on what he considered to be the best course of action. He would, while everyone was enjoying themselves find Zawi Chemi, the eldest and wisest of the witches at Court and talk over possible options with her. For years she had nurtured a soft spot for him, having proposed to him on three separate occasions, and he knew she wouldn't be able to resist the twinkle in his eye. Mind made up, he headed towards where Michael was sitting, doing a very convincing job of looking drugged, he thought to himself humorously.

Michael, Dan and Hazel watched Abednego approach and wondered if something was wrong.

Drawing up a chair, he leaned forwards, careful that no-one else should hear what he was about to say. "I'm going to find Zawi Chemi. I think she might have information on the tablets, or the very least, be able to provide me with something to counter them." He whispered, barely audible to the three of them despite sitting so close.

"Shall we come with you?" whispered Michael, his eyes bright with excitement at meeting a real live witch.

"No, it would be easier if I went on my own," he replied, his eyes darting round the Hall, checking that no-one suspected anything.

"Well," Hazel cut in, "do you think anyone would mind if we left with you to go to our rooms, only we're really rather tired."

Without hesitation Abednego agreed to the request, glad for the opportunity to remove them from the danger of Hargrin and Raglin, especially as he wouldn't be there to protect them.

Despite not being consulted, Michael and Dan thought it a wonderful idea; the image of nice warm beds being far more appealing than another hour of play acting in a noisy room. Rising together, they informed the King they were retiring for the night, and then left the Hall as discreetly as possible, though they knew some people would be watching with interest.

Noticing them leave, Sophie scoured the Hall to make certain that neither her mother nor sister were paying any attention to her; they weren't. Discreetly sidling along the side of the Hall, seemingly invisible as usual, she departed through the side door just moments after Michael and the others had left.

Resting against the brickwork of the hallway and sighing with relief, she spied Abednego go one way, while Michael, Dan and Hazel walked in the direction of their rooms.

Scuttling to catch up with them, she halted when she overheard their conversation.

"We're only going back to our room to collect your map of the castle, remember the one you did when we found the prisoner." Hazel hissed, barely loud enough for Sophie to hear.

"I thought we were going to bed." Michael muttered, his legs and posture seeming much more stable than it had appeared in the Great Hall, Sophie thought.

"And do what?" Her frustrated hand gripped onto the bottle Sophie had given her, now full of liquid and hidden under her borrowed cloak.

"Oh, I don't know! Sleep?" Michael retorted sarcastically.

"And miss this opportunity!" Hazel declared, "never!"

"What opportunity?" Dan's weary voice asked, "it's night time, an event that happens at the end of every day!"

"Very funny!" Hazel stopped them for a second by grabbing their arms to halt their progress. Frightened of being caught, Sophie moved into the shadows at the side of the wall, behind a polished suit of armour and listened, for clearly Hazel had something important to say or do.

"Abednego's busy and the King and his Ministers think we're going to bed."

"Not a bad assumption," Dan muttered, "for that's what I thought as well."

"Which means we're free to do what we want!" Her shoulders were raised so they almost touched her ears, Sophie could tell from the tone of her voice how excited she was and smiled at her zest for adventure.

Neither Michael nor Dan answered but Sophie could see the exasperated expressions which had contorted both their faces.

"So I thought we could get the directions and try to save that guy in the cells... as we promised," she added to give extra weight to her argument.

Both relaxed slightly, for although what she was suggesting was dangerous, they had felt guilty about doing nothing to help him when they had promised they would. "I suppose," agreed Michael.

"By my reckoning we've about an hour until the feast finishes which gives us plenty of time to go to our room, collect the directions, and make our way to the secret tunnels. Then it doesn't matter how long we take, as long as we're careful not to get caught by those awful hogs or whatever they are."

Gradually won over by her persuasive arguments, Dan and Michael raised little protest. "Then all we have to do is wait until everyone's asleep before we return. No-one need ever know we've been anywhere. Abednego won't wake us to check on us at such a late hour, and nobody else ever visits our room."

Hazel made it seem so easy that Michael and Dan wondered why they had considered it dangerous in the first place, until a thought struck Michael, "How are we going to release him?"

"Your ring of course," she said as though it was the most obvious answer in the world.

"But nobody's supposed to know I've got it! So I can't be letting a strange man in prison know it's in my possession, Abednego will go mental!" Michael reasoned, determined neither to let Abednego down, nor to put the lives of himself and his friends in danger.

"Come on guys," Hazel retorted, "if the prisoner wants to escape, as I'm sure he does, I'm positive he won't mind closing his eyes whilst we use the ring's power. Admittedly he might think it a little odd but, he's unlikely to question it too much, if it means he'll be released."

"Suppose," muttered Michael, who wasn't too taken with this part of the plan.

"Okay," Hazel replied. "I for one can't bear the thought of that man being locked up for no reason. Can you? "

"No," they both agreed.

"And I think that as we know where he is and we have the opportunity and means of helping him escape, we should at least try. Don't you agree?"

"Suppose," Michael muttered again, while Dan responded with a mere incline of the head.

"That's settled then, we'd better hurry, we're not going to get anywhere by discussing things in the hallway." Hazel instructed, marching purposefully forward towards their room.

Digesting what she'd just heard, Sophie's mind was whirling; secret passages in the castle? Underground prisoners? A ring which could unlock cells! Waiting for a few moments to elapse, Sophie followed closely behind, keeping an eye on the hallway, watching what passages they turned down until she saw them disappear into a room. Once outside, she waited patiently for them to emerge, for she had decided that rather than follow them secretly as she had been doing, she would confront them with what she'd heard, and ask them to take her with them. With her knowledge of the castle and of the people in it, she might be able to help.

Grabbing the notebook containing the directions and instructions, Dan scanned the first few lines to familiarise himself with the journey. "Ready?" he asked, slightly more confident now he had his notes with him. Taking the lead, he opened the door, and came face to face with Sophie, waiting patiently outside.

"W... w... what are you doing here?" He stuttered, unable to fathom how Sophie had made it to their room so quickly. Then a terrible thought occurred to him, "Did you just hear...?"

For a while she said nothing, questioning her earlier resolve to tell the truth. Would they hate her for eavesdropping? Would they turn her away? She was tired, her head was muddled and she was having trouble thinking. Lacking the energy to make up lies, she decided it would be better for all concerned if she told the truth. "I'm sorry, I heard everything you said, about the secret passage, a prisoner and a ring." She hung her head in shame, "but I promise, hand on heart, I won't say a word... not to anyone"

Scrutinising her, Dan saw the shame etched in her eyes and instinctively knew she was telling the truth. Yet still, her knowledge was dangerous, and he wasn't sure how far she would hold up if interrogated by someone determined to extract information from her. "Okay," he replied. "We believe you, but you must go back to your room and pretend this conversation never happened."

"Oh, but I can't do that," she exclaimed, "I want to come with you, help you release the prisoner, see the secret passages."

"We can't take you with us," Hazel reasoned, "it's far too dangerous!"

"It's no more dangerous for me than it is to you, is it?"

"Well... erm..." Hazel muttered, but she knew Sophie was right.

"Please let me come," she begged, "I know some of the people here and I can tell you almost anything about the castle grounds. I know I don't know about the secret passages, but I might be able to help you with other things." She smiled sweetly, her cheeks dimpling and her green eyes, looking expectantly at them.

"Oh, all right," said Michael and when neither Hazel nor Daniel argued with his decision, she couldn't help but throw her arms around Hazel, her eyes alight with joy, her face full of excitement.

"I suppose it would be better for you to be with us where we can keep our eye on you. At least you won't be with your mother and Viola where you might be tempted or forced to let things slip." Dan's reply was cutting, the implication clear and her heart sank. The feeling of being distrusted wasn't a pleasant one and her face fell. Removing her arms from Hazel, she dropped them to her side, not sure she even wanted to go any more.

Mortified at the way he had sounded and upset at the hurt etched on her face, especially as he had caused it, Dan was quick to apologise. "Sorry, I didn't mean it to come out like that. It's just that... well... if any of the information you've just heard fell into the wrong hands, our lives could be in danger."

"That's okay." Sophie replied, overawed by the importance of what she's just overheard. If it was that serious and their lives were in danger, she could fully understand why he might be a little tetchy.

Attempting to dispel the remaining tensions, Hazel, as enthusiastic as always, prompted them to get going for time was of the essence and she wanted to be safely in the secret passageways before the feast finished. And so along the passageways they moved, Dan leading with his notebook from the front, taking them through the labyrinth of corridors. Again, they noticed the metal plaques on some of the doors, but this time recognising some of the names, and as they passed through the more ornately decorated hallways where gilt framed portraits hung amidst a backdrop of velvety paper, Sophie pointed out some of the richer families who resided there, telling them the positions they held at Court. Finally, as they headed further from the rich section, the passages became smaller, and their fear of being discovered eased.

Suddenly, without a word of warning, Hazel surged forwards and headed towards a cold metal statue of a bearded horse. "I've found it!" She exclaimed excitedly, her hand rubbing the smooth metal, eager to turn it.

"I was just about to..." Dan started, but was cut off mid sentence for Hazel had already pulled the statues right ear in an anti-clockwise direction to reveal the opening from before. This time they weren't as fearful and Hazel stood aside, allowing Dan to take the lead once more through the opening in the wall. Sophie followed at the back, her heart pounding at this discovery, her nerves a little frayed.

Once they had all entered, the wall behind them closed leaving them trapped. This time much more confidently, but still slow due to the dimness of the tunnel, they headed along the passage. Candles flickered from the walls, their small flames licking up into the air, emanating some light and warmth, though not as much as they would have liked.

Unused to the unevenness of the floor, Sophie slipped a couple of times, but remained upright by clutching at the damp walls. Winding along the passage, they were careful not to go too far too quickly, for they could barely see more than a couple of metres in front of them and they last thing they wanted was for anyone to become separated.

The deeper they ventured, the more uneven and dangerous the walls, with rocks jutting out, scraping their sides and hands as they felt their way further into the darkness.

"Are they icicles hanging from the ceiling?" Sophie whispered to whoever could hear her.

"Think so," Michael replied, trying not to get too distracted.

"How can there be icicles in the middle of a castle during summer?" she asked.

"Don't ask us," responded Michael, "we're still trying to get our heads round secret passages, talking door knockers and food that appears on command."

"Oh..." When he put it like that, she could see how everything she had previously taken for granted could be questioned, and she had no idea how to explain any of those occurrences at Court. Continuing to follow from behind, Sophie wondered how long the passage went on, but didn't want to ask too many questions for fear of irritating them. Instead, she wiped her rose blonde hair from out of her face and strained to see how far in the distance the candles went on for. The occasional drip of water rolled off the tip of the icicles onto her face, but she didn't dare take her hands from the steadying walls to wipe the water away.

Finally they halted while Dan indicated that they had reached the stairwell they were to descend. Turning to face Sophie behind him, Michael informed her that the stairs were steep and slippery and warned her to be careful. Nodding silently at his words of warning, Sophie couldn't help but wonder if she had made the right decision, for right now she could be snuggled up in bed and... oh no! What would happen when her mother and sister returned from the feast and discovered she wasn't there? Anxiety descended upon her as, for the first time since venturing after them, she considered the consequences of her actions. However, it was her turn to move down the stairs, and for that she needed her full concentration.

The further they descended, the darker the staircase became as fewer candles lit their way. By now Sophie's feet were soaking as she trod in puddles full of dank water and algae, her hands pressed fiercely against the walls to stop her slipping onto the others below her.

It wasn't long before they were all standing at the bottom, once more in a tunnel which expanded hundreds of meters in either direction. The high ceiling removed any feeling of claustrophobia and small lanterns accompanied the flickering candles providing much more light than they'd previously enjoyed. Paving slabs had replaced the rocky ground, making walking and remaining upright much easier.

"Shall we get into a boat now?" Dan asked, thinking it would be much easier for them to move along the passage that way without being seen, for the hog guards could appear at any moment.

"Let's just take a little stroll." Hazel suggested, wondering if they could take another peek at the library with all the magical books.

Chapter Thirty-eight: Potions

All four walked along the canal; beautiful boats floating under small bridges to one side; wooden doors intermittently on the other. "The laboratory's down there!" Hazel pointed, but could tell by their response they weren't in the mood to take another look. So, much to Hazel's disappointment, they walked straight on past when she added, "shame, wasn't that the place the woman gave Hargrin the tablets used for drugging us? Would have been nice to get some or to take a look at what other drugs are in there..." she sighed, leaving the thought planted in their minds.

Once more, Sophie was out of her depth, not knowing what they were referring to, but not confident enough to ask.

"Perhaps we could just take a little look..." Michael agreed, thinking how exciting it might be to find secret potions.

An argument formed on Dan's lips about how it would waste time and about the possibility of getting caught but decided against it. Once Hazel was determined upon something, there really was little hope of holding her back. Resigned to their fate, he swivelled back and headed to the door. Inching it slowly open, eyeing inside to make sure it was empty, Dan opened the door enough for them to enter. Inside, they once more faced shelves and cabinets adorned with bottles and jugs. This time, they noted that the huge white table in the centre of the room was clear of clutter. The machines to their left, however, still flashed silently although it was a blue rather than red steam which was, this time, being emitted.

Too curious to hold back any longer, Hazel surged forwards towards the shelves to take a closer look at the contents of the bottles. Many of the granules were quite ordinary looking so she moved to the bottles with the frothy liquid. 'Invisibility.' One bottle said, 'energy', boasted another. Other labels had still to be stuck on for the bottles, although full, they had nothing on them to indicate what they contained. Snatching a few from the shelf, Hazel shoved them in the bag Sophie had lent her and which still contained the bottles holding their drinks from the feast, laced with memory loss solution.

Checking to make sure none of the others had witnessed her 'borrowing', for she knew they'd only tell her to put them back, Hazel patted the bag, a grin on her face at the thought of not getting caught by Dan. Then walking to where the others stood, she joined them in watching the flashing lights on the machines.

"This is amazing," Sophie whispered in wonderment.

"Isn't it?" Agreed Dan, who since his stay at the castle, had given up trying to think of any explanations for what they were encountering other than magical. "Come on, we'd better get going in case we get caught." His insistent manner was enough to prompt the others into action and even Hazel raised no qualms about leaving.

Outside they walked past the library which Hazel had also wanted to visit, but which they insisted on leaving until another time. Not so upset at this, Hazel once more patted her bag, for little did the others know that last time she had acquired three books from there. These were also inside her bag, so when Dan had collected his notes, she had sneakily shoved them into her satchel, ready for their journey.

Next they passed the room with the skulls, which they refused to enter. Finally, giving up hope of entering any more rooms, they clambered into the nearest boat, decorated with a green leafy design. Crouching down, Hazel once more unhooked the rope which moored it in place. The ripples moved the boat lazily downstream, past others still tied to their posts, along the increasingly darkened passage. Wrapping her arms about her, Hazel shivered, having forgotten that the deeper the boat passed, the more the damp penetrated their bodies. Beside her Sophie was doing the same while neither Dan nor Michael appeared to feel the chill in the air. 'Typical,' Hazel thought to herself, 'always the women who suffer!'

Once more, droplets of water fell intermittently onto their heads, dripping down their faces and at just the moment when one found its way directly into Michael's eye, he felt the warmness of the ring by his chest. Fumbling round for it, all was darkness as the boat ventured into the tunnel and any light was extinguished.

Anxious for their well-being, Sophie's heart pumped as she noticed a closed door in front of them. "How will we get past?" She asked, concerned that the boat would collide into the barrier.

Silence ensued, none of them wanting to be the one to break their secret and tell her about the powers of the ring, and then it happened. From the ring on Michael's hand, a red light shone illuminating the whole of the crumbling tunnel. Her face aghast, Sophie looked at each in turn amazed, and then focused on the huge door which had started to open of its own accord, allowing their little boat passage through. As soon as their boat had passed into another, dustier passage where moths congregated around the flickering flames, the doors closed.

The splashing of water droplets onto the floor and into the moat were the only sounds they could hear. They breathed a sigh of relief that so far, they hadn't been caught.

"How... why..." Sophie stuttered, her eyes focused on the Michael's ring which he quickly replaced in his pocket

"We'll explain later." Said Dan who was busy looking out for signs of danger, "now's not really the best time to get into a discussion," he hissed as his eyes darted about, scouting for danger.

Her pretty face screwed up in distaste as the smell of damp pervaded her nostrils. Eager not to annoy Daniel, who she was still somewhat in awe of, she accepted what he said dutifully and followed as they made their way along the passage, taking the trouble to avoid scraping into the cobwebs, which adorned the wet, moss covered walls.

Suddenly and without any warning, a grunting noise filled the air; realising it was the sound of the hogs, Michael and Hazel lost no time in rushing towards the boat from which they had recently alighted. Sophie, completely unaware as to what was happening, stood glued to the spot, unable to move. Her chest had clammed up, and her breathing had quickened. Next to her stood Dan, who had been tempted to run to the boat like Hazel and Michael, but hadn't wanted to leave Sophie on her own, and so he had stayed, although he wasn't quite sure how he was going to protect either of them. As before, the guards were adorned in red and green, their long pointed ears protruding from their green metal helmets. But this time, their ears stood erect, as though they were listening out for something.

Dan pulled Sophie towards the wall in the hope that the shadows would hide them from view. Unfortunately this wasn't the case, for as soon as their snouts sniffed the air around them, it was clear they sensed someone was near. Their faces sneering in delighted contentment, the fatter of the two spoke, "I think we have company!"

The hog on the left, wiping his brow chuckled, replying, "A little bit of fun at last, always nice to have something to break up the monotony of the day."

Holding their breaths, Sophie and Dan slid along the side of the wall, until they were just metres from the boat. Then, in a somewhat feeble attempt to make it to the vessel without attracting their attention, they surged forwards, only for the hogs to turn around and spy their intended prey. Realising that to enter the boat would be to endanger the lives of Hazel and Michael, they instead both grabbed an oar and turned to face the creatures who were steadily closing in on them.

More frightened than she had ever been in her life, Sophie edged forwards in an attempt to appear confident and defiant, hoping to confuse the hogs. Watching, and impressed by her bravado, Dan did the same.

In one giant leap the hog to the right almost reached Sophie. Quick to react, she raised her oar high into the air, and then brought it down with an almighty thud onto his head. Arms shaking nervously, she fought to overcome her nerves. Once more she lifted the wooden weapon, then watch bemused, as her own hands brought it crashing down on onto the hog's head a second time, eager to ensure victory.

Meanwhile to her side, Dan ducked as the second hog attempted to hit him. Bent low, he immediately brought his oar crashing round the back of the animal's legs, just at the point where his armour would fail to protect him. Yelping, the beast's snout creased in pain while his eyes glared in fury. Stumbling, the hog reached out to the wall to maintain his balance while Dan took the opportunity to stand upright in readiness to inflict more damage.

By this point, having defeated her attacker, Sophie noticed the other hog's lack of composure and instinctively swung her oar one last time. Her aim just as accurate as before placed the thick wooden slate directly on the side of its face. Stunned from the onslaught, the hog's head snapped to the left, his legs stumbled and his hands fell from the wall. Like his friend, he fell to the floor, landing in a heap not two yards away from her previous victim.

Exhausted by the force of her actions, the oar slipped from Sophie's grasp, and she fell to her knees, unable to comprehend what she had just done. "Please tell me they're not dead." She whimpered, her eyes welling up with tears as she looked down at the beasts. For although she knew they would have shown her no mercy, she still wouldn't be able to forgive herself if she'd taken a life.

"They're alive," Dan reassured her, for their chests were faintly rising and falling, "although I think we can safely say they'll be out cold for quite some time." Reaching out to Sophie, Dan comfortingly placed his arm on her shoulder as Michael and Hazel both approached. Signing with relief, Sophie regathered her composure as Dan helped her to her feet.

"Wow," exclaimed Hazel, "you were both amazing." Her voice full of praise, proud at how well they had managed to take on the guards and glad that no harm had come to them.

"It was Sophie really," said Dan. "I didn't do that much."

"Nonsense, it was a joint effort," Sophie corrected him. "If you hadn't been there and taken out the back of his legs, I wouldn't be here to tell the tale." Her green eyes smiled. He smiled back, impressed at the way she had handled herself and feeling quite taken by her pretty face.

"Well, enough of the congratulations," a composed Dan said, "it won't be long until they come round and they'll be sure to report back what's happened, and when they do? Well, let's just say it doesn't look good for us." His stiff tone betrayed none of his anxiety.

"I don't think we've got to worry," said Hazel, and before anyone had a chance to question her. Hazel's hand had slipped into the satchel beneath her cloak, rummaged round and pulled out a bottle. Inside were the contents of their drinks from the feast, still contaminated by the memory loss potion. Her face grinned as she inspected their surprised expressions. "I'm sure just a few mouthfuls of this will be enough to secure our anonymity."

"Excellent," exclaimed Michael, "what a great idea!" Eager to get it over with, Michael lifted the head of one guard and opened its mouth while Hazel poured some of the red liquid down his throat, meanwhile Dan and Sophie did the same to the other hog.

Once they had positioned the beasts comfortably on the floor, a thought occurred to Dan. "I can't believe that the two of you," he said, looking first at Hazel then Michael, "let Sophie and I face them on our own." His serious tone indicated his annoyance at their cowardly actions.

"Firstly," responded Hazel, matter-of-factly, "you can't blame Michael and I for instinctively trying to make it to safety. Most people would have done the same? And secondly, it was better that at least two of us to remain unseen. After all, if they'd arrested you, then you would have needed us to come and save you, which we couldn't have done if we'd been taken as well."

"Suppose you've got a point," Dan riposted.

"And you have to admit that at no point were your lives in danger. You both did so well against them from the start, they never had a chance. Do you honestly think that if we'd seen them hurt you, we would have done nothing?" Hazel's bright eyes implored.

Dan wanted to believe her, but he wasn't sure how they could have helped had the beasts got the better of them. "I understand your logic, but I'm not sure how useful you would have been if they'd badly injured us," he countered.

"You know that wouldn't have happened," ventured Michael, "if necessary, I'd have used the ring against them."

Again, Daniel could only agree and his dark mood lifted. Sophie saw no reason for her to doubt them. "What about the ring?" she asked, so far they had talked about it being able to release the prisoner, and now they were saying it would have helped them against armoured guards, and she had already seen it glow and open a huge gate.

They were torn between telling her and keeping their promise to Abednego, and whilst they could understand her inquisitiveness and her right to know, and she had certainly done enough to earn their trust, they just couldn't bring themselves to break their promise to Michael's great Uncle.

"Our main priority's finding Grimbald and getting out of here. We can talk later, if that's okay?" Dan asked, his tone rather more gentle than the last time she'd enquired. Her recent actions sufficiently quelling any niggling doubts he'd had about her trustworthiness.

Hazel looked at Michael, pleased at Dan's change in attitude. Of the three, Dan was the most suspicious and cautious by nature and the least likely to divulge any information. Yet since getting to know Sophie and especially after her bravery, if he felt she should be told, then she saw no reason to withhold anything from her.

"That's great," Sophie responded, eager to help anyone who needed rescuing.

"To Grimbald!" Pointing her finger forwards, Hazel was just about to head to his cell when Michael held her back.

"Wait a minute." Kneeling by the hogs, he felt around their belt and, as expected, found a set of keys jangling from it. Carefully releasing the catch which secured them to the leather, Michael manoeuvred them off the guard's person, he then returned to the others.

"Good thinking Sherlock," Dan smiled at the exultant expression on the pale, delicate face.

"Well, with you and Sophie beating armoured beasts into unconsciousness and Hazel bringing along a potion to keep them from remembering what happened, I had to do something to contribute didn't I?"

"You've got the ring! That's plenty to guarantee you a place!" Dan had almost added that as King of Kilion he had an automatic right but thought that in light of Sophie's company, the less said, the better!"

Chapter Thirty-nine: The Secret Passageway

Within minutes they reached the cell in which Grimbald sat, his face looking dejected.

"Cheer up!" A jubilant Hazel almost danced as she approached, "surely that can't be the expression of someone who's about to be released from prison!"

Caught off guard, Grimbald jumped at the intrusion into his thoughts of the good days. Swivelling slowly round to see who had spoken to him, his eyes lit up as they fell onto the three teenagers he'd spoken to the previous night. It was then that he noticed behind them, slightly obscured from view, was a pretty blonde haired girl who hadn't been with them previously. Curious, but too tired to comment on their new acquisition, he rose to his feet and shuffled towards them.

"You remembered! And you risked your safety for me! I appreciate it but I can't possibly let you suffer on my account. You see we need special keys to get me out, and the cell is protected by armour clad guards so I guess we or rather I, am stuck. His eyes reflected the sadness of his words, and it upset them to see how in just a couple of days, he had resigned himself to lifelong captivity.

Anxious to dispel his worries, Michael held out the keys for Grimbald's inspection before briefly explaining what had happened. Moving towards the lock, he smiled at Grimbald and told him not to worry, he would soon be free.

Unable to believe his luck, the older man watched the keys, one by one, being tried in the lock. Nearing the end of the bunch, he'd almost given up hope thinking that they might have the wrong set, when finally the lock clicked and the door creaked open, allowing Grimbald his freedom. Rushing out, he flung his arms wide open like a newly released bird, then twirled around with his face upturned, eyes alight with excitement. Unable to hide their grins at this spontaneous show of joy, they watched the amusing sight, for it was clear that his huge frame of over six feet was not supposed to move that quickly.

Swiftly locking the cell, they kept hold of the keys in case they needed them for any other area of the castle. With the hogs having no recollection of losing them, they thought it unlikely that keeping them would make the situation any worse. Extracting them from Michael's shaking hand, Hazel dropped them into her satchel, which was getting rather full and was starting to pull on her shoulder.

"What are we going to do now?" Michael asked, "go back to our rooms?"

"Good suggestion. I think enough time has lapsed for people to have gone to bed. If we creep back quietly, no-one need ever know of our night time wander." Dan replied.

"But what should I say to my mother and sister? They're bound to have noticed my absence!" said Sophie, chewing her fingernails nervously, not a habit that she was prone to but it was the only comfort she had, as all her earlier fears had returned. How was she going to explain going missing from the feast and returning back late without incurring her mother's wroth? The thought of the confrontation was not one she relished.

Considering her predicament for a moment, it wasn't long before Dan had a solution. "We could go with you and explain that we were feeling ill and, not wanting to disturb her or Viola who were deep in conversation, we asked if you could take us outside to escape the stuffiness of the Hall. Michael could say how we lost track of time because you were telling him about the castle and Viola, but that eventually, you realised it was late so we hurried to get back in case they were worried."

Amazed at such a good plan conjured up so quickly, Hazel had to agree it certainly sounded plausible. "I'm sure they'll be fine if they think you've been helping us and telling us good things about your sister."

Feeling much happier, Sophie's spirits rose, and she even forgot to ask when they would tell her about this mysterious magical ring. "Sounds good. So how exactly do we get back?" she asked, thinking that as the water in the moat was flowing in the wrong direction, they wouldn't be able to return that way.

"Just you watch," said Michael, excited about once more stepping on the slightly discoloured paving slab and watching the wall open before them.

"But what about Grimbald?" Almost forgetting his existence, Hazel now turned to face him, "what are you going to do?"

"Don't you go worrying about me, young lady. I've a wife at home who is probably worrying herself to death. I told her I'd be a couple of hours and that was a couple of days ago. I can just imagine the state she'll be in!" Eager to get back to Ragetta, he was just about to work out an escape route when a thought struck him. "Before you go, can I just ask... last time we spoke, you said you couldn't remember anything, is that still the case?"

Nervous about what Grimbald might ask if he told the truth, Michael almost considered lying, but then thought how the poor man had been imprisoned because of him, so felt it only fair he answer truthfully. "No," Michael replied, "we have our memories back."

"In that case, can I ask... who your father is?"

"Why do you want to know?" Michael was nervous and looked at Hazel and Dan for help but none was forthcoming. If he said 'Mathis' in front of Grimbald and Sophie, it would alert them immediately to the fact that he was the heir to the throne of Kilion. He could make up a name and end any speculation, but although he knew he should lie and continue the story Abednego had concocted, his heart raced, for he couldn't bring himself to do it. The man standing before him seemed so genuine and Sophie had risked upsetting her family to tell them what she knew, she'd even been attacked by guards. It hardly seemed fair to keep anything from them. So instead, he said nothing and waited for Grimbald to answer.

"I was just wondering, like. It's just that I used to be the personal companion and servant of a Prince, his name was Mathis, and it broke my heart when he left for a place called England. That's why I left the castle, couldn't bear to work here doing anything other than serving him. I know I'm waffling, it's just that you look so like him, I couldn't help but wonder, if maybe, you know, he'd met someone there and had a child." A drop of water splashed onto his dirty face where some of the grime from the castle moat had dried on his skin.

Michael's mind was troubled. Half of him desperately wanted to tell him that Mathis was his dad, whilst the other half warned him of the potential consequences.

Sensing his friend's confusion, Dan answered for him. "Mathis was his father." The revelation startled Grimbald, who clicked his fingers nervously, whilst Sophie clasped her hand to her mouth to stop herself from making any comment.

Hazel couldn't believe that it had been Dan, ever the cautious one, who had finally divulged the information that they had pledged to keep secret.

"Y... y... you're really his son?" A gobsmacked Grimbald stammered; unable to believe that his inclinations, seeming so unlikely, had actually been true.

Relieved it hadn't been him who had broken the promise to Abednego; Michael nodded in confirmation and watched the strain lift from the older man's face.

Grimbald bending down on one knee, his thick, chestnut hair tangled and in disarray, his hotchpotch of new and old clothes stained and torn, and his weary face creased and dirty, pledged his life in support of the new King.

Nails in her mouth once more, Sophie, realising the importance of the slim blonde boy before her, also fell to her knee.

"Please get up," Michael instructed, feeling awkward at such acclamation. "I'm just ordinarily like you; I live at home, in a two-bedroom flat with my mum. I go to an ordinary school, where I am bullied, and I have no television or car, or any other modern technology that most people my age have."

"But you're not ordinary," Grimbald replied. "You're the son of Prince Mathis, God rest his soul, which means you have a stronger claim to the throne than Mazarin."

"Please," said Michael, "can we keep this secret? I only found out this morning, and I'm still trying to get my head round the whole situation. The last thing I want is to cause any trouble in Kilion, and I really don't think that at fifteen, I have the ability to rule this country properly. I think it would be best for everyone involved, if at least for the moment, my identity was kept secret. Please don't tell a living soul who I really am. I need time to figure out what to do." The thought of his secret becoming common knowledge upset him so much his face was flushed. "Please, please promise me that not a word of this will leave your lips?"

His heart filled with compassion, Grimbald put aside his plans of helping Michael acquire the throne and agreed immediately. Sophie likewise nodded in agreement, her actions automatic as her mind was still trying to grasp the fact that this boy was really the King of Kilion.

"Could you at least put my mind at rest about your poor father's death? Grimbald asked, "you see, here in Kilion, we were told of the unprovoked attack on the Prince, but they said they couldn't bring his body back for a proper, Royal burial as he'd been buried in England. Me and my wife, see, we were distraught because we'd have loved to say goodbye to him, properly like." Tears welled up, for although his murder had been years before, thinking about it still managed to stir his emotions.

Michael face took on an expression of surprise. "I... I'm n... n... not sure what you m... m... mean," he stammered, "my dad just disappeared. He was supposed to be coming home from work one night and he never made it back."

Confused, Grimbald asked, "We were told he was mugged but it had gone wrong and he'd been killed in the struggle."

"But how would you know that when even my mum never found out what happened to him? Who told you?"

"Richard, the Gatekeeper told us. He had a farm nearby; it was his job to make sure no harm came to your father. It was he who brought us the sad news," Grimbald explained, thinking it odd that he hadn't actually seen Richard since.

At the mention of the farmhouse, Michael's hand flew to his mouth and he stumbled backwards. Fortunately Dan was on hand to steady him. So that was it? Suddenly it all clicked into place, his dad's untimely disappearance, the police finding nothing and the local news article in the paper reporting the 'farmyard slaughter' that same night.

Eager to find out what had caused Michael to react so badly, but not wanting to pressure the boy who was clearly upset, Grimbald laid his hand on Michael's arm and waited patiently for him to compose himself.

After a couple of deep breaths, during which time Michael had organised his thoughts, he explained everything he knew about the night his dad went missing. He spoke of the report on the farmhouse and how the farmer's wife and two children had been discovered, murdered, in the hallway. He said how the police had found the bodies, each with a single gunshot wound... and that there had been blood stains which had failed to match the blood of any member of the Arkwright family.

"What about Richard and Mathis?" Grimbald enquired.

As Michael slowly turned his head to look into the kind eyes of the older man, he whispered, "Their bodies were never found and neither was the weapon."

At that, the realisation hit all five at the same time, "So, if Mathis wasn't buried in England, and he wasn't buried here, do you think there's a chance he might still be alive?" Sophie whispered.

Wary about raising his hopes, but unable to contain his excitement at the prospect, no matter how small, that he might still have a father, Michael responded breathlessly. "I hope so."

"Given what's just been said, he can't have been killed when they said he was," Hazel said, stepping closer to Michael, "for if they'd killed him, surely to stop any questions, it would have been easier to produce his body as evidence."

"Makes sense to me," agreed Dan. "I can't see any reason not to bring the body of someone back if they were dead, unless they were still alive."

By this point, Michael's eyes were wide open, his heart was pounding furiously against his ribcage and his hands were trembling with excitement at the thought that he might, just might, still have a dad, Michael said, "I can't stay here and do nothing. I've got to try to find him."

The same thought had crossed Hazel's mind. At least that had been before common sense had taken over. How would they find a single person, in a country they didn't know, with no method of transport and no idea what he now looked like. "I see where you're coming from," she soothed, "but I really think that searching aimlessly will achieve nothing." Sensing he was about to protest at her refusal, she quickly added. "Now we've discovered he may be alive, although a lot can happen in fourteen years, I think we should stay at Court, keep up the pretence of you being the great nephew of Abednego, and make subtle enquiries to try to find out where he might be or at least work out a starting point."

As Michael opened his mouth with a counter-argument, they heard a noise behind them and immediately stopped talking, leaving a deadly silence to encase them. Nervously, their eyes flitted around the passage, their pupils dilated, their senses alert to potential danger. Gloominess however, was the friend of their foe and had enabled its accomplices to remain safely hidden. Just then three guards appeared from out of the shadows. Their eyes were as cold as ice, boring into them as their huge, armour clad frames approached.

Frozen to the spot, unsure of the way in underground tunnels, they eyed the approaching guards cautiously, assessing for potential weaknesses. Stopping abruptly, just yards away from where they were huddled, the guard in the middle sneered, "Do you honestly think we're going to let you have your freedom? That we'll stand aside as you try to find your poor, pathetic father? You underestimate Raglin if you think this is an option!"

As the middle guard roared with laughter the slightly shorter guard to his left continued. "Indeed, it's our intention to escort you and your... assortment of friends to his apartment. I'm sure he'll be wanting to get involved in any decisions concerning your future." Joining in the laughter of the middle guard, he added, "and with five for the price of one, I think we can expect some hefty rewards for our good work tonight, don't you think?"

Feeling his ring light up, Michael jerked into action, discarding his worries about the rings discovery. He rubbed the ring on his finger and closed his eyes, concentrating his anger on the guards, the ring began glowing. His blood boiled at the thought of being deprived of his dad's company for these last fourteen years. Initially the guards looked stunned, then excited as they realised what Michael possessed, but then as they surged forwards, their weapons threatening Michael and his companions, an avalanche of rocks from the ceiling above fell directly onto them; some landed on their armour and slithered off, others crashed into their faces, causing temporary blindness as they yelped in pain. Slipping and sliding on the damp floor, they crashed into each other like skittles, confused and dazed and unable to concentrate on anything except preventing injury.

Seizing the opportunity, all five ran from the guards, down the passageway, uncertain as to where they were going. None of them had any idea of the dangers lurking there but they figured if they wanted to escape, they had no option but to continue heading into the unknown. Occasionally scraping themselves along the wall where rocks jutted out, it wasn't long before they were panting, frightened for their lives.

"Quick, here," Dan, who had been at the front of the group, indicated an opening to his right.

Following behind, anxious to avoid the guards who had regained their composure, they took a turning down an even narrower path. The floor was just as uneven as before, the walls were much closer and the ceiling much lower, creating a feeling of claustrophobia. Once more Michael's ring glowed, allowing them some light. He could feel it tugging him, just as it had on the evening they'd entered the farmhouse. The others stepped aside as Michael took the lead, allowing the ring complete control over his movements. The ring was leading them through more turnings, the passages becoming smaller, and soon Grimbald had to hunch his head and shoulders through the confined space until finally, they reached a ladder which allowed their ascent. Before them was an opening where they could see the outline of two moons in the sky.

The fresh air caressed their faces as one by one they made their way into the open, finding themselves in an unfamiliar section of the castle grounds. From where they were standing, they could barely make out the faint silhouette of the fountains and statues residing in the back courtyard of the castle. Instinctively they knew that to save their lives, they needed to head away from the castle. Any option of returning had been taken from them the moment the guards had overheard their conversation about Michael's heritage.

Momentarily they faltered, unsure of where to go. They felt trapped, the castle was surrounded by a huge moat and wall, which none of them except perhaps Grimbald was able to cross. The only alternative was the huge wrought iron gates guarded by the King's own men and it was unlikely they would allow Mazarin's guests to escape in the dead of night.

Fortunately after a few moments of indecision, the ring worked its magic and Michael was once more content to allow the ring to pull him in the direction it obviously thought best. And so it was that Michael led the others through the trees, being careful not to tread on the pretty flowerbeds randomly scattered on the luscious green grass. Soon they realised they were in familiar territory, as Michael remembered exploring this area during Viola's tour. In the distance, Dan spotted the door to the secret passageway which Viola had excitedly pointed out to them yesterday, but recalled how it hadn't been used for years and then... the ring!

In tune with Dan's thoughts, Michael and Hazel headed towards it without hesitation, hoping their instincts would be proven right. As soon as they approached, the ring glowed as brightly as it ever had done and the stone slab, bedecked in italic writing, although in a language none of them could decipher, rolled aside allowing them access. Michael was the first to descend the muddy steps followed by Sophie, Dan and Hazel, with Grimbald following at the end. He thought that if the guards were to catch up, he would have the best chance of fending them off. Fortunately, the guards remained out of sight as Grimbald clambered in and returned the slab to its resting place.

Pausing to catch their breath, they rested against the walls, physically and mentally exhausted from the evening's events, aware there was little chance of getting any rest for quite some time.

Ashamed, Michael bowed his head, his hands clasped in front of him, trembling and blaming himself for their predicament. If he'd lied to Grimbald and stuck to the story concocted by Abednego, nothing this bad would have happened. The guards would still have found them but may well have taken them to Mazarin who would probably just have lectured them for wandering around, but by telling Grimbald the truth, not only had he provided them with evidence about his parentage, but also the whereabouts of the ring. Guilt at his stupidity gnawed away at him, and nothing anyone could say would make him feel any better.

"Perhaps," said Dan. "It was the incentive we needed to get out of the castle. It was full of danger anyway." Casting his dark eyes along the new tunnel, he wondered where it would take them, but felt happier knowing that no-one else could gain access, which meant they were safe for the moment at least.

"Suppose," Michael mumbled, "but I think we should try to find my dad."

"I understand why you want to find him, but our main priority needs to be making sure we're all safe."

Sophie, who until now had remained silent, finding it a lot to take in, murmured agreement with Hazel. She for one, didn't want to die or find herself locked up. "First of all we should find ourselves a hideaway, where no one will find us."

Determined to have his input, Dan added, "Let's follow this tunnel and see where it takes us."

"I'm sorry," muttered Grimbald, "If I hadn't asked Michael who his father was none of this would have happened."

"Let's stop worrying about blame. None of us could have foreseen what was going to happen. So we were heard... the main thing is that we've all escaped unharmed. Let's just do as Dan says, and find out where it takes us then decide what to do from there," Sophie asserted, discarding her usual mild manner to take control of the situation.

"What about Abednego?" Wiping the dirt from her hands onto her cloak and readjusting the handle of the bag which was digging into her shoulder. Hazel couldn't help imagining the poor old man visiting their room tomorrow morning only to find them gone. "What if he thinks we've been kidnapped, or murdered? Or that we've run away without telling him? Isn't there some way we can let him know we're alright." Despite delighting in this adventure, which was the most exhilarating thing she'd ever been part of, she was aware of the very real dangers they faced. Really it would be better if they had Abednego with them.

"Don't worry, we'll figure out a way of letting him know where we are. It's recently caught my attention that little Michael here..." Grimbald patted him on the arm, "seems to have possession of Mathis' ring. That at least should be able to help us get some kind of message to him. Don't you think?"

Gladdened by the thought, Hazel couldn't help but remember the others who weren't so fortunate; Catherine, Mary, her dad and nanny Rose, to name a few.

"Come on," Grimbald prodded at Dan who was barring the way. "Let's get moving." Figuring they should put as much distance between them and the castle as possible, they cautiously made their way down the tunnel which seemed to go on for miles, until they came to a dusty and cracked wooden door.

***

Pushing at the frame, expecting it to be locked, Michael was surprised to find it opened easily. Peering inside, the room was pitch black. Fortunately his ring was still glowing, providing adequate light.

As the others tumbled in behind, they were surprised to witness candles and flames lighting up, one by one of their own accord! The room was so bleak they thought they were probably in a basement somewhere. To the back a narrow staircase led upwards, out of sight. The wall to their left was completely covered in bookcases, although the titles of the books were obscured by cobwebs and dust. The furniture seemed in good condition, but again was so dirty, no one wanted to sit down. It was clear no-one had visited there for quite some time. To their right was a small opening, indicating the presence of another room. Eager to discover what mysteries it held, they traipsed into it, only to find a small kitchen. Against the back wall a grimy old cracked cauldron hung above some half burned wood, which could be used for cooking, but first they would need to get some food as the cupboards were bare.

With little else in the room to hold their interest Hazel and Michael were eager to investigate upstairs, while both Sophie and Dan were slightly more cautious. "What if something dangerous is up there?" said Dan, who was he knew, being a overly vigilant after the events of that evening.

"I'm sure there's no need to worry," Michael responded. "If there is something awful up there, I'm sure it won't take them long to figure out that only a staircase separates them from us." Michael chuckled to himself, his humour having returned after his earlier worries.

Clambering up the stairs, Michael in front and Hazel behind, they emerged onto the landing of the next floor, only to discover that the upstairs was as empty and unimpressive as it was below. Shouting down to the others, telling them it was safe, it wasn't long before Sophie, Dan and Grimbald converged on the upper floor, all eager to find out whether it led to any more secret passageways. After thoroughly searching the rooms, they were a little deflated to discover nothing of any importance. It seemed the only way they could get out other than the passage back to the castle was the front door.

Without asking permission or indicating her intention, Hazel zipped over to the front door and peered outside. Expecting some magical, mystical place, she was unimpressed to find that outside there was nothing more exciting than a few similar houses in the centre of a small, quietly sleeping village. Opening the door further, she stepped into the fresh air in the hope that a better view would allow her to find a huge building or something magnificent, which might explain why this house had been chosen as the end of a secret passageway. She could see nothing except for clusters of dainty houses.

"Close the door!" ordered Dan. "What if the guards go past and see us? We'll be arrested. We've got to be really careful, for Michael's sake." Irritated by Hazel's complete lack of concern for their safety, Dan huffed and retreated downstairs back into the passageways.

Closing the door, the others followed Dan downstairs where Michael used his ring, which he was starting to get the handle of, to light the logs in the fire, creating small crackling flames which went some way to providing some warmth.

Exhausted and unable to think properly, they rested there a while, busily trying to formulate a plan, and so, sitting around the fire, they listened as Grimbald told them stories of Mathis and his elder brother Melchior in their younger days, of their feats of bravery and shows of kindness, of the wars which beset Kilion, the death of the King and how his ring had never been found. He told how Azarel had been cursed and badly disfigured before vanishing from Kilion. They all listened intently as Grimbald described how Mathis had rejected the troubles of Kingship and had opted for a life free of power and politics. They all hung on his every word, caught up in the history that had shaped this, the future, and wondering what had happened to the other ring.

Chapter Forty: A Change of Plan

His neck ached where he had fallen asleep awkwardly at his desk. Arousing slowly from his slumber, in the dead of night; Richard stirred and opened his eyes, looked at the table beside him and fell back asleep. It took a few seconds for his brain to compute that something was wrong. Opening his eyes once more, adjusting to the darkness of the room, he tried working out what it was that was different, but for the moment his mind was befuddled from exhaustion.

Rising to his feet, he stretched his arms in the air and yawned as the bones in his shoulders clicked back into place. Pushing his chair under his desk, he instinctively went to grab his keys and that's when he discovered they weren't there!

"Jasper!" He yelled down the corridor to get the attention of his limping attendant.

"What's wrong?" A croaky voice responded after a short pause.

"Do you have the keys to the cell?" Richard asked, praying fervently that Jasper had taken them to do some chore or check on Mathis.

"No," his response was immediate and certain, "you locked up tonight, remember."

Richard's heart sank from the answer he had expected, but had still hoped would be different. Maybe he had put them down somewhere. It wasn't beyond the realms possibility,after all, he was tired and had been known to lack concentration when suffering from sleep deprivation.

With that thought, and hope, in the back of his mind, he scoured his room, but it didn't take long, for it was so sparsely decorated there wasn't much to search. First he looked under the bed, then under his covers, in the cupboard and finally in his drawers but the keys weren't there.

Starting to panic, he headed out of his room and took the stairs two at a time. He checked in the kitchen, the cupboards, then by the fire, but once again, he was left unsuccessful. He then tried scouring the small living room, but again found nothing.

"Don't just lie around doing nothing!" Richard shouted, at the top of his voice. "Get yourself out of bed and start helping." Realising it was his fault, he knew he had no excuse for being so sharp to the ever faithful Jasper, and even contemplated apologising, but couldn't bring himself to do it. He was so worked up and annoyed at himself, all common sense and politeness had fled. He was enraged that after fourteen years of keeping Mathis safe, of securing his person behind bars, now was the time for the keys to go missing. Why were things going wrong now?

The blood drained from his face at the thought that somehow, the prisoner might have escaped. Turning on his heel, he bounded down the stairs to the cell to find... an empty room. He looked around, knowing that if Mathis had been there, he would have seen him straight away but he checked again anyway

"No!" He yelled in despair, "he's gone." He felt faint, all his energy deserted him as he slumped to his knees on the cold, crumbling stone floor. Chills travelled up his spine and crept through his body as he realised the full extent of the devastation which would come his way if this wasn't corrected. He had two options: he could either search for the prisoner on his own in the hope that he or Jasper found him; or he could send word immediately via his hunting hawk to Raglin and prey a full scale search would ensure the capture of the Prince whose life had cost him so much.

With each precious second that passed, the Prince would be further away, he needed to decide quickly and he knew how much his future depended upon his choice. After just seconds he reasoned it would be better to tell Raglin immediately, because if he didn't find Mathis and then later had to confess he'd had waited to tell him, the penalty would be far, far worse.

Hurtling up the staircase, Richard grabbed some parchment, pen and ink, and then scribbled a quick note outlining how Mathis had gone missing. Addressing it to Raglin, he sealed the note then whistled for his hunting hawk. Attaching the rolled script to the right leg of his faithful bird, he indicated where it should go and watched as it flew gracefully out of the window into the night sky.

Grabbing his coat, he quickly shoved it on before making his way outside. Jasper followed as he headed deeper into the forest, tip-toeing through the trees and thickets, trying to be as quiet as possible. The last thing they wanted was for Mathis to hear them and hide among the dense undergrowth, that way they would never find him. Richard hoped fervently that in his poor condition, Mathis wouldn't be able to get very far or run from them if they caught sight of him.

***

As usual, Raglin's window was open, for he was determined that he could be reached at any time by his Master, who although within the castle could only reach him using a specially trained bird. It was more than his life was worth if his Master sent for him and he didn't respond immediately.

With the moons still high in the sky, Richards hawk soared through the gap, into Raglin's apartment and landed on his bed, screeching loudly enough to wake the old Courtier. Surprised by the shrill noise, Raglin grabbed the sword by his headboard and held it aloft to protect himself from intruders. Relieved at the sight of the bird, Raglin wondered what could be so urgent that he should be awakened at this time of night. Grabbing the parchment attached to the birds leg, he broke the seal and scanned the writing.

His face turned white with fear then red with fury as the implications of what had been written sunk in. Heading for his desk, he wrote a brief response, instructing Richard and Jasper to search as far as possible and informing them that he would arrange for reinforcements as soon as possible. Desperate to take command, he quickly got dressed and dragged his travelling cloak around his shoulders.

Heading along the passageway, within minutes he reached Hargrin's room. Fortunately Hargrin was a light sleeper and answered almost immediately, although Raglin sensed that the younger man was far from amused at having his beauty sleep disrupted. However, irritation slipped away when he realised it was Raglin standing at his door and immediately feared the worst.

"We have problems," he said, his voice brisk.

"What's happened?" Hargrin asked.

"Mathis has gone missing! I'm heading straight over to his cell to lead a search, but first of all, I need you to check that Michael and his friends are safely tucked up in bed."

"Why wouldn't he be? He knows nothing about the prisoner, does he?" Hargrin replied as he ran his hands though his dishevelled hair, which was usually so well groomed.

"I know there's no reason he shouldn't be there, but the same could be said for Mathis. I just need peace of mind.

"What if he's not there?" The thought of finding an empty room filled the Minister with dread, the last thing he wanted to do was to make a wrong decision and incur the wrath of Raglin and the Master.

"Then wake Abednego and find out what he knows, but hopefully it won't come to that." Anxious to get going, he made to leave when his arm was gripped by a fearful Hargrin.

"What if the old man knows nothing?" he ventured, his mind flitting through endless possibilities. He knew he was being stupid, there was probably nothing to worry about, but it didn't stop these scenarios swimming in his head now the seed of doubt had been sown.

"Then use your initiative and think for yourself; do something to find them. My immediate priority is making sure Mathis is caught before he is discovered. If Michael and his friends aren't in their room, and Abednego doesn't know where they are... I don't know... find Zawi Chemi... see if she can give you anything to help. Use your initiative." Frustrated and worried that he'd have to inform the Master of this turn of events, he turned on his heel and left the room.

Heading down the hallways to the front of the castle, he attracted the attention of a loyal guard and instructed him to ready his mount. It would have been far too cumbersome and noisy to take a carriage and he knew his horse would be much swifter through the forest.

It was just a few minutes before his horse was brought to him and Raglin mounted as swiftly as a man half his age. Bending to whisper orders in the guard's ear, he made himself comfortable before galloping in the direction of the cell.

***

They hadn't been searching long when Jasper happened to come across the sleeping form of Mathis who had curled up by a tree and fallen asleep, exhausted from the exertion.

Calling out to his Master, Jasper was overcome with excitement at finding the prisoner. He realised that he could well have secured the safety of both he and Richard, for if they had lost him, who knew what penalty would have been inflicted. Once more his fate seemed secure, for Jasper had been eagerly anticipating the day when he would finally be free to do what he wanted, to make his own decisions, to no longer be tied to living on his own, in a dangerous forest with no friends or company save his Master, who rarely even deigned to acknowledge his existence, despite owing him his life.

Hurtling through the trees, Richard joined Jasper and a genuine smile spread across his wrinkled and weary face, and for the first time since they had been living there, he threw his arms round his servant and hugged him. Jasper stumbled, his weak leg barely able to take the weight. Regaining his posture, Jasper said nothing, too taken aback by Richard's emotional response, for never once had Richard showed any sign of possessing any feelings.

"Quick," whispered Richard holding out some rope, "tie his hands, it'll make it easier for us to lead him back." Tugging none too gently at Mathis wrists, they woke the sleeping Prince.

Eyes focusing on the two faces peering down on him, Mathis couldn't believe his attempted escape had been discovered so quickly. Tears sprung to his eyes and this time he made no attempt to struggle. Fourteen years ago he had fought back and for that he had been rewarded with a knife through the shoulder; he wasn't about to make the same mistake twice. Then he had been young and agile and had only faced one man. This time, his body was tired, weak and lacking any energy; this time there were two of them. Unable to look them in the eyes, his head hung limply on his chest. His body was like putty as they pulled at his arms and with savage brutality bound them together tightly. The ropes scraped his fragile skin, allowing traces of blood to seep through, and through all of this he said nothing, he had no intention of letting them know how much they were hurting him.

Pulling him to his feet, they escorted him back. Richard took the lead at the front while the feeble frame of Jasper lumbered beside him, helping to hold him upright. If Mathis hadn't known better, he would have called the assistance an act of kindness by the grey, greasy haired servant, but Mathis knew the only reason he was helping him was because of the accident which had left him limping so now he couldn't walk too fast.

It wasn't long before Mathis was being pushed back into his cell and once more, his feet felt the cold stone slabs beneath him. Struggling over to his mattress, he collapsed on it exhausted. Physically and emotionally drained, he closed his eyes as a feeling of desolation swept through his whole body; he felt empty. All he could do to keep himself going was to focus on what it had been like, for that brief period of time, when his eyes had been able to gaze at the stars and the moon above, when his cheeks had felt the freshness of the grass against them, and the night air had blown on him, caressing his skin, welcoming him back to a life of freedom. It seemed so cruel that it had been snatched from him so quickly, and that he was once again incarcerated in this cold, dreary cell, awaiting a fate that was in somebody else's hands.

Unable to contain himself, he cried. Not just silent tears rolling down his face, but uncontrollable sobbing, causing his whole body to heave and shake with the effort. It was the crying of a man so desperate and yet so afraid of death becoming his only welcoming friend. He knew that from now on, his captors would be ever more vigilant to make sure he didn't escape. Tonight had been his one chance and he had let it slip through his fingers, like fine sand on a golden beach.

**

From the branches above, in the deathly arms of the skeletal trees, Siddons had watched as they had bound his wrists and hauled him away. He couldn't believe that in just half an hour, so much could have changed; how freedom could turn to captivity, how overwhelming joy and excitement could be transformed into the depths of despair.

It didn't seem fair! He'd left Mathis to rest while he had scoured the local area, and his journey had been a success, for he had found a secluded area, made sure it was safe from local creatures lurking in the undergrowth and then worked out a safe route there. It would have given Mathis time to recuperate, at least a few hours until day break. His heart brimming with joy and excitement, he had headed directly back to where Mathis lay, eager to wake him and lead him there. Then, just as he approached, he'd heard the voices.

Carefully gliding to a halt, and landing on branches high above the ground, he'd searched below to discover their whereabouts. His heart had plummeted as his vision had rested on the two men binding his arms. He'd desperately wanted to help, to do something to save him, but what? He was just five inches tall and as much as he'd considered all options possible, he couldn't see how he could have done anything to prevent them capturing him. Dejected, he'd flown to the nearest tree and prayed for a miracle that would stop them taking Mathis. God hadn't answered his prayers.

Since then Siddons had remained on his branch unable to move, not knowing what to do. He couldn't bring himself to face Mathis once more in his cell, couldn't adorn the happy face he knew he should wear for the occasion. He knew he should offer some comfort, but just couldn't face it. What if Mathis asked about another attempt? How would he say that the chances of a second escape were unlikely? He just didn't have the strength of character to deal with it at the moment. Yet he couldn't go back to his village either, for they had disowned him. He, like Mathis was alone, and he didn't know how he was going to cope.

Tears rolled down his furry face, dripping off his nose and onto the floor below. He couldn't just sit here, open to the elements; he needed to go somewhere to think, to hide from the forests dangers. So, with no destination in mind, he flapped his wings and flew aimlessly through the trees and bracken, all the while secretly hoping to bump into a vampire or another creature that might end his misery. Finally, his wings exhausted, his eyes tired from the late night and weeping, he landed by the stump of a tree. Nestling himself down, it wasn't long before he had cried himself to sleep.

***

Rearing his horse in front of Richard's house, Raglin wasted no time in dismounting and tying its reins to the nearest tree. Stumbling towards the building, with his anger all consuming, he barged into their kitchen unannounced and came face-to-face with Richard, who along with Jasper was slumped at the table, waiting for him to arrive.

"Why aren't you searching for him? I thought I made it perfectly clear he's to be found immediately." Raglin roared, blood flowing to his face, turning it as red as the misty sky earlier that evening.

"We have him. He's safely secure, back in his cell." Richard answered, his voice slightly resentful at the obvious lack of respect accorded to them by the over mighty noble.

Sighing with relief, Raglin's tense shoulders relaxed, and yet, not ready to believe their reassurances until he had seen the evidence for himself, he made his way to the cell and was relieved to find Mathis curled up like a baby on the mattress, just as he had been the last time he'd seen him.

Returning once more to the kitchen, his anger still unsated, he roared, "How did he escape?" His body bore down on them, his thick set physique and stormy eyes no less intimidating than it had been fourteen years before when first they had incurred his wroth. Raglin hated incompetence of any kind, and he considered the crime even worse when the result was the escape of a valuable prisoner. For with only one set of keys in existence, it was clear that some ineptitude had been responsible.

Exhausted from the events of the night and the worry they had suffered, Richard had hoped the visit would be brief and that he would be allowed to crawl into the safety of his bed. With difficulty Richard managed a modicum of deference in his whispered reply, "I've no idea, my lord. The keys were next to me when I went to sleep. Yet, when

I woke up, they had gone. We rushed straight to the cell only to find it empty. I wrote to you immediately to ensure the quickest search for his return. Once that had been done, Jasper and I searched for him and found him sleeping under a tree."

"I didn't ask what happened! I asked how it was that he was able to escape!" Raglin roared.

"I don't know," Richard unwillingly conceded, "no matter how hard I think, and through all the possibilities I've considered, I can't work out how he got the keys from my desk, and that's the truth." His last statement was delivered with some force, as was his stare which Raglin rightly interpreted as a challenge to question his story.

Unwilling to get into an argument, especially as the prisoner was once more secure, Raglin ignored Richard's lack of deference and focused on more important issues. "Where are the keys now?" His voice had calmed, yet he still felt irritated at being called out in the middle of the night to deal with this fiasco.

"I don't know. We've searched both him and the cell, but can find nothing. So to secure him, I've placed a new padlock on his door; that should prevent him escaping again but as for the keys? It's a mystery."

Exasperated, Raglin slumped onto a seat beside them and considered what course of action he should take. It was clear that someone or something was trying to help the Prince escape, which was the last thing he could afford to happen, for it would completely jeopardise their plan.

"Someone, get me some parchment and ink," he demanded, then watched Jasper rise from his seat and limp out of the room, only to come back a few minutes later with a quill, ink and some scroll. Making sure they weren't looking over his shoulder as he wrote, he scribbled a note to his Master, indicating that he considered it time to introduce Mathis to his son, or if not his son, someone sufficiently like him to convince Mathis that it was in fact, his child. Tonight he would have the ring and the password! He knew the plan was being rushed. He just hoped Hargrin had sufficiently ingratiated himself with the boy to coax the password from him once Mathis passed it on. It wasn't ideal, but he had to do something lest Mathis escape a second time. Raglin, convinced it was the only sensible option open to him, summoned Richard's hawk, tied the note to its leg, whispered its destination and watched as the bird flew out of the door towards the castle.

Relieved that the night was turning out slightly better than expected, Raglin decided he would be best served waiting with Richard and Jasper; it wouldn't take their Master long to arrange for Hargrin to bring the teenagers to him, afer all the younger Minister would already have them in his company. And despite Hargrin not knowing where the cell was based, he shouldn't find following the hawk too difficult. Most likely, the other Courtiers would remain oblivious as involving too many might arouse the boy's suspicion.

His throat dry from the journey, Raglin demanded a drink then allowed himself to think of his hopes of the future. Tonight was the night all their plans would start to reach fruition. Tonight, he'd reunite Michael with his long lost dad and watch Mathis give up the password for the ring. Once this was complete, he'd witness Mathis' life being taken from him. Finally, with the gateway opened, he would be the one to obtain the healing waters which would herald the rule of Azarel as Kilion's new King.

Chapter Forty-one: Following his Lead

Determined to undertake his task while arousing as little suspicion as possible, Hargrin visited the rooms of Michael, Dan and Hazel personally. Initially his knock was quiet, to make sure no-one else was woken by the commotion. However, after receiving no answer, he tapped slightly harder; again, no answer. Slightly concerned, he wondered whether the memory loss tablets were causing them to sleep deeper than normal. So, for a third time and a little harder than before, he rapped at the door. Still there was no answer and a niggling sensation of fear crept into his thoughts. Wondering what to do, for the door was clearly locked, he stood for a few moments in contemplation. Then, removing a bejewelled brooch from his cloak he carefully manoeuvred the pin into the lock and was relieved to find his old skills had not deserted him.

Pushing at the door carefully, he tiptoed into the dark room and headed straight to the bed in front of him. He was shocked to discover it was empty. Moving to the other bed at the side of the room, he staggered back after finding that it this too remained vacant. Lastly, he approached the adjoining door and shoved it open, turned on the lights and stared at the third bed which was also bare.

Despite having asked Raglin questions about what he should do if this situation arose, he hadn't actually considered it a possibility. After all, what were the chances that they, as well as Mathis would have disappeared the same night? Especially as to his knowledge, neither knew of the other's existence; it seemed so ridiculous that initially he was at a loss. He needed to act quickly. At dinner time he had felt so near to achieving the glory that he had aspired to his whole life, and now he could almost feel it. Yet just hours later, unless he found the boy, his chance at greatness was going to slip through his fingers. Okay, he tried to calm himself, remember what did Raglin tell me to do if this happened? His mind went back to their earlier conversation; should he visit Abednigo in the hope he knew something? Or Zawi Chemi, the wise woman of the Court?

Rushing from the rooms, he flitted through the castle as quietly as possible until he stood outside Zawi Chemi's room, he decided that given the circumstances, magical assistance might be a wise option and help any visit he had to make to Abednigo.

No sooner had he approached her room than the door swung open for him, as though somehow she had been expecting his arrival. For a while neither spoke, Hargrin needed time to decide how best to coax the favour he required from her, Zawi Chemi had equally important decisions to make. As the silence grew, she looked him up and down and assessed the extent to which she would allow herself to become embroiled in the intrigues which were being played out at Court. Her memory flitted back to her earlier conversation with Abednego: she had been horrified to discover the real reason for Hargrin's acquisition of the memory loss tablets, and had promised him she would do nothing further to assist the Courtiers. However, sensing the sorry state of Hargrin, who now stood depleted before her, she couldn't help but feel some sympathy for him. And so, she beckoned him to sit, willing to at least listen to his woes, and probably the favour he was bound to request.

"I assume there's a reason for your visit at such a late... or rather, early hour?" she enquired, her steely grey eyes focused on those of the man before her.

Adept at lying, it was with ease that Hargrin regurgitated a mass of untruths to the crinkled woman who had always proven susceptible to his charms. He told her of his worry for the safety of the teenagers, how he had thought he'd been helping them by acquiring the memory loss tablets; but now that he had witnessed the effects they were having on them, he was becoming ever more worried about their health and well-being. He confessed his naivety, how he'd believed himself to be acting on the King's behalf, but that after careful consideration, he was starting to wonder whether this was in fact, the case.

Conscious that he was rambling, he paused in the hope that a response from the old woman might indicate her initial thoughts. To his disappointment, she offered nothing and so it was with trepidation that he continued, though he kept the rest short. "After noticing the early departure of the youngsters tonight, I was worried that it might be the tablets making them ill. Imagine my dismay! I mean, I've grown fond of them; I even took them on a tour of the castle grounds today. The thought of harm coming to them... well... it's just awful. So tonight after the feast, I lay in bed but rest alluded me, my mind kept wandering and I couldn't help but suspect that someone... I won't mention any names for fear of being wrong... might be, you know, not acting in their best interests."

"So what is it you want from me?" She asked, half-believing his story but wondering how she could possibly help if he was telling the truth.

"I was hoping you could supply me with an invisibility potion," he requested, and then added as she raised her eyebrows speculatively. "You see, I have an inkling they might be having secret meetings, and if my suspicions are correct, Michael might well be a topic that is high on the agenda. I thought, if I were invisible, I could unsuspectingly gatecrash one of their rendezvous and find out their intentions. Then if, as I suspect, there are plans involving Michael, I will be able to inform the King or Abednego immediately."

"I see," the wise woman mused, more to herself than to him. "There is clearly logic in your suggestion, but tell me, why not go straight to the King, or Abednego with your suspicions?" Her question was a simple one, one he had expected.

"I had considered that option, but after some reflection, I realised that the only real evidence I have is my own instincts and their strange behaviour at the end of the feasts, which isn't really sufficient evidence to go around making serious accusations. And then, even if the King does believe me and interrogated the Courtiers, I suspect it highly unlikely any confessions would be forthcoming, and what would be worse, is that they'd be even more careful knowing that there was suspicion clouding them. Their tracks would be even harder to follow." Feeling he had sufficiently dealt with the 'why' he hadn't told Mazarin, he moved on to the issue of Abednego, playing on her soft spot for him and the possible impact on his health, "as for Abednego; he's not as young as he once was and I wouldn't want to worry him unnecessarily. Of course as soon as I discover any concrete evidence, he'd be the first person I'd inform, but if I find nothing, at least I'd be able to put my mind to rest."

"Clearly you've considered your options, but how do I know you speak the truth?"

"I have no hard evidence. I'll understand if you refuse my request, for I appreciate I am placing you in a rather awkward position, and for that I am sorry. Look, forget what I've said..." He cast his eyes downwards, revelling in the successful deception of a witch, "I'm sure I'll think of some other way to put my mind at rest." He made to bid her farewell as he rose from his seat.

"Wait," she commanded, "I hope you're speaking the truth about your desire to help them, for I cannot bear the thought of anything happening to a relative of Abednego's, especially a boy so young." Zawi left the room, but was gone no more than a couple of minutes before returning with a tiny bottle filled with green frothy liquid. Placing it gently in the palm of his hand, she carefully folded his fingers around the bottle, and then looked at him squarely. Her white wispy hair escaping from the bun she always wore it in. Hargrin noticed that she looked all her years and more. "I'll help you for the sake of Abednego, and I trust that you're not deceiving me, for if I find out you've misled me, and that you use this potion for anything other than helping the children, I promise you'll regret you ever made my acquaintance." With that warning she bid him farewell.

He was shaking as he left the room, his hands quivering violently as he deposited the bottle in his pocket beneath his cloak. Never before had he been talked to in such a venomous tone, and never before could he remember ever feeling physically sick at a threat.

Blanking it from his mind, hoping that the near future would bring him such power as to remove all fears of her warning, it was with trepidation that he made his way to Abednego's apartment, fully armed.

Once more he knocked quietly, praying the old man hadn't absconded with the children; then he waited a while, not wanting to appear impatient and all too aware of how late the hour was.

Inside his room, Abednego had lain awake, unable to sleep, fearing for Michael's safety. His mind was replaying the conversation he'd had with Zawi Chemi, and since retiring for the night, he had done nothing except try to work out the best way to remove his great nephew from the dangerous Courtiers without attracting suspicion.

Hearing the banging at the door, his mind was brought back to the present and he slowly rose from his bed, his limbs aching with age. Walking as quickly as his legs would carry him, he expected to find Michael, Dan or Hazel, or even the King on his doorstep. What he didn't expect was that he would be faced with the slimy Hargrin, who made his flesh crawl.

"What do you want?" His tone was harsh, his eyes unforgiving. Yet noticing the unkempt hair and the expression of worry etched on the younger man's face, Abednego knew that whatever it was, it had to be serious.

"Do you know where Michael and his friends are?" Hargrin asked. His speech was rushed and his tone was one of panic.

"Why, what' happened? Isn't he in his room?" Now it was time for Abednego to start worrying.

"No, I've just checked, and they're not there." Running his hands through his chestnut hair, Hargrin couldn't shake off his feeling of desperation. He could tell immediately from the reaction of the old man that Abednego was as much in the dark as he was about their disappearance.

"But why would you check on them this time of night?"

Unable to explain the real reason, Hargrin skimmed over the issue in an attempt to address the important part; where was the boy? "There's no time to go into it now, but suffice to say that Raglin got an inkling that something wasn't right and sent me to check on them. And he was right, for when I entered their room, they weren't there." Hargrin heard the words escape his lips and knew how lame they sounded, but fervently hoped Michael's disappearance would be enough to distract Abednego from questioning him any further... to his relief he was right.

Unable to take in the implications of their disappearance, Abednego stumbled back and fell onto an armchair. His breathing became laboured as he held his hand to his throat. The thought was too much, to think that his guests had gone missing, where could they be? Guilt enveloped him, for if he hadn't found Michael and given him the ring, none of this would have happened and he would be safe at home with his mother and friends, enjoying a nice summer holiday.

"Are you okay?" Hargrin rushed forward towards the old man, but kept some distance, for he knew of Abednego's dislike of him and the last thing he wanted was to antagonise him.

"I'll... be... fine." His speech was jolted for he was finding the delivery of his words difficult. His only consolation was that at least he knew that Raglin and Hargrin hadn't got their hands on the young teenagers, for if they had, why would they be waking him in the middle of the night to find out where they were? Perhaps sensing the danger they were in after their discoveries during the day, they had decided to escape. Thinking about it logically, perhaps it was best for all concerned that they were out of the way, but why hadn't they told him?

Knowing how much power the Courtiers possessed, and how important Michael was to them, Abednego knew he couldn't just leave them to defend themselves. He had to know they were safe, and so he decided, after some consideration, that as soon as Hargrin left the room he'd find them and offer his services.

"What should we do?" Hargrin demanded, increasingly aware of the seconds ticking away, half suspecting Abednego was playing for time.

"I... I... don't k... know." Stammered Abednego, "I need time to think, to come up with something..." He added. Closing his weary eyes, he sat deep in thought while Hargrin looked on, remaining silent, out of his depth and contemplating his next course of action.

Hargrin was certain he wasn't going to let the old man out of his sight. "Is there anywhere they might have gone?

To a relatives perhaps? Back home?" He suggested, desperate to uncover any evidence which could help locate Michael.

Abednego had initially thought they might try returning to England, back to their parents, but he knew by their very presence at Court they had no idea how to return home, and so it was with complete honesty he was able to respond, "None of them have any family close by and I'm certain they've never been further than the trip they took with your good self. I wouldn't know where to begin looking for them." Resting his head in his hands, he hoped Hargrin was buying into his expression of worry. "Perhaps we should inform the King?" He continued, "he will surely be able to get his men onto it straight away!"

As the old man had expected, Hargrin was loathe do so such a thing, arguing it wasn't necessary to worry the King so soon when they might well return before morning. Neither believed it, but it suited both of them to keep the King out of it.

"Perhaps they'll return of their own accord before morning, as you say," agreed Abednego, "and if they don't, we could say nine o clock to meet and discuss strategies?" Eager to be rid of Hargrin so as to begin mounting his own search, Abednego, rather rudely and completely out of character, opened his door to indicate that Hargrin had overstayed his welcome.

Obediently leaving the old man's apartment, Hargrin considered how the conversation had gone, replaying it over in his mind. He was content in the belief that Abednego, like himself, knew nothing of their disappearance. Yet he couldn't help but wonder whether the old man knew more than he was letting on about where they might be. For although he himself had a perfectly sound reason for abandoning the idea of involving the King, surely Abednego would want a full scale search to be launched as soon as possible... unless of course, he did know where they might be. So as soon as the door closed, Hargrin retrieved the invisibility potion, removed the stopper and took a swig of the liquid. A tingling sensation overwhelmed his body, spreading down his throat through his veins and to the extremities of his body. After a few moments he lifted his right arm, then left leg and peered down at them. He saw nothing! Amazed at the speed with which the potion had taken effect, he cautiously waited a few more seconds before once more knocking on the old man's door.

Inside his room, Abednego scoured his drawers and retrieved a ring from his late wives favourite trinket box. Just as he placed the ring on his finger to help him find Michael, he was disrupted by yet more knocking. Under his breath he cursed whoever was at the door this time and was tempted to ignore it. Not wanting to take the risk of whoever it was bursting in on him whilst with the second ring, he shoved the ring that Melchior had bestowed on him just before his last battle, into his pocket.

Answering the door, Abednego was confused to say the least, for there was nobody there, nor was there any sign of anyone down the corridor. Thinking it must be his mind playing tricks on him, he closed the door, not for one moment sensing the invisible form of Hargrin slip past him.

Focusing once more on finding Michael, Abednego removed the ring from his pocket and slipped it onto his wedding finger, oblivious of the unwanted presence.

Initially Hargrin had taken care to place some distance between him and Abednego, while remaining focused on every movement the old man made. Watching him remove the ring from a pocket under his cloak, Hargrin had to stop himself from exclaiming in delight at his discovery of the lost ring. Sensing his opportunity, he decided to grab the jewellery and scarper, thinking he could take it straight to Raglin and thus dispose of any need for Michael. As he lurched forwards, he accidently trod on Abednegos overlong cloak and Hargrin felt his body weight become feather light; his whole being, still attached to Abednego's cloak flew through the air, streaks of light flashing past him, the wind slapping his face.

He had no idea what was happening or where he was going, all he knew was that he had found the magic ring.

Chapter Forty-two: Finding Michael

The stars in the sky had reached their zenith, their lights shining more brightly than they had for some time. It was as though they had foreseen this was going to be a night of legends and had crowded into the sky to watch events unfold. The red mist had evaporated, leaving in its place a clear view of the two moons, luminous in the sky.

Inside the mud house, Hazel yawned while Michael's head kept jolting as he fought the battle against sleep. Watching the teenagers before him, Grimbald felt a feeling of tenderness and knew that sleep was calling. Rising from the hard, wooden seat and adjusting his huge cloak over his coat, he coughed then said, "Right, we all need some beauty sleep. I'll tell ya more stories tomorrow if yer like but I for one need to visit the land of nod." Heading towards the fire to put out what was left of the fierce, red burning embers he added, "no use us trying to conjure up amazing plans for our survival if we're too tired to think straight, now is it?"

"No," Hazel drowsily agreed, desperate for sleep but not at all sure she could even be bothered to move.

Sensing how comfortable the two girls seemed where they were, Grimbald said, "My thoughts were men upstairs, ladies downstairs. If that's okay with you?"

"Fine by me," Sophie mumbled, for her attention had started to wane and as much as she had enjoyed listening to tales of Mathis and Melchior, sleep was even more inviting.

"Tell you what," Grimbald continued, looking at Michael affectionately, "why don't you and Dan get yourselves upstairs and get ready for bed. I'll be up in a few moments once I've given this furniture a quick wipe over. Can't be letting these young ladies fall asleep in so much dirt now, can we?" Heading to the kitchen to find a cloth or towel to wipe the surfaces, he set about making the place a little more hygienic. The last thing he wanted was for anyone to catch a disease from the filth there.

Saying good night to everyone, Michael and Dan ascended the stairs and looked around to find the best place to sleep. "I'll have a quick look in that room," suggested Dan as he disappeared from view, hoping to find a soft surface to sleep on.

As Dan left the room, Michael heard a banging at the door and the faint croak of Abednego's voice. Astounded that the old man had discovered their whereabouts so swiftly, especially when they hadn't even thought he'd know about their disappearance yet, Michael scuttled to the door to let him in.

Throwing caution to the wind, forgetting to check for danger, Michael flung open the door and greeted the old man enthusiastically.

Shivering before Michael, his eyes half closed through weariness and his clothes dishevelled, Abednego stumbled forwards, his limbs tired but his heart filled with joy at the knowledge that Michael was safe.

But before Michael even had a chance to help Abednego inside, the old man's head suddenly jerked to the right hitting his shoulder and he slumped to the floor.

His mouth opening and closing, Michael wanted to scream yet his voice had deserted him. Anguished at Abednego's strange fall, Michael's leaden legs just about managed to stagger towards the unconscious body. His hands fumbled clumsily under Abednego's armpits to pull him into the safety of the house. Finally finding his voice, he shouted for someone to help him as he started to heave.

Hearing Michael's cry for help, Dan emerged from the room and asked what was wrong, but before Michael had a chance to respond, he felt an almighty thud across his right temple. Dropping Abednego, he clutched his hand to his head, stumbled to his right, then collapsed beside his great Uncle. His head was throbbing and he could feel warm, sticky blood trickle from a cut just above his eyebrow.

In the background he heard Dan yell followed by the thudding of footsteps. Michael willed himself to get to his feet but could barely move and before he was able to roll onto his side, he felt himself being lifted into the air.

His eyes half-closed and his vision blurred, he couldn't see what was carrying him.

He could hear Dan shouting for him to be put down, but his demands remained unanswered. Michael felt his strength ebb away, felt himself become increasingly weaker as he was slung like a sack of potatoes over something hard, then whisked away. The wind stung his face, drying the blood on his skin, but even the stinging sensation it brought wasn't enough to rouse Michael from his lethargy. The last thing he remembered was a frothy liquid being poured in his mouth and a tingling sensation flowing through his body before he gave way to nothingness.

***

Yelling at Michael to come back, Dan had rushed after him, running as fast as he could to catch up with his friend who was suspended in mid-air. Yet his attempt had been futile, for within no more than a minute he had watched as Michael had vanished, disappearing from sight before his very eyes.

Back in the house Hazel, Sophie and Grimbald who had heard the commotion from downstairs, had reached the top floor and watched Michael vanish and Dan halt abruptly, his body hunched forwards in despair.

As they awaited Dan's return, Hazel was astonished to notice the fallen body of Abednego by the front door. Picking up the old, limp man up in his strong arms, Grimbald carried him inside and gently placed him on the floor. Lying the cloak over his frail body Hazel and Sophie wiped his face and talked soothingly to him.

Full of frustration and anger, Dan returned to the house, his throat hoarse from shouting and his body tense with frustration. Sitting next to Hazel and Sophie, he stared at the old man, willing inspiration to come to him.

In the background Grimbald cursed under his breath, chastising himself for failing to protect the son of Mathis. It felt like he'd let his friend down a second time, for he should have been there to stop it. He knew he had to do something, to try to rescue him, but how? "Did you see what they looked like lad?" He asked Dan.

"That's... erm... no..." He stuttered, images of Michael aloft in the air still visible before him. "Whoever, or whatever it was, they were invisible and so was Michael after a while." Slumping onto the wooden floor, his dark hair straggling across his even darker eyes, he rested his chin on the palms of his hand, looking no less dejected than Grimbald.

"What do we do?" asked a horrified Hazel, images of a tortured Michael pervading her inner thoughts.

"I don't see there's much we can do!" Grimbald replied. If Michael was invisible then how could they find him? "I don't think we should go putting any of ourselves at risk at the moment, that won't do him any good at all, now will it?" Grimbald grunted, hating having to say it, for he was desperate to find Michael and get revenge on whoever was trying to harm him.

"I'm sure Abednego would know what to do," Dan's tone was wishful. "We just have to wait until he comes to." And so they sat in the dark, dusty room waiting for Abednego to regain consciousness. It wasn't long before sleep had taken them into her embrace.

***

Halting abruptly, Hargrin eased Michael from his shoulder and lay him down gently on the grass, uncertain about what he should do next. He'd rescued the boy safely, as Raglin would have wanted. But despite this achievement, he had no idea where he was or where he should go, for Abednego's ring had transported them to the cottage so quickly, he hadn't had time to get his bearings. He had no idea where they were in relation to the castle, or even where Raglin would be. His body, aching from carrying the teenager so far, scanned the vicinity before concluding it to be sufficiently safe to rest while collecting and processing his thoughts.

Yet try as he might, he was finding concentrating difficult; his mind just wasn't functioning properly. He was exhausted from having so little sleep, and for all this he was still considered relatively young, being only in his thirties, he wasn't used to being awake at such a late, or indeed, early hour. Above them, the darkness was fading and the moons beams were dimming, as the faint light of dawn spread its wings throughout the sky.

His initial instinct had been to try finding his way back to the castle, but with Michael still out for the count, and his body too tired to carry the boy much further, the thought was postponed. With no horse or Hunting Hawk, Hargrin couldn't see what else he could do, other than sit and wait to be found.

So he spent the next couple of hours struggling to keep his eyes open. Hargrin knew that if Michael gained consciousness and escaped while he slumbered; it would be more than his life was worth.

***

With the chirruping of birds signalling the advent of the sun, Michael finally awoke, his head feeling groggy. The invisibility potion had recently worn off both him and his captor and it was with little surprise Michael found himself face to face with Hargrin, whose charm seemed to have faded with the potion.

"Where are we?" Michael croaked, his eye sore from the thump he'd received at Hargrin's hands.

"Don't know." The Minister grunted, still worried about how they were going to get out of there. At least now Michael was conscious he would be able to walk.

Just then, as Hargrin heaved himself to his feet, he heard the galloping of hooves approaching and was barely able to contain his excitement when he saw Tacitus riding a dappled grey stallion and leading Hargrin's own mount.

Grabbing Michael's arm, making sure he couldn't escape, Hargrin hauled him to his feet and waited for the Minister to approach. The dappled horse soon reared up close enough for them to converse.

"Just had orders from the Master to come and collect you and the boy." We're to head straight to Raglin who is waiting with you know who." His voice was conspiratorial, and his face glowing with pleasure. Hargrin heaved a huge sigh of relief, for clearly like he, Raglin had claimed his prey.

"How did you know where I was?"

By the time Raglin got to the cell, the prisoner had been returned, but the escape attempt prompted the Master to bring the plan forward. Fortunately for you, it was as the hunting hawk was delivering this order the he glimpsed you. So, he came to find me and was able to lead me here, and now I have come to collect you and take you both to Raglin." Tacitus paused to catch his breath before adding, "We must hurry, Raglin's expecting us as early as possible." Dismounting, he tied the reigns to a trunk, and then grabbed hold of Michael's arm as Hargrin mounted his stead. Once he was comfortably in position, Hargrin clamped his hand round Michael's forearm whilst Tacitus grabbed hold of Michael's hips. Between the two of them they hoisted him onto the horse, positioning him in front of Hargrin to make escape impossible.

Untying his own horses reigns, Tacitus mounted before whistling shrilly, indicating for the horses to canter. Michael made no attempt at escape; with his head throbbing and Hargrin's arms clamped round him so tightly that breathing was difficult, he didn't like his chances.

The journey took quite some time and it certainly wasn't the most pleasant ride Michael had ever experienced. Soon enough he found himself being thrust off the horse, and his arms once more being gripped so tightly that he thought his blood supply would be cut off.

Between Tacitus on his left and Hargrin on his right, he was pushed into a small house, similar to the one he'd left behind. He was led through a hallway, and then manhandled down some stairs, where to his dismay, he noticed Raglin chatting animatedly with a middle-aged, stocky man. Hearing the arrival of his guests, Raglin looked up and smiled at Michael, "Just in time! Excellent job. Hargrin, keep him there just for a moment, won't you?"

While remaining encased in Hargrin's strong grip, he couldn't take his eyes off of where Raglin was standing. Behind him were steel bars, just like the ones which had kept Grimbald prisoner. They're going to lock me up! He thought to himself, and then peering inside the cell, he noticed a small basin, an old mattress and... there was already someone in there! Sitting on the bed, his back hunched forwards, was a skinny, dirty man, who when he looked up at the sound of footsteps, under his mass of scraggly hair, reminded Michael of... him!

Chapter Forty-three: Mistaken Identity

As dawn broke, Ragetta and her mother Estella were already awake, rattling round their hidden house, gathering everything they might need.

"Knife."

"Check." Ragetta said as her trembling hand wrapped some scrap cloth around the blade. "Why exactly did we have to take this knife?" She asked, still wondering why her mother had insisted they spend nearly an hour looking for this particular one earlier that morning.

"Ah my dear... you see, it's a special knife that can cut through metal. So, if your husband is, as you suspect, imprisoned, we can use it to get him out!" The wrinkled face smiled at her daughter affectionately, her eyes glistening with love for the first time in years. What joy it was to have company, and how much better it was that the company happened to be her daughter!

"What a... I can't believe it!" Stammered Ragetta, stunned at her mother's innovation.

"Thought it might be easier than trying to locate a key!" Estella added, revelling in the excitement; a stark contrast to the monotony which had been her life for more years than she could remember. Since entering the forest on her self-imposed exile, her days had merged into each other, with little to distinguish one from the next. She closed her eyes and recalled how once she had been the wisest witch in the coven, working on new potions, revelling in her discoveries.

Flinging her arms around Estella, Ragetta thought the one positive thing that had come from her husband's disappearance was at least finding her mother. If successful, perhaps in future, she could have both in her life!

"Come now Raggie, we've work to be doing if we want to get this husband of yours back." Removing herself from her daughters incredibly strong clutches, she tidied her clothing and wiped her silver hair from her face.

"Yes mum." Composing herself, she returned to the open bag on the table.

"Memory loss potion," the old woman continued.

"Check. And these are for?"

Sighing, Estella sometimes wished her daughter wasn't quite so inquisitive. "It's so if anyone encounters us trying to rescue them, we can slip them some, so they won't remember we were there." Her voice was hurried, her tone a little sharper than she had intended.

"Oh yes. Sensible, I see." Ragetta agreed, "sorry, I know we're in a hurry. I just can't help myself!"

"I know dear," Estella smiled.

"Food."

"Check."

"Water."

"Check."

"Underwear."

"For goodness sake, do we have to go through all of this? We've got everything, let's go!" Anxious to depart, Ragetta tied the cords of the bag and threw it over her shoulder as she made her way up the ladder.

Following behind, though not quite as quick on her toes as her daughter, Estella couldn't help but worry in case they had forgotten something. Well, it was too late now she thought to herself, we'll just have to make do with what we've got.

"To the castle," She heard Ragetta shout over her shoulder, and wondered if her daughter had remembered anything she'd been told the previous evening about the importance of secrecy.

Clambering out of the stump, Ragetta noticed a small blue, furry creature resting under the branch. "Shhhhh!" She whispered to her mother, who was less than graceful as she stumbled out and landed on her behind.

"W... what... who's there?" a scared, bulbus-eyed Siddons stammered, pushing his back further into the trunk, hoping it would eat him up.

"Mother! He's seen us!"

"Who are you?" he asked again, his nerves calming down slightly, for neither Estella nor Ragetta looked particularly menacing.

"I'm Ragetta," the younger of the two women answered, her face and eyes both kindly looking.

Still shrinking away from these humans, he wondered what their business was in the forest and more to the point, what they were doing inside a tree stump.

"Nice to meet you but I'm afraid we must go, we need to be somewhere urgently," Striding forwards without a backwards glance, she regretted not paying more attention to the tiny creature.

Sensing his chance, thinking that maybe he had bumped into them for a reason, Siddons started gabbling. "Please, I need your help, I... erm... I need to help someone escape from prison."

The plea caught Ragetta's attention. Stopping, she turned to face this furry creature that was wobbling on shaky legs. "A man? Late forties?"

"Y... y... yes." He stammered uncertainly, wondering if he wasn't the only person who knew of Mathis' captivity.

"You mean he's here, in the forest?" her shrill voice becoming excitable at the imminent prospect of seeing her husband.

"Now, dear," Her mother soothed, rubbing her shoulder affectionately, "don't get yourself so worked up."

"Quick, we must help him." Siddons asserted, his eyes wide with pleading. "He's being held there by some Court men and now he's tried escaping once, I'm certain they won't let him live much longer." Catching his breath, he was anxious for them to follow him.

"It's him, it's got to be!" Ragetta shouted ecstatically, grabbing her mother's arm and swinging the old woman round in a circle.

"Please stop," croaked Estella, "you're going to have me over."

"Sorry," she apologised, forgetting her mum wasn't as young or agile as she used to be. Changing her focus back to Siddons, she asked, "can you lead us to him?"

"Yes, yes, yes," he said, his cheeks creasing where just hours before tears had wet his fur. Anxious to get going, he fluttered his wings and flew before them, leading them through the brambles and bracken.

Stopping occasionally, waiting for Ragetta and Estella to catch up, he tried taking them on the easiest route to the cell, a route away from any pixies and other forest creatures, though fortunately most slept during the day.

Finally they were there, outside the bars through which Siddons had flown. Approaching the cell, treading carefully so as not to alert anyone as to their presence, they were just about to peer through the bar when they when they heard voices. "They're with him now," Siddons whispered, his voice frightened. "Poor Mathis, do you think they'll kill him? Can't we do anything to help him?" Fluttering his wings in agitation, he paced up and down before them.

"Hang on a minute..." Ragetta whispered as softly as she could manage "did you just say Mathis?"

"Yes. Why?" And then the thought struck him, what if they hadn't been talking about the same person?

"Well... erm..." She stalled, her mind all at sixes and sevens. "Mathis, alive! But how? When? The boy? Grimbald... where is he?" So many questions flooded her head, she didn't know where to begin.

"Calm yourself dear," commanded Estella. "Now we're here we should at least try to help him. If the Court men are here, they can't be with your husband as well, can they?" The old woman reasoned.

"S'pose not," Ragetta agreed, but her thoughts were once more interrupted by the sound of voices, although this, time, those inside the room.

All three sat transfixed, listening to the conversation beyond the bars. They weren't sure what to do for the best; if they tried to help there was a distinct possibility they might be captured or killed. If they did nothing, Mathis could be killed. Waiting for inspiration, they remained seated and listened as it all unfolded, too nervous to intervene.

Chapter Forty-four: Gate to Dragon Falls

Raglin glanced at Michael who was still being clutched firmly by Hargrin. Leaving Richard mid-conversation, he dismounted the stairs and unlocked the new padlock, allowing him access to the small cell. The middle-aged man followed obediently, still conversing with the Courtier who was no longer listening. Michael had no idea who he was, but by the look of his clothes, he was certain that wherever Raglin knew him from, it certainly wasn't the castle.

As the door to the cell creaked open the prisoner slowly turned to face his captors. His eyes like hollows in his head, red rimmed from crying. Enlightenment dawned on Michael who instantly gasped, he so wanted to shout and ask the prisoner if he was his dad, but before he even had time to draw breath, Hargrin clamped his hand so hard over Michael's mouth he could barely breathe.

"You dare say a word." The threat was whispered harshly in his ear, every word emphasised for effect. Michael was scared to even breathe too loudly. He nodded his head weakly and watched as they pulled the door shut behind them.

"I'm going to ask you one more time," said the overly polite voice of Raglin. "Give me the ring, and the password."

"No," the prisoner's voice was hoarse, but Michael could still hear the determination in his refusal to divulge the knowledge they so clearly wanted.

"Tell us," he shouted, "how to get to Dragon Falls," all politeness had disappeared.

"I would rather die than tell you anything."

Michael watched in admiration. You would be forgiven for thinking him weak; to look at him was to see nothing more than a dejected, undernourished body, yet his concise answers proved otherwise. It was clear that despite his lack of physical strength, there was a lot of fight in him emotionally.

"Why don't we just kill him?" Richard asked "Now that we have…"

"Shhhh," scolded Raglin. "Keep your mouth closed. Since you've not extracted a single piece of useful information, I think it best if you leave the rest to me."

"As you wish," Richard responded. Michael heard the grudging acceptance, but it was obvious to anyone listening that there was certainly no love lost between the two of them.

"I don't have the ring so you might as well kill me now, if that's what you want." A defiant Mathis said from his mattress.

"Raglin!" Hargrin shouted from behind the bars cell. I know…" Michael felt the clutch of his captor stiffen while a smile spread across his tired face.

"Please Hargrin, keep out of this. I'll call for you when I need you."

"But…"

"Keep quiet I tell you and let me deal with this." Raglin roared, losing his patience with those around him. His face was getting hotter and he was becoming increasingly frustrated with Mathis' refusal to tell him where the ring was; the last thing he needed was for Hargin to interrupt him when he was trying to work.

Hargrin's hand, if possible clamped even tighter over Michael's mouth who was finding it harder and harder to breath. Desperate to tell Raglin about Abednego's possession of the ring, he had to clench his teeth to stop himself from shouting to the older Courtier. If only Raglin would listen to him, there would be no need to carry on as they were; they could discard Mathis and Michael, get the ring off the old man and get the healing water.

To keep his mind occupied, Michael returned his attention to the goings-on inside the cell where Raglin strode towards Mathis; leaning over him like a towering giant.

"Bring him in Hargrin," Raglin commanded, his eyes glistening with malice as he waited for his star guest to appear.

Hargrin was so annoyed, he was half-tempted to ignore the request, but decided that at least if he did everything Raglin requested, he couldn't be accused of doing anything wrong. With one hand clamped on Michael's shoulder and the other tightly over his mouth, Hargrin pushed the boy down the steps and shoved him through the door. There Michael was better able to witness the cold, damp cell that the prisoner had been forced to endure.

"Mathis, meet your son, Michael, Michael meet Mathis, your dad."

Dumbstruck by the turn of events, Mathis opened his mouth, but nothing came out. His heart raced with excitement and his eyes tingled as tears appeared. His eyes devoured the boy's slight frame, his blond hair flopping over his eyebrows and the intense eyes which stared questioningly in his direction. Instinctively he knew it was his son. A feeling of shame swept over him as he considered how he must look. He clasped his arms around his knees, bones protruding from the little flesh left in his arms. He pushed back the mass of hair which looked like a mane around his face, then stroked his long bristly beard which was overgrown and untidy. Even the thought of escape had not aroused as much emotion as this meeting. Still, he could find no voice when he had so much he wanted to say.

"Dad!" Michael tried to rush forward to feel the embrace of the father he couldn't remember, but was held back by Hargrin's strong grip.

"You're not going anywhere boy, you're staying here." The harsh words instructed, and Michael felt the grip on his shoulders tighten.

He didn't try again, fearing that if he fought against them, they might hurt his father who looked too weak to protect himself. It would be too much for him if anything happened to Mathis because of him, he'd never be able to live with himself.

Instilled with a new lease of life, Mathis' mind was once more alert. Why would they bring his son to him? They must want something, and then he pieced the jigsaw together, they were going to use Michael as bait as a way of extracting the information they wanted from him.

"Pleased to meet your son?" Raglin questioned. "What about an exchange? For something so special, I assume you'd be willing to sacrifice quite a lot?"

Mathis knew exactly what Raglin wanted, and was loathe to give it to him.

"I don't want to waste time. You want your son and I want the ring and the password to Dragon Falls, as far as I'm concerned, it's a simple swap."

"I'm not lying." Mathis reiterated through clenched teeth, "I really don't know where the key is." His voice was almost a growl, increasingly antagonised by their refusal to believe him. "I haven't seen it since you got him," Mathis nodded in the direction of Richard who was listening intently to the confrontation, "to attack me, and half kill me in the process. It could have been found by anyone."

"Still playing games are we? Well, if you're not prepared to share the information on those terms, perhaps I should change them." Retreating to where Hargrin still clutched a trembling Michael, Raglin produced sharp, shiny silver blade from his belt and held it threateningly to the teenager's throat.

Trembling violently, Michael breathed as shallowly as possible for fear of the blade puncturing his skin. Then suddenly, Raglin changed tact. Dropping the knife from Michael's throat, he patted the boy on his back before striding towards Mathis. Still clutching the knife, Raglin hauled Mathis up off the mattress, his bony legs shaking so much they were barely able to stand. Positioning the blade at his captive's throat, he sneered, "How would you like your son to witness your death on your very first meeting?"

Not having foreseen this sudden change of tactics, Mathis' mind was chaotic. He couldn't bear to have his son watch him die, yet neither could he tell them what they wanted to know." His breathing quickened until he was panting, he didn't know how much more his frail body could take.

"Please." It was the first sign of submission he'd shown since his capture, and Raglin knew he was finally making progress. "Please, I'm not lying; I really don't know where the ring is."

"Stop," Michael yelled, "stop it, remove the knife and I'll tell you where it is." He knew he had promised Abednego he'd keep it a secret, but how could he watch his dad suffer and say nothing? The thought of watching his dad die and knowing he could have prevented it would be far too painful.

Gently removing the blade away from Mathis throat, Raglin shot Michael a piercing glance. "Are you telling the truth lad?"

"Yes... I am, just let him go. Please. I'll tell you everything you need to know."

"Michael please don't give it to them, you can't let them get it. If they get their hands on it they'll only use it for power and glory. Believe me; death will only bring me peace."

"Dad, I can't and I won't let them kill you!" His head was pounding, his eyes full of confusion and his heart full of pain. He knew he shouldn't tell them, he should do as he was told, but he needed his dad alive and he'd pay any price to make it happen."

"Well," Raglin demanded, irritated by the conversation "enough with the sentimentality, just give me the ring!"

Michael's nervous hands slipped it from his finger and held out the gold ring with the Ruby encased in the middle; the key to Dragons falls and the reason for their plight.

Raglin's eyes gleamed with pleasure. Who could deny him power now?

In a flash, he was by Michael's side. Grabbing the ring from his delicate hands, he held it aloft for all to see. Twisting the ring over in his hand, he smiled with malicious pleasure at the knowledge that it wouldn't be long before he became the second most powerful man in the country.

"The password boy, give me the password," he demanded.

Michael's face fell and his eyes flitted from side to side nervously. "I don't know," he said, "I've never had to use a password before, it just does things when I'm angry or need it to."

"Stupid boy, that's the small simple magic, we need a password if we're to get to Dragons Falls. Now give it to me, or as God is my witness, your dad will die." The knife, once more by the fragile mans throat, pricked his father's skin and Michael watched, mortified as a trickle of blood slid down the translucent neck of his father. He saw Mathis wince, but no complaint escaped his lips.

Michael couldn't bear it, "I don't know it, please, stop. I've given you the ring but I really don't know the password."

Then, with a flash of inspiration, Raglin dropped Mathis slight frame to the mattress and instead encompassed

Michael in his arms. "You might not know the password, but your father does, don't you Mathis?" His lips raised into a smirk.

Amidst the madness and threats, Hargrin wondered if it was the same ring he'd seen with Abednego. If it was, how hadn't he noticed Michael remove it from Abednigo's limp body? Perhaps it was the second one, which meant he alone knew of the whereabouts of both rings. He decided not to speak, knowing that Raglin wouldn't listen. And why shouldn't he keep it to himself? Why shouldn't he have the power? His mind made up, he remained near the cell wall, closer than he'd like to Richard and the man peering from the doorway, whose greasy grey hair hung limply across his eyes.

With the knife once more at his neck, Michael held his breath in anticipation. He was only fifteen, he didn't want to die. He didn't even want to be King. He just wanted to go home and be with his mum, to be like any other boy of his age, but it was no use trying to convince Raglin, who was determined to gain access to this Dragons Falls, or whatever it was.

"So Mathis, changed your mind about the password yet?"

Sickened by Raglin's evil grin, Mathis wondered what sort of person could derive pleasure from threatening to kill a boy. But he knew he was caught as Raglin was one to carry out his threats. He abhorred the idea of helping them enter Dragon Falls, and to give them the power of the ring and eternal life would be disastrous. They would take the throne and no doubt bring upon Kilion a multitude of horrors, but he couldn't let Michael die. He knew as a Prince, he should put his country first, but as a father, he couldn't sacrifice his son.

Feeling disgusted at what he was about to do, he closed his eyes to shut out their faces. Then as quietly as possible he whispered the password.

The attempted escape and now this, was just all too much for him. Unable to cope with the strain, his weak body slumped to the floor. He felt as though the last fourteen years of silence had been worth nothing; they had won. He had provided Raglin with the passport to power and evil. All he could do now was pray that they'd leave and let him and Michael get re-acquainted.

Clutching the ring, Raglin whispered the password. Nothing.

Michael, realising how desperate the situation was, lurched towards Raglin. Closing his hand around Raglin's palm, he tried to reclaim what was rightfully his. He tugged at it violently, but wasn't tall enough, or powerful enough to succeed. He was no match for the older man who, despite being nearly 60, was much stronger than Michael.

If only Dan had been here, or Grimbald, with their athletic physiques; they would have stood a much better chance, but they weren't there, so Michael put up the best fight he could muster.

Annoyed that the password hadn't worked, Raglin wondered if Mathis had lied to him, but surely he wouldn't, for he must have known Raglin would try it immediately. Even Mathis, as stubborn as he was, wouldn't risk his son being killed. Maybe he hadn't said it loud enough or, and a thought occurred to him, maybe it needed to be said by the rightful owner. He needed Michael to say it, but how?

Amused at Michael's ludicrous attempt to steal the ring from him, Raglin had knocked him away with his elbow, sending him sprawling across the cell as he continued to make his way towards Mathis.

Sensing the Minister approach and inspired by Michael's attempt to get the ring, energy he didn't know his body contained flowed through him; Mathis rose to his feet and lunged forward. His attempt was as feeble as Michael's, as he was neither as strong nor as nimble on his feet. Raglin's amusement turned to anger as he could ill afford to lose the ring, and he didn't like his chances against the two of them.

Hargrin and Richard watched the events unfold. They both considered whether they should help but both decided to refrain from doing so. If Raglin wanted their assistance, he could ask for it, and if they stepped in without permission, Raglin might consider their intrusion impertinent, or assume they thought he couldn't cope. It was too great a gamble.

Remembering the knife clutched in his hands, he rammed it into Mathis' flesh. Yelling in agony, the already weakened man clutched his side as deep red blood seeped through his fingers. The hollow eyes looked at Michael in despair as the pain wracked his body, draining his life from him. Disengaging from the entanglement of bodies, he stumbled backwards and collapsed onto the mattress; landing on a broken coil, his head hit the wall, enough to hurt but not enough to knock him out and deaden his pain. In fourteen years he'd not shed a single tear, and yet for at least the second time that day he felt yet another stream of salty water slide down his cheeks and onto his lips.

Staggered by Raglin's cruelty, Michael ran to help his father who was writhing in pain. His slim arms encased the dying man as he muttered words of reassurance. He couldn't stand the thought of losing his dad a second time.

Sensing this as a perfect opportunity, Raglin's strong arm yanked Michael back. "Want to help him do you lad?" He smiled at the look of despair engrained on the boys face. The boy would be putty in hands, as long as he thought he could save his dad.

"Simply say the magic word and get the ring to open up the gates to Dragons Falls. There, you'll find the water you need to heal your father."

Hearing every word, Mathis wanted to shout out and warn Michael not to do it, but he was too weak and his faint groans went unheard.

Michael stammered, he had to decide quickly. If he opened the gates he'd lead them straight to where they so desperately desired. If he refused, he'd never forgive himself for his dad's death. Like a set of scales, he weighed up the options, eventually deciding to obey Raglin.

"Can you promise my dad will live?"

"I certainly can, but we must be quick." Raglin said, his grip on Michael's arm getting tighter the more excited he became. He was so close to his plan coming to fruition. "We have got to get going. The quicker we get there, the quicker we'll bring the healing water back. It can heal, but it can't bring people back from the dead."

With no alternative available, Michael tentatively touched the ring and whispered the word under his breath. They waited in anticipation.

A bright light illuminated the small room with shades of pinks, purples, reds and yellows, blinding them. Holding his hands over his eyes to protect them, Michael stumbled backwards, shying away from the fierce heat. Soon it faded to reveal a sparkling, golden gate shimmering in the light. Pearls adorned the top of the marble poles creating such a beautiful object Michael couldn't quite believe his eyes.

"Quick, lad!" pushing the boy through the gate, Raglin indicated for Hargrin and Tacitus to accompany them. Both stood motionless, staring at the magic gateway. Frustrated, Raglin stormed over to them, grabbed both Ministers and managed to get them through the opening. It had already been far too long since Michael had gone through and he was worried that he would already be lost to them on the other side. Shoving them through, they just managed it before the faint gold of the gate faded into nothingness. And so, while Mathis lay in agony and Richard and Jasper stood in astonishment; Tacitus, Hargrin, Raglin and Michael disappeared from view. Once more the cell was no more than a dim, gloomy and cold prison.

Groaning, Mathis was filled with despair so deep it plunged his soul into a darkness from which he doubted it could ever return. Richard and Jasper, standing in the doorway, wondered whether they should kill him now, or keep him alive as Raglin had implied . Not prepared to risk killing the prisoner without Raglin's direct orders, they went upstairs, in search of something to stem the flow of blood.

Chapter Forty-five: Re-united

She didn't know how long they'd slept, but the sun was still low outside and the birds had yet to cheer them with their morning melodies. Hazel, determined to find Michael, woke the others. It was imperative that no time was lost in finding their bestfriend. Her dark hair hung over her face as she rushed around, nudging people, ordering them to prepare to leave.

"Errrr... err," murmured a concussed Abednego as he slowly opened his good eye.

All eyes focused on the semi-conscious man, hoping he had fully recovered from the blow to his head. "M... Mi... Micha...?" his voice was slurred, but his mind was starting to focus.

"He was taken..." sobbed a distraught Sophie, rubbing the old man's forehead with her sleeve to wipe away the dirt and blood.

Gradually regaining his strength, it was only a few minutes before he had hauled himself into a seated position. His old body was still weak and slightly concussed, but bit by bit, memories of the previous night pieced together until the puzzle was complete.

"Would you like something to drink?" a concerned Hazel enquired, still worried about him, there was a nasty bruise that had formed on his head by his right temple, and his eye was swollen.

"There's no time for drinks..." He chided, "we must get Michael back."

The others looked at each other, sympathising with his plight. "I'm afraid," began Dan, "that whoever or whatever took him, was invisible. We couldn't see where he went."

Raising his leaden head and looking at them one by one, Abednego was startled to see Grimbald and Sophie with them, and wondered what they were doing with his great nephew. Surely Michael would have chosen to take him, his great Uncle before either of these two! Slightly upset and not a little indignant at this discovery, Abednego almost questioned their presence. Reason however prevailed, and saving Michael was much more important than his pride. Pushing his jealousy aside he coughed to clear his throat. "We don't need to know where he's gone," he stated. Waiting for the inevitable questions, he was somewhat surprised that no-one said anything, they just listened intently. "I have the second ring; it will take us directly to him just as it brought me here."

Catching their breath, the knowledge that Abednego possessed Melchior's ring was a bombshell they hadn't foreseen.

"So, for the last fourteen years, you've been a keeper of both the rings?" Dan asked incredulously, wondering why Abednego had not used them sooner.

"I prefer to think of myself as Keeper of the Keystone, for as you're probably aware, it is the stones which have the power. They were simply placed in a circlet of gold to make them easier to keep on a person. The most important power they possess individually, is their ability to open the gate to Dragon Falls. Used together they can open the door to places much greater than even that."

Intrigued by their power and Abednego's possession of them, Hazel was careful to refrain herself from bombarding him with questions, for each one would keep them longer from finding Michael.

Sensing their inquisitiveness, Abednego threw them a painful smile, "I'll tell you everything, don't you worry, but another time. First we must save my great nephew. So, make sure you've a firm hold of my cloak." Holding out the thick material, he inspected them to make sure they were all clutching it tightly before adding, "and if I were you, I'd brace myself for the wind, which at force, can be rather vicious." With that he grabbed the ring from an inside pocket and concentrated his thoughts on finding Michael.

Flashes and streaks of light in the air, and then grumbling sounds so loud that it shook their bodies , and yet all the while the cold slapping sensation of the verocious winds attacked their faces. It took no more than seconds for the ring to transport them from the safety of the dusty cottage to the smaller damp cell which had housed Michael just moments before.

Landing with a thump, the five intruders opened their eyes and inspected their bleak surroundings. Nobody recognised where they were, but one thing was for certain, Michael wasn't there.

It was the bright red, stickiness of blood that caught Abednego's attention. As he heaved his body into a standing position, he noticed that it came from a scrawny man lying in a foetal position on a mattress in the corner of the cell. Still wobbly, it was with difficulty that Abednego staggered over to offer assistance.

As he slowly approached, he heard the muffled grumbles from the man, cursing Raglin and crying out in pain for Michael. Placing his arm lightly and comfortingly on the injured mans shoulder; he tried to soothe him, to offer support and to find where the wound was.

Sensing the old man's kindness, Mathis mustered enough energy to crane his neck wearily around. Barely conscious, at first Mathis wondered if it was his imagination playing tricks on him as his eyes met those of Abednego. Their eyes locked as recognition dawned on both men. Their hearts stopped, stunned as they gasped at the others appearance.

Shocked to his very core, Abednego stumbled backwards, his hands clasping his throat as he struggled to breathe. In his wildest dreams he hadn't expected to see him still alive. All those years ago, he thought he had witnessed the death of his only remaining nephew. Since that stormy night, visions of the attack had invaded his memories, had permeated his dreams, turning them into nightmares and had left a hole in his heart. Countless nights afterwards he had spent hours awake crying, weeping, asking for forgiveness and almost every night since he had prayed for his soul; witnessing a scene so horrific is something you never recover from. The closest he had ever come to reconciling himself to the fate which had befallen his nephew, was knowing he would spend his life doing everything in his power to protect Michael, and preparing him for when he gained his rightful inheritance of Kilion.

Fourteen years of suffering, of mourning his death, of recriminations. Fourteen years of his life he had lived and believed a lie, and now so unexpectedly, his whole life, and everything he had thought to be true had been proven a lie. Ten years he had searched for Michael, three days he had known him and in a couple of minutes he had lost him. Yet with the snatching of Michael had come his reunion with Mathis.

If only he had known Mathis was alive! He would have searched for him, dedicated his life to finding him. If Mathis had kept the ring, he could have reached him and saved him all those years ago, but for the sake of Kilion, Mathis had discarded the Key, allowed Kilion to live in peace, and forsaken his future.

The old man inspected the cell, disgusted by the cracks imprinted on the damp walls and the cold stone floor. Tears of sadness and regrets streamed down his bruised face and landed on the floor. He didn't know what to say, words stuck in his throat.

"Is it really you Abednego?" The injured man rasped. His deep, listless eyes implored, wanting it to be true. "Please help!" His tone was so desperate. Abednego knelt down by him and clutched his cold hands. Bringing it to his cheek, he rubbed it, trying to give the Prince comfort.

"You're alive! What's happened to you? Where's Michael?" He halted, allowing Mathis time to process the questions.

"Quick, over here." He shouted at the other three, who until that moment had been glued to the spot. Snapping back to life, Grimbald was first by Mathis' side, his strong arms gathering Mathis up protectively, clutching him to his strong frame. Worried by the size of him, Abdenigo had yelped in consternation. Yet Grimbald was as gentle as he was big. His grip was soft and his manner caring as made sure he held Mathis as sensitively as possible, worried that his fragile physique might snap in his embrace.

As Grimbald gazed down at the shell of the Prince; Ragetta, Siddons and Estella stormed through the house into the cell. Having waited for Raglin and Hargrin to depart, before braving entry, they had wasted no time in entering as soon as the Courtiers had vanished through the gateway.

"Grimbald, thank God you're safe!" Ragetta panted, her face flushed, "I was so worried!" She was just about to thrust her arms around her husband's neck when she noticed who he was cradling like a babe in arms. "Mathis. Dear Lord, is he alright?" Her voice was full of concern. The shock of discovering Mathis was still alive and fresh in her mind. Only minutes before she had sat shivering outside, praying for Michael and Mathis to escape, or for Raglin to show compassion. She had winced at the shouting and shuddered as the cold steel had entered the flesh of the Prince who had looked so weak. She was sure he couldn't survive.

"He was stabbed," she mumbled, "Raglin stabbed him. He did it to force Michael to open the gate." Her composure collapsed as sobs escaped her exhausted body.

"Calm down dear," a reassuring Grimbald comforted. He knew he should wrap his arms around his wife, but couldn't take them from Mathis. He hadn't been there for him before, but he was determined to protect the man he had sworn to serve above all others. Today, even if it was his last, Mathis would know he wasn't alone, and that he, Grimbald would always be there for him. He would be with Mathis to the very end.

Fluttering above, his fur wet with tears, Siddons flew to this Master.

"Quickly, let me through, let me through. We don't have much time," Estella commanded.

As he stumbled back from Mathis to allow the old witch access, Abednego retreated to where Sophie, Dan and Hazel stood nervously. Sophie and Hazel each placed an arm around the old man, sensing how much their support was needed.

With Ragetta also retreating from the weakening body, Estella positioned herself next to Mathis who was still encased in the strong, comforting arms of Grimbald.

The wrinkled face assessed him, her look one of concern. She knew saving him would be difficult. His aura was fuzzy, and his future unfathomable. There was no certainty he would live. Using the corner of her cloak she wiped away the sweat and blood that still trickled from the wound. "Leave this to me. Abednego and Grimbald, you need to concentrate on bringing Michael back. He went through the gate to that place, Dragon Falls. You must get him."

Persuaded to leave Mathis in the capable hands of Estella, Grimbald gently let go of Mathis, laying him once more down onto the old mattress. He didn't want to, but knew Estella could help Mathis more than he, or anyone else he knew could.

"Dragon Falls," Abednego whispered. Deep down he had known that would be their destination, but it hadn't stopped him from praying otherwise.

Eager to justify Michael's actions, Ragetta sobbed, saying he was forced into opening the Gateway by Raglin.

Abednego responded quickly. Commanding Estella to do whatever she could to keep Mathis alive, he played his hand over the ring and whispered the password; he had hoped he would never have to say it, and that it would be forgotten in the annals of history. But now he said it to save the lives of both Michael and Mathis.

A flash of light as bright as before infused the cell, temporarily blinding those in its presence. Finally it faded and a gate was revealed. Looking back once more at Mathis' listless body, and wishing he could stay to tend him, Abednego's loyalties were torn. It was only the knowledge that he was in the capable hands of Estella, whose healing powers had been legendary, that gave him the strength to make the hardest decision he had faced since watching Mathis lie dying in the alley. Like then, he felt he was abandoning Mathis and he could only pray he was making the right choice.

Both his head and his heart told him he couldn't leave Michael in Dragon Falls on his own any longer than necessary; Michael needed his help. Fortunately neither Raglin, Hargrin nor Tacitus could use the ring there without him, as the legitimate holder of the Keystone, all magic had to be performed by him. Yet despite this, Abednego worried at his vulnerability. No fifteen year old lad could fight against the persuasiveness and threats of such evil men. His only hope was that he got there before they forced Michael into doing something he might regret.

As the seconds ticked by, Abednego and Grimbald disappeared through the gateway, leaving a stunned Dan, Sophie and Hazel watching in horror as they left. Were they to be stuck there, in the cell? Reading each others thoughts, as Estella and Regatta tended eagerly to Mathis, the three youths walked towards the gate, making it in just before the gateway vanished.

Too late to stop them, Estella watched tearfully as her son-in-law and the others had disappeared into a realm she knew to be fraught with danger and prayed for their safe return. She knew her place was in Kilion, trying to save Mathis. Her only consolation was that no more would she be consumed with loneliness for Regatta, for she was there to help her in this time of need. Bending down, she helped the weak Prince to his feet and then stared at Richard and Jasper, who appeared in the entrance of the cell. For an awful moment she thought they were going to try to stop her, or even worse kill her, but they didn't. They stood and stared, their faces confused as she and Regatta held Mathis up, with Siddons flying ahead and leading the way up the staircase.

They left the building with Mathis clinging onto them. His feet were dragging, life barely in him. Outside they lay him down in the fresh air in the hope that it would warm his body and lift his spirits. Rubbing her hands together to heat them, Estella lay them on the Prince and felt them tingle. She knew it wouldn't be easy, but she was determined to keep him alive until they returned with the healing waters he so desperately needed. Keeping him alive would be hard, but even harder to bear was not knowing what was happening to those she loved; of not being able to help them against the horrors and traps that littered the miracle that was Dragon's Falls.

"Let's just pray they choose the right door. God knows what horrors they'll be forced to endure if they choose any of the other ones."

"They will live, wont they?" Regatta asked.

"I don't know," the older woman answered truthfully.

"Can't they just get the waters and return?"

"It's not that simple I'm afraid. The Gate will lead them to four doors. Only one leads directly to the healing water. The other three lead them to trials which must be passed; many of which are life threatening and are set within the deadliest of terrains. Then, if you are fortunate enough you will reach the dragon that protects the waterfall. This will need to be passed in order to collect the healing waters. Only those who prove themselves worthy will be able to pass the dragon."

Colour drained from Regatta's face; she may never see Grimbald again. For the first time, she cursed the day he had ever noticed Michael. If only she could turn the clock back, but she knew she couldn't. All she could do was wait and pray for Grimbald and Michael, for his friends and for the forlorn figure of Mathis whose was the only fate she might be able to control.

The End

Printed in Great Britain
by Amazon